PRAISE FOR BOO WALKER

An Unfinished Story

"Walker's attention-grabbing and surprising plot highlights the engaging characters in this tale of second chances. For fans of women's fiction such as Nicholas Sparks's and Kristin Hannah's work."

—*Library Journal*

"*An Unfinished Story* is an immersive tale about a quest to find something real and true after life turns upside down. Boo Walker has written a book with a tender heart, cast against the soft background of coastal Florida, a setting rendered with a hand for delicate detail. A great story of redemption that carted me away."

—Barbara O'Neal, bestselling author of *When We Believed in Mermaids*

"*An Unfinished Story* is the perfect mix of character-driven, heartstring-pulling drama and sharp-witted humor. I was thoroughly entertained and found myself in awe of Walker's talent as a writer. I'm not even sure where to begin . . . His storyline was poignant and meaningful. His prose was masterful and full of gorgeous imagery that made the setting come alive for me. His pacing was spot-on. The dialogue was brilliant—deep and soulful at times, witty and amusing at others. On top of all that, he has created a complex and marvelously memorable character in Whitaker Grant, who charmed and amused me at every turn. I could go on and on. At the end of the day, this was a wonderfully enjoyable book. Clearly, Boo Walker is an author whose time has come."

—*USA Today* bestselling author Julianne MacLean

"I love books with breathing characters you can root for, a narrative of human life to which you can relate, a conclusion that can stop the heart, and an author who can bind them all together with passion and soul. Boo Walker proves he's that kind of writer with *An Unfinished Story*."

—Leila Meacham, bestselling author of *Roses* and *Titans*

"Grieving widow Claire Kite and frustrated writer Whitaker Grant cross paths in Boo Walker's moving novel *An Unfinished Story*. Accurately conveying the complexity of human emotions, this story of love and healing kept me turning pages and tugged at my heart. Not to be missed."

—Karen McQuestion, bestselling author of *Hello Love*

"If Nicholas Sparks and Maeve Binchy had a baby, he might sound a lot like Boo Walker. *An Unfinished Story* strikes a perfect balance between humor, warmheartedness, and the daily pathos of being human."

—Jodi Daynard, bestselling author of *The Midwife's Revolt*

The Singing Trees

"Walker's (*An Unfinished Story*) beautifully written coming-of-age novel is set during the Vietnam War . . . Ideal for book groups and for readers who enjoyed Taylor Jenkins Reid's *Daisy Jones & the Six*, Susan Elizabeth Phillips's *Dance Away with Me*, or Nicholas Sparks's novels."

—*Publishers Weekly* (starred review)

"A heartwarming read."

—Historical Novel Society

"*The Singing Trees* is a beautifully crafted coming-of-age story set in working-class Maine during the seventies, a time of intense turmoil and transformation in America. It is a heartfelt, complex tale of chasing your dreams without forsaking your roots, and I was swept away by Boo Walker's deft storytelling and incredibly complex characters. Soulful but also full of sharp dialogue and humor, *The Singing Trees* is exactly the sort of book you get lost in, then mourn when it is over."

—Suzanne Redfearn, #1 Amazon bestselling author of *In an Instant*

"*The Singing Trees* is more than a poignant coming-of-age story; it is a deep exploration of the intricacies of personal growth, family ties, and that most elusive and extraordinary of human gifts, forgiveness. Walker's lively cast of characters centers around the young artist Annalisa, whose vibrant, yearning nature lights up this story. I cared for her from the first page as she struggles, as we all do, to protect herself from heartbreak only to find that an open heart is a necessary condition for her art, and, ultimately, for happiness. Book clubs will enjoy second-guessing Annalisa's choices, and readers everywhere will be enthralled by this clear-eyed journey into the lessons of the heart."

—Sonja Yoerg, *Washington Post* bestselling author of *True Places* and *The Family Ship*

"Boo Walker is that rare writer who is both a master storyteller and wordsmith all at once. Set against the backdrop of small-town Maine, *The Singing Trees* is an uplifting story about the juxtaposition of love and great art, and the possibility of second chances. This is a book to bring you to tears but leave you with a light in your heart."

—Eoin Dempsey, bestselling author of *White Rose, Black Forest*

"Boo Walker's *The Singing Trees* filled my heart with a song that echoed inside me long after I'd read the last sentence. With his skill at storytelling on display, Walker deftly takes the reader on a journey through the choices and sacrifices facing those who are caught in creativity's siren call in this tale of love, sacrifice, and ultimately forgiveness. Bring tissues because there will be tears, but the good kind—the kind that let you know you are alive."

—Emily Bleeker, *Wall Street Journal*
and Amazon Charts bestselling author

A

SPANISH

SUNRISE

OTHER BOOKS BY
THE AUTHOR

Writing as Benjamin Blackmore

A

SPANISH

SUNRISE

a novel

BOO WALKER

LAKE UNION
PUBLISHING

Published by Lake Union Publishing, Seattle

www.apub.com

Amazon, the Amazon logo, and Lake Union Publishing are trademarks of Amazon.com, Inc., or its affiliates.

ISBN-13: 9781542037921
ISBN-10: 1542037921

Cover design by Caroline Teagle Johnson

Printed in the United States of America

For Ruth Chiles, who is proof there are angels

The twisted tree lives its life while the straight tree ends up in planks.

—*Chinese proverb*

Chapter 1

AND THEN THERE WERE TWO

Baxter Shaw's fear that he had failed as a father gnawed at him as he pushed open the door to his daughter's classroom. Finding it empty, he called out over the drumming of the rain on the roof, "Hello? Anyone here?" Only twenty minutes earlier, Mia's teacher Ms. Mecca had called and asked to see him, so he knew he was expected. Mia had apparently hit another student.

Assuming Ms. Mecca would be there momentarily, he walked to the windows overlooking the playground and watched the rain fall, his mind running rampant with thoughts of where he'd gone wrong. Was there anything more painful than knowing that your eight-year-old was struggling and that you were not only responsible but also unequipped to help? His little Mia, the sweetest girl in the world, a budding chess maven, a homemade jewelry and origami enthusiast, the inventor of the forever puppy, still with a closetful of princess gowns . . . hurting another student. How had it come to this?

He didn't want to think it possible that his daughter would do such a thing, but he knew better. Her behavior had been on a downslide for the last six weeks or so, since late August, and he couldn't figure it out. That was when the nightmares had started, too, these visions she was having of her mother. Of course it was all related.

Sure, Mia had every reason to be struggling, but with the power of passing time, the work she had done with her therapist, and Baxter's efforts to entomb the memories of the past, he had thought they'd broken through the worst of it.

But the horror of what had occurred three years ago had sent them into a tailspin from which he'd begun to worry they would never recover. He'd given up everything to dedicate his life to her, leaving his band and tossing away the only aspiration he'd ever had, but it hadn't been enough. What else was there then? What else could he give?

What he knew and what kept him up at night was that he should have given up his dreams the moment he'd met Mia's mother, Sofia— *not* the moment he'd lost her.

"Hi, Mr. Shaw," Ms. Mecca said, entering the room. "Sorry to keep you waiting."

Baxter spun around to greet her. "Hey there."

She had a wonderful and warm smile that always allayed some of Baxter's worry. What was it, the fourth time in six weeks they'd met like this? Every time he saw her, he thought the same thing: thank God Mia had someone like Ms. Mecca, because she and Mia's psychologist were the only positive female figures in her life.

From the moment Baxter had mentioned Mia's nightmares, Ms. Mecca had jumped into helping—and that was shortly before the behavioral issues had started. In a way, the nightmares had been the omen of things to come. She had even gone out of her way to connect with Mia's psychologist, and they'd been speaking on a weekly basis since the issues had begun. Their combined efforts were enough to make Baxter tear up.

As they made small talk about the weather, Ms. Mecca dragged two of the students' small chairs into the middle of the room and encouraged him to take a seat. Baxter's lengthy torso threatened to snap the little plastic chair at any moment, so he sat as gently as possible and then crossed his arms, bracing himself for what she might have to say.

Mr. Shaw, she could start, pulling off her glasses and glaring at him. *No one said it would be easy, but wow. Just wow. This whole father thing just isn't working out, is it? You're a chip off the old block, aren't you?* Of course, she didn't know Baxter's father.

"I can't believe she hit another student," Baxter said. Actually, he kind of could. Mia's nightmares had led to a lack of sleep, which led to a groggy and often grumpy child who had little interest in getting up in the morning, let alone going to school. Not only had her grades slipped and she'd lost interest in hanging out with her friends, but she was also exhibiting behavioral issues for the first time in her life. It had begun at home with her demeanor: almost instant mood changes, often turning uncharacteristically vicious—at least, little-girl vicious. He'd ask her to clean her room and she'd erupt, saying that she already had. Or he'd ask her to take three more bites of her green beans or bring her plate to the sink, and she'd have a complete meltdown.

Then she'd begun exhibiting issues in class like circle-time disruptions, ignoring Ms. Mecca's requests, and refusing to do her classwork. Lately, Mia didn't even want to go to school, but Baxter wouldn't allow that. What? Was she going to ride around with him in his truck all day?

"I'm so sorry," Baxter continued. "I signed her up for some self-defense classes over the summer, and they may have gone to her head. I suppose they should have taught her some accompanying restraint. Was it bad?"

"Mia punched the student in the throat. But . . ." Ms. Mecca bit her lip and stared down toward his left arm, as if she were attempting to interpret one of the tattoos that crawled out his sleeve. She finally looked up. "It's bigger than that, though. Look, Mr. Shaw, I may have made a mistake." She crossed her arms, as if guarding herself. "In late August, around the time Mia started having her nightmares, we did a family tree exercise. Something I've done with my third graders as long as I can remember."

3

"Oh boy." He instantly got an idea of where this was going and felt Mia's pain so strongly that he wanted to run to find her in the principal's office and sweep her up into his arms.

"It was just a quick exercise. I didn't even think about Mia losing her mother. It didn't come to mind when you mentioned Mia's nightmares. We draw a tree and populate it with our family, and I do a little genealogy lesson. It wouldn't have been an issue had another student not said something to Mia that . . . that I think is the root of what she's going through."

Baxter dug his fingers into his Levi's.

She continued, "It only came to my attention today after an altercation with that same student. I had a chat with Mia in my office. I guess she's been keeping a lot to herself. Apparently, they were still talking about the exercise at recess that day, because this other student said something about how . . ." She paused.

"About?" Baxter said.

"How her mother died."

At Ms. Mecca's words, his throat tightened, and he felt as though he were being strangled. He'd told Mia that her mother had died in a car accident.

"She knows now, Mr. Shaw. The other student said something about it again today, and that's what caused her to lose her temper."

Baxter felt the strain all over his body. He should have told her. Just as her psychologist had suggested toward the end of her first year of work with Mia, he should have told her. But he'd kept putting it off. What he'd been waiting for he didn't know. Just a few more days and weeks when she could enjoy a life where such violence didn't exist.

He blew out a gust of air. "Yikes." Rubbing his hands together, he wondered why Mia hadn't said anything. He searched the laces of his caramel boots for an answer, a sign of what to do next. She'd been doing so well, he thought. In fact, they barely talked about Sofia anymore—not since moving to Greenville, away from all the reminders of her mom in Charleston.

"I know it's a lot," Ms. Mecca said, "and I'm really s—"

"You have nothing to be sorry for," Baxter interrupted with a gentle wave of his hand, knowing any blame was his alone. "I don't know why she didn't tell me."

Ms. Mecca looked relieved to be off the hook. "She said you've been really stressed lately and had enough on your plate."

"Oh, Mia. You'd think she's raising me and not the other way around. I wish she'd let me do the adulting."

Ms. Mecca shook her head. "I know. It's a very sweet and mature gesture . . . I think it's more than that anyway, though. These are big emotions for a girl her age. She might be trying to forget it."

That was exactly what he'd been trying to do too. "So . . . who was the kid who said it?" He immediately felt guilty for putting Ms. Mecca into an uncomfortable position. "You don't have to answer that."

"I'm sure it wasn't meant to cause such damage," she said carefully.

Baxter started to stand. "I guess it's time to have the talk I've been putting off for way too long."

Ms. Mecca rose with him. "Don't beat yourself up, Mr. Shaw. And please let me know what I can do to help."

"You know I will, and seriously, don't think twice about the lesson. We're lucky to have you in our lives." He meant it.

"Thanks," she said. "We're here if you need us."

Baxter offered a last wave. "Don't worry, I got this."

Those last three words fell out of his mouth and thumped onto the floor like clumps of wet clay.

The principal, who was probably a decade older than Ms. Mecca, peered over a laptop computer at her desk and said in a childish voice intended for Mia, "There he is."

Baxter smiled at her and then found Mia on a purple couch on the opposite wall, her head buried in a notebook that she'd been drawing in, probably another unicorn. She loved unicorns right now. "Hey, sweetie." He heard more pain than he'd intended coating the fringes of his voice.

She looked up, her face showing relief and even happiness that he was there. He saw for a moment the dimples that she'd inherited from him. But her expression quickly melted into hesitance, the darkness under her eyes from a lack of sleep becoming more evident, as if she only then remembered what she had done.

"Hi, Daddy."

Her long hair was frizzy, as it was when it rained. As usual, she wore an array of colors that had turned her into a walking rainbow. Ever since she'd started dressing herself at four years old, she'd always tried to see how many colors she could squeeze into one outfit, a habit that even losing her mother hadn't broken. Today, along with her purple rain jacket and yellow sneakers, she wore a pink shirt buttoned all the way up, with an orange belt and white jeans.

He approached her and put a loving hand on her head. "You ready to go home?" He saw that she was indeed drawing a unicorn.

"Am I in trouble?" Mia asked.

Baxter glanced at the principal, then back at Mia. He lowered to one knee and found his daughter's brown eyes, the ones that looked like they'd been plucked from her mother. "No, you're not in trouble, honey. But I'm gonna take the day off so we can spend some time together."

"You're going to take the day off?" Disbelief coated every syllable.

This topic was the low-hanging fruit of their relationship, and the guilt trips she delivered never failed to hit hard. If only she could understand. Adults work, that was what they had to do. And when you didn't have a partner, you had to work twice as hard.

"Let me rephrase," he said. "I am going to work as little as possible today. Okay?"

She nodded, snapped shut her notebook, and hopped off the couch.

After Baxter thanked the principal for watching Mia, the two of them walked hand in hand through the office to the front desk, where Baxter returned his visitor tag. At the exit, he helped Mia button her purple rain jacket and then retrieved an umbrella from where he'd left it by the double doors. Popping it open, they dashed out into the Carolina rain toward his truck. He lifted her up into the back of his shiny black four-door Chevy Silverado, helped her click her seat belt, then raced around to his side.

Once he'd shut the door, he twisted to her. "We have a lot to talk about, don't we?"

She glared at him, which meant she wasn't interested in talking about what had happened.

He nodded sympathetically. "Let's wait until we get home."

"Or not," she said with another shot of her mother's attitude.

Letting it go, Baxter said, "I have a serious question."

"Here we go again," she said dramatically.

He pretended not to know what she was referring to. "What?"

"I already know what you're gonna do," she said with mild disgust.

He formed a straight line with his lips. "What is the purpose of a porpoise?"

She nearly gagged. "Dad joke four hundred and fifty-nine. Someone save me."

"It's a good one, no?"

"No. There's no punch line."

"The punch line is the question." He tapped his head, assuring her of his brilliance.

"It doesn't work that way," she said. "Um, do I smell french fries? I want some."

"Nope. Kale chips."

"Right." She eyed him like she wasn't going to play his games.

"Nothing gets by you, does it?" He'd just gotten busted for cheating on his diet today. Typically, he avoided bread and potatoes, but it was an eff-it kind of day, and a chicken sandwich had seemed to be the remedy.

He reached into the Chick-fil-A bag, pulled out the rest of his waffle fries, and handed them to her. "All yours."

She set them in her lap and drew one out. "Ketchup, please."

"Coming right up." He peeled back the top on a dipping pack and gave it to her. "Let's do our best not to get any all over my truck or your white jeans, okay?" She nodded as she dragged her fry through the puddle of red.

He reached for his phone in the cup holder. "Give me just a minute before I pull out."

"I thought you were taking the day off," Mia said, and without turning, he could imagine what kind of know-it-all look she was giving him.

"I am," he muttered, stabbing out a quick email to Dr. Carr, suggesting they set up a session ASAP. After a little more than a year of visits, Baxter had stopped taking Mia to see her. Mia had seemed to be doing okay, considering their loss, and she seemed to have adjusted to their life in Greenville without too much trouble. The two of them could go a full week without saying a word about Sofia. Of course, the day after the nightmares started, Baxter had reconnected and Mia had been seeing her ever since.

Dr. Carr's initial impression was that Mia was suffering from a delayed form of grief, a sort of PTSD, as she was only now getting old enough to truly process what had happened. That may have been true, but as Baxter had learned today, there was more to it than that.

Trying to get everything out of the way, Baxter spit out a round of text messages. See if you can get them by early next week. Another: Let's stick with the sheets of drywall for now. I'll let you know if I think of anything else. To the guy who'd installed the wrong gutters on a house, he texted: Let's just get them replaced and move on.

A few weeks after they'd lost Sofia, Baxter had left his very successful alt-country band and bought out the contracting business of a guy he'd worked for growing up. That was what had taken him and Mia from Charleston to Greenville, and it was a decision he questioned daily, because the stress he'd taken on with managing construction projects was slowly killing him.

That was when his phone rang—Alan. Baxter held up his finger to Mia. "One sec and we'll be out of here." He accepted the call, and his right-hand man's southern drawl came oozing out of the phone like Grandma's Molasses. "Baxter, we got a problem."

"Only one?" Baxter said, speaking loudly enough to cut through the noise of the rain. To be a contractor was to run a hundred miles an hour all day long, constantly taking calls just like this one.

"We just got to Carter," Alan said. Baxter had convinced several investors to go in with him to build three spec homes in a new development south of town, and one of them was on Carter Street.

Though the chance to become a premier builder for the development had been a heck of an opportunity—a potentially life-changing one—Baxter had put every bit of cash he had into it, and the feeling of being strapped was starting to get to him. What if he couldn't get that cash back? It sure didn't help that lumber prices had skyrocketed shortly after he'd broken ground or that the Fed was talking about hiking up interest rates yet again, which would kill this already-stumbling real estate market. As if Baxter should have been surprised that the boom was slowing just as he slid all his chips into the center of the table.

"Winslow didn't get in there last night to pressurize the gas line, and I can't get in touch with him," Alan went on. "If he doesn't show up in the next hour, we'll have to cancel the inspection. God knows how long it'll take to reschedule. Which means we'll have to push the slab pour back—"

"And the drywall guys," Baxter added. "I get it." He thought quickly, knowing the first thing he had to do was calm Alan down.

"Let's take a step back for a minute. See if you can get ahold of his wife. Maybe he forgot. In the meantime, let me call Mitchell and see if he can get out there. He owes me a favor. Don't worry, we'll figure it out."

"A'ight, I'll report back."

Baxter ended the call and pushed the keys into the ignition. "I'm going to try very hard not to answer any more calls, honey."

"It's fine. Can we listen to Katy Perry?"

So sweet and understanding was her tone, but it brought up a sickening guilt. He knew he worked too much—his own therapist had said so, up until Baxter had run out of time for their weekly appointments.

Baxter didn't want her to know what was on his mind, so he addressed her musical request instead. "Katy Perry? Again? What about Bob Dylan or Paul Simon or Neil Young? You love Neil. Have I ever played you *On the Beach*?" Shaking off the yucky feeling still clinging to him, he sang a few lines of "For the Turnstiles." She was the only one he sang for anymore.

Mia shook her little head. "I really do like it, Daddy, but . . ."

Need she say more? The truth was he didn't listen to much music anymore anyway. He just liked giving her a hard time.

"All righty then," he said. "Katy Perry it is."

Chapter 2

THROUGH THE GATES WE GO

Driving past downtown in a particularly reflective mood, Baxter remembered what it was like growing up in Greenville, when the city was showing faint sparks of life but a long way from the hip spot it was today, what with the development around the Swamp Rabbit Trail, the growing list of festivals and events, and the seemingly countless cool markets slinging local fare. He remembered how excited every adult in town had been when BMW had announced over thirty years ago that it was opening up a plant. They'd turned out to have good reason, as the car manufacturer's arrival had kick-started a boom. Now *Greenville* rolled off the tip of the tongue with cities like Nashville and Asheville, and publications touted it as one of the best places to raise a family in the United States.

He felt like he might have been the same as Greenville back then, with the guitar in his hand, showing some sparks of a kid breaking through, but he was mostly just a punk with long hair and a couple of homemade tattoos, trying to learn a 360 kick flip on his skateboard like Tony Hawk, sneaking Salem Lights from his alcoholic mom or Camels from the guys on the construction sites where he'd worked growing up.

By the time Baxter and Mia reached the guard gate that led into their neighborhood, the rain had slowed to a drizzle. With Katy Perry still singing, Baxter waved at Sam, who wore an oversize gray uniform featuring a gold badge. The gate and the large homes and the expert landscaping and the streets void of trash made one feel safe, as if a friendly voice said as you arrived, "Welcome to Willow Ridge, Baxter. Leave your worries behind."

With the gate there, it was also nice to know that his parents wouldn't be waiting at his doorstep, ready to beg for money again. His guitar was such a joke to them until they'd realized that he'd made it. His father's gravelly southern voice always distantly called out, "Just a few bucks, Bax. I'll get you back."

After six turns and twentysomething speed bumps, they arrived at their 3,300-square-foot brick home, which had been built only two years before he'd bought it. It was way more house than they needed, but it was the typical size in this neighborhood of southern yuppies—a stereotype he was squeezing into more and more every day. There was even a sense of pride in doing so, because it meant that Mia wasn't growing up in a trailer park like he had.

He'd bought a golf cart with oversize tires and a nice stereo the year prior. He'd even hung on top a flag of his alma mater, the University of South Carolina. Though he didn't regularly participate in the text thread going between him and his former bandmates, he'd sent them a picture of the golf cart, and they couldn't get enough. Former front man to a renegade alt-country band now rolling around in his dolled-up golf cart through his gated neighborhood on the way to the pool for a turkey club sandwich and a Michelob Ultra.

"My move," Mia said, climbing down from the truck and running to the door. She was very into chess these days, and they'd left a match going from earlier.

Still in the truck, he watched his little girl as she keyed in the code and entered the house. During the drive, he'd considered how to broach the subject of his wife's death. He'd not forgotten something Dr. Carr had told him when they'd first met: to trust his instincts. She'd made the point that instincts come from the deep brain, the intuitive part that is much wiser than the analytical side.

He understood her suggestion because he believed good lyrics came to a songwriter in much the same way. Actually, he'd paid for this house with the leftover money from touring and the royalty checks from songs he'd written for his own band and ones he'd sold to various Nashville artists. These were tunes that had come to him before Sofia passed; he hadn't written anything since.

His best songs had always come from out of the blue, like magic. Not that the feeling was fresh in his mind. He hadn't written or even played much since leaving the band, those fun days of youth a distant memory, his Martin guitar stowed away in a closet, collecting dust. But when Dr. Carr had told him to trust his fatherly instincts, it had hit home. With as much doubt as he felt these days, he just hoped he was reading the signs right.

He found Mia sitting on the bench at the dining room table, staring at the half-played match of chess on the black-and-white board. A bouquet of yellow and red wildflowers they had picked on a walk the evening before sprang from a vase on the other side of the table.

Without looking up, she said, "Pawn to B5, your move."

He sat across from her, gazing over the figures. As a way to find something they could do together, Baxter had given her the chessboard the previous Christmas. He'd had no idea how much she would love it. She'd spent the rest of the Christmas break and many days after school in the following months studying the game on YouTube. In fact, Baxter was no longer letting her win or even seeing ways to teach her, and last night she'd beaten him in eight moves.

"I'd like to talk about what you told Ms. Mecca," he said casually.

"Do we have to?" She glanced at him before returning her attention to the board. Then she began to hum. She'd been doing it for weeks now. According to Dr. Carr, humming was a form of disassociation.

"I know you'd rather not talk about it, but we have to. You know that." He was completely unsure of where to start or how detailed to be, but he knew this was the time to have the talk he'd dreaded for three long years. "Why didn't you tell me what happened at school?"

Her shrug catapulted him back in time.

Five years before Sofia's death, Mia's arrival had come as a cataclysmic surprise. They'd been married only two years, and the idea of having kids was something they'd talked about as if it were a decade away. Baxter was touring heavily with his band, Cactus Road, and they'd finally broken into larger venues after years of dragging their equipment from one smoky and shady bar to another across the Southeast.

Wasn't that when the curveballs came? One night after a show at the Amway Center in Orlando, as casually as if she wanted to know, *Sushi or Thai?*, Sofia had asked him, "Where would you put a crib on the tour bus?"

Not that he wasn't excited—he remembered lifting her up and spinning around, singing, "You're gonna be a mom! I'm gonna be a dad!"—but as all surprise pregnancies did, it had made them reevaluate their plans. Sofia traveled with the band everywhere, and he loved their time together, but adding a little one promised all sorts of complications.

In the months that followed, Baxter strongly considered leaving Cactus Road. It was a beast of a decision, a war in his head. Music had saved his soul, and until then he'd dedicated his life to it. What if he left the band and resented Sofia and Mia for it?

But always and forever in the back of his mind was his arduous upbringing and how he'd told himself that if he married and had children, he would do everything he could to give them the opposite of the life he'd known. Where Baxter's addict parents had been checked out half the time, their double-wide trailer a swinging door to drug deals, Baxter wanted to be an engaged father who raised his child in the safest of environments.

And yet he didn't know what else to do with his life. With Sofia leaving her job to become a stay-at-home mom, his best bet of giving them financial security was staying put. How many meals had his family skipped when he was Mia's age? How many times had he drenched his butter pasta in ketchup and covered it in bread-and-butter pickles, just to have a little extra food on his plate? He couldn't let his daughter experience that hunger in her belly, even for a minute.

With Sofia's full support, Baxter chose not to leave the band. But once she was gone, he had little choice. Of course the touring life was no life at all for a motherless little girl, but there was also another factor at play. Losing Sofia had knocked the creative wind out of him. He didn't want to play anymore; he had nothing left to give. When he picked up his guitar a few days after she'd died, all he'd felt was that he was holding the instrument of her destruction. He should have left the band the first time he'd considered it, case closed.

Baxter couldn't tell his daughter everything. Hell, he could barely sit with the memories himself.

"What did the kid say to you?" he asked. He had no idea how much detail she might know.

Mia's eyes darted left to right on the board, searching for her move. "What did Ms. Mecca say he said?"

A *he*, Baxter thought. He felt his mouth go dry as he said, "That he told you your mother was killed by a bad guy."

After a long few seconds, she moved her pawn again and said, "Yeah."

"Why didn't you tell me, honey? How in the world have you kept this a secret?"

"Why didn't you tell *me*?" She looked at him with eyebrows curled in anger, more anger than which he thought she was capable. "Is it true?"

He held her gaze. Mia had every right to be angry with him. He was angry with himself. "Your mother did not die in a car accident. She was shot by a sick man in a Target parking lot while you were in day care."

The memory was a dull blade into his chest. Images as black and white as the board flashed before him: Baxter stepping away from a sound check for their first appearance at *Austin City Limits* to answer Sofia's call. Her voice had faded by the second as she'd attempted through gurgling and coughing to tell him what had happened. The call had abruptly ended—maybe she'd hung up—and he'd tried her back, over and over, disappearing backstage because the guys in the band were still messing with their instruments and giving Baxter a hard time. ("Bax, she's got you wrapped around her finger!") He could still hear the crack of the gunshots, the wailing of the sirens, and the life leaving her voice as she told him to take care of Mia.

Give her the best life, Bax. The best you can.

Casting his own emotions aside, he stood, rounded the table, and sat on the bench next to Mia, straddling it so he could face her. When she looked at him, he could see that her eyes had given way to vulnerability. This was exactly why they didn't talk about Sofia anymore. It was too painful.

"What did Mommy do to him? Why did he hurt her?"

Baxter hid his sadness by speaking almost matter-of-factly, as if talking about that day didn't crush him. "She didn't do anything. She was walking into Target to get me a new shaving razor, and this guy was really angry."

"At who?"

Baxter inclined his shoulders. "No one. He was just . . . sick and angry and confused and decided to open fire on a bunch of people in a parking lot. He'd been let go from his job and his girlfriend had dumped him and he was really messed up. I didn't want you to ever have to go through what I went through, thinking about him, thinking about her in such a way."

She put her hand on her queen, almost like she was unfazed by what he'd told her. He knew that wasn't the case, though. Could she actually grasp what he was saying? Or was she disassociating again?

"Where's the bad guy now?" Mia asked.

"He's in jail for the rest of his life. Two life sentences."

He couldn't believe he was telling her this—that he *had* to tell her this. All because he'd chosen to hold on to his dream of music. He should have been the one buying the goddamn razor.

He leaned in and pressed his forehead to hers. "I'm sorry."

"I didn't tell you that I knew," Mia said, "because I didn't want you to be sad."

He sighed as sorrow and anger swelled around his cheeks. "Honey, you don't need to worry about me. I'm fine." Trying to lighten things up, he curled his tattooed arm into a bodybuilder move. "Besides, look at these puppies. You don't ever need to protect me."

She didn't find his gesture funny at all.

He said, "And this is why it's always been best that we don't talk about your mom too much. It's just better that way, right? We have to be strong for her." He touched her chin. "Right?"

"Yes, sir."

"Now will you tell me the truth about your nightmares?" he asked, knowing they had to have the conversation. At least once. "What do you see?"

A long pause. Then with her eyes still on his chest, she said, "I just see someone shooting Mommy."

Tears pricked his eyes. He saw the same thing, day and night. "I'm sorry, Mia. I'm so sorry."

"It's not your fault, Daddy."

He looked at her. "It's not about fault, honey. It's about . . ." He squeezed his eyes shut. "Why did you even believe the kid in your class? What if it wasn't true?"

"I knew it was true because it was Philip who told me."

He heard his voice rise an octave. "Alan's Philip?"

Mia gave a nod.

Baxter turned away. The reason he had met Alan in the first place was that their kids were the same age. Baxter had met Alan's wife, Amy, at the day care Mia attended at the time. Alan and Amy knew damn well that Mia didn't know the facts of her mother's death, so why had they told Philip?

"I guess it doesn't matter," he finally said, looking back at her.

But it did matter. He felt a flash of anger toward Alan but more so at himself. He shouldn't have lied to her for so long, and maybe not at all. Mia's anger at him drove the stake only deeper.

"Who else knows?" Mia asked.

He'd been dreading the question. "It was in the news, honey. Most adults know. All the adults you know."

"And they were lying to me too? How about the other kids in my class?" Her forehead creased with embarrassment. "Do they know?"

Baxter shook his head. "I . . ." This was hard to admit. "I reached out to the parents in the class and asked them not to talk about it with their children yet, not until I'd spoken with you." As a matter of fact, he'd messaged them in a group email. The idea had seemed good at the time. He was even proud of how successfully he'd protected Mia from knowing the specifics of her mother's death, an effort that had required making sure everyone in Mia's life knew not to broach the topic. As he heard himself talking now, though, it felt more like he'd been conspiring against her.

Mia stared into the middle distance.

Was she too young to be able to process her feelings? he wondered. Or was she checked out? Or angry?

Baxter swallowed. "I was doing the best I could, sweetie. I swear to you. There are no . . . instructions for what to do when this happens. All I wanted to do was protect you."

She didn't even blink. After a beat long enough for Baxter to once again properly scold himself for his failures, she said, "I just wish I could remember her better."

No, no, no, he thought. That was not at all what she should be wishing.

"I kind of remember her," she said, "like, I see her face and I remember being with her, but I feel like I'm forgetting her. I keep seeing her up in heaven frowning, thinking I'm"—her eyes finally lifted—"not a good daughter."

With a heaviness pressing down on him, Baxter pulled her into his chest, sliding her toward him. "Honey, nothing about you would make your mom sad. Those are just yucky thoughts."

"I just . . . I just . . ."

"What?"

"I don't want her to go away."

The hollowness in his chest swelled. He thought of the day he'd started erasing Sofia from their lives—the photo albums, the framed pictures, throwing them all away. Bagging up her clothes and tossing them in the trash can outside because he couldn't bear the idea of donating them and someone else wearing them.

"Honey, that's just the way it is. We both have to let her go. Thinking about her all the time—talking about her—it only makes it worse. Now that you know what happened, there's nothing left to wonder about . . . nothing more to know."

With her face against his neck, Mia nodded. Baxter pressed his eyes together hard, feeling his failures like never before.

Chapter 3

23andMia

While Mia napped on the couch, Baxter retreated to his home office and tried to distract himself with work. He waded through email hell for a good forty-five minutes, delegating what he could and trying to prioritize the rest of the requests. Until recently, he'd been good at multitasking. Maybe not as good as Sofia, but good enough to manage thirty to fifty simultaneous projects. With Mia's issues cropping up, though, he'd lost his groove, and the decisions and issues he faced often came at him in a chaotic and unmanageable blur.

Honestly, what did any of it matter if she wasn't thriving? If one more person told him kids were resilient, he was going to explode. It was his job to make it so that she didn't have to be resilient. And if he couldn't figure out a solution soon, he'd probably have a heart attack as opposed to exploding. That was what the burning in his chest lately was telling him.

Giving up on work, he googled *anxiety*, and the results led him down a rabbit hole of information. Apparently, anxiety was a normal reaction to stress, a feeling he was not short on. Searching for remedies, he ignored suggestions to go to the doctor and clicked deeper into the more holistic-looking sites, with suggestions such as spend time walking, spend time in nature, stare up at the sky, meditate. He didn't know which was worse, being poked and prodded by doctors or one of the latter options.

Reading an article about how less work can make you more productive, he was about to throw the computer across the room when he noticed an alert notifying him of a new email. Just when he'd finally gotten his in-box under control. Unable to let the message sit there unattended, he navigated to his mail app. The email was from 23andMe, something about a compromised password.

A sharp pain ran up his spine as memories came rushing back. It had been Sofia's idea to do the test not long before she died. In fact, when they'd first met, she was upset because she'd only just found out the day prior from her mother, Dotty, that she'd been adopted from a convent in Madrid while her father was working as an American diplomat stationed at the embassy there.

Nothing came of it, though. First, with the help of a translator, she'd reached out to the convent. They'd been less than helpful, stating that all adoptions were closed. Then, using his email address to sign up, she and Baxter had both taken tests. To no one's surprise, Baxter had learned that he was mostly English and Irish. He'd even found two third cousins, who'd also taken the tests. Considering his lineage was bogged down by drugs, alcohol, and abuse, he'd opted not to reach out to them.

Sofia was mostly Iberian, meaning Portuguese and Spanish, which was not a surprise considering the story Dotty had told her. To her dismay, her family tree was blank. She'd been pretty bummed about that. Ultimately, they'd never been able to locate her biological parents, and it had been a sore spot in Sofia's life. She'd always felt like she didn't belong.

Maybe like how Mia felt now.

Baxter felt sick inside. Even the image of Sofia's face in his mind was enough to kill him. He shook his head, thinking more stress triggers were the last thing he needed. He decided he'd better deal with the password issue now and be done with it, so he logged on to the site. It was Sofia's account that it defaulted to, so her name was at the top right: Sofia Shaw. Baxter wondered if there had been any updates to Sofia's family tree, but the less going down memory lane, the better.

He dragged the cursor up to the notifications bell to figure out how to close her account but saw a notification below: A relative has sent you a message.

As much as he didn't want to, he couldn't help himself. There was something tempting about finishing the work they'd started years ago, finally solving the mystery of her origins, even if she wasn't there to experience the victory. He couldn't just pretend that he hadn't seen the communication. It would haunt him. And so, against the wishes of half of him, he navigated that way.

Someone named Ester Arroyo had written.

Looking away to the wall left of the monitor, he resisted for a moment. He could still back out. Close the computer and walk away. Then, when he was in a stronger place, come back and delete the account and move on.

However, a stronger force, one of curiosity and maybe even hope, tugged him in the other direction. Without his exactly willing them, his eyes drifted to her words.

> Hello, Sofia, my name is Ester Arroyo, and I received a message that we are related. I've been looking for my daughter, who I gave up for adoption in Madrid in 1982. Could that be you?

Baxter lost his breath. *Madrid.* Part of him wanted to call Dotty, both to see if she knew more and perhaps to unravel some of the mystery for her. But because Dotty had hidden Sofia's adoption from her, the topic was a tremendous sore spot. Only when Sofia had expressed interest in taking a DNA test and learning about their heritage had

Dotty felt forced to confess the truth. Bringing up anything to do with the adoption would certainly do no good. Even more, Dotty would most likely pull back even further from Mia, which was only barely possible.

Sofia's mother was now on her fourth marriage and had moved up to the Santa Ynez Valley, and she was almost as checked out as Baxter's mother. Though Dotty had come to the funeral and even stayed for a week, she'd been in so much emotional strife that she was barely there at all. And she'd gone back west and separated herself by the day, to the point that Mia had been lucky to get Christmas and birthday gifts. Though Dotty'd never admitted it outright, it seemed to Baxter that her guilt over hiding the adoption, coupled with Sofia's murder, had completely broken her past the point of fixing.

When he'd gotten himself together enough to think, he clicked on Ester's profile and suddenly felt like he'd been struck in the back of the head. Loss and longing raced to the surface like an amateur scuba diver whose tank had gone empty.

A dark-skinned woman with long black hair striped with ribbons of gray stared back at him with brown eyes that Baxter saw every day on his daughter's face and every night when he dreamed of the woman he'd lost.

"Earth to Dad," Mia said. "Who is that? She looks just like Mom."

Baxter froze.

Mia had appeared out of nowhere and was standing next to him. Before he could close his laptop, she was reading from Ester's profile.

"I'm trying to find my daughter, who was born on November 3 of 1982. I gave her up for adoption at the Santa María Convent that same day." Mia put her hand on her dad's shoulder. "Who is that?"

"Nobody, honey," he replied quickly, feeling like he'd just been caught sifting through Sofia's ashes. He shut the laptop. "Nobody."

"Why did she look just like Mommy?"

"I don't think she did." His heart burned and his mouth went dry. He didn't want to lie to his daughter, not again. Not today. But she was far too young for this.

"Yeah, she did. Look." Mia slid her finger under the laptop lid and began to open it.

"Stop," Baxter said, more harshly than he'd intended.

"I just wanted to see the picture, gosh."

The way he'd just snapped at his daughter snapped him out of his trance, at least long enough to realize that he shouldn't hide what he'd found from her. But wasn't what he'd told her earlier enough for today?

Taking both Mia's hands and staring down into her eyes, he said, "That's my personal stuff. My computer, okay?" He changed his tone. "Now, what are we doing for dinner?"

He could see that she wasn't satisfied with his response, but thankfully she let it go.

⁓

Later, Mia walked into the kitchen. "Daddy, I'm still thinking about that picture on your computer."

Baxter dropped his head. He stood at the counter, cutting slices of meat off a baked ham that he'd bought the day before. It was the gift that kept on giving in their household, and Baxter had a hundred ways he could put the ham to work: sandwiches, soups, casseroles, meat and threes. Tonight he was making paninis with white Vermont cheddar and the bread Mia liked from Publix.

Something had told him several times in the last hour since she'd seen that photo that she wasn't going to let it go. In fact, he'd even thought of what he could say to curtail her curiosity: that it was Sofia's grandmother in the photo, Dotty's mother. And when Mia asked to see the photo again, he would show it to her one last time and then be done with it.

It occurred to him that it was during a meal with one of the many baked hams that had filled their refrigerator since losing Sofia that Baxter had finally found a way out of their misery. Along with casseroles, southerners loved to bring over these hams to show their love. The first had been a gift from their neighbor, and on this particular night, he'd served it to Mia with mac and cheese and broccoli. It had been three weeks since the murder, and he'd been down twentysomething pounds and still wasn't eating—other than an occasional bite of something to keep his stomach from burning.

Between bites, Mia had been asking what Mommy might be doing in heaven when Baxter had had to excuse himself. He'd rushed to his room and folded onto the floor, curling up into a ball and crying. When he'd heard the door swing open a few minutes later, he'd looked up to see Mia staring at him. He'd forgotten to flip the lock.

To this day, he could still hear the creak of the door hinges as she came into the room. The sight of his little girl looking down on the one person she needed to count on had triggered something in him. He'd instantly seen himself at her age, looking over at his glassy-eyed parents on the couch as they disappeared from reality with beer and weed. He knew exactly the feeling of needing someone to count on but not having them, and he'd do anything to protect Mia from knowing even another moment of it.

He'd pushed up from the floor with a clear vision of what to do. For one, she would not see him cry again. He had to be strong. To do that *and* to move on, they would stop talking about Sofia. It was time to bury her for good. And one of the first ways to do that had been to sell that cursed house, get rid of her belongings—her Honda Passport, her clothes, the surfboards, the computer—and get the hell out of Charleston. No more would Mia see a weak father who was as lost as she.

Here they were almost three years later, more baked ham on the counter, and Baxter was still lost and still trying to extinguish Sofia's memory.

He set the knife down and went to the sink to wash the ham off his hands. As he dried them with a dish towel, he said, "You're not going to let it go, are you?"

"I don't understand why you won't tell me." She surely wasn't disassociating now; she was determined.

Guilt rushed in. Not necessarily the guilt of lying in the first place—she had been five and needed protecting—but he should have said something sooner. He should have kept Mia with Dr. Carr and worked on how to break the news. He could have spared Mia the embarrassment of finding out from a classmate, and he could have saved her from the nightmares.

"C'mere, let's sit down," he said, scrambling to figure out what to say. How could he explain all this to Mia in a way that would reveal the truth but also allow him to put an endcap on her questions?

They sat a foot apart on the couch. She folded her legs under her. Baxter rested his forearms on his thighs and turned to her. "You know how you were working on the family tree in Ms. Mecca's class? How you're at the bottom, and then one side is me and then Cassie and Pops and then their parents? And then how another branch goes to your mom?"

Mia dipped her chin while repeatedly flicking her thigh with her middle finger, a nervous habit that, like humming, she'd picked up recently. Baxter wondered if what he was about to say was too much for her. Then again, he couldn't bear telling another lie.

Hoping he wasn't making a grave mistake, he said, "There was something your mom found out when she was older, actually the day before she and I met." He paused, a foot hanging over the ledge. "Your mother was adopted."

Mia stopped the motion with her hand. "What?" She looked confused, but he knew she understood. One of her friends was adopted.

"Grandma Dotty is actually her adoptive mother." Baxter resisted the urge to say, "Doesn't that explain a lot?" He smoothed his hands together as he continued to lean toward his daughter. "Have you ever heard about 23andMe?"

She shook her head.

"It's a way to test your genes, to see where you come from. You know about DNA, right? It's the . . ." He stopped, realizing he must have been writing songs during his biology class at USC. "It's the little bits in your body that make you who you are. 23andMe can take your spit from your DNA, analyze it, and then tell you everything about your family. It goes back thousands of years."

She looked at him skeptically. "Your spit?"

"You spit into a vial and stick it in the mail. They send you the results. Back around the time your mom and I started dating, genetic testing was getting kind of popular, and she'd been thinking about doing it, curious about her ancestry."

Baxter sat back. "After she found out she was adopted, your mom got so excited about finding her real family." He didn't say that Sofia's eagerness to find her family was because she'd never felt like she belonged in the family who'd raised her. "So we eventually took the tests."

"And . . ."

"And . . . we didn't find anything. In order to find a connection, other people in your family have to do the same test." With every word, Baxter wondered how in the world he was going to bring the conversation to a close. This was far more than he'd thought about Sofia in a long time, and he felt like he was in danger of offsetting his own progress as well.

"Anyway, I just happened to be on the website—this 23andMe—because of a random security email, and I saw that someone had reached out to your mom. And it may . . ." A sudden and overwhelming wave of something—*Was it sadness?*—or whatever it was rushing through him felt awful. Swallowing it back, refusing to let Mia see it, he said, "I think it might be your mom's real mom. That's why they look so much alike."

"What? Holy cow. So that would make her my grandmother?" The question marks in her eyes turned to flames of excitement.

"Could be. I don't know."

"Can I see her?"

Nope, he thought. This was not going as planned. If only Mia had been satisfied with what he'd told her.

He grabbed his computer and returned to the couch. She squeezed next to him as he opened the laptop and navigated back to Ester Arroyo's profile.

"Whoa," Mia said. "She looks just like Mom."

"Yeah, I know. Kind of wild, right?"

"So she's looking for Mom?"

"Yeah, apparently. We can't know for sure that she really is your mom's mom. I can't imagine they always get it right on this website."

Her inner lawyer came alive. "They look alike, though."

"That they do."

"And she wrote a note?" Mia's demeanor had taken a U-turn from earlier in the day, and she was suddenly engaged and interested.

Baxter suppressed an urge to tell her not to get too excited as he navigated to the messages. Mia read it out loud and then said, "We have to write her back."

There it was, Baxter thought. He knew that was coming. As successful as he'd been at protecting his daughter by blocking off the memories of Sofia, it seemed she had found another way in.

"That's the thing, honey. I don't think we should."

"Why?"

"Well, for one, she might not speak English. She lives in Valencia, Spain." That rationale didn't work, and Baxter realized it only after he'd said it. Ester had written them in English. Of course, it could be she'd used a translating tool.

"No problemo," Mia said. *"Yo hablo español!"* It was true—she was learning Spanish. One of the perks of Mia's school was that they were strong advocates for foreign language.

"Okay, here's the real reason. She's looking for your mom, honey, and she's not going to like what she finds. In fact, the truth will break her heart. You know how badly it hurt us when we lost Mommy. We don't want her to go through the same thing. I don't think your mom would want her to either."

Mia slunk into the couch.

"I know it stinks and I know . . ." He stopped before he said something negative about Mia's existing grandmothers and their lack of participation in Mia's life. "I know it would be neat to exchange a couple of notes, but we have to do what's best for this woman. Do you understand?"

Mia frowned.

With his own broken heart, Baxter wrapped his arm around Mia and pulled her in. An eight-year-old couldn't understand how painful dredging up the past could be. Even seeing the photo and reading Ester's words sent memories of Sofia rushing up into his mind, forcing him to dodge them like someone swiping at him with a knife. Going any further wouldn't be good for either one of them.

Mia put her fingers on the trackpad and clicked on the photo of Ester. They both stared at the woman for a while, and the longing coursing through him served as proof to how dangerous memories could be.

Shutting them out once again, Baxter folded closed the computer. Feeling instantly more at peace, he said quickly, "Okay, wanna help me cook the paninis?"

Chapter 4

SHE DREAMS OF BUTTERFLIES

Baxter finally got Mia to bed around nine, a practice that had become a full-time job. After the lengthy process of getting her to brush her teeth, go to the bathroom, and dress in her pajamas—tasks hindered by countless distractions—he lay next to her in the bottom bunk bed of her room, which, with the dollhouses, trampoline, and shelves and baskets spilling over with toys, could easily double for a toy store.

Mia lay on her back, a small stuffed panda named Roger tucked into her right arm. An armada of other stuffies lined up on the other side of her. He was reading her a bedtime tale, pulling off an impressive—if he did say so himself—German accent for King Jonas in the story, when Mia interrupted him with the ever-so-simple "Daddy."

As soon as the word left her mouth, he knew he was in trouble. He could feel her little brain spinning. "How dare you interrupt my performance," he said. His accent might have sounded more French than German, come to think of it.

"Would you still be playing music if Mommy hadn't died?"

Setting the book aside, Baxter rolled toward her, inches from her face. He instantly worried that he'd made a mistake by telling Mia about the adoption and about the note from Ester Arroyo. Had he made the situation—as grave as it already was—even worse?

"I don't know," he admitted. "The tour bus life gets old quickly, trust me, all the travel, the eating out. You were on the bus sometimes, though you don't remember. I like sleeping in the same bed every night, and I love having a morning routine, chatting with you while you eat your cereal, my Peloton ride. And what's better than coming home to you?"

He partially believed what he was telling her, but it was complicated. Music had been everything to him, and they'd broken through. How many bands had fallen short of achieving their aspirations? Baxter and the other guys had done it, making the kind of money they could have only dreamed of when they'd started putting around in that old blue van in their early twenties.

He sure as heck hadn't imagined it when he'd bought his first guitar, an electric Peavey, and a ragged old Marshall amplifier from a pawnshop downtown. A hundred bucks for both. His dad had called it a waste of money; his mom hadn't even noticed. From the moment Baxter had plucked the first string, though, he'd found safety from all the bad things going on inside his house. As long as he had a guitar in his hand, he could drown out the screaming between his stoned or drunk parents, and he could forget about the last time his father had hit him or his mother had told him, "I knew you were a mistake."

Not that he'd completely stayed out of trouble. He'd gone to jail three times before he graduated from high school, once for breaking and entering, another time for getting caught with a bag of weed, and another for spray-painting the word ANARCHY on a patrol car. At least he'd graduated from high school, which was more than he could say for most everyone in his family and in their circle. Hell, he'd even gone on to get a degree in music from the University of South Carolina. More than once, he'd told the story of what his father had said when he'd told him he'd gotten a scholarship: "They'll let anybody in these days, won't they?"

That was okay, though, because by then he wasn't out to prove his parents wrong or to achieve the impossible and make them proud. By then all he cared about was conquering the world one song at a time.

These were things Mia couldn't know. Because yes, dammit. Yes. He would still be playing music if Sofia hadn't been gunned down.

"But you're always so stressed when you get home," Mia said. "I know you don't like your job." He could smell her bubblegum mouthwash.

"Well, sometimes, but . . . you'll see when you get older. No matter what job you have, it's not always exactly what you want to be doing all day. In theory, playing music is a really fun way to make a living, but after a while, all the driving and staying up late and spending all your time with four other guys starts to grate on you."

Was that true? he wondered. Though he'd been telling himself that, he recalled such fond days on the road. Mia didn't need to know that, though.

"And when you fall in love with someone like your mom and have a little girl like you, everything you thought you wanted changes. I could have been playing the Royal Albert Hall to the king and queen, and I would have rather been with you two." At least, in hindsight, that was the truth. How he wished he'd seen it more clearly then.

If that had been the case, he wouldn't have been on the road when Sofia was killed. He very well might have been with her, or better yet, been shopping on his own to buy a razor. Either way, he sure as hell would have stopped that bastard. He would have . . .

A great gasp of air escaped him as he nearly folded over.

"Are you okay?" Mia asked.

"Yeah, sorry." He gripped the flesh of his left thigh and squeezed tightly, attempting to let the physical pain take him away from the agony of the past.

Shaking it off, he touched Mia's nose. "When I wake up in the morning, the first thing I think about is you. *You* are what matters now."

"Why do you work so much then? I barely see you sometimes. You pick me up from school and then work even more."

More guilt pounded him. He hated how he felt, as if he were neglecting her. He wondered if there was any way to effectively communicate the whys of working hard. He'd been making great money in his late twenties and thirties. Their tours had become incredibly lucrative, and he was selling three or four songs a year to big country artists. And for the record, unlike a lot of the stuff clogging the Nashville airwaves, the songs he was writing for them had heart and soul. He'd found a niche in writing stuff that walked the fine line between being satisfyingly esoteric and intelligent while also having enough of a hook to enjoy heavy rotation on the radio and streaming services.

The royalty checks BMI was cutting him had grown absurdly bigger every month, to the point that before Sofia was killed, the hot topic in their house had been whether to upgrade their existing home or buy a beach house down near Beaufort, a little place where they could escape the traffic of Charleston.

Well, the checks were smaller now, and Cactus Road was disappearing into the back of people's memories, and he wasn't writing any more songs, and the fear of falling back into the poverty of his youth was just about killing him, so the only thing he knew to do was to give his all to his new company, at least until he'd built a team that could get through a day—hell, an hour—without needing him.

"That's part of taking care of you," he said. "I work hard so you don't grow up like I did, so we can live in this awesome house and you can go to your very expensive school. So I can retire at an early age and leave you some money one day. Cassie and Pops have always struggled, and we skipped meals, and I didn't get to go to a good school, and I didn't get birthday presents . . ."

He wished he could explain things better, but the truth of how bad his youth had been wasn't something he ever wanted to share with her. "Listen, Mia, it's a much bigger discussion than we have time for tonight, but know that, even though I might seem a little bit"—he searched for the word—"a bit agitated at times, I'm very happy with my life—with our life. Don't worry about me. All you need to worry about is getting a good night of sleep. I'll take care of the rest."

He picked up the book again and found his page. "Okay, let's figure out what happens with King Jonas."

After he reached the happily ever after, he stood and turned out all the lights, save the one dimming lamp in the corner, enough light to keep her from being afraid. He pulled the covers up around her and her stuffies and kissed her forehead.

Through a yawn, she asked, "You're singing me a song, right?"

"When do I not sing you a song, my little dove?"

Mia was quite possibly his biggest fan in the world and had worn out every Cactus Road album, memorizing every single word—including a few curse words he wished his younger songwriting self had withheld for the sake of his daughter.

On a stand next to the bedside table stood the pink three-quarter-size guitar he'd bought her the year before. He picked it up and sat on the bed, turning to her. Though he occasionally broke rank with something different, she typically wanted the lullaby he'd written for her when she was a few weeks old. Even now, almost eight years later, the tune could put her to sleep in minutes, often before he'd made it to the second verse.

Of course it was a silly little song—he'd written it for a baby—but it was catchy too. Knowing he had an uphill battle to get her to fall asleep tonight, he got right into it, singing,

> Close your eyes, our little Mia
> And find the world of sleepy dreams
> Your unicorn is saddled
> She wears flowers in her mane
> You can set off toward the stars together
> Make your way around the moon
> You can chase a bolt of lightning
> While we're singing you this tune.

Baxter barred an F chord and could hear Sofia joining him for the chorus, just like the old days in Mia's sky-blue room in Charleston. He could feel her hand on his shoulder, and he wished he couldn't. He wished he could just play the song for Mia's sake without it having to stir up so much of what went wrong.

Mia joined in, too, as he sang,

> When Mia dreams she dreams of butterflies
> And drifts away to this lullaby
> When she wakes she's glad to be alive
> And her mommy and daddy are right here by her side . . .

It took two more verses before Mia drifted off, hopefully riding off on her one-horned mare into a place far away from today. He'd never seen anything as beautiful as his daughter sleeping, her innocent face, the rise and fall of her chest, her heart full of love.

Then he was reminded of the dark things that visited her at night, and he hoped tonight might be different. Every night after he sang her this song, he hoped and prayed she might sleep through the night. Every three days or so, it happened. She'd wake refreshed, and he'd wonder if it was the calming tea he'd given her or the dinner he'd prepared. Or something he might have said or the way he'd sung her the song.

Perhaps tonight it might be different.

⌒

"Daddy!"

Baxter's eyes opened as if he'd been waiting for it. The clock on the bedside table read *2:14*.

A moment later, Mia rushed in from the hallway like someone was after her, Roger the panda bear clutched in her arm, tears streaming down her cheeks.

She reached the bed in desperate fear. "I was calling for you."

He rubbed his eyes, feeling the sand in the corners. She climbed up into the bed, slipped into the soft down, and wrapped her arms around him. It had happened so often in the last six weeks that this whole thing was like a dance routine between two partners who'd been practicing together all year.

"Everything's okay," he whispered, feeling her shake, wanting to ask her about the nightmare but not wanting her to relive it. "Everything's okay," he said again, kissing her head. So much for the truth setting them free.

When her trembling subsided, he started on her song again, petting her head. "And when she dreams she dreams of butterflies . . ." Soon she drifted off.

As usual, Baxter worried this might be it for him, his last chance to sleep. If his mind started up too much, he'd be a goner, and he was already thinking a mile a minute. Much more and he'd give up, get up, make coffee, and accept it was time to start the day. Lord knew even twenty-four hours weren't enough to accomplish all the things he had to do.

Baxter eventually fell into another half sleep but opened his eyes when he heard Mia stir. She muttered something like "stop" and then rolled over. His eyes watered as he looked at his little girl fighting through her grief. Then she groaned and moaned, and Baxter got ready to wake her, to pull her away from whatever she was experiencing. It was all this damn rehashing of memories that was making it worse.

Then a startling scream rose from her mouth—an agonizing, fear-laden scream—and Baxter's arms flew open to pull her in. His heart broke into a million pieces as he put his hands on her face and kissed her forehead. "It's just a dream."

She opened terrified eyes. "I don't like it."

"Me either, sweetie." He held her tighter, her back to him, and he whispered to her, repeating that everything was okay, as if it really were.

Trying not to move a muscle, he waited, breathing quietly, thinking he had to figure out how to fix this, whatever it took. How monumentally he'd screwed up by not telling her sooner. None of this would be happening. Breaking the news could have been a concerted effort in which Dr. Carr could have been there, and Ms. Mecca and the rest of the school could have been standing by, ready to support Mia.

Instead, a clueless kid had broken the news, and Mia had made the unbelievable decision to keep it all to herself. *Oh God,* he thought. Sofia would be so disappointed in him. Why couldn't it have been him who had been shot? She was the one who should be raising Mia.

If he hadn't laid down such roots with their house and new company, he might be of the mind to pack everything up and move to another state, somewhere even farther from the memory of her mother.

The only solution that seemed to make sense to him was to minimize all this talk about Sofia. Now that the truth was out, it was time to move on.

Chapter 5

THE REAL WORLD

The chirp of the alarm at six thirty felt like a drill sergeant screaming in his ear. He glanced at Mia, who slept next to him. "Time to get up, buttercup," he said, forcing a chipper tone, almost believing it himself. "Open those eyes, time to rise. Feet on the floor, though I love your snore."

"I don't snore," she said, her eyes peeling open with the sass one would expect of a teenager.

He pinched his fingers together. "Just a little bit. More like a . . ." He made a sound like a kid learning to whistle.

"Yeah, right." She rolled over, burying her face into the pillow.

"Seriously, time to get up."

"I don't want to go," she said in the pouty voice he knew all too well, her eyes still closed, her face half-swallowed by the down pillow. When he tried to wrangle her away, she finally looked at him. "Not today, okay?" Then she attempted to make her case.

Baxter stopped her. "Mia, no way. We're not doing this."

"Doing what?"

He shook his head, clinging to his patience. "I just need some help, honey."

Mia lifted her head off the pillow. "I still think we should write her."

"Write who?"

"Mom's mom."

"Mia, we already talked about this." He sat up and took her hand. "Please, give me a little bit of a break today. I need you to get up and get ready for school."

Mia sighed like he'd asked her to mop all the floors. "Fine."

As he thanked her, she slipped out of bed and trudged toward the door. What a way to wake up, feeling like he'd already let her down.

"Oh," she said, "if we have time, will you help me finish that necklace for Ms. Mecca? I need your help making it beautiful."

He was already running through his checklist of what needed to be done to get out the door in time. "You need *my* help making it beautiful?"

She nodded as her bottom lip pushed out.

He stared at her for a long time. If she only knew. No, he thought, he couldn't do it this morning, and she'd have to understand. "Look, not this morning. I've . . . My day is just . . . I have to do a million things before we leave. But remind me tonight, okay?"

She backhanded the air with both hands. "But I told her I'd bring it to her today."

"I understand. But we probably should have thought about that yesterday, right? I'm sure she'll understand. Now, please. We need to move quickly this morning. We're in a rush."

She let her hands fall to her sides. "We're always in a rush."

"Welcome to life, my little daughter."

With slumped shoulders, she twisted toward the door.

"Hey, Mia," he called.

"Yeah?"

He touched his nose. "I love you."

She touched her nose back and whispered, "Love you, too, Daddy."

As she disappeared down the hall, his thoughts rushed over him. Being a single parent wasn't easy. It was almost comical, and yet it was gut-wrenching at the same time. He never could seem to get away from hearing Sofia's last words, her asking him to give Mia a good life.

Sometimes it hurt so badly inside, this fear of failing his daughter, whom he loved beyond words, and failing his wife, who would demand more of him. Not that Baxter wasn't trying, even giving it his all, which was more than he could say about his father, but it was like he didn't exactly comprehend how to do it right. All the determination in the world didn't matter if you didn't know where you were going.

And this whole thing with 23andMe . . . he felt his cheeks quiver at the thought of actually connecting with Sofia's mother. That was the last thing he wanted to do. And the last thing Mia needed.

Times like these he just wanted to bury his head in Sofia's lap and cry it out. And he sure as hell couldn't put any of this heaviness on Mia. He couldn't let her know how much he was still hurting. It was a lot right now, digging up the past, having to relive it again.

He clenched his fists and tightened his whole body, wishing it all away. *Fuck!!!!* he screamed in his mind.

Then, as he'd done every morning since Sofia had been gunned down, like Siduri speaking to Gilgamesh, he said out loud, "Pull it together, Baxter. You've got a little girl out there who needs you."

⌒

"You look rode hard and put up wet," Alan said as Baxter climbed out of his truck at one of their jobsites, a house halfway framed. "Another bad night?"

"Another bad night, yeah, you could say that." Outside, in the sun, it was hot enough to still be summer. Fall must have been stuck somewhere.

He eyed the house, hearing the hammering from the guys inside. It was one of three spec homes they were building.

When he'd first heard the Avery Group was developing the massive neighborhood, he'd done everything he could, including beg, to be a part of it. The developers had offered several contractors opportunities to be one of the premier builders for the new community, which guaranteed work for at least a decade. Baxter was not among the chosen ones.

It wasn't going to stop him, though. Already tired of the sales part of the job, he wanted this gig, and he'd pushed the Avery Group until they'd finally relented, accepting him on a temporary basis until he could prove himself. Baxter was pretty sure it was because of his past success as a musician that he'd been allowed in the door. One of the higher-ups had been a fan.

Damn if they didn't ask a lot, though. They wanted him to buy ten lots and put up three houses before the end of February. If he could do that without any problems, they'd consider bringing him on, keeping him busy quite possibly until retirement. They weren't the most artistic or rewarding houses to build, but a project like this could finally give him the break he needed. He'd hastily agreed to their terms, perhaps too hastily, because it was going to take every dime he had and then some.

If things went sideways, he'd be in trouble. Not only had he liquidated his mutual funds and Sofia's 401(k) and drained his savings accounts, but he'd also convinced several investors to get on board too. The Avery Group had the Midas touch, so it was a good bet. Surely he could get these houses up and sell them for a profit, but what if something went wrong? Forget not becoming a premier builder. What if he couldn't sell the houses at the right price? A lot of it came down to the real estate market and stabilized material pricing, both variables no one man could control.

Had this been his only project, it might not have felt as risky, but this opportunity had landed at the worst of times, just when he'd already been pushing his unseasoned team, stacking extra jobs on every one of his four overworked project managers. How many times had he given them all motivational speeches lately, assuring them that if they pushed through, they'd be living the good life in a couple of years?

Baxter faced Alan, seeing firsthand how the extra workload was taking its toll. "You don't look much better than me. You keeping it together?"

"Tryin' to." Alan spit chewing tobacco into the gravel, then adjusted his yellow hard hat. He was Baxter's most reliable project manager, and certainly a friend as well. He was what Baxter would call a good ol' boy. His Carhartt pants had holes in them, and there was a permanent circular mark in his left pocket from where he kept his can of Copenhagen. A flat orange pencil stuck out of the pocket of his collared blue shirt.

He was not a handsome guy. He had a double chin, though he was skinny, and his nose was almost as crooked as the way his hard hat rested on his head. He had big ears too. Despite all that, he was married to a younger, beautiful woman who couldn't have loved him more. At the core, Alan was a sweetheart and as reliable as any man Baxter knew, which made what he had to say all the more complicated.

Not that he wasn't used to confrontation—he and Alan had butted heads a thousand times over work-related issues—but this one was personal.

"Wellllllll," Alan said, the four-letter word lasting a good three seconds, "I'm about to go find some more two-by-fours. The delivery was short. Then I got my standin' meetin' with the Prices at eleven. Somehow, I gotta find the time to . . ."

They discussed business for a little while, until Baxter seized a pause. "Look, I gotta talk to you about something."

Alan pulled his hard hat off, showing a messy head of hair and a sponge of sweat above each ear. He'd probably been working since six. "What's going on?"

Baxter found the dark of Alan's pupils. "Did Philip say anything about Mia hitting him yesterday?"

A light of recognition came on in Alan's eyes. "I knew about some-one hitting him, but he wouldn't tell us who. The teacher sent home an incident report."

"Yeah, well, there's more to it. I just found out Philip said some-thing to Mia in August about how her mom died, how she was killed. And I think he said something again yesterday."

Alan frowned as he tossed his hard hat to the ground. "Oh shit. I'm sorry, man."

Baxter raised frustrated hands, palms up. "How does Philip even know?"

Alan sighed. "I think he overheard Amy and me talking a couple of months ago. I didn't say anything because I was hoping he didn't hear."

Seeing how much this bothered Alan, any frustration Baxter had felt dissipated. "Yeah, he heard."

"I really am sorry," Alan said sincerely. "And we'll talk to him."

"It's not your fault, bud. I should have told her a long time ago." Hammers banged inside the house. "How did it even come up?"

Alan half smiled. "Well, frankly, Baxter, we're worried about you. Amy and I were talkin' about what we might do for you, how we can—"

"You don't need to worry about me."

"I tend to disagree. And that was before this whole sleep thing. You're burning it at both ends, buddy. Look at you. We were talkin' 'bout how you needed to take better care of yourself, go out and have some fun. Let loose a little bit. Maybe even go on a date. Lord knows there's a lot of women anxious to see that day. I was saying how Mia was getting older and was ready for the truth when I noticed Philip standing there at the door."

Baxter shook his head. He had had it up to his ears with people telling him how to live. Soon as someone loses a spouse, everyone in their life has all the answers. Every one of his bandmates *and* their wives had tried to get involved: "This is what I'd do, Bax," or "Trust me, time will make it better." Baxter had stopped answering their calls for a while. They'd gotten the message and backed off.

"Though this isn't how I would want Mia to find out," Alan said, "she was bound to. Not that I'm making excuses. I should have been more careful. But, Baxter, maybe I'll take this opportunity to tell you what I was tellin' Amy."

"I'm not sure that I want to hear it."

Alan met his eyes with a rare firmness. "I'm going to say it anyway. You've looked like hell for months. Since this sleepin' thing came up, it's only gotten worse. I've never seen you drop balls until recently. And here we are taking a big bite out of a new project I hope to God we can pull off. No offense, and I'm no poster boy for perfection, but you being at the helm of this thang, you need to take care o' yourself."

Trying not to get defensive, Baxter ran his eyes past the freshly paved road to one of the empty lots waiting for a house. He knew there was truth to what Alan was saying, but Baxter was doing the best he could.

He said, "I know I'm pushing my limits, believe me. As soon as I get Mia feeling better and we can get a few of these houses sold, then I'm gonna sit back and relax, work on myself."

"Forgive me for sayin' so," Alan said, "but I think you might need to find some balance in your life a little faster than that. Or you might not make it until all this is done. Mia needs her dad, maybe more so than this job needs you. You said she's goin' through another bout of grief. I wonder if you are too—"

"It was only three years ago, Alan. I don't think grief is that easy to let go. But more than anything, we've got a lot going on right now. It feels like make-it-or-break-it time for the company."

"That's why we're workin' our asses off for you. I'm just sayin' you might be able to handle it better if you take care of yourself. Amy would tell you to go spend a weekend at the spa, get a massage, a facial. I'd tell you to go find a good woman. Get yourself out there." He pointed a finger at Baxter's chest. "Tell me this. When's the last time you picked up a guitar? Wrote a song? Hell, did something for fun?"

"I play Mia a tune or two every night," Baxter said, as if he'd just served an ace on the tennis court. He so wished everyone would worry about themselves. If they really wanted to help, just leave a casserole or a baked ham at the door and move along.

Alan picked up his hat and dusted it off. "I hear ya. It just seems like you're distracting yourself from living sometimes, but what do I know."

Baxter swallowed, more defensiveness rising up in him, and searched for the right words to show how he felt. "Look, I appreciate you caring. And I don't want you to beat yourself up about the thing with Philip. It was gonna come out one way or another."

"Still, I'm sorry," Alan said. "You know me 'n' Amy are pulling for you and would do anything to help both of you."

"I know. How is Amy, anyway? How's her mom?"

Alan set his hat back on his head, and it rested again crooked. "The doctor thinks she's losin' the battle. They caught the cancer too late, you know."

Baxter bit his bottom lip. "And here I am stuck in my own stuff. I'm sorry. Y'all let me know if I can do anything."

"Hey, we all have our cross to bear, don't we?"

"That we do, brother."

~

Baxter picked Mia up late from aftercare at 5:37. She was the last one there, and he apologized profusely to the teacher. As they crossed the parking lot to his truck, Mia said, "I'm not going to the skate party tomorrow."

"What?" He stopped and turned to her. "Honey, Lucy's your best friend. You have to go."

"She's not really my best friend. And I *definitely* don't have to go." Her tone said it all. She was ready to fight if he took the bait. They'd been here far too often lately.

He found the last-second strength to resist telling her that she had to do whatever he told her to. Instead, he asked calmly, "What happened between you and Lucy? And don't you like to laugh at me being tortured by the moms?"

She seemed to back off from her attack mode. "Nothing, and I just don't want to go."

The last thing Baxter wanted to do was force her to go places, but he was worried about her socialization. All she wanted to do lately was stay at home and play chess, or make bracelets or necklaces with beads, or sleep.

Dr. Carr had called Baxter during lunch and stated the obvious, that finding out the details of her mother's murder had brought her grief back up to the surface, and the best thing Baxter could do was to be there for her. "Get on the floor with her," she'd said. "Play with her. Talk to her. Listen to her. Give her all you got."

Baxter had gotten frustrated. "I do give her all I've got." What did she think he was doing?

"When you take her to the playground, instead of sitting on the bench, maybe get on the swing next to her." Was that what Mia had told her? Dr. Carr had said something else that had gotten under his skin too. Baxter had expressed his regret at not telling Mia sooner about her mother, to which Dr. Carr had replied, "It's spilt milk, Baxter. Nothing you can do now."

What in the hell did that mean? Had he ruined Mia for good? That was what it felt like.

When he'd told Dr. Carr about Mia seeing over his shoulder the picture of Sofia's potential mother, he heard the excitement in her voice. "Oh, well, this is great. What a wonderful way to connect with her mother. I think you should let her write her. All these things that can keep Sofia alive can be great for her."

Baxter had never agreed with Dr. Carr with regard to keeping Sofia alive, but he'd chosen not to argue with her. She'd probably win, anyway. "That's the thing," he'd said. "This woman looking for her daughter doesn't know that she's dead."

Dr. Carr had replied, "That's tough, Baxter. I can't make that decision for you. I can understand your hesitation, though." If only making decisions were as black and white as his memories.

He'd spent the rest of the day trying to ignore the notion, but it kept niggling at him like a relentless vole in his lawn that wouldn't stop poking its head up in a new place. At one point, he'd wondered if he couldn't get rid of the thought because it was supposed to be there. Or . . . maybe Sofia was the one who kept driving it to the surface.

Glancing over at his daughter, he could feel her resentment toward him. He'd been in the doghouse with Sofia a thousand times, and he'd never liked it. He wished he could swear to Mia that he'd never lie to her again, but life was too complicated for such promises.

Instead, he asked, "Are you upset that I lied to you?"

She cast a look out the window, as if she didn't want to talk about it.

"Or that I won't let you write the woman from yesterday?"

She shrugged, and he was pretty sure that meant *both*.

"I get it," he said. "I should have told you sooner. I'm so sorry, honey, more than you could ever know. And the thing with 23andMe . . . I don't know what to say."

He heard her start to hum, and that was what did it. There was nothing he could do about how he'd lied to Mia, but maybe he could at least turn around her day if he let her write to Ester. Surely a little pen pal thing wouldn't hurt, would it? Perhaps he'd overreacted. Anything to stop the humming, which was the ultimate spotlight on his failures.

With no shortage of hesitation, he said, "So I was thinking . . . maybe you're right. Maybe we should write to Ester. Just to see where it goes."

Mia inflated as quickly as an airbag in a fender bender. "Really?"

"Why not?" he said, figuring he could probably write a whole book of why-nots.

"That would be so awesome, but what about having to tell her what happened?"

Baxter took a pensive breath. This point had been at the center of the debate in his head. "Honey, I think in this case she'd rather know."

In the kitchen at home, with a Stouffer's beef Stroganoff heating up in the microwave, Baxter drew out his laptop. Mia was nearly climbing on top of him to see. "Can you believe it, Dad? I wish Mom could be here."

"You and me both." The sinking feeling inside him was awful, but seeing his daughter light up offered a bit of hope.

He typed:

> This is Mia's father. She's standing next to me. My wife, Sofia, was adopted and grew up in Venice Beach, California. Perhaps we should speak on the phone?
>
> Baxter and Mia

She read it out loud. "Yeah, okay. But don't you want to be a little nicer?"

"Okay, fair enough." He added: It's so lovely to meet you.

When Mia gave her approval, he moved the cursor over the send button. He could feel his heart beat hard. Maybe this wasn't a good idea. Then he felt Mia's hand over his, and before he could stop her, she'd pressed down his finger and sent the message.

Chapter 6

THE INVITATION

Part of him had hoped Ester wouldn't respond, but she sure had. Quickly too. Baxter had woken up to her message Saturday morning and read it without notifying Mia.

> So happy to hear from you! Yes, I would love to talk. We are six hours ahead of you here. What time would work? We can use WhatsApp.

Shaking his head with regret for what he'd gotten them into, he'd called Mia over from where she sat at the dining room table studying a YouTube video about chess openings. They read the message together, Mia bubbling over with glee, and Baxter had suggested he and Ester speak the next day.

Fast-forward a little over twenty-four hours to Sunday morning, and Baxter was in his office, slurping down coffee, getting ready for Monday and waiting on the call. Though Mia had begged to be a part of it, Baxter wasn't about to let her talk to Ester without screening the situation first, so she was with a babysitter—a teenager who lived two doors down—and they were probably watching cartoons.

Right on time, Baxter's cell phone came alive, lighting up on the center of his desk. A shock of nerves zapped him. Was this really happening? He pulled off his glasses—the ones forty had forced him into—set them down in front of him, and accepted the video call.

"Baxter?" Ester said warmly.

Baxter took her in for a moment and caught himself before gasping. He knew she was Sofia's mother like he knew Mia was Sofia's daughter. Along with her slightly angular features, it was her eyes that were most familiar, the way they formed on her face like exquisite knots in driftwood, so wonderfully crafted by nature, so wholly wise and curious and alive.

As nice and comforting as they were to look into, as if Sofia were visiting him from wherever she'd gone, the experience was incredibly unsettling, so much so that he had to look away.

"That's me."

"It's a pleasure to meet you, Baxter."

Baxter dragged his gaze back to the screen. "And you too, Ester."

She wore a conservative black dress. Her long hair fell well past her shoulders. Her full lips shone a deep velvet, the lipstick slightly glossy from the light overhead.

She corrected his pronunciation of her first name. "Almost like Fred Astaire. The emphasis is on the second syllable."

He tried again and she gave a nod of approval. "This is . . . kind of . . ." He stopped, unsure what to say.

"Strange?" she said, filling in the blank.

"Yeah, that's one way to put it." What shocked Baxter almost as much as her resemblance to Sofia was the woman's age. He'd expected someone in her seventies for some reason, but Ester looked to be in her late fifties, perhaps. She must have had Sofia when she was very young.

He realized he was repeatedly clicking one of his Shaw Building pens and dropped it like it had suddenly turned hot on him. "Your English is amazing, though. Did you live over here at one point?"

"I went to the University of Cambridge in England."

"Ah, impressive." He heard the trace of an English accent clearly then. And now he knew where Sofia got her smarts.

They both stumbled over each other's words for a second until Baxter took control of the conversation. "Sorry, there's a little bit of a lag. But I just want to say . . . well, not that I doubted the DNA tests, but I wasn't sure until today. You are certainly Sofia's mother."

Ester sat up with a subtle yet powerful smile. An eternity of pain seemed to wash away from her face, as if she'd been looking for Sofia for many years. He was about to stomp on her happiness, though, and the thought pummeled his heart. Part of him wanted to get it over with, and the other wanted to push it off as long as possible. Aside from not wanting to crush Ester's hopes, there was nothing he hated more than having to speak of Sofia's death.

"Where is she?" Ester asked, making the choice for him. "May I talk to her?"

He let out a breath, stalling. There was no way out. "I'm afraid she passed away."

Her face, nearly the same as Sofia's and even Mia's, melted into sadness, as if those few seconds had acted like years on her age. She looked off to the left, visible regret and guilt washing over her.

"This was a while ago," he said, filling in the silence. "Three years or so." Keeping the phone camera directed to his face, he stood from the chair, letting it slide back to the wall. "I'm sorry to have to tell you. I wasn't really sure what to do." As if his delivery choice mattered.

She finally turned back, her dark eyes now moist. Pacing the room, he apologized again as she wiped a tear from her cheek. Knowing she needed to hear more, Baxter went on: "We married ten years ago. Met in South Carolina, which is where we are now. As you have figured out, we have a daughter. Mia."

A warmth rose over Ester's teary face as she tested out saying her granddaughter's name. "Mia. How wonderful."

"And she wants to talk to you very badly. In fact, she wanted to be on this call, but I . . ." He shook his head. "I wanted to tell you about Sofia first. Mia's doing well, but losing her mom's been hard."

"I can imagine."

He found himself impressed by how Ester took the news. Though he could sense its heaviness bearing down on her, he could also see—even over the phone—clear evidence of her strength. Knowing Sofia, he shouldn't have been surprised.

"How did she die?" Ester asked, cutting deeper into the marrow.

Baxter couldn't stand the question, and people asked often. It seemed to be such a curiosity when he met new people. Knowing he was a widower wasn't enough. They wanted to know *how*, which was such a rubbernecking and invasive question. He tried not to blame them when they asked, as it was human nature. Their question usually came with a disclaimer, too, like, "Do you mind if I ask . . . ?" His answer was always as short as possible and usually enough to terminate what invariably felt like an interrogation.

He had a much different reaction when Ester posed the question. Though he sure didn't want to relive the memory again, she deserved to know, and he felt a need to say it in the gentlest way he could muster. And then he could line up a quick call with Mia and wrap this whole thing up.

"It's not . . . it's . . . ," he stuttered. "It's hard to talk about. She was killed." *Killed* was a much less violent word than *murdered*, and he used it strictly for her and other people's benefit.

Ester's face drooped.

Having worn out the tile with his pacing, Baxter returned to the chair and slid it under his desk. "Maybe it's something we could talk about later?" In fact, he'd be happy to *never* talk about it again. She didn't need to know the details.

She shook her head. "Please tell me."

As much as he didn't want to think about that day another moment, he knew he had no choice. And he went about it like a nurse applying first aid to a wound. "A mass shooting. A man on a run of bad luck went on a shooting spree in the parking lot of a shopping center in Charleston, South Carolina. You could find it in the papers if you wanted to. It was big news over here for a while."

Ester pinched the bridge of her nose and let her eyes close. Baxter paused out of respect, not knowing if he should say more.

When she looked at him again, she said, "I don't even know her. I don't know anything about her. And she's . . ."

"I know," Baxter said. "I know." He drew in a big breath and then let it out all at once. Maybe it wasn't such a good idea that he'd responded to her note. She might be better off not knowing.

For Ester's sake, he begged a smile into existence and allowed himself to speak of Sofia for a moment. "She was one of a kind, a big bright star in my universe." Oh, how words fell so short, he thought, when he tried to describe his wife.

Ester offered a smile at his attempt. "I had her when I was very young. And I was . . ." She stopped and changed directions. "Tell me more."

He'd already had enough and didn't feel obligated to become Ester's therapist, holding her hand as they walked through the past. "Look," he said, "I know you'd love to know all about her, but I'm just not . . ." He searched for how to say it without sounding like a jerk. "Mia and I have worked hard to get past what happened and . . . I've found it's just easier if I don't go too much into it. She lived a great life and made a beautiful daughter." What else could he say to bring their conversation to a close?

Ester nodded, and he could see that he'd let her down. What else was new? She'd better get in line.

"I was going to name her Lita," Ester said out of the blue.

Lita.

Without understanding why, the idea of Sofia growing up some-where else, having a different life, a different name, potentially never finding Baxter, hit him hard, so much so that he was tempted to hang up on her. This is what it was like for a sober alcoholic to hold a bottle to their lips.

"But I like Sofia even more," Ester continued.

Baxter stretched the corners of his mouth into a smile. It felt more like stretching putty. He didn't respond.

Ester wasn't done. "You seem like a good man. I'm sure Sofia was very happy. Can I just ask . . . how did she get to South Carolina? When I returned to the convent in Madrid last year, they wouldn't tell me anything, and I've always wondered what happened."

Whatever he needed to say to get off the phone. "Her adoptive father worked for the US government and was stationed over there. He worked at the embassy. Something happened with their marriage, though, and they got divorced shortly afterward. I think he might have cheated. She—her name is Dotty—left him and took Sofia back to where she'd grown up in Venice Beach, California. Sofia didn't know about the adoption until the day before I'd met her."

Ester stared blankly into the phone's camera. Had she imagined a better life for her? Either way, it just wasn't his problem. He had his own.

Realizing how rude he must be acting, he offered a little more infor-mation. "She wanted to meet you. She wanted to find you."

"Why didn't she?" Ester asked, fresh pain creasing her forehead.

"She tried. We both did the test years ago. But there was no one on the other end. And we tried to find something through the convent, and that led to nowhere . . ." His voice trailed off.

Ester let her eyes fall closed, like curtains being drawn. Baxter thought he had a good idea of what she was thinking: how things could have turned out so differently.

Wanting to spare her more agony, Baxter pressed on. "Only when I happened upon the site randomly the other day did I find you. Actually,

Mia's only now learned the truth about how her mother died. It wasn't something I was eager to share."

"I don't blame you," Ester replied, releasing some of the pressure from which he'd been unable to escape since Ms. Mecca had called him over to the school. "Could I meet her?"

As if he had a choice now. "Yes, let's make it happen." For the sake of Mia, who wouldn't sleep a wink tonight otherwise, he said, "We could do something later today if you'd like—if that doesn't feel rushed. I'm not sure Mia will forgive me if I tell her we put it off." And he really just wanted to get it over with so he and Mia could move on.

"Please, let's do that." Her excitement radiated through the phone.

"Yeah, okay." He thought about what the rest of his day looked like, then factored in the time change. "Could we do something later your time, like after dinner?"

"*Sí, claro*, we stay up late here. It's Spain."

"How about nine your time?"

"*Perfecto.*"

Swallowing all the fresh pain that had surfaced, he said, "It's really nice to talk to you. I'm sorry to have told you about Sofia, but . . . for what it's worth, you gave birth to an amazing woman who changed me in ways I couldn't even begin to describe. I'm a musician, or I used to be, and she was so encouraging. She always pushed me to chase my dream."

When he said that last part, he realized he had to end the call. Yes, despite how his dream had destroyed them, despite how the life of a musician is not one for family, she'd pushed him. And she'd done so because she loved him more than anyone ever had, and she wanted him to realize his dream, even if it meant hurting their own.

And that thought right there was exactly why it did no good to keep talking about the past. He'd need a therapist all over again. The further away from it he could keep Mia and him, the better.

Ester touched her heart and smiled. "I want to hear so much more."

He cleared his throat and just about hung up on her. "That's the thing. I'm so sorry, but I just don't want Mia having to relive it all. I'm fine with you meeting, but I'd rather you not talk about her mother. I can't tell you how much effort I've put into helping her, and I'm already worried that her meeting you is going to cause problems."

Ester looked puzzled.

Baxter raised a hand. "I want you to talk to her, believe me. She's very excited. I'm just asking you to . . . keep the conversation about her, not her mother."

Seconds passed as they looked at each other. Then she nodded. "I understand."

"Thank you."

"Ciao, Baxter," she said sadly.

"Ciao." He barely got it out as he ended the call, dropped the phone hard onto the desk, and sat there, stewing in grief and guilt.

He hoped it wasn't a huge mistake to have written her.

Chapter 7

I Am Girl

When the phone rang later, Mia snatched it out of Baxter's hand. It was still light outside, and the sun came in through the skylights in the great room and cut an obtuse triangle of light in the middle of the hardwoods. They were both on the couch and had been waiting for the call. After tearing her way through the closet, leaving a hurricane-worthy aftermath, Mia had settled on her turquoise socks, yellow jeans, white belt, and blue I Am Girl, Hear Me Roar shirt. A pink elastic band held back her hair, which, according to the babysitter, had been extra wild today and required a generous amount of water in the taming.

Ester appeared on the screen, and Baxter turned to his daughter to see her face, surely a mirror of Ester's youth. Mia cracked a smile. "Hi."

"Hi, Mia," Ester responded, shining equally as brightly.

Baxter was not as thrilled. This was a big chance he was taking, letting them speak. What if all this dredging into the past made her nightmares worse? What if she became even more withdrawn?

"You're my grandmother?" Mia asked, leaning into the phone without any jitters at all.

Ester laughed. "*Sí*, yes. I'm your grandmother. In Spain, we say *abuela*. Can you say that?"

"*Sí*. I'm taking Spanish at school."

"You are? Oh, *Dio*, I love you already."

Love? Baxter thought. It was a big word to use for knowing someone only a few seconds.

"If I could," Ester said, "I would reach through the phone and hug you. And your shirt, let me see your shirt."

Mia held the phone out away from her and straightened her shirt so Ester could make it out. "My dad bought it for me."

"I love it," Ester said. "I love your whole look. Your father is teaching you well, apparently."

Mia nodded and brought the phone back to her face. "I can't believe you're my *abuela*."

Baxter saw through the phone, through all those miles, this word, *abuela*, wrapped around Ester like loving arms. "*Abuela*, that's right. Yes, I'm quite certain of it, Mia. In Valencia, grandmothers are called *Iaia*. Like a yoyo but *yaya*. Would you like to call me *Iaia*?"

"*Sí, Iaia.*"

Baxter thought the idea was quite presumptuous of Ester. *Let's not get carried away.* It wasn't like they were going to talk on a daily basis.

Mia asked, "And how about my grandfather? Is he there?"

A pregnant pause consumed the moment as Ester seemed to take small sips of air. Finally, she said, "No, but you have lots of family here."

"Like how much family?" the girl who had barely any family at all asked with eager anticipation.

Baxter felt like he'd needed to jump in and referee. He'd wanted the call to go in the direction of a quick question-and-answer thing like a onetime interview, but it seemed both Ester and Mia were talking as if this wouldn't be their last call.

"So much family," Ester said. "My daughter and son—your aunt and uncle. And you have so many cousins from my brother's side. Guess what . . . you are my first grandchild."

"Really?"

"*Sí,*" Ester nearly sang. "We also have a farm of animals: wild horses and donkeys, chickens, geese, ducks, dogs."

"No way." Mia gleefully looked at Baxter.

Baxter couldn't even fake a smile this time. *Her first grandchild?* What did that mean? Was Ester after more than just a call? He wanted to rip the phone away from Mia and say, *Look, with all due respect, we are not the people who can help you assuage your guilt. We're about to say goodbye for good.*

"Can I come meet them?" Mia asked.

"What?" Baxter put a tense hand on her arm. "Honey, no, no, no—"

Ester held up a finger. "I want nothing more than for you to come. You can even stay with us."

Mia nearly leaped into the screen. "We'd love that, wouldn't we, Daddy?"

Before Baxter could respond, Ester said, "If you come soon, you could see the harvest. We grow olives here. And we have a very large house with extra bedrooms. Your aunt and uncle and everyone else would be thrilled."

What in the hell was happening? He'd completely lost control. Did Mia think that going down this road was going to bring her mom back? And didn't Ester realize that such an invitation could completely thwart Mia's progress?

"Can we go, Daddy?" Mia asked, tugging at his shirt.

He stopped and started several times, then blew out a blast of air. "No, honey, we're not going to . . ." Oh God, he didn't want to ruin the moment. She was so happy. So he lied instead. "I'm sure we can once things settle down. Maybe even next summer."

Mia frowned. "Next summer?"

He threw up his hands. "Spain is a long way away. I'll have to look at tickets, check out the calendar." She gave a look that said, "I hear you, but I'm not listening."

Baxter was on the edge of a panic attack, his entire body wound up, his vision blurring.

"It's not that far away," Ester said. "Just across the pond, as they say in England. Besides, fall is stunning here, especially during harvest. The sooner the better."

Had they lost their minds? Who was this woman to come into their lives like a wrecking ball? As much as he wanted to snap at her, he couldn't in front of Mia. But she sure as hell was going to get an email from him later. She had no idea what Mia was going through.

Mia was still tugging on his shirt when he said as politely as possible, considering the tension in his jaws, "We'll talk about it later, y'all."

She turned back to her grandmother. "He'll come around. He's just hardheaded sometimes. He works all the time. Like, *allllllll* the time. And he's always overthinking things."

"Yes," Ester said, "apparently he was working on a Sunday."

Mia was talking with her free hand now, really laying it on. "He works every Sunday. *Todos domingos.*"

Ester laughed, then leaned toward her phone, her face growing larger on the screen. "Sounds like he needs a break."

"Yes, ma'am, I think you're right."

Baxter felt like he was watching a squash match between the two, his head going from the screen to his daughter, back and forth. He was dizzy with guilt, though, so much so that he couldn't bring himself to end the call. Here Mia was the happiest she'd been in weeks. How could he take it away from her?

"So tell me, Mia," Ester said, "tell me all about your life."

With Baxter trying to extricate himself out of his shock, Mia opened up in a way he hadn't seen in a very long time. Ester prodded her with endless questions, devouring Mia's answers like caramels passed through the phone. They talked about Mia's love of chess and the music she liked and her brightly colored wardrobe. Ester asked about Mia's favorite subjects in school and who her friends were and what she liked to do with her father.

Though Baxter felt afraid of this budding connection, he couldn't bring himself to take his daughter away from her suddenly blissful mood. They were both laughing about how Mia was better than her father at chess when Mia said, "You look a lot like my mommy."

There was the line. Baxter turned to stone.

"I do?" Ester asked. "I would love to see pictures."

Baxter instantly became much more clearheaded. This ended now. "Okay," he said, reaching for the phone to bring the call to a close. "I think that's enough for now. Ester, we have a few things we need to do."

"But—" Mia started.

"Mia," Baxter said quietly. "It's time to say goodbye." He left no room for argument.

When they looked back at the phone, Ester asked, "Could I speak to your father for a moment?"

"Yeah, okay." Mia waved. "Goodbye, Iaia."

"Ciao, mi cariño."

Once Mia had left the room, Ester said to Baxter, "She's just lovely, Baxter. Lovely."

"Thanks. But as you can see, this isn't a good idea. I'm so sorry."

"Forgive me for arguing, but I don't see how coming to visit could hurt. She seems very happy to me."

"I'm sure she does." It took all his effort not to let her have it.

"I'm very serious," she pressed. "There's a great deal of change coming here. So many things to say in person. And I think the two of you should come."

Did she not hear a word he was saying? This was it. He was going to write a note to her after the call, saying as much. This wasn't about lost connections; this was about saving his daughter. And what the hell did she mean, *so many things to say . . . I think the two of you should come?*

Baxter glanced back at the closed door, wondering if Mia was listening.

Ester kept going. "We've already missed so much of each other. Let's not waste any more time."

"Ester, it was very nice to meet you," he said quickly. "And I'll be in touch." With that, he ended the call.

—

At five in the morning, Mia jumped onto the bed and proceeded to play drums on his back. "I'll go to school if you agree we can go to Spain this year."

"No, no, no," Baxter replied, sitting up and looking out the window, noticing the sun wasn't even peeking over the horizon yet. "You're not doing this. Going to Spain is not something we will negotiate." The night before, he must have said "we can't right now" fifty times. He pulled a pillow over his head.

Kneeling, she ripped away the pillow. "Fine, then I no longer negotiate going to school."

If only Mia could live in his skin for a few minutes, she'd understand you can't just hop on a plane and go on vacation whenever you want—especially to see Sofia's lost family. He pulled his face away from the pillow and found his beautiful daughter staring down at him.

"For someone your size," he said, "you sure can be intimidating."

She gave a grin as words bubbled out of her mouth. "When do we leave? Tomorrow? Next day? Next day after that? I do need time to pack. I hope I have enough clothes."

He pretended to search her arm. "Where's your power switch? It's got to be somewhere."

She giggled and then changed her tone. "Mom would want us to do this." Though Mia might have been right, she was not playing fair with such a statement. Sofia would have first considered the psychological effects such a trip might play on Mia.

Baxter pulled sand away from the corners of his eyes as he rolled over. "She would want you to figure out this sleeping thing and not miss any more school. And for me to finish what I've started with work." He wished he could tell her that Sofia would want him to keep all these old wounds from opening.

"That's what you always say." In her best imitation of him, she said, "I'm dying at work right now. So much going on. Let me just do this and this and then I'll do this and then I'll be ready. And I'm just waiting, Daddy. All I do is wait."

Feeling a burn behind his rib cage, he attempted to center himself. "I promise it'll get better. I know I'm working too much. Believe me, I don't want to be. This is not what I signed up for; it's just gotten out of control. Bottom line, we're not going to Spain right now."

Her entire demeanor changed. Her shoulders slumped. A frown followed. It was almost more than he could bear, his failures coming to the forefront. He didn't know what else to say.

"I know it's my fault."

"What's your fault?" *Here we go,* he thought.

"That you have to work so hard."

"What are you talking about, it's your fault?"

Her gaze went down to her knees. "If I hadn't been born, then you could still be playing music and not having to do a job you hate to take care of a handful like me."

Nothing anyone had ever said had cut deeper. He pulled her down and wrapped his arms around her. "Don't you ever think that, honey. It's just not true. If you hadn't been born, then I would never know what it's like to love you. Me leaving the band had *nothing* to do with you." More lies, but what the hell else was he supposed to say?

She pushed back up, her legs folded under her. "Maybe it did."

"Well, yes, I guess, but it was me making a choice. Like I've told you a hundred times, I didn't want to be out on the road and give you that kind of life. And you come first. You always come first." At least now she did, he thought. Always and forevermore she would come first.

The other piece he couldn't say was that Sofia had been his muse, his fuel, his everything. There were no lyrics worth writing after her. There were no notes worth playing. Aside from playing for Mia, he could barely stand the sound of his own voice, or even the feel of his Martin in his hands.

He didn't want to tell these things to Mia, because he didn't want her to know how broken he was, even after three years. Blaming his retirement on priorities seemed to show strength, while admitting he'd lost his creative spirit showed only defeat. He had to show Mia there was a way out of her grief, even if that weren't true for him.

Look at her now, staring at him, waiting for direction, *needing* direction.

It became abundantly clear that all he'd done was put up a big facade. He'd pretended he was okay, without believing he'd ever be okay. There was something wrong with that, wasn't there? And he'd lied to her about how Sofia had died, and he'd forced everyone in their circle to go along with it. The wheels were coming off . . .

Baxter swallowed back the failure slithering up his throat and looked at his daughter again, feeling such overwhelming love, wanting to give her everything. In a moment of clarity, he wondered if what he should give her was this trip to Spain. And maybe he needed it too. He winced as he thought of how rude he'd been to Ester, hanging up on her.

"What, Daddy?" Mia asked. "Are you okay?"

His stomach twisted into knots, thinking about being so far away from his projects, but he drew in a deep breath, trying to let the worry go. For God's sake, it was so nice to see the old Mia when she was speaking with Ester. He'd tried everything else to help her. Was this the only way?

Taking a one-eighty he hoped he wouldn't regret, he brushed a strand of curly hair from her face and said, "I don't want you to think you've won this negotiation and that you can get whatever you want out of me, but maybe I can work something out."

The risks he took by even saying this idea out loud were beyond worth it to see the eruption of joy on her face. "Really? When can we go?"

He visualized the calendar in his head. "Well, your fall break is coming up, right?"

"Yes, sir." She hugged him.

"I'll see what I can do. Only for a few days."

She threw her arms around his neck. "Thank you, Daddy! I'm so happy. *Estoy feliz!*"

"Oh God, I've already lost you to Spain, haven't I?"

Letting go of him, she asked, "How were my negotiation skills this morning?"

"Not bad," he conceded, shaking his head, "though you did attack me at five in the morning, before I was able to mount my defenses."

She wagged a finger at him. "Timing is crucial. That's what you always say."

"You, my dear, are the reason I'm going gray. You and you alone. And now it's payback time." He flipped her onto her back and launched into a tickle attack that brought out every last giggle she had.

If only he could have been laughing too . . .

Chapter 8

The Road Home

The wheels of their Boeing 737 hit the runway in Madrid only three weeks later in late October, which was a testament to Mia's gung ho attitude about their ten-day sojourn. As the plane came to a stop at the gate, the anxiety of leaping into the unknown with his fragile daughter and also being so far away from the goings-on of his company struck Baxter like a blunt force object across the head.

It hadn't helped that he'd gotten a call on the way to the airport from his least-favorite client, a guy named John Frick. He had insinuated that Baxter hadn't signed off on a change order for a massive remodel he was doing for him. Though Frick had a good reputation around town, Baxter worried he was going to try to weasel out of paying Baxter the eighty thousand and change he owed.

The truth of it was Frick had completely altered the design of the main bed and bath after he and Baxter had agreed on a price of the home build. That was okay and it happened. Typically, Baxter would pause the project while he repriced his work. Then he'd have the client sign the change order before continuing. A month earlier, Frick had begged Baxter not to slow down and had assured him he was good on his word. The two men had shaken on the deal, and Baxter had figured it was enough. Without a signed change order, Baxter would have a hard time proving that his charges were fair, which meant court and lawyer fees and an even-more-strapped financial situation.

This wasn't some exceptional incident either. Clients refusing to pay, other clients complaining about the work that had been done, subcontractors not showing up, permits not being issued, employees leaving for greener pastures. This was every freaking day, and this was exactly why he shouldn't be frolicking around Spain right now.

He turned on his phone and waited for it to connect and download his new messages.

And ten days . . . what was he thinking? The flight had been nearly half the price for those particular days, which was what had gotten him even considering it. He further justified the length by telling himself he and Mia needed that time together anyway. If things went wrong with the family, they could always head back to Madrid or drive up to Valencia. The Airbnb he'd booked was barely a hundred bucks a night, so the loss wouldn't be disastrous.

It was just after nine in the morning in Madrid, a little cloudy but warm, if judging by the airport workers on the tarmac wearing short sleeves under their orange vests. Pulling on their backpacks, he and Mia followed the crowd off the plane and walked hand in hand through the airport. He looked over at her, in her bright rainbow top and hot-pink backpack, a walk that was almost a canter, and he hoped this journey would live up to how excited she'd been about it.

From the moment he'd given in, Mia had been returning to her old self. Her nightmares were less frequent. She was going out of her way to listen more. And Ms. Mecca had even reported a very positive turn at school. Hopefully, their journey would be the final blow to her grief.

The first time Baxter had gone to Europe was in college, when he and a buddy had backpacked from Lisbon to Copenhagen one summer. He and the band had done two European tours, bouncing around tiny clubs and playing to mostly expats. The fourth trip would have been one he and Sofia had planned to Paris, but she'd not lived long enough to board that plane.

As they followed the crowd toward customs, the memory hit him hard, Sofia and him sitting at a booth at Rue de Jean, their favorite French restaurant in Charleston, sharing mussels and *frites* and deciding over a bottle of champagne to take their delayed honeymoon in Paris. He saw it so clearly, but as always, the scene was black and white in his mind.

When he and Sofia had eloped a year before that dinner, Cactus Road was in the middle of a summer tour, so they only had time to sneak over to Aspen for the weekend after a show in Denver. Once the band played the last show of that run, he and Sofia had opted to buy a house and further postponed the honeymoon. The memory turned to a shard of glass embedded in his heart.

Paris never happened.

Was it any wonder he didn't like traveling anymore? Like the music he used to enjoy so much, the joy of setting out on the open road had lost its spark. Mia and Alan and the other people who knew him well would never have believed how much he used to love climbing onto the tour bus to start a new tour. He could almost touch that feeling, he and his bandmates off to take over the world. And then the memory was gone, the sweet appeal of adventure fading on his tongue.

Unable to help it, Baxter caught himself falling back into the all-too-familiar abyss of what-ifs. What if he'd been the one who'd made the run to Target? Or what if he'd been in the parking lot? What if she'd left their house five or ten minutes later? What if the gunman had chosen a different store?

Baxter tried to snap himself out of it, squeezing Mia's hand, but his thoughts snowballed to fears, and he felt very far from his comfort zone and utterly lost and doubtful. Who was he kidding? He couldn't solve his daughter's issues by taking her to Spain for ten days. Hell, he probably wouldn't even win her trust back.

He sighed when he saw three hundred weary-eyed and jet-lagged people waiting in only two very long lines at customs. "You have got to be kidding me."

"What's wrong?" Mia asked, her eyes taking in the sights as though they were delectable macaroons.

"A mild mental breakdown," he muttered to himself.

"What?" she asked, not understanding him.

"Nada, honey. It's all good." He looked at his phone. The messages finally poured in. He scrolled through, looking for any emergencies. For a brief moment, he thought he'd actually escaped unscathed. But then he noticed an email from Airbnb.

He clicked on it and read. With each word, his stomach twisted more. Due to a plumbing issue, the host had canceled their reservation. "Oh, c'mon." He looked up at the customs officers reading passports in slow motion. This country might just kill him.

Another email confirmed that he'd been refunded. As they settled into the back of the line, Baxter searched for a new place. There was nothing near Cadeir; the closest accommodations were thirty minutes away. Attempting not to let Mia see how frustrated he was, he stabbed out a WhatsApp message to Ester: Hi there! We've arrived in Madrid but just found our Airbnb canceled on us. I'm trying to find another place. Do you have any leads?

Back to his search he went, but Ester replied a minute later: Please do not waste your money. As I told you, we have a very large house with several extra guest rooms.

He replied back: I wouldn't want to impose. The truth was that he wanted to test the waters first. This was a big step for him to take his daughter here. What if the initial meeting didn't go smoothly? What about her nightmares? He wanted a safe place to be able to get away.

She responded quickly: Whatever you prefer.

He shook his head and put his phone in his pocket.

Mia must have sensed his mental breakdown and put her hand on his arm. "It's okay, Daddy. Everything's okay."

"I know. It's just . . . our house fell through, so . . . I'll figure it out."

A spark of even stronger excitement lit up her face. "Why don't we stay with Iaia? She asked us."

"I know that. It's just not very polite."

"I think it's rude not to stay with them."

If she could only understand. It was one thing to share a few meals and see the estate, quite another to spend the night in their home. Twenty minutes in Spain and he was already at his breaking point. Sure, he might need a vacation, but this journey wasn't that. It felt more like he was going to war to save his daughter, and he just might not survive to see if it worked.

He continued to search, as if a place would suddenly pop up on the map. Maybe they could just stay with them for the first night until they got their bearings. He sent Ester a quick thank-you and said that they'd try to find a place for tomorrow. She sent a simple thumbs-up.

An hour passed before they finally walked through and then went on to get their bags. Or bag, Baxter soon learned. Mia's bag had come through perfectly, but his was missing. He looked everywhere, marching from carousel to carousel, hoping to see his black bag among a sea of them. Giving up hope and agitated beyond words, he tugged Mia by the arm in a march worthy of General Patton's praise to the baggage assistance desk.

"*¿Perdón, hablas inglés?*"

"Yes, of course," a Delta Air Lines employee answered in perfect English.

"Thank you. It looks like they've lost my bag."

"I'm sorry, sir. Let me see what I can do." She asked for his information with all the calm in the world.

Her patience with his frustration worked to cool him off some, and he thanked her kindly.

The woman typed for a while and then finally looked up. "It looks like your bag is still in Atlanta."

"I see." Baxter offered his best smile, which was the same one he put on when one of his clients back home told him they'd changed their mind about the height of the kitchen hood.

"It will be"—she typed and clicked her mouse—"on the first flight tomorrow."

Baxter's fake smile melted away like butter in a pan. "We're leaving Madrid and headed to our family's—" He stopped himself. *Our family* was too much to say. *Waaaaayyyy* too much to say. He started again. "We're connecting with some people at their place in Cadeir, outside of Alcoy."

She brushed a hand through the air. "Not a problem. We can send the bags there as soon as they arrive in Madrid."

"Great," he said, wishing he hadn't checked their luggage. "And thanks for the help."

She gave a genuine smile. "Travel is not easy these days."

"No, it's not." Baxter gave himself a proverbial pat on the back for his own outstanding show of patience.

They passed through the last security check and entered the main terminal of the airport. All Baxter could think about were the omens smacking him in the face. No place to stay and no luggage. Could there have been any clearer sign that he'd made a mistake by bringing her here?

Following the signs, they found the rental car kiosks. Every counter was closed, and he just shook his head. Give him a month and he could have this airport running like a top.

"How is this country functioning?" he asked, more to himself than Mia. "It's almost ten in the morning, and everything is closed. What are they waiting for? Mañana?" He cut a look at Mia, and the way she looked at him was a mirror reflecting his inner unraveling.

"Am I being impatient?" he asked.

She pinched her fingers together. *"Un poco."*

He showed both racks of teeth. "Yeah, I thought so. Have I mentioned being an adult isn't easy?"

"Not in this specific conversation."

A couple dragging roller bags brushed by him. "But I have before?"

"Once or twice."

He inclined his eyebrows. "Don't ever grow up, trust me."

"As if being a kid is easy," she said. "No car, no credit cards. Everyone always telling you what to do." Her eyes narrowed. "Remember what you always tell me?"

"Oh, I can't wait to hear some of my previous wisdom."

She clapped her hands. "Buck up, buttercup."

"Buck up, buttercup? Okay, if I ever tell you that again, I will give you fifty dollars. And do I really clap my hands when I tell you?"

"Every time."

"I have no idea how you put up with me. And before you respond, shall we move along?"

Baxter asked for directions from a security guard. Though he was a long way from fluent, working in the construction industry had taught him a thing or two. *"¿Dónde está Europcar?"*

The jovial security guard pointed outside, and they walked that way. Correct that—Baxter continued his obstinate march, and Mia strolled with curious eyes. He couldn't let go of not having a bag, wondering what he would wear in the meantime.

The Europcar building was more like a trailer. He and Mia stepped inside, where a man boasting a Kelly Slater–worthy wave of hair made possible with a generous amount of gel stood behind the counter scrolling through his phone.

The man didn't move when Baxter said hello. He stood there patiently, only once turning back to Mia and shaking his head.

A minute passed before he tapped on the desk. *"¿Estás abierto?* Are you open?"

The man looked at the clock that read *9:58*. "Two minutes, por favor."

Baxter turned and lowered his eyes to Mia. "This is me being extremely patient. You can take notes if you want."

Forty-three seconds after ten, the man said kindly, "Hello, your name?"

"Shaw," Baxter said, sliding over a sheet of paper and his passport.

The man proceeded to type an endless string of keys and click more clicks than had ever been clicked by a mouse. It was as if he had to write the back-end code for his software. Finally, the guy reached for a set of keys off the wall.

"What am I driving?" Baxter asked.

"An Opel Corsa."

"Okay, I'm assuming it's a large car?"

"It should be fine, yes, sir."

After a few signatures, he and Mia went to find their car. Not to Baxter's surprise, it wasn't in the correct stall, but he pressed the "Unlock" button until he saw the flashing headlights of a tiny purple car.

Baxter felt his teeth grind, wondering if he could even squeeze behind the wheel of this sardine can. "You're kidding me, right?"

"I like it. It's cute!"

"That's not the point. I paid for a large car. This is *not* a large car." He felt his heart flutter.

Taking a deep breath, he said to himself, *Ten days. All you have to do is make it ten days.* He felt so embarrassed at his own meltdown, but he couldn't help it. He was in quicksand up to his neck, gasping for air.

Back in reality, he made a fast decision. "Honey, I know you're anxious to get on the road, but I'm not driving this car. I could literally toss it into the back of my truck."

"You said *literally*," she told him. "You owe me five bucks." They'd both been big offenders of overusing the word, and it had taken imposing a hefty five-dollar fine to finally break each other of the habit.

"Fine, Mia. Five bucks. Let's go see what else they have."

Back in the trailer, the man listened to Baxter go on about how he'd paid for a large car. When Baxter was done, the man said, "Give me a moment, please."

"What's so funny, sir?" Baxter asked, noticing the upward curl of the man's lips.

"Just that the Americans always want bigger cars. Please forgive the stereotype."

Baxter let out an exaggerated laugh that was louder than he'd intended. "Ha, that is funny. You'd think you would have had a larger car waiting on me, since you know I'm American. Especially since I paid for one."

The man acknowledged Baxter's idea with a nod and then went back into his computer. Baxter was beyond mortified at his own behavior but couldn't seem to stop it, the quicksand swallowing the last of him.

Eventually, the man said, "I do have an Audi SUV, but you will need to pay the additional amount."

Baxter cocked his head. "You're joking, right?"

"Daddy," Mia said, taking his hand.

"Yes," he said, changing the tone of his voice for her, raising it several octaves. He might have gone a little too high, because what came out sounded more like a bird chirping. *Yes?*

"Please take a deep breath." Maybe he should steer Mia toward a gig recording meditations.

After he lowered his anxiety level from a seven to a four, he asked with a measured amount of calm, "How much in addition?"

"Three hundred and forty-two euros."

"You know what," Baxter said, almost at the breaking point, "give me the Audi. I will happily overpay to get the car I originally chose—and paid for—in the first place." He reached into his wallet and slammed down his American Express business card, because you're damn right, he was writing off every single cent of this journey.

Then, because he was driving himself crazy, he added, "I'm sorry for my lack of composure. The flight must have taken it all out of me."

"No pasa nada," the guy said, which meant something like "no big deal."

Settled into the Audi, which was a much more pleasurable experience, he plugged the directions to Cadeir into his phone and prepared to make the four-hour drive to meet Sofia's family. A British woman with a robotic edge to her voice guided him out of the city, mangling the Spanish names with reckless abandon.

Twenty minutes later, Baxter stopped at a gas station to get a bite to eat and a coffee. Parked on the side facing a group of teenagers smoking cigarettes, Baxter and Mia both tore into a *bocadillo* with *jamón*, which was a ham sandwich for the uninitiated.

Baxter said with a full mouth, "I have to admit, they might not have any clue about expediting anything, but they have the sandwich thing down, don't they? Good God, that's good." He took a sip of his cappuccino and was blown away by the flavor. "Espresso machines in gas stations. Why can't they put this level of seriousness into everything else?"

Baxter gave himself an attaboy for turning his attitude around. *You're a good daddy,* he heard a voice say, mocking him. *Good Baxter! Good Daddy!*

In the back seat, Mia tore into a Kinder egg, checking out the surprise inside and then biting down on the chocolate. "Hmm, I could live here forever."

"In Spain?" He started up the car. "You could live here forever because they have Kinder eggs?"

She nodded, taking another bite.

"Aye, aye, aye," Baxter said. "Look, Mia. I'm sorry. I know I'm being . . . like, not totally fun. This is hard for me, to leave everything behind. And to step back into the past like this, to meet your mom's family."

As he said it, he realized this fear might be the root of all his anxiety right now. Yes, there was his company hanging in the balance and his daughter's future, but he had to admit, dredging up old memories and diving back into Sofia's life was . . . unsettling. He'd worked very hard to bottle up those memories and to separate from them. Never would he forget how awful that first year after her death had been. He couldn't go through that again.

"I didn't notice you were being annoying," Mia said with a mouthful of chocolate.

He found her eyes in the rearview mirror. That smirk of hers. "Thank you. Now . . . I have a serious question for you."

"Not this again. I thought we were leaving dad jokes back home."

He held up his finger, as if this joke was certainly worth her time. "How tall is shortbread?"

Mia dramatically slapped her forehead. "Oh, what a mac-and-cheese fest! Please don't share your jokes with our Spanish family. I'll be mortified."

"Mortified? How old are you anyway? And are you embarrassed of me, my dear? I think my jokes will be a hit here."

Mia sighed. "What am I going to do with you?"

Back on the highway, he locked in the cruise control, rolled down the window to let in the dry air, and tried to chill out. Was this really a peek at Baxter on vacation? A man who couldn't step away from work for a few days without losing his mind? Hopefully, he could settle in, and the rest of the trip would run smoothly. In a perfect world, the family would be super accommodating and there would be no awkward moments. Mia would have the time of her life and sleep through every night. And Baxter, in the meantime, could somehow manage his company from afar and make sure it didn't go out of business.

It didn't take long for Mia to start making song requests, and he let her be the DJ as they drove through a long patch of farmland. He realized this was the first time he'd taken in the view without being lost in his head. They drove by herds of cattle and horses grazing on endless fields of grass and grains. He passed the time singing along with Mia and checking out the foreign cars: the Fiats, SEATs, Mercedes, and Peugeots, becoming aware how very American he was in this giant Audi SUV. He might as well have raised an American flag off the hood.

The landscape soon gave way to hillier terrain and gradually rose into low-elevation mountains, the sight of which seemed to shake something loose in Baxter. This was pure desert country, dotted with terraced olive groves and sagebrush and patches of cypress and pine trees, and it was absolutely splendid. Every mile seemed to shed the angst he'd felt at the airport.

No doubt the Spaniards had mastered the art of building, and he was becoming increasingly self-conscious of what he was currently working on back home. The cream- and blush-colored villas roofed with terra-cotta tiles tucked into patches of trees at the end of long drives captured the essence of Spain so perfectly. Baxter could only imagine the many generations who'd occupied them. And he had to admit, though he'd already seen multiple examples of European bureaucracy at work, the roads were in fine shape. He could do this drive all day long.

With about an hour left, Mia fell asleep, and Baxter found himself with nothing to do. It was too early to make calls. Shocking even himself, he decided to listen to some tunes. He went straight to his idol, Mr. Bob Dylan. As the *Desire* album played, Baxter stepped even deeper into the Old World and thought it curious how amazingly well Dylan's music fit into the Spanish world. Was it the modal sound over the simple drumbeats, or the way Bob sang so gruffly, like an old gaucho, or was it the dusty, windblown lyrics that sounded like the best desert music that could ever be written?

One thing was for sure: music hadn't sounded so wonderful in a long time, and Baxter wondered for a brief moment if Spain and this journey might truly be good for him too.

Chapter 9

Familia de Arroyo

As they broke off the highway a couple of stops past Alcoy, Baxter and Mia were drawn like the opening of a fairy tale by the beauty of the area. The October sun shone warmly over a landscape blanketed with vineyards and olive and orange groves and even palm trees. *How could there be such a place?* Baxter wondered, pulled further away from all the worries of home. This kind of landscape must have been what Alexander the Great and Julius Caesar and Napoleon had sought.

Though they were in the mountains of Alicante, far above sea level, they weren't far from the Costa Blanca—maybe an hour or so—and with the windows down, the breeze carried a faint scent of the Mediterranean, and with it a taste of the Balearic Islands of Ibiza, Mallorca, Menorca, and Formentera, places Baxter had read about on the way over.

Following the winding roads over tall bridges spanning deep ravines, Baxter turned deeper into the mountains and entered a forest with leaves painted the colors of fall. This was a *long* way from the mountains of North Carolina, where he used to take a guitar and tent into the woods as a teenager. This was more like what he remembered of Colorado through the window of the Cactus Road tour bus, the dry air, the jagged peaks. *Those were good days,* he thought warmly, feeling a surge of youth. The guy in that bus could never have known that he would soon meet a woman who would change the course of his life.

Any comparison to the States was a stretch, though, because this was the Old World, where the present intertwined with the past, and whispers rose from the old castles and ruins, telling stories of the Roman and Moorish influence and the countless wars fought over this land and the many men and women who'd farmed it for as far back as anyone could remember. He could feel here a hint of inspiration, a spark igniting, as if the man who once wrote songs called out to him from a decade ago, begging him to reawaken to the magic of life.

It was a fleeting thought, because an open gate and a sign appeared on the right reading FINCA DE FAMILIA DE ARROYO, and suddenly Baxter was asking himself what he was doing here and what he'd been thinking to jump from a DNA test to a trip to Spain.

Mia yelped. "There it is, Daddy!"

He turned down Son Volt, who were singing about living free. "Still time to turn around," he offered. "Last chance."

She hit the top of his head. "Are you kidding me? Hit the gas, Pops."

A hard right led them through the gate, and Baxter heard in his head a voice very different from the one that spoke to him in his neighborhood back home. This one had a Spanish accent. "Enter at your own risk."

Ignoring the warning, he drove the gravel road that wound deeper into a forest. A crumbling stone wall about knee high lined both sides. They bumped along until it opened up to a grove of ancient olive trees lining up and over a gentle hill. The knobby and gangly trunks with banyan tree–esque disorder looked like giant hands had reached down and twisted each of them, a failed attempt to pull them from their roots. The branches were full of sage-colored leaves, and swollen olives hung in loose clusters.

They crossed over a small creek on a stone bridge that could have been built a thousand years ago. Once on the other side, the villa came into view. Ester's photographs had not painted the true picture. Baxter estimated this grand home measured about six thousand square feet. It must have been added onto over the years, the original at least two hundred years old. Vibrant ivy with dark-green leaves climbed up every visible wall of the terra-cotta stucco. The closer they came, the more he saw that the beauty of the building came with inevitable aging. Some of the stucco had broken off; part of the roof needed replacing. The landscaping needed work, too, and it occurred to Baxter that this place must have once been worthy of the king and queen, but it had lost some of its sheen.

"There they are!" Mia yelled.

Baxter looked past a fountain and toward a huge pergola. To his surprise, about thirty people were gathered together in the grass, circled around several long tables with baskets and bowls and plates of food and bottles of wine and olive oil. A circle of children was attempting to keep a soccer ball up in the air, much like it was a hacky sack. Everyone was dressed like they'd come from church. Their heads swiveled like pinball flippers as they heard the Audi approach. The ball the children had been playing with rolled to a stop. The entire sight made him feel a bit jittery, as if he hadn't quite understood what they'd be walking into.

The driveway led up to a U in front of the house, where several cars were parked. Baxter stopped behind a beat-up Land Rover Defender with mud splattered above the wheels. They climbed out, and Baxter breathed in the scent of the place: roses and citrus and herbs.

A black-and-white curly-haired dog broke away from the crowd and ran toward them. Mia fell to her knees, giggling, and let him lick her face. She'd been begging for a dog ever since they'd moved to Greenville, but he just didn't have the time or energy to take on another heartbeat at the moment. Baxter saw Ester coming their way, moving slowly, just shy of a limp. He wondered if she'd hurt herself. She wore velvet lipstick and a dark dress.

With her eyes falling on Mia, she exclaimed, "*Dios mío*, you truly do look like one of mine. Come give your *iaia* a hug."

Mia looked at Baxter for permission. He gave a quick and perhaps nervous nod. Ester hugged her granddaughter long and hard, more so than Sofia's adoptive mother or Baxter's parents had ever done. He hoped Mia was doing okay.

When Ester finally let go, she said, "I am thrilled you're here." She looked down at the curly-haired dog, who was squeezing his way into the action. "And apparently, so is Paco."

"What kind of dog is he?" Baxter asked. "He's beautiful."

"*Un perro de agua,*" Ester replied, petting Paco's head. "A water dog."

Ester turned back to the family, who waited like a pack of dogs held back by a leash. "We're all happy you're here. This is my brother, Mateo, his wife, Isabel, and then their three children . . ." She kept going, introducing the entire Arroyo bloodline in one fell swoop.

Baxter saw a little bit of Sofia in many of them, which set off his anxiety. Forget about remembering names. He was just trying not to lose his mind.

He smiled awkwardly at everyone and gave a wave. "We're happy to be here too." As if it was needed, he said, "I'm Baxter and this is Mia."

Ester approached him and kissed one cheek and then the other, an act Baxter fumbled through. Holding up two fingers, both with large rings, she said, "Two kisses here in Spain. Left and then right. You'll learn." She hugged him hard, and Baxter did his best to return the effort, despite the resistance he felt inside.

Mia beamed as her family bombarded her with greetings, and despite his nerves, Baxter felt a surge of pride as he saw Mia conduct herself with both quiet confidence and refined southern civility, blending "yes, ma'ams" and "yes, sirs" with every bit of Spanish she knew. In fact, seeing her thrive seemed to quell his anxiety some.

Ester introduced the cousins, who stood there obediently like her little soldiers and responded with "hola" as their great-aunt called their names. "Mia, meet Francisco, Salvador, Maria, Lila, Amparo, Lola, Carmen, and . . . where's Alfonso?" She surveyed the immediate area and then looked out through the groves. "Anyway, you'll meet him later. He's probably climbing trees."

A savory note hit Baxter's senses—like meat on the grill—and his eyes sought the origin. Beyond the others waiting to say hello, he saw a man in a mustache standing over a giant paella pan, working the contents with a utensil nearly the size of a tennis racket. There were three other paella pans next to him, all resting on standing burners connected to propane tanks.

The introductions ensued, and Baxter did his best to repeat everyone's name as he shook hands and kissed more cheeks. Thankfully, most of them spoke English—or at least enough to say hello. The kissing on the cheeks was something that took some getting used to, but after about six or seven more people, he became a pro. Still, this was like stepping into the Twilight Zone, meeting people from a life Sofia could have lived.

A man handed Baxter a silver can of beer, a Turia Märzen, which he accepted graciously. He took the first sip with the same gusto, thinking a cold beer was the antidote to a long flight and family reunions, and then he heard Ester calling for him.

After looking Mia's way to make sure she was okay, he joined Ester. She stood next to a very prim and proper man Baxter recognized from the pictures Ester had sent as Sofia's half brother, Rodolfo. He wore a waxed hunting jacket over a crisp white shirt, with dark jeans and polished leather shoes. His hair looked impossibly perfect, and he wore a neat mustache that matched his manicured eyebrows. His sideburns ended in an angle below his ears.

Baxter put out his hand and turned up a smile. "Very good to meet you, Rodolfo."

"And you as well," he said unenthusiastically, as if he had a better place to be. With their hands clasped, Baxter noticed the man was missing his middle finger, only a small stump remaining. He also caught a big whiff of his heady cologne.

"It's a beautiful place you have here," Baxter said, trying not to look at the finger.

Rodolfo steered his eyes out over the property. *"Sí."*

Attempting to break through the ice, Baxter put in extra effort with an even wider grin. Any farther and the corners of his lips would connect behind his head. "Is this as weird for you as it is for me?"

"Un poquito, yes," Rodolfo admitted, drawing out a fancy silver lighter and cigarette and lighting up. Once it came to life in a puff of smoke, he turned to his mother and said something in Spanish with the speed of a machine gun firing. Ester hit him on the arm and responded with equal linguistic rapidity.

"I'm gonna have to learn to roll my *R*s like that," Baxter said, wondering why Rodolfo seemed put off. Had he not known about Sofia? Was that it? Baxter had done his best to screen the situation, but each time they'd spoken, he'd stopped before prying. Oh God, was everyone here just finding out about Sofia?

"¿Dónde está tu hermana?" Ester asked her son, cutting the palpable tension. Baxter understood: *Where is your sister?* He hoped she might be a smidgeon kinder than Rodolfo. Otherwise, it was going to be a long ten days.

Rodolfo answered his mother and then strutted away, smoke drifting up over his head. Baxter thought he might have seen the straw edges of a broomstick protruding from his posterior.

He couldn't resist calling out, "Great to meet you. Thanks for having us."

"Don't worry about him," Ester said. "He'll come around. Alma skipped church, as she's getting ready for harvest. I'm sure she'll be here shortly."

"Does everyone speak English?"

"No, not everyone, but I'm a strong advocate, so most everyone. How was your trip?"

She was holding her side and winced like it might be hurting her, so before he answered the question, he asked, "Are you okay?"

Nodding, she glanced sideways at her arm. "*Sí*, just back troubles. The fifties are not easy."

"I'm trying to avoid them." He moved along. "The trip was good, except the airline lost my bag, and we lost our rental. You sure it's okay we stay tonight?"

He really hoped she'd suggest something else, but she grinned and waved off any other option. "*No pasa nada*. As you can see, we have plenty of room. And I'm sure we can find you something to wear. The stores are closed today, but Rodolfo can take you into town tomorrow if you'd like."

Baxter would rather wear the same pair of underwear for a month. "I can run into town tomorrow in the Audi, no big deal."

She flipped up a hand. "You don't want to drive our skinny streets in your large car. Americans have died between those walls. And you can find something of my husband's to wear in the meantime. Ah, there she is."

Ester looked down one of the dirt roads leading into the groves. A woman in a straw hat strolled toward them through a ray of apricot sunshine. Her dark skin glistened from a day of work. The sleeves of her scarlet-red button-down shirt were rolled up to her elbows. She wore black boots and faded jeans with holes in the knees.

When she looked up, his heart skipped a beat. He'd not considered the grandness of meeting Sofia's half sister, but it came down hard on him as she followed her mother's waving hand. He'd seen pictures of her, and she didn't much look like Sofia, but something in that moment reminded him of her, maybe the way she moved.

Alma's hair was cut at the shoulders, whereas Sofia had always let hers fall well down her back. Her face was softer than Sofia's and their mother's. More like Mia's, come to think of it. The high cheekbones were there but warmer and more rounded, her face less chiseled.

"*Buenas,*" she said, drawing closer. Her eyes were green, a soft sage almost, not brown like Sofia's, and they gave off a vintage warmth and soul, like what a record player puts out spinning vinyl. Without hesitation, she leaned in and kissed both cheeks.

"Very good to meet you," she said with a strong Spanish accent. "Long journey?"

It took him a moment to respond. He barely got out, "Yeah, long journey." He touched his chest, knowing he'd made something of a scene. "Forgive me. It's a little heavy meeting all of you." He attempted another swig of the empty beer, wishing for a drop to calm his nerves.

"Mia!" he called out, his voice cracking like a pubescent boy. "Come meet your aunt." Thankful to have successfully diverted the attention away from his own vulnerability, he watched his daughter run over.

Alma lowered to her knees, opening her arms. "Very good to see you, Mia. We are excited to have you." Her English was certainly more broken than Ester's.

"Thank you," Mia responded politely. As the two embraced, Baxter watched Mia for any troubling signs. To his surprise, she seemed to be doing much better than him.

Letting go and holding Mia's shoulders, Alma said, "What a miracle you are here, truly. How was the plane ride? Did you get to watch any good movies? I love drinking Coca-Cola and watching movies on planes."

"Yes, ma'am, me too—and I love Coke—but my dad only lets me watch one movie and have Sprite, because Coke has caffeine."

"Oh, that's fair. You had an overnight flight, didn't you? You must be tired."

Putting a hand on Mia's shoulder, he said to Alma, "Yeah, an overnight flight and we're both exhausted." Turning to Mia, he said, "But we're hanging in there. Right, sweetie?"

"I'm not tired," Mia said.

"Of course not," Alma replied. "When I was your age, I never ran out of energy. Is that how you are?"

"Yes, ma'am," Mia replied.

"And she didn't even come with a power switch." Baxter's joke fell hard on the pine needle–covered ground.

Ignoring it, Alma leaned forward to meet Mia's eyes. "I can't wait to get to know you. And I want to hear about your mom, if you feel like talking about her."

Baxter froze. Would he have to deflect Sofia's questions the whole time? He worried how Mia might respond, but she did great. "Sure."

Alma frowned. "I so wish I'd met her."

When she turned to Baxter, the sadness on her face assured him this meeting wasn't only difficult for Baxter and Mia. Whether or not Alma had known she had a sister, she certainly hadn't known until very recently about the murder.

"Sofia would have loved it here," Baxter finally said, breaking up a silence that was fringed with all sorts of loss. "She would have loved meeting everyone."

Alma's warm eyes showered over him. "We can check you in and give you the tour after lunch." Taking Mia's hand but keeping her gaze on Baxter, Alma drew in a lengthy and amazingly peaceful breath, one that benefited Baxter and surely Mia as much as it probably did her.

"For now, just relax," she said with an ease as pure as a mountain breeze.

Wouldn't that be nice, Baxter thought.

Chapter 10

Fideuá

Baxter and Mia sat with Alma, Ester, and Rodolfo at one of the three crowded tables that each featured a massive pan covered in foil. Next to the pan sat bottles of wine and bright-green olive oil, both without labels, and a wide stainless steel salad bowl filled with purple and green lettuces and shaved carrots. Wooden cutting boards overflowed with baguettes and slices of Manchego cheese and paper-thin folds of Iberico *jamón*, which Ester had explained came from pigs fed acorns and chestnuts. Baxter kept popping olives from the bowl in front of him into his mouth. They were the best he'd ever had, and after about ten, he'd gotten used to spitting the pits, or *huesos*, to the ground.

"This is called *fideuá*, typical of the Valencian community," Ester's brother Don Tomas said from across the table, two of his grandchildren flanking him on either side. Baxter had learned a few moments earlier that "Don" and "Doña" were used as terms of respect, much like using Mr. or Mrs., but Ester had told him that she didn't like being called Doña Ester, that the title made her feel old.

Don Tomas was certainly older than Ester, well endowed with a belly he carried like a badge of pride to prove his love of food. His pockmarked face seemed to hold a permanent smile, showing that between food and this giant family of his, life was pretty good.

He pulled off the foil to reveal the contents of the paella pan in front of him. The steam billowed up and filled the air with the smell of the sea. He scooped portions onto plates and passed them down as Baxter tried to work through why he felt so uncomfortable inside. Was it just that he'd put so much hope into this trip helping Mia?

"*Fideuá* is like paella, but we make it with broken spaghetti instead of rice," Alma explained, sitting at the end of the table next to Mia. "There's a story about a cook on a boat—in the 1930s, I believe. His captain always ate too much paella, so the cook switched pasta for rice, hoping the captain wouldn't eat more than his share. It was a success and caught on in Valencia."

In moments, everyone had a plate stacked high with this wonderful concoction of broken spaghetti mixed with vegetables, mussels, scallops, shrimp, and fish.

Baxter noticed a slice of red pepper on Mia's plate, and he stabbed it.

"You don't like the belly peppers?" Alma asked her.

"Belly peppers?" Mia said with a smile. "You mean bell peppers?"

"Ah, bell peppers. *Sí.*" Alma bit her lip, then finally admitted, "I thought they were belly peppers because they're shaped like bellies."

Mia broke into a laugh. "Who has a belly shaped like a bell pepper?"

The laughter around the table forced Alma to blush. "And moving on," she said, pouring Mia a generous portion of olive oil next to her bread. "If you eat good *aceita de oliva* every day, you will live a very healthy life. Our oils are very high in polyphenols, which are good for your aches and pains, your heart, your head, even your soul." She broke off a chunk of bread and handed it to Mia. "Try it and tell me what you think."

Everyone watched as Mia sponged up the vibrant oil and bit into the doughy goodness. Her eyes fell closed. When she looked back at Alma, she asked, "You made this?"

"We all did," Alma replied. "Well, we grow the olives. The mill in town crushes them for us."

"Alma is too modest," Ester said, pouring herself sparkling water from a bottle. Baxter noticed she didn't drink wine like everyone else. "She is the *granjera* here," Ester continued, "the head farmer. Just like her father, your aunt has a gift for understanding those trees out there . . . understanding everything that grows here."

Alma leaned toward Mia. "Tomorrow, I can take you on a tour of our farm, if you'd like."

"Yes, ma'am, I'd love that." Mia dragged her chunk of bread back into the olive oil.

In the spirit of kindness, Baxter asked Rodolfo, "And what do you do?"

Rodolfo wiped the corners of his mouth with a napkin. "I sell the oil." He'd taken off his jacket and rolled up his sleeves.

Ester patted Rodolfo's arm, which were both shaved and shaped like a swimmer's. "Alma runs the farm," Ester said, "Rodolfo sells the oil, and I make sure the two don't kill each other."

A nervous chuckle scratched the air, then . . . near silence. The songs of the birds in the groves were the only sound. Baxter could see that Ester wasn't exactly joking.

Mia didn't let the quiet last too long. "What happened to your finger, Uncle Rodolfo?"

Uncle? Baxter thought. Was Mia that desperate for family that she would claim just anybody so quickly? And what was Baxter thinking? How had he not seen the possibility that Mia would want more long-term relationships with these people? Even as they pulled in, he was thinking more in terms of this trip being a quick fix.

And as far as bringing up the missing finger, when it came to elephants in the room, Mia was like a safari guide standing up at the front of the Jeep in the Serengeti, pointing them out the moment they appeared.

He held up his hand. "A tractor accident, *cariño*."

Having worked in the construction business since he was a kid, Baxter had seen his fair share of missing fingers. The thought sent him back to the worries of being so far away from his team. *Please,* he thought, *don't let anything happen that I can't fix from over here.*

"And *this* is why he is the salesman," Alma said, attempting to lighten the mood but failing epically. Rodolfo glared at her with angry eyes. Not for the first time, Baxter wondered what he and Mia had walked into.

Mia asked for the specifics, and Rodolfo explained he'd been changing an implement on the tractor, and his finger had gotten caught between two pieces of metal.

Trying to let the image go, Baxter poured himself a generous amount of oil, dipped his bread, and took a bite. He had to admit it was tasty.

Alma was staring him down like a chef would when you taste their food. Baxter gave a thumbs-up. "Though I'm not an expert, I'm certainly impressed."

Alma thanked him. "I hear you're in the construction business."

"That's right." Baxter tore off another piece of bread. "Feel free to put me to work. As Mia will eagerly tell you, I have a hard time sitting still."

"Is that true, Mia?" Alma asked her.

"He's like the Energizer bunny," Mia replied.

"*Sí,*" Alma said, "but I was thinking more like Tim the Tool Man."

Baxter smiled. "How in the world do you know about Tim the Tool Man? I grew up on that show." He was referring to *Home Improvement.*

Alma scooped a forkful of *fideuá* and held it out in front of her. "American television is how we really learned English, Baxter the Tool Man."

Baxter side-eyed his daughter. "It doesn't have quite the same ring, does it?"

"I think it works," Mia replied. Then to Alma, she announced, "He doesn't like his job. It's *very* stressful."

"It can be," Baxter admitted.

"Can be?" Mia said. "See all those gray hairs around his ears?" Everyone rewarded her with a laugh. "Yeah, there's the proof."

When Alma finished chewing her bite, she asked Baxter, "What got you into the construction business?"

"Same as you. My father was a builder and taught me from a very young age."

"My dad was a rock star," Mia added with a mouthful of broken spaghetti, eating more than he'd ever seen her consume back home.

"Is he?" Alma asked, looking at Baxter in jest.

He gave Mia an overly dramatic evil eye. "Will you stop trying to embarrass me, Mia?"

His daughter took his question as encouragement. "He was in a band called Cactus Road. They were *huge*."

Baxter almost shushed her again, but how dare he do that to his number one fan? Instead, he attempted to downplay it. "We were kind of big for a minute in some circles."

"What did you play?" Ester asked.

"The guitar, mostly acoustic." He felt himself getting hot, almost itchy. Thinking about those days with the band was almost as bad as falling back into the memories of Sofia.

"You'll have to play for us," Alma suggested.

Baxter raised his hands. "Maybe I'll bring my guitar next time." *Next time?* he heard himself say. There wouldn't be a next time.

"We have one," Alma said. "My father's. He was an amateur guitarist, but he has a very nice guitar."

Of course he does, Baxter thought. Just his luck. If she only knew. He had no interest in anyone's guitar.

"My dad quit after my mom died," Mia said, clearly intent on trying to make Baxter's face flush red.

Ester crossed her arms and said to Alma, "Your father may have been a terrible guitarist, but he was a masterful lover."

"Mama!" Alma said, reaching to cover Mia's ears. Rodolfo muttered what sounded like a string of Spanish curses, and everyone within earshot exploded in more laughter.

When the excitement at the table settled down and people began to slide their forks under more *fideuá*, he asked, "Do y'all get cell service around here? I seemed to have lost it as we pulled in."

Rodolfo pointed behind him. "You have to go toward the neighboring property."

Panic set in, like a sharp gray fin had risen through the surface of the water. "You mean y'all don't get any service anywhere?" Then Baxter added somewhat sarcastically, "How do you get anything done?"

Alma grinned. "That's exactly how we get things done. We have a landline and Wi-Fi inside, though." She pronounced *Wi-Fi* like *weefee*. "Usually it works once you get close to the pile of rubble in the meadow," she added.

"Okay," Baxter said, "no big deal." And yet it was . . .

‒

After the last of the *fideuá* was scraped from the pans, the kids left the table one by one. Alma called out to a boy spinning a soccer ball on his finger. "Alfonso, *ven aquí!*"

The boy, who Baxter realized was the one who had been missing earlier, the one Ester had said must be climbing a tree, rushed over and stopped in front of his aunt. He had a thick head of straight brown hair that came over his ears and nearly covered his big eyes.

Alma placed her hands on his shoulders, facing him. "Have you introduced yourself to your cousin?"

He shook his head and then shyly turned to Mia. *"¿Quieres jugar?"*
Mia looked at her father and Alma before responding. *"Sí."*

She slipped off her chair and followed him hesitantly toward the other kids playing in the grass by the tree line.

Coffee seemed to appear out of nowhere, and adult conversation ensued. Baxter was the target for a while, and he spoke about life back home: American politics, favorite cities, sports.

Ester bailed him out and spoke about her deceased husband, Jorge, how he'd been the fourth generation to run the estate and had breathed new life into the farm and into his family's brand. "He died in a plane crash over Salzburg, Austria, in December," she said. "He was going skiing with a friend."

"I'm so sorry," Baxter said. "How long were you together?"

"Aside from breaking up for a couple of years when we both went to university, we dated since we were fourteen years old. Can you believe that?"

Baxter had opted for sparkling water, or *agua con gas*, over coffee. He held the glass in his hand, turning it slightly every few seconds. How unbearably human it was to know that at best in life, you fall in love, but there was no way of avoiding losing that person down the line.

"Jorge loved this place even more than his father," she said. "He reinvented the way they farmed. He became the talk of the olive oil world."

Baxter looked past Rodolfo to the house. He followed the ivy up the walls to the terra-cotta tiles. Had things been different, Sofia might have grown up under that roof and had very different parents.

Pulling himself back to the conversation, he said, "I just never would have thought that there was such a thing as the olive oil world. Sounds like wine in a way. Shows you what I know."

"Yeah," Rodolfo said, "but people don't easily understand the romance of oil like they do wine."

"Not yet, anyway," Alma said.

Rodolfo lit a cigarette and said through a cloud of smoke, "I don't know that it will ever change. What our family has been making for so long isn't appreciated like it used to be. People aren't willing to pay the prices, especially with all the dirty competition out there." He laughed to himself. "Americans think they're buying olive oil. No, no. They're not buying olive oil. It's seed oil that's been deodorized in Jaén. There's no regulation, and without enough interest in the product, Americans, and even Europeans, don't know what to look for or how much they should be paying. They don't know that you can't make a liter of good oil for two euros. And with your American tariffs going up twenty-five percent, it becomes impossible."

"Challenging but not impossible," Alma said. "I pray there will always be a place for good olive oil."

Another sarcastic laugh. "My sister is such a dreamer."

"Like her father," Ester added.

Alma looked up to the sky. "In a way, I feel like he's watching me."

Rodolfo scoffed. "He's only shaking his finger at you, *hermana*."

Alma almost said something but stopped, clearly resisting the urge to take his bait. Rodolfo said something else in Spanish, and Ester silenced him with the wave of a hand and a rapid-fire assault in Spanish. Baxter couldn't help but think Ester's invitation should have come with a disclaimer. *Ten days,* he thought. You could bet he'd be back on Airbnb's website as soon as he could plug in.

"Well," Baxter said, standing, "as much fun as this has been"—he waited for a smile but none at the table came—"I'm going to check on Mia."

"Please stay," Ester said. "I'd like to hear more about Sofia while the kids are away. If it's okay with you."

No, it wasn't okay with him. This was enough for now. With all of Sofia's family around, they might as well dangle pictures of her in front of him.

He looked over to where Mia and the other children had disappeared into the olive trees. "I just want to make sure she's okay. It's a big deal for her to be here."

"Oh, she's fine," Ester said, waving a hand at him. "*Tranquilo.* Let her have some fun."

Baxter thought Ester sure didn't comprehend boundaries. Was that the Spanish way? He tried a different approach. "Honestly, I'm feeling a little bit worn out. It was a long travel day. If you don't mind, I'd love to get Mia situated, maybe let her take a nap. And I could use a shower."

Ester backed down, and Baxter turned away before everyone at the table sensed that there was more going on than his weariness. Without turning back to them, he said, "I'm just gonna grab Mia."

Following her path into the groves, he called out, "Mia!"

There was laughter, but she didn't respond. He followed the sounds of the children as he walked farther in. It was probably beautiful, but he barely noticed.

"Mia!" he called out again.

She finally yelled back, and he went that way. A hundred yards farther in, he saw the colors of the children's clothes standing out amid the natural scenery. And then he saw that they were climbing trees.

He found Mia sitting on a low branch with Alfonso. "Hey, honey." He was about to ask her to get down when he noticed the smile on her face.

"Hi, Daddy."

"Are you okay?" It was an absurd question, because she looked more than okay.

"Yeah, come on up." She patted the limb. "There's room right here."

Baxter gave a half smile. "No, thank you. I just wanted to check in. We should probably get a nap. It's been a long two days of travel."

"But we just got here. I'm okay."

He wasn't about to argue with all the cousins watching him. And she did have a point. Dreading a return to the table but not seeing a way out of it, he said, "All right, a little bit longer and then I really do want you to get some rest."

"Yes, sir. Don't worry, I'm fine."

He turned up one corner of his mouth. "I can see that."

Slightly puzzled and yet happy that she seemed to be more than okay, he meandered slowly back to the table.

It didn't take long for Ester to return to her interrogation. At least, that was what it felt like to Baxter. The other tables had their own conversations going, but the adults sitting at Baxter's table, including Ester, Alma, and Rodolfo, waited with watchful eyes and bated breath for him to talk about their lost family member.

Accepting that Ester wasn't going to quit asking and that he couldn't exactly ignore her requests to know more about her daughter, he decided to get it over with. "This isn't stuff I like to talk about around Mia, but I know you'd like to know more." He took a centering breath. "Along with being the most loving mom and wife in the world, Sofia was my greatest cheerleader. And Mia's. Really, she pulled for everyone around her. And she was one of the few people who could make me laugh to tears. Had a very witty sense of humor, a way with puns."

He momentarily lost himself in a contrapuntal memory of how dedicated she'd been to her work before she quit. He'd given her a hard time over being so serious about a presentation she'd been working on for a cat food company. She'd snapped at him: "So you think what you do is more important?" He'd bought himself a week in the doghouse for that one.

Realizing everyone was still staring at him, he said, "She was very serious too. A businesswoman. Highly organized and driven, almost superhero status. The complete opposite of me and I loved it . . . and needed it. I was playing music, touring, so she was on her own a lot, raising Mia. Still, she managed to keep her job part-time, working from home. She did branding for companies and was really good at it. She could do it all so effortlessly. I really admired that about her. I always knew we'd fall apart without her . . . and we just about did."

As he said it, he felt his eyes swell with sadness, and he bit down on his tongue to keep from falling apart. The last thing he wanted was for these strangers to see how weak he still was.

"She sounds like me," Ester said. "Before I agreed to marry Jorge, I'd planned on law school. I was a fighter."

He released the bite on his lip and tried to smile. "Really? She was a fighter too. Not the kind of person you could say no to easily. If you crossed her, she wouldn't let you get away with it. Almost like she was on a mission to make things right in the world, and if someone broke the laws of humanity, she would not let it stand."

Baxter suddenly shocked himself with a smile. "No one broke lines in front of her and got away with it; no one littered; no one screamed at their kids. I loved her fire and fight; it was very infectious. Sometimes uncomfortable but so admirable that I enjoyed it."

Ester and the others were silent in a way that made Baxter think they could listen to him talk about Sofia forever. He didn't have much more in him but pressed on. "And she was beautiful, just like Mia. Thank goodness she doesn't look like me," he added in a failed attempt to be lighthearted.

Everyone at the table granted him a courteous and charitable chuckle.

"Sofia was a skater and surfer girl," he said, trying to smother the awkwardness. "That whole California thing. Her favorite band was the Red Hot Chili Peppers, if you know them. Her favorite food was Mexican. She went to UC Santa Barbara and landed an internship for a marketing firm that was working with a lot of the production studios in Hollywood. That's when the business bug bit her. But she never lost that surfer girl side of her. When she moved to Charleston, she brought her longboard and rode it just about every morning before work. I'll have to see if I can dig up any pictures of her riding waves."

"Please," Ester said, coming around with her own smile. Though he'd shared a few, Ester had continued to beg for more pictures every time they spoke on the phone.

An image of Sofia in her wet suit sprang to life in Baxter's mind. He could see her coming out of the water, her board tucked under arm. Baxter used to take his guitar out there and watch her surf as the sun rose over the horizon. Those were some of the best songs he'd ever written.

Baxter forced himself to look at Ester, and he felt sheepish and small, knowing that they'd seen his true colors just now. He was not the man he wanted to be. And he couldn't talk about her without his whole world coming down on him.

"Anyway," he finally said. "That's enough of that for now." That was about all he could say, and thankfully the family seemed to get the message as they pulled their eyes away from him two by two.

Chapter 11

Tranquilo

After everyone had left, Baxter and Mia grabbed their things from the Audi and followed Alma, Ester, and Paco inside the house. He had been glad to hear that Rodolfo lived in the city center, so they wouldn't be sharing the same lodging.

Up the front steps and pushing through the door, they came directly into a massive living room made up of several sitting areas. It smelled of burned wood, smoke, and sage. Oriental rugs covered much of the slightly uneven tiled floors. Baxter was mesmerized by the very fine furniture and exquisite antiques. The walls were stuccoed white, and random spots of naked brick and stone peeked through in the corners, evidence from centuries of patchwork. The sloppiness didn't detract from the artistry, though—perhaps even enhanced it.

Thick wooden beams he would have paid a fortune for back in the US stretched across the twenty-foot-high ceilings. A regal golden chandelier hung from the middle. Straight ahead soared an immense wood fireplace that wouldn't have been allowed under code back home. A cutout to the right held a stack of wood taller than Mia. Through the windows on either side of the fireplace was an outdoor courtyard. Giant cypresses grew around the edge, and a lone olive tree stood in the middle, like an ancient statue.

"On the other side of the courtyard are the offices," Alma said. "I'll show you tomorrow when you're rested. We can taste the oils."

"We'd love to," Mia said. "Wouldn't we, Daddy?"

Baxter reluctantly nodded. Though he was a long way from Greenville, he still had work to do.

They found themselves in the kitchen, which was a work of art. Bright brass pots and pans swung alongside dried herbs above a counter made up of navy-blue tiles. Two copper stools edged against a butcher block island that showed gashes and cuts from decades of use. A dozen or so eggs filled a *cazuela* to the right of the farm sink. A small breakfast table with four chairs hosted a basket that spilled over with oranges, which is exactly what Baxter smelled at the moment.

They ascended the creaky stairs, the planks worn down by the years. Mia's was a simple room with an arched ceiling of white stucco lined with wooden beams. A well-treaded yet fancy rug with gold patterns woven into a background of a light red covered most of the floor. On the tables flanking the four-poster bed were matching lamps with jewel-covered shades. At the end of the bed was a small trunk topped with a cushion to sit upon. Above it hung a chandelier that looked like a crown suspended in the air.

Mia noticed none of these things, though. She raced directly to the pile of books and toys waiting for her in the cushiony chair by the bathroom. "These are for me?"

"Of course they're for you," Ester said. "I've got a lot of catching up to do, as far as being your *iaia*."

Beaming, Mia held up a 3D puzzle. "How did you know I love puzzles?"

Ester looked incredibly happy as she approached Mia. "Because your aunt loved them too."

Mia smiled and went one by one through her gifts. The last gift Baxter's parents had given her was three years earlier, a lamp that had come right off one of their own tables in the trailer in Aiken, where Baxter had visited exactly once.

Leaving Mia with her grandmother to unpack, Baxter followed Alma into a room next to Mia's. A colorful blue-dominant fresco decorated the border of the two windows that overlooked the front of the estate; long beige drapes hung on either side, their thick rods capped with elaborate gold finials. The dark-oak headboard of the bed was carved in floral patterns. Above it hung a tapestry with women in headscarves filling baskets with olives gathered from under their trees.

Desperate for a good night's sleep, Baxter tested the mattress and nearly broke his fingers. Nope. He wouldn't be sleeping well at all. He was the prince and the pea when it came to all things bedding.

"Will this be okay?" Alma asked.

He set his messenger bag on the bed. "It's great, thanks."

"About your bag. You've called the airline. Not much more we can do. I would be patient. You're on Spanish time now. I'll see what I can find of my father's in the meantime. You can leave your clothes outside the door, and I'll run the laundry tonight. Everything will be dry by tomorrow afternoon."

He felt his eyebrows squeeze together. "Tomorrow afternoon? Are your dryers powered by gerbils?"

She laughed at his awful joke. "You Americans and your dryers. We don't have a dryer."

"No dryer?"

"No dryer," she said with a sadistic and subtle grin.

"So it's the twenty-first century and you still hang things?"

"Yes, we hang things. On lines."

"Why no dryers?" He was truly curious.

Alma shrugged. "We have different priorities, maybe. Or maybe we're not as worried about doing things so quickly over here. I enjoy the process."

"Fair enough," Baxter said, feeling like the butt of a joke. "Maybe I'll absorb some of this easy-living stuff before we leave. By the way, could I trouble you for that Wi-Fi password?"

"Let me see if I can find it." She raised a finger. "For now, disconnect for a minute. You're in Spain. Repeat after me. *Tranquilo.*"

"*Tranquilo,*" he said.

"There you go, Baxter the Tool Man. Relax. Go take a bath, clean off."

"A bath?" he said, the idea hitting him like the taste of a bad oyster. "Baxter the Tool Man doesn't take baths."

The notion apparently entertained her. "I guess you'll have to get used to it. Ester has the only shower in the house, and she doesn't like anyone going in her room."

To confirm he was showerless, he inspected the bathroom. Sure enough, a claw-foot tub short a showerhead and shy of four feet in length filled the corner.

"You know how to work one, right?" Alma asked from behind him.

He turned back to find her grinning at him.

"Are you having fun with this?" he asked.

"I think you're a slightly high-maintenance American, and yes, it's fun."

"I'm glad I entertain you," he said.

"It's like Tim the Tool Man has stepped out of my TV," she said, backing away from the bathroom and turning to go. "You're the most American American in all of America."

He faked a laugh, but his mind had returned to Mia. Was she getting on as well as she seemed? Was she really having the exact opposite experience as him? Or was she the world's greatest child actor?

"Make yourself at home and we'll talk later," Alma said. He thanked her as she left the room.

After settling in, he found Mia curled up in her bed, playing with a Rubik's Pyramid—another gift from Ester. She said, "I already know what you're gonna say."

"Oh, is that right?"

Lowering her voice an octave, she asked, "How are you, Mia?"

Baxter chuckled; she was right. "How did you know?"

She twisted the base of her toy. "You always ask me the *same thing*, Daddy. How are you, Mia? How are you, little princess? How are you, peanut?"

He stepped toward her. "I think asking how you are is a reasonable question. Is there something else you'd rather me say?"

"You could change it up some." She switched to an adorable robotic voice. "Greetings, earth daughter, how was your day?" With her best attempt at a deep voice, she said, "Or . . . what's up, girl?"

He pressed his hand down on the bed. "Um, I will never say to you: *What's up, girl?* If a boy ever says that to you, you let me know, okay?"

"Why?" She kept fidgeting with her toy.

"Because." He held back from telling her where his protective-father imagination had just taken him. He had yet had to talk to her about boys, but he was pretty sure he wouldn't let her even talk to boys on the phone until well into high school. Dating could begin in her early thirties.

"*Because* isn't actually a reason."

He shook his head at her. "Eight going on eighteen, aren't you?"

She shrugged with the same sassiness that her mother could harness at a moment's notice.

He sat on the bed and gently pried the Rubik's Pyramid from her. "You sure everything's good? I know this is a lot."

Her beautiful little eyes found his. "It's fine."

Eight-year-olds were so hard to figure out. Sometimes Mia spoke like a teenager or even older, talking about her feelings like someone who'd been seeing a therapist for years. And then other times she'd answer with, "It's fine," or, "I don't know how I feel. I don't know why I did that. I don't know, Daddy!"

He set the Rubik's Pyramid on the bedside table. "If you'd rather stay somewhere else tonight, we can."

She shook her head. "No, I like being here."

"You do?"

"Of course. Everyone is so nice."

"They are, aren't they? You just let me know if anything changes. We can always get out of here early."

She made a face like he'd said something preposterous.

"Wanna sleep with me tonight?" he asked.

Mia shook her head. "No, thanks. You can just tuck me in. Iaia said she'd read me a book."

"Oh, is that right? Have I been replaced?"

She shrugged.

Read her a book? he thought. It wasn't so strange on the surface, but Ester sure had jumped right into her role, hadn't she? The boundaries seemed to fall away by the second around here. Well, they hadn't come up against Baxter Shaw yet. He knew how to put up walls. Hell, he did it for a living.

⁓

Turned out jet lag wasn't good for insomnia. Two a.m. and Baxter was wide awake. Alma was unable to find the Wi-Fi password, so he'd done as much work as he could without a connection, mostly billing stuff and writing a few emails he'd queued up to be sent out later. He couldn't wait to check into a new place with internet, which felt more essential than hot water.

Now he was stirring in a whirlwind of thought, second-guessing the whole trip. Well, second-guessing for the hundredth time. He'd walked in on Ester and Mia earlier while they were supposed to be reading. Instead, Ester was asking Mia about her mother, asking if Sofia ever read to her. Baxter felt like Ester had defied his request that they not talk about Sofia. Mia didn't seem visibly upset, but Baxter had quickly suggested, "Okay, time for lights-out."

In the quiet, the house seemed to talk, gentle creaking and settling, as if it were on the move, shifting from the uncomfortable position of sitting there for hundreds of years, almost like a yogi whose limbs had fallen asleep.

Knowing that he probably wouldn't fall asleep, he was tempted to go downstairs, just for a change of scenery, but he'd probably wake up someone. And he didn't want to leave Mia, just in case she needed him. She was exhausted, though, so maybe she'd get a good night's sleep.

Or not.

Mia's scream slashed through the quiet rustling of the house. Paco's bark immediately followed. Baxter raced out of bed and out of the room. His heart pounded as he entered her bedroom. She was hugging her legs and crying.

"Sweetie," he said, "it's okay." He climbed into the bed and sat against the headboard, then pulled her into him and cradled her with his right arm. She wept hard, gushing out tears. He wiped her cheeks and looked at her, making sure she'd woken from this dream. Helplessness and guilt in equal parts clawed at him with their talons.

Mia wiped her eyes on her pajamas. "I wish Mommy were here."

"I know you do." He wished she were here too. And that was the problem with being here, that though it was so very distant from everything Sofia had known, from her childhood in California all the way through to Charleston and the end, they were still excavating her roots, dragging up memories and feelings that Baxter had worked hard for three years to protect them both from.

The nightmares might get worse from here. This moment was validating his concern. In that instant, he wondered how he could pull off leaving early, like only after two or three days. How could he even make the suggestion without upsetting Mia? He wasn't exactly worried about the feelings of the Arroyos. This was about his daughter.

"Just know that you're giving her a huge gift by being here," Baxter said. "If she was here, she'd give you a huge hug and thank you like crazy." He didn't know what else to say.

"I just don't understand why she had to die," Mia said through sniffles. "She could be here right now, meeting her mom and sister and brother and everyone . . . she'd be soooo happy. I don't understand why that guy would want to hurt people."

Baxter had spent plenty of time wondering the same thing. He noticed he was rocking her as he said, "There's not always a reason. It's taken me a long time to accept that." His mind went there, back to those days. By then, with the growing number of mass shootings, the media was doing their best to avoid making a spectacle of the shooters. Though they'd covered the day from a thousand different angles, they'd published only one photo of the shooter.

Eric Mendecki. A twenty-eight-year-old loner from Tallahassee, Florida. It didn't seem that he'd come from a broken home, but his father, an electrical engineer, and mother, a high school arts teacher, had given interviews and spoken of the darkness and depression that had always been inside of their son. Seeing how destroyed they were that they'd raised a murderer, Baxter had found a way to let go of his anger toward them, but he'd never forgive their son.

Mendecki had moved to Charleston to follow his girlfriend, who was a nurse at MUSC. According to interviews with her, she'd already broken up with him and told him not to come to Charleston. He'd ignored her, moving into a small apartment in James Island and taking up a job as an Uber driver. When she refused to see him, he began to stalk her, once breaking into her apartment on Spring Street. She obtained a restraining order against him, which was what had pushed him over the edge.

In his apartment, the police had found three guns, one of which was a semiautomatic like the one he'd used on Sofia. They'd also found a one-page letter written in clean cursive, a declaration of hate for humanity. The media did not print it, but the families of the victims were offered copies. Baxter didn't have a choice but to read it. He had to understand why this man had taken Sofia's life.

As outlined in the letter, Mendecki wanted to "wake the fucking deaf and blind masses." They—the contents of the entire letter—were the words of a madman, and Baxter had crumpled up the piece of paper, none the wiser as to why Mendecki had chosen to hurt random people or why it had to be Sofia who'd been put into his sights. All Baxter had been left with was further evidence that he should have been the one in that parking lot.

"Where did the bullet hit her?" Mia asked as she wiped her nose.

Baxter was so lost in his own nightmare that he barely heard her and had to drag himself back. He felt like his chest was caving in with hate and sadness. That fucking Mendecki. If they ever let him out, Baxter would be waiting for him.

And now Baxter and Sofia's precious and sweet baby girl was forced to ask questions that no one should ever have to ask. But she had to because she needed to understand, just as he'd needed to. The thing was, though, like Baxter, she would never understand. More information wasn't the answer.

Still, he'd hidden the truth about her mother's murder for too long, and look what it had done. He might be able to help her forget her mother, but first she had to know the truth.

"In the chest, baby doll." As he said it, he saw an image of the bullet leaving Mendecki's AR-15 and tearing into Sofia. He saw her fall onto the pavement, her head bouncing on impact. It was all black and white. And he saw Sofia digging in her purse for the phone as a pool of crimson blood collected around her.

"Baxter," she'd whispered when he'd picked up. "I'm . . ." She was coughing.

"What's wrong?" he'd asked, knowing instantly that it was severe.

"I've been shot."

Baxter felt a deep burn in his chest as he pressed his eyes and lips together, forcing himself not to fall back into the weak man he'd been in the months afterward. He moved a strand of hair from his daughter's face and stared into her, wanting to show her more than anything that he would always be there for her.

She was off somewhere else, though, staring at the wall in front of her. He touched her chin and tilted her head to him. She finally looked at him, and he opened his mouth to speak but came up short of words. What could he say? That he wished he'd been the one who'd taken that bullet? All he managed to get out was, "I'm so sorry." He was sorry it wasn't him. He was sorry that it wasn't Sofia raising her now. He was sorry that he hadn't been a better father since then.

The floorboards creaked. Someone else was up. He drew in a deep breath and tried to pull it together.

"Why did you have her cremated?" Mia asked. "Why not bury her? I wished you'd buried her."

"Oh, sweetie pie." He kissed her forehead. This wasn't fair, any of it. What kind of world makes a little girl grow up trying to make sense of her mother's murder? He wasn't about to tell her that he'd cremated her because he couldn't bear the thought of his Sofia lying in the ground all alone. Her mother had wanted her buried back in California, but Baxter wouldn't allow it. That was another reason Dotty had pulled more out of their lives.

Answering as best as he could, Baxter said, "Your mom and I had never talked about it, so I had to make the decision. I didn't like the idea of her being stuck in a coffin. Why do you wish I'd buried her?"

She spoke slowly and sadly. "So that she wasn't gone."

He put his head against hers and said something he wasn't sure he believed, as if his vocal cords were just doing whatever it needed to do to rescue his daughter. "She's very much still here. Just in a different way. She's in our hearts and all over this place. Her body was only a small part of her."

"Still, I think she would have liked to have been buried and not burned."

Had he made the wrong choice? Maybe Mia was right. The idea of Sofia burning was harrowing. Why hadn't he thought of that? And he wasn't sure that he'd even taken into account what Mia would have wanted.

Paco came around the corner and jumped up onto the bed. Mia smiled as he licked her face. Seconds later, Ester followed, wearing her nightgown. "Is everything okay?"

"Everything's fine," Baxter said, pushing Paco and his wet tongue away. "She's just having a tough time sleeping. I think it's the new environment and jet lag." He didn't feel like sharing more. Baxter realized he was wearing Don Jorge's blue boxers and white T-shirt. His own clothes hung on a line outside his window.

Ester didn't seem to notice or care as she slowly rounded the bed and took a seat. She'd explained during dinner that she'd been experiencing lower back issues, and though they were clearly bothering her tonight, she didn't hesitate in pulling Mia onto her lap. "Come to your *iaia*. Tell me what's wrong."

"I had a nightmare."

"You did, did you? Don't we all, sometimes. Do you know how to say them in español? *Pesadillas.*" Ester rocked Mia back and forth, only glancing at Baxter for a moment. He was so surprised by her audacity that all he could do was force a close-lipped smile.

Ester broke into a quiet lullaby in Spanish, a beautiful melody that calmed Mia as successfully as the unicorn song. He'd wanted to yank Mia out of her arms, but he couldn't now.

More creaking and then Alma appeared at the door. "What's going on?" She wore a long T-shirt that fell halfway down her thighs.

Baxter crossed his legs and lifted his knees some. What in the world was going on? Worst decision ever to stay here. In Baxter's mind, the conductor of this awkward train called out, "All aboard."

Mia said, "I had a nightmare about my mommy." Not only didn't Mia seem bothered, but she seemed grateful for the attention.

"Oh, *cariño*." Alma followed the same path Ester had around the bed and put her hand on Mia's back. Ester said something to her in Spanish, and the two talked for a moment. As much as Baxter felt bothered by their disregard for boundaries, he felt a lot of love in that room.

Alma left a minute later, and Ester looked over at Baxter. "Would you mind if she came and slept with me? If she'd like that."

Baxter was about to shake his head when Mia sprang up like a puppy who'd just heard a squeak. "Really?"

"*Sí. Claro.*" Other than *sí*, he'd heard two words said countless times since their arrival, and he now knew what both meant. *Vale* meant "okay," and *claro* meant "of course."

Ester turned to him. "Only if it's okay with your father. Alma used to have bad dreams, and she always wanted to sleep with me. I think it might help."

Baxter could feel his daughter's eager eyes waiting for his approval. He looked at her and started to say no, but she said, "It's okay. I want to, please."

He rubbed his eyes, if only to hide from the moment. He was having to make all these fast decisions right now, and he hoped to God he wasn't screwing up. To say yes would put her in a possibly fragile position, but to say no would bolster her sadness.

Taking a leap and hoping he wasn't wrong, he said, "Okay, fair enough. But I want you to go pee and let me talk to Ester for one moment."

"Yes, sir."

He thanked her as she climbed out of bed and disappeared into the bathroom. Then he turned to Ester, who was standing up from the bed. "Thank you for helping, really." He meant that. "But please just be careful. This is a lot. I . . . I really don't want her talking about her mother."

Ester looked at him quizzically, as if passively challenging this request, but thankfully she finally accepted a boundary and said, "Of course."

When Mia came out, he handed her Roger the panda bear, and she tucked him under her arm. Baxter kissed her forehead and then watched Ester lead her down the hall, Paco and his wagging tail following closely behind.

Chapter 12

THE LAYERS PEEL BACK

Baxter woke to the crow of a rooster and the smell of burning wood drifting up through the floorboards. Though he'd eventually fallen asleep, the jet lag had wreaked havoc on him, and it took him a few moments to find his bearings. He reached for his phone on the bedside table, and for one blissful moment he imagined he had cell service. Or at least Wi-Fi. Nope, nada. Nadadamnthing. It was 7:15, probably the latest he'd slept in maybe two or three years, which didn't mean much, because he'd been up most of the night being strangled by two hands, one being the worry over his company crumbling without him, and the other his worry about Mia's emotional state.

He wanted to go walk down the hall to check on her but didn't feel comfortable enough to barge into Ester's room. What had he been thinking, letting a stranger take his daughter? Okay, maybe Ester wasn't a stranger. She had the same blood as Sofia, and he supposed that was enough for him to give her the benefit of the doubt. All he could do was hope that Mia had slept through the rest of the night and felt safe with Ester.

And today he'd find another place to stay.

He dressed in more of Jorge's clothes, a pair of pants cut short at the ankles and a pink collared shirt tight in the arms and chest. For the benefit of anyone still sleeping, he crept down the hallway and down the stairs, but the noisy floors sounded like a four-hundred-year-old wooden orchestra belting out the climax of a Mahler symphony with each step. Paco certainly heard him from downstairs and let out a good morning bark.

As Baxter reached the bottom step that fed into the living room, he smelled coffee and smoke and saw that a fire glowed in the fireplace. On the mantel was a line of thick cylindrical candles of various colors, the wax caked down the sides. The two windows facing the courtyard showed the golden fog of the morning.

Paco met him with a wet tongue, and Baxter rubbed his head for a minute. "Morning, buddy."

"Buenos días," a voice said from one of the chairs facing the fire.

Baxter found Ester holding a mug of coffee, the steam rising up into clouds.

"Good morning," he said. "How'd she do?"

"She's up there sleeping away," Ester said proudly. The firelight flashed on the smooth skin of her face.

Baxter stepped toward the fire and reached for the poker and straightened a log. "Was she able to go right back to sleep?"

Paco curled up on the small circular rug at her feet and rested his head on one of her slippers. "It took a little while," Ester said. "She asked if we could make pancakes. I told her I didn't even know how to make pancakes, but I have something much better. And I shared with her about what Alma was like at her age—how much she liked to play outside, that she was a tomboy. Eventually, I looked over and she'd fallen asleep. I left a note on the pillow so she'll know I'm downstairs."

Relief came over him as he leaned the poker back up against the wall. "Good thinking."

"As I mentioned, Alma used to have trouble sleeping, slept in my bed a lot too. Children need a sense of safety sometimes."

Baxter didn't like the insinuation and worked hard to avoid coming off prickly as he said, "Yeah, she's slept with me a lot lately, but I'm trying not to let it become a habit. Is there more coffee?"

"Help yourself. It's on the counter to the right of the stove."

He returned a moment later with his own mug, still bothered by what she'd said. He sat in the other chair, facing the fire. It crackled and popped as it pushed warmth out into the cold room. Apparently the temperature dropped dramatically in the evenings here, as he'd heard happened in the desert.

"What's going on with her?" Ester asked. "These nightmares are happening a lot?"

He glanced at her for a moment and then back to the fire. "Just lately. They'll pass."

There was abrasion in his voice, and she surely heard it. Not wanting to be a jerk, he said, "She's been having them since August. I knew they were about her mother, but I didn't know the details." Baxter gave her a very brief synopsis of what had transpired since that first nightmare.

Ester sighed. "Seems like you've been doing a lot of this on your own. I wish I'd found you earlier, but I suppose it wasn't meant to be."

"Thanks," he said, appreciating the validation. She was right; he had been alone in raising his daughter. He put his lips to the mug, but the coffee was too hot to drink. "I've been trying hard to protect her, but that day has once again found its way in and is trying to wreck our lives. When I told her her mom was adopted and that she wanted to find her family, she was ecstatic. You know most of the story from our calls."

"I think coming here will be so good for her."

"I hope so."

"And how about you?" Ester asked.

Baxter stared into the fire, the flames licking the stone above it. "With so much going on back home, that's yet to be determined. My business is still so young, so we're still trying to catch our groove." He took a sip of the hot black coffee, welcoming the warmth and surprising sweetness. "But I'm happy to get to know Sofia's family, all of you, and it's nice to get away from work and to spend some time with Mia." Ready to move on, he said, "That's great coffee. You put sugar in the pot?"

"It's *café torrefacto*, the typical way here. They roast the beans with sugar, giving it a glaze. You like it?"

"I like everything I've tasted since I landed."

They were quiet for a while, letting the fire do the talking. Baxter wished that he could be as relaxed as her, but this just wasn't easy. For a guy who'd successfully broken through his grief by cremating many of the good memories along with his wife's body, sitting here with Sofia's biological mother in the house she could have grown up in was not something for which he was emotionally prepared. His old therapist would probably be driving a victory lap, saying that Baxter hadn't broken through the grief as much as circumvented it, and an occasion like this had proved Baxter's method faulty. Baxter, on the other hand, would say three years just wasn't enough time.

Mia and Alma would be up soon, and then he'd lose his chance to satisfy a curiosity, so he said, "May I ask you something without offending you?"

Ester smiled, as if she welcomed serious talk in the morning. "I'm not easily offended."

He nodded. "Did your family know about Sofia?"

She made a small noise of acknowledgment, a hum in her throat. "Until earlier in the year, no. Only my mother and father, who took the secret to their graves. But I did tell Alma and Rodolfo in May, just before I started searching."

"What brought all this about?" If she wasn't afraid to ask the hard questions, then neither was he.

A log fell in the fire, shooting up a burst of sparks. He saw the flames dance in her eyes. "I've lived a lot of my life ashamed for abandoning Sofia, and the time came to try to do something about it. I suppose once Jorge was gone, I felt more freedom. It was time to make—" She stopped abruptly, casting a look over his shoulder. "Well, it was time."

Baxter wondered what she was holding back and turned to see what had caught her attention. On the kitchen side of the living room, there was a sitting area with four chairs facing a sofa pushed up against the wall. Above the sofa hung a large painting of a mustachioed Don Jorge in a dark suit and red tie. It looked like he was watching over the room.

Her husband was a striking man, someone who exuded not only confidence but almost dominance. It hit Baxter that she was far more freshly widowed than he, and yet here he was making every conversation about Sofia and Mia and him. It hadn't even been a year since she'd lost him.

"My husband would have been very angry that I hid Sofia. But he would have been just as angry had he known."

Baxter took a long sip of the sweet coffee and said exactly what he was thinking. "I'm sure it was hard losing him."

"We both know what it's like."

Baxter nodded in agreement. How many times had he woken to reach for Sofia in the bed next to him, only to touch cold sheets?

"But," she said, "my Jorge and me, we were different. I loved him, most of the time. But he was a hard man to love." Baxter had picked up on some of that struggle from Rodolfo at lunch the day prior. She continued, "I was certainly sad, but I think what you had with Sofia was much stronger, so I suppose it cut much deeper."

Baxter thought it was a very nice thing to say. He couldn't imagine two people loving each other more than Sofia and he had. It was the little things they did for each other, the extra efforts, the breakfasts in bed, the well-thought-out gifts, even the tiniest gestures, like when Sofia would leave him love notes in his guitar case or how he'd have an orchid delivered every time he left for a tour. Even the taste of that feeling was too much to recall, though, so he moved on.

"May I ask who Sofia's father was?"

She gripped the armrest rather harshly, like her chair was about to launch. "A one-night stand my first year of school in Cambridge. He was Spanish, from Salamanca. I never knew his name, never saw him again. I was a wild one when I was eighteen, finally getting out of this little town. Jorge and I had just broken up. He'd gone to school in Berlin the year before. Sofia's father was the only other man I'd ever slept with."

What a big secret to keep, Baxter thought. "How did Alma and Rodolfo take the news?"

She finally let go of the armrest. "As you can imagine. I suppose Alma took it better than Rodolfo. He and Jorge had a difficult relationship, so he very much leaned on me growing up. And when he found out, it hurt his feelings. I think I disappointed him."

Baxter knew exactly what it was like to be disappointed about your parents and felt a twinge of sympathy for Rodolfo. No man becomes so jaded without being betrayed at some point. "Yeah, I have to say . . . he doesn't appear thrilled about our arrival."

She shifted in the chair, as if the topic of her son was the source of her back pain. "It has nothing to do with you. He just wants the best for this family, and I know the responsibility weighs on him. I'm afraid he sometimes comes off the wrong way because of it."

Rodolfo didn't seem upset about losing his father. Was he that bothered by finding out about Sofia? Or was there something else going on?

There was another question that had been lingering in Baxter's mind: What had Ester told the other people in town about Baxter and Mia's arrival? Being such a small town, he and Mia would surely stick out. He hadn't yet found a chance to ask when a car horn honked outside.

"Ah, there's Alberto."

Paco popped up to his feet, launching a series of warning barks as he ran to the front door.

"Who's Alberto?" Baxter asked, hearing the driver honk again and again.

Ester grimaced as she stood from her chair.

"Here, let me help." Baxter sprang up and offered a hand.

"He's the bread guy."

"You have a bread guy?"

"Eight thirty every morning. The best bread in the entire *comunidad de València*. Would you mind running out there? Let me get some euros."

Baxter offered to run upstairs for his wallet, but she insisted on paying. He followed her into the kitchen and watched her dig into her purse. Drawing out a bill, she handed it to him. "Get the croissants, the *chapata*, and a couple of baguettes."

As Paco and Baxter descended the steps to greet the man in the white van, Baxter breathed in the chilly morning air. This reminded him of California weather, and he was taken back to the time Cactus Road opened up for Bob Weir of the Grateful Dead at the Santa Barbara Bowl. He remembered how cold his fingers and vocal cords were once the sun had gone down. But they'd killed it that night, and Bobby had even invited Baxter out to sing "Jack Straw" with him at the end of the night. He and Bobby sharing a microphone, belting out that chorus with every single one of those fans in that packed amphitheater. Afterward, when Bobby had thrown his muscular arm around Baxter's neck, and as they'd waved at the crowd, Baxter had felt more alive than he could ever remember. He'd done it, dammit, he'd done it. He'd climbed out of all the shit with his childhood and done something right with his life.

And it was a night he could not think about for another moment.

Alberto shut off the engine and climbed out. He rounded the vehicle, whistling a tune, and approached with an infectious smile. "Buenos días!" he said, giving Paco a quick pet on the head. Alberto the happy bread man had chubby cheeks that looked like they'd been stuffed with ping-pong balls. Cheeks probably looked like that after a lifetime of such smiling, Baxter decided.

Alberto said something that sounded like, "You must be the Americanos."

"Yep, that's us."

Alberto said something in Spanish about playing music, and Baxter took it as a question. "Yeah, I play. Well, I used to." Baxter thought this must be the smallest town in the world for the biggest news to be that an old has-been musician and his daughter had come to town.

"*Conoces* Carrie Underwood?" Alberto asked, his cheeks inflating even more.

"*Sí.* Not personally, but sure, I know who she is."

Without a moment's hesitation, Alberto belted into the chorus of "Before He Cheats." The man had a great voice—even pulled off the twang—and was not afraid to use it. Even the rooster quieted.

When Alberto was done, he looked at Baxter with a questioning eye. He jabbed a thumb to his own chest. "*American Idol?*"

Baxter grinned at him, thinking he liked Alberto very much. "You would have a good shot. And if your bread is as good as your voice, then I'm ready to see what you have in the back of this van."

Alberto didn't seem to pick up on Baxter's subtle suggestion. "*Me gusta* Eric Church *también.*" He was saying he also liked Eric Church. Apparently this was the last stop on Alberto's bread route, because he had no interest in rushing out of there. Baxter had no intention of telling the guy that he'd written a song for Eric Church years ago, a cut on his second album.

Holding his hands out in front of him to guide his notes, Alberto started into an Eric Church tune and sang two verses and a chorus. Baxter felt like Simon Cowell and wondered if he should offer a comment at the end. A very natural performer, Alberto held the last note of the chorus and then looked at Baxter for approval.

Accepting that he was on Alberto time, Baxter offered a few claps. "Bravo, sir."

Alberto took that as a request for an encore and belted out a few lines from "Lost Highway"—and pulled it off pretty well.

"I think you belong in Nashville," Baxter said. In hacked Spanish, he asked about the bread again, perhaps a little too eagerly.

A bit let down, Alberto got the message and led him to the back of the van. As the door swung open, the yeasty deliciousness of simple carbs wafted out. Baxter made a mental note to not miss a run this week.

"Oh my," he said, gawking at the stacks of plastic crates spilling over with limitless variety. "You could feed all of Spain. I know I want croissants and a *chapata*. Two baguettes. What else? My daughter would kill for one of those doughnut things."

Alberto bagged everything, then waved a baguette at Baxter and said something about it going well with tomatoes and salt and oil. He kissed his own hand.

"Sounds amazing." Baxter held up the bill Ester had given him. "Is this enough? I can go back and get more."

Alberto waved him off with the baguette. "No, no, no. *Es un regalo*, a gift."

"Really? That's very kind, thank you."

Alberto then said something about Baxter's missing bag, and Baxter spent a minute figuring out that Alberto delivered more than just bread and would bring his bag when it eventually made it to town.

After a long goodbye, Baxter turned, hearing the bread man whistle as he returned to the truck. Before Baxter closed the front door, he turned back. Alberto was waving at him and then rolled down the window. "*¿Te gusta* Johnny Cash?"

"*Claro.*"

Alberto looked beyond satisfied. He waved and then turned up the volume of his radio. Suddenly Johnny Cash was singing, and Alberto jumped in to join him. Baxter broke into a laugh as Alberto sang all the way out of the driveway, his hand waving like a madman out the window. He was a man who'd realized his potential and was doing exactly what he should be doing. Must be nice.

Returning to the house with Paco, Baxter was delighted to hear his daughter's voice, coming out chipper from the kitchen. When he rounded the corner, he found her standing next to her grandmother, cracking eggs into a bowl.

"Buenos días, sunshine." He kissed her head and hugged her. "How'd you sleep?"

"Fine."

"Fine?"

A nod, like it was no big deal. "Iaia said I can stay with her tonight too."

"Oh, did she?" He plopped the bread down next to the bowl of oranges, unsure what to make of Mia's answer. "The secret powers of grandmothers, huh?"

Mia shrugged, but he saw so much more. He thought he saw pride on her face. Now whether that was because she'd survived the night or found a grandmother and felt loved or whatever else, he didn't know.

A few minutes later, Alma entered the kitchen, dressed for work. A flannel shirt was tucked into old jeans. A knife in its sheath dangled from her belt. He thought it was quite a sight to see such a beautiful woman dressed as a farmer. She reminded him of Sofia going out to her garden boxes in Charleston.

"You look chipper," Baxter said.

"It's gonna rain today."

"Oh, is that good news? I've never known someone to love rain."

"When you live in the desert and grow olives, rain is the best thing in the world." Then she added, "As long as it's before we start harvesting."

"Then let it rain." He held up a baguette. *"¿Tienes hombre?"*

She looked at him very strangely. *"¿Como?"*

He repeated himself, feeling like his pronunciation probably needed some work. *"¿Tienes hombre?"*

She cracked a grin. "You're waving bread at me and asking me if I have a man?"

His face blushed with embarrassment. "No, I'm asking you if you're hungry."

Alma stepped up to him, so close he could smell the minty freshness from her toothpaste. *"Hambre.* Not *hombre."*

He heard Mia and Ester laughing behind him. "Ah. *Hambre."* He said it again. *"Hambre."*

"Hambre," she whispered back.

He jabbed a thumb at his own chest. *"Yo soy un hombre. Yo tengo hambre."* I am a man. I have hunger.

She smiled approvingly. "There you go. Another five years and you'll catch up with Mia."

"Five years?" Baxter said in a high pitch as he looked over to a very happy Mia.

"Have you tried his bread yet?" Alma asked him.

Baxter turned back to her and shook his head. "No, I ate so much *fideuá* yesterday. I need to lock it up today."

"You're missing out."

She reached up into the cabinet and brought down a jar of dark honey. She ate a spoonful with her eyes closed and then reached for the bottle of olive oil on the counter, pouring a generous amount in that same spoon. He couldn't help but wonder if she did have a man, but he pushed away the question like it was a glass of turpentine.

"Is that your breakfast?" Mia asked her.

"This is . . . how do you say . . . a morning ritual. One for allergies, one for health. Want to try?" She took another spoon from the drawer and fed Mia honey and oil. Then she poured the oil into one of Mia's hands and helped her rub it around like lotion. She then proceeded to paint Mia's face with even more oil. "This is how you'll stay young and beautiful forever."

Glowing with all the oil, Mia looked happier than she'd ever been, and Baxter couldn't make sense of it. Maybe it was just getting away from everything back home.

Alma rubbed her own hands with more oil. "Who wants to go take a tour of the farm after breakfast? Before the rain?"

Mia couldn't have raised her glistening hand faster. Baxter didn't understand why all this was so easy for her, but he was happy to see it.

And he was also happy that Ester had kept insisting that he ride with Rodolfo to pick up toiletries and some clothes, because he now had the perfect excuse. When they all looked at him, he said, "No, Rodolfo and I are going into town." He could already sense that wonderful feeling of his phone finally downloading messages. Even if something had gone wrong, at least he would no longer be in the dark.

Alma severed his excitement. "Not this early. Stores don't open until ten."

"Ah, of course not. I'll just brush my teeth with Paco's tail."

"Eww," Mia said.

"You're on for a tour then?" Alma asked.

Baxter felt Mia staring at him, expecting big things from him. And he wasn't about to let her down. "You know what? Why not?" Maybe if he showed some engagement now, he could get away with working later.

Mia actually clapped for him. "Yay, Daddy!"

There she was, adulting again.

Chapter 13

ALMA'S FARM

With Paco running up ahead, Alma, Mia, and Baxter strolled up the gravel road deeper into the estate, past a long line of cypress trees and up to where several tractors rested in an open shed. Really leaning into his commitment to engage, Baxter asked about the two larger yellow ones with what looked like wings made of tarps folded out in front of them.

"Those are our umbrella harvesters," Alma answered. "Have you not seen them work on YouTube? They open the tarp around the trunk of a tree, then wrap their arms around it and shake, causing the olives to fall. It's one of the few modern practices I like, as it's more gentle on the fruit."

Truth be told, Baxter did find the process interesting. Had he not had so many other things going on, he could almost have been having fun.

A man covered in grease looked up from one of the harvesters and offered a wave. Alma said something to make him smile, and then he went back to work. Baxter could see that she was a good boss.

She said, "Francisco has to make sure the machines are working perfectly, as timing is everything. Once I'm ready to pick, it's a race to the mill in order to protect the quality of the fruit. I can't have a machine break."

Yeah, Baxter knew the feeling, and he wondered if her team here was more reliable—or more seasoned—than his back home. There were so many potential things that could go down while he was away. The thing with John Frick possibly not paying him held the number one spot for potential disasters.

Trying to pay attention, Baxter looked to where Alma pointed past the shed to a forest that led to the mountains in the distance. He shut out his other thoughts and focused on her voice. "Our land bumps up against the Parque de la Sierra de Mariola. The entire area has more, emm, medicinal wild herbs than anywhere in the world. Their . . . emm . . . essence is soaked up by the trees through their leaves and roots, which gives the olives and our oil much of its complexity."

They came upon a fenced-in garden, where a large gray guard dog named Dalí watched over flocks of geese, chickens, and ducks—maybe thirty total. Baxter noticed the proud rooster he'd heard this morning strutting near the henhouse. Past him was an extraordinary garden. Long lines of vegetable plants grew out of bright-red soil, all under cover of a tall grapevine canopy used to protect them from the desert sun. Though he kept looking at his watch, he was truly impressed with what Alma was doing here.

Dalí met them at the gate, his giant tail wagging. He was much bigger than Mia, but she did a good job of not letting him knock her over as he nearly smothered her with licks. While Paco and Dalí played together, Alma gave Baxter and Mia the tour of the garden.

Alma pointed out all the veggies they'd grown through the year, like the withering pole beans climbing up the trellises and the last of the cherry tomatoes looking lonely on their vines. With winter coming, only a few plants were still productive. Mia followed Alma's finger with rapt attention, while Baxter was getting antsy, feeling for his phone in his pocket, wishing he could just check in.

As if knowing what he was up to, Mia took Baxter's hand. "My mommy had a really nice garden, didn't she, Daddy?"

"That she did," Baxter said. A vision of the day he and Sofia had built garden boxes together came soaring into his mind. He remembered smacking his thumb with a hammer and Sofia rushing inside to get some ice. How come, even here—maybe even especially here, thousands of miles away—he couldn't escape her memory?

While Alma and Mia collected chicken eggs from the henhouse and duck eggs from under a nearby bush, Baxter thought, *Okay, enjoyed the tour. Now, let's wrap it up.*

Not feeling that same sense of urgency, Alma led them up the road to what she called the upper groves. She showed them the piles of fermenting and pungent compost that she aged for two years before spreading around the trees as fertilizer. And then she led them past the electric fence and into the grove of olive trees, pointing out the different varieties, or cultivars.

Baxter sensed a shift in him. He was dwelling less on what could go wrong back home and found himself feeling a little envious of Alma, if he was being honest. There was a kind of poetry here, showing itself in the way this woman and her team cared for their land. And if he thought about it too much, he'd start regretting the life he'd created in Greenville, one sustained by eighty-hour workweeks and the construction of cookie-cutter houses.

While passing through a patch of olive trees Alma called Picuals, Mia broke away to play fetch with Paco. Baxter was suddenly alone with the person responsible for these uncomfortable feelings rising inside of him.

He tried hard to listen as she said, "It was my father who started farming holistically. His father was always after the biggest yield, so he could make the most money. He had no problems using pesticides and herbicides, anything to make it easy. But this is not a way to treat your land . . . or the animals and people who live on it. He died of leukemia, which very well could have been from the chemicals he used. My father changed everything and restored the order."

Baxter's mind was a busy battlefield, and he wondered if Alma could see that he was only half paying attention. He could see her mouth moving and hear her speaking, but a second train of thought was running at a much faster pace. It was that he wanted to be interested. He wanted to say, "Yes, I have the same unrelenting passion for life as your father and you," but he couldn't. Those days were long gone.

She gestured to one of the trees in front of them and spoke with so much pride and love for her babies that Baxter could barely take it. "Look how beautiful these trees are," she said, "how happy and healthy. We want the farm to behave as nature intended, the way it did before us. When my father took over, he said he could sense the land dying. He said the olive oil had lost its power. *'Tu aceite es tan bueno como el amor que pones en la tierra,'* he'd say. Your oil is only as good as the love you put into the land."

It was a similar thing with music, Baxter thought. Your music was only as good as the dedication you put into your craft. If only his dedication hadn't ruined everything. This was probably why Alma was single. It was almost impossible to become a true artist while at the same time have enough gas in the tank left for loved ones.

He heard Mia giggling and turned to find her playing tug-of-war with Paco. The dog held one end of a four-foot branch between his teeth and was pulling so hard his legs were slipping out from under him in the leaves. Baxter wasn't sure which one of them was happier, Mia or the dog, and the sight triggered a voice in his head. A female voice. Sofia's. *Give her the best life, Bax. The best you can.*

⌇

Back near the house, they climbed into Alma's tan-colored Defender, with dirt striped along the sides. Paco jumped in like he'd done it a million times before.

"I'm sorry it's such a mess," she said. "This time of year doesn't leave much room for doing the little things."

Baxter climbed up front, situating his feet around a half-empty gasoline container. There were green tape and clippers on the dash. With the windows down, they drove over the creek they'd crossed the day before, and she pointed out the neighbor's house. "Don Diego was my father's best friend. They grew up playing together. You may meet him, but he keeps to himself these days. He was hurt very much by my father's passing."

At the two-lane road that led to town, Baxter realized he might find some service and dug out his phone so quickly one might think it had turned into a live grenade. Holding it discreetly between the door and his right leg, he stared at the screen, hoping to see a bar or two appear, but none came.

Alma saw what he was doing. "No, sorry, you have to go a little farther down."

"Oh, okay. No big deal." He hoped Mia hadn't noticed as well. He slipped the phone back into his pocket as Alma crossed over the road and drove through a patch of thick forest for two hundred yards until they reached another grove of olive trees, each gangly tree spread out twenty feet apart from one another.

Determined to do a better job at being present, Baxter put all his effort into listening to Alma and absorbing the sights.

"These are our oldest trees," Alma said. "Due to their age, they don't produce like they used to, but their oil is like nothing else you've ever had."

Indeed, the trees looked like old wise men, waiting to share their secrets.

"This is one of the disagreements my brother and I have," Alma continued. "He'd prefer to rip them out and replant."

Kind of sounded like what Baxter had done, ripping out the roots of their Charleston life, replanting in Greenville. Sometimes that was what you had to do. He remembered driving out of Charleston on I-26, glancing in the rearview mirror as if an open-mouthed monster were chasing them.

An electric fence ran along the outer edge of the tree line. She opened the gate with a remote control resting in the cup holder, and then they bumped along the road, driving deep within the trees. She stopped when the horses came into view. There must have been fifteen of them, all black, grazing on the grass. Then they caught sight of the two white donkeys lingering nearby.

Mia could barely contain herself as she unclicked her seat belt and thrust her body up between the two front seats and squealed. "No way! They're so beautiful."

Who was this little girl? Baxter wondered. He hadn't seen her this way in months, if not years.

Alma switched off the engine. "I think so, too, *cariño*."

The three of them climbed out and walked toward the animals, but they proved to be very skittish and slunk deeper into the trees. Alma explained they weren't used to humans, as they'd never been ridden or even domesticated.

It was a mighty sight to behold, these wild animals wandering the groves. Baxter could see in everything Alma did with this farm that growing good oil was more an art form than anything else. This farm was indeed holy to her, like a cathedral is to a priest, and Baxter couldn't ignore how inadequate it made him feel. He wanted to say to her, "I once had this too. The stage was my cathedral, and I used to be somebody. I also used to break bread with the majestic."

Instead he found himself asking the most ridiculously unimportant question while also falling into the box of brutal American clichés. "How many acres do you have?"

Alma didn't seem to mind. "I don't know acres, but we've got six hectares of trees, and another twenty-five of land, split by the road we just crossed."

"How many trees?"

"A thousand, most of them centennials." She turned to Mia. "That means over one hundred years old. Can you believe it?" Speaking to both of them again, she said, "We've had many of them tested, to identify their cultivars, and some don't even have names yet. In other words, they are the only of their variety. Now can you start to understand the miracle of this place?"

Baxter looked over at Mia, as if the question was for her only.

"Yeah," Mia said. "I get it." Then she seized Alma's hand and bounced alongside her as they walked along a gravel road. It was as if Mia were right at home.

In an instant, Baxter felt a change come over him, as if someone had slipped him a drug. He saw Sofia in place of Alma, saw Mia looking up at her mom with huge admiration, saw them smiling at each other, laughing. It was the three of them and their dog walking up the hill in the Spanish countryside. It was gray out, but there was so much color, the green of the leaves brilliant and beautiful, the golden hue coloring the air, and their smiles—Sofia's and Mia's—even brighter, rainbows bursting from their lips.

It was as if Sophia had been a long way from the parking lot and the shooting. Instead of being in the wrong place like she had, she'd picked up Mia from day care and made dinner like she always did on Thursday, and then they'd continued with the rest of their lives. Maybe he would've stuck with the band, maybe not. In a way, it didn't matter, but he sure wasn't building cookie-cutter homes that he didn't believe in. They were much happier and Mia was strong and she wasn't having nightmares. And Baxter was on top of the world.

Then he heard the crack of the semiautomatic weapon, and like a filter had been dropped down over his eyes, his vision turned to monochrome, and he heard Sophia on the phone telling him she loved him, and he heard another crack before the line went dead. He saw himself calling her back, over and over, his shaky fingers jabbing desperately at the digits. Black and white, black and white.

"Daddy?"

A hand reached through time and dragged him back to the present. Baxter shook it off, seeing the golden hue was gone, too, and before him stood Mia and Alma, both staring at him.

"Was just daydreaming, sorry." He could only imagine the look on his face. *Get me out of here,* he thought.

They kept going, though, and Alma stopped in front of a particularly twisted and knotty tree. She reached up and plucked one of the olives. "See how they are just turning, showing this, emm, how do you say . . . marbling? It's a sign they're ready. Some growers wait until they're nearly black, but then you lose the health benefits and that great bitter quality."

"Oh, how interesting," Baxter said, cringing at his obviously fabricated excitement. He really wanted to be the kind of guy who could stand there and be truly interested and learn all about the process, but he wasn't at the moment. At the forefront of his mind was getting linked up so that he could find a place to stay and also make sure he still had a job to go home to.

Alma kept going: "The other producers laughed at my father for picking earlier. They called him Don Quixote. Mia, that's like calling him *un hombre loco,* a crazy man."

"Why were they so mean?" Mia asked. Baxter watched their exchange as if Mia and Alma were on the television and he were physically separated from them.

"Because innovators are always laughed at in the beginning. They soon realized his oil was better, and they stopped laughing, wanted it for their own." She tossed the olive to the ground. "They're almost ready. Just a few more days. The rain today will plump them up to perfection."

Mia had plucked an olive and was staring at it. "How do you know?"

"Well, of course, we do tests, but the trees tell us too. They're alive, Mia. Just like you and me. They have vascular systems like we do. They draw in their environment through their roots and through their leaves. When you treat them with love and respect, they not only talk to you, they sing to you."

She smirked at Mia as she said the bit about singing, as if she was telling an old wives' tale. Baxter faked a smile, one he knew both Mia and Alma read right through. If he wasn't careful, Mia was probably going to bring up his lack of participation later. She had an uncanny ability to detect when he was checked out.

If she could only understand. The whole experience this morning had seemed to put his life onto an operating table, bright lights, scalpels, and all. Truthfully, he hated the man he was without music, without this passion that radiated out of Alma. Being around all this just made him realize how much his life kind of sucked. Not the Mia part, of course, but the rest of it.

A welcome drop of rain splattered onto Baxter's forehead, and he reached for it. "There's your rain." No doubt he was ready to go.

Alma looked up to the sky and opened up her arms, as if all her prayers had been answered. She was silent for a while, and Baxter watched the rain land onto her face for only a moment before turning away. Was he really jealous of this woman?

When she lowered her gaze from the sky, the peace on her face made Baxter wonder if she'd just seen God. One side of her mouth curled. "Let's go taste some oil."

Taste now? Baxter thought he'd be done. If there were anything he could have said to get out of it, he would have, but he just couldn't allow himself to spout out an excuse. Not after his poor performance this morning.

Alma turned to Mia. "And then I think your dad better clean himself up." She waved her hand back and forth in front of her nose. "He smells way too much like *los burros*."

"*¿Los burros?*" Baxter asked, trying to act like he was there with them.

"*Los burros,*" Mia answered. "The donkeys, Dad. Get with the program. He doesn't like baths, thinks they're a waste of time."

Baxter worked hard to joke with them and offered a smile. "That's not true. Well, kind of."

Alma took a step toward him. "Then perhaps we could take you up to the barn and hose you down."

Mia laughed out loud, and the sound of it calmed him. Determined to climb out of his funk, he whipped his head to her. "Oh, now Alma's the funny one? Don't make me share a dad joke." He could hear the shakiness in his voice, but at least he was trying.

"Not to hurt your feelings, but she *is* a little funnier than you."

Dipping his chin, he glared at them. "I see how it is."

Alma smirked, then took Mia's hand and led them back toward the Defender. Baxter could see so clearly how badly Mia needed a female figure in her life, especially when the only male figure in her life was Baxter Shaw.

~

In the back of the villa, there was a separate entrance to what they'd turned into the offices for the Familia de Arroyo estate. The tang of pipe smoke permeated the air; a string quartet played from a record player on a table under the window—apparently Rodolfo was a fan. Fancy boxes with the family's logo, surely all loaded with oil, towered toward the ceiling on one wall. An exquisite brass chandelier hung above them.

Rodolfo poked his head up from a desk on the other side of the boxes. He said something to his sister in Spanish, and she snapped back at him. Baxter watched with surprise as Mia raced over and threw her arms around him.

Rodolfo smiled. "*Hola, Mia! ¿Qué tal?*"

"Muy bien."

Baxter appreciated that whatever antagonism Rodolfo felt over the arrival of the Americans didn't show in his interaction with Mia. Otherwise, he and Baxter would surely have an issue.

While the two spoke in Spanish, Baxter turned back to Alma, who extracted several bottles from various boxes and placed them on a long table, where a line of small wineglasses waited. The bottles were made of dark glass and featured bright-yellow labels decorated with the family's regal logo.

Alma poured three equal shares of a very bright green oil into the wineglasses. "We make four different bottlings, only one monocultivar from the trees my father planted as a boy." She handed him the first glass. "This is from the lower grove."

Baxter couldn't get himself to make eye contact as he took the glass. He didn't want her to see what was going on behind his eyes, specifically his lack of patience with their leisurely morning. He couldn't believe he was eager to get in the car with Rodolfo, but a chance for cell service and to finally get out of Don Jorge's underwear was far more tempting than tasting oils. No offense to Alma, who seemed like a lovely person.

Giving it his best effort, he stared at the green and cloudy liquid and asked, "Do I swirl and sniff like wine?"

"Cup it in your hand for a minute to bring up the temperature. Then, yes, swirl it to lift out the bouquet and take a sniff."

Baxter followed her instructions and took a sip, then offered his best smile. "That's great." It really was, he thought, still tasting the unctuous oil coating his tongue. As Ester had mentioned the day before, olive oil was the gold of the Old World, a product that had been around since the ancient Egyptians, and he could tell, even with his limited experience and distracted mind, that what this family made was very special.

"The bitterness you taste," she said, "that's what it's all about. Those are the polyphenols that are so healthy for you. They act as, emm, antioxidants and anti-inflammatories. This is why olive oil is good for your skin and your digestion and your heart, among so many other things."

Baxter thought how it would take a whole lot more oil than was made here to heal his heart. Trying not to latch on to these negative thoughts that kept springing up, he put every effort into listening. An artist of her caliber deserved that level of respect.

She moved her hands to the rhythm of her voice. "The problem is that the oils most people are drinking are past their prime and don't have this level of polyphenols. Most people, Americans and Europeans included, do not understand how much it costs to make good oil. They buy the cheapest on the shelf without doing any research. They need to understand good olive oil—from the right farming and a good growing area—is not cheap. And people need to understand that oil has a shelf life. Time and light are the enemies. You don't want to be using anything much older than a year. It won't hurt you, but it won't help you either." She held her glass up to her nose. "People live richer lives when they have good oil in their kitchen."

Baxter sniffed again. "I guess the problem is we don't have anyone telling us this back home. Maybe you need to go get on a plane."

She twisted the cap on the last bottle. "It's all about education. You're right. We don't have enough ambassadors sharing the story. In my dream world, restaurants would have oil lists and oil sommeliers like we have with wine." Pressing her lips together, she cast a look up to her left. "One day, maybe."

Baxter studied her profile, seeing a woman who cared relentlessly about what she was doing. He remembered how passionate he used to be, how outspoken on everything, constantly studying the news and devouring books, looking for the truth between the lines and slyly slipping it into his lyrics. There was a time when he thought he could actually make a difference.

Oh, how distant from that man he felt now.

Chapter 14

In the Shadow of a Masterful Lover

Around ten, Baxter left Mia with Alma and climbed into Rodolfo's Smart car to ride into Cadeir. The man wore a pressed blue shirt, a cardigan, and tight-fitting brown trousers. It seemed amazing to Baxter that he cared so much about his attire but was willing to massacre his appearance by driving this sardine can—albeit a very clean sardine can.

He had to give the man credit, though. Rodolfo had great skills behind the wheel. Balancing a cigarette with his left hand and working the stick shift with his four-fingered right, he used both knees to turn the steering wheel. Despite the light rain, he drove like he was running speed trials at a Formula One race. Though Baxter was equally enthused about getting this over with quickly, he winced at the thought of running off the road in this tiny car.

At least he'd die with his phone in his hand, he thought, reaching into his pocket with a level of satisfaction that was almost embarrassing. That was the way it was, though, for an entrepreneur. You had to be plugged in. Once he confirmed that all was well, he could settle back and relax. But for God's sake, it had been almost twenty hours since he'd gotten an update. A lot could go wrong in that amount of time.

Hold up . . . his right pocket was empty. He looked down in the crack between the door and the seat and didn't see it. He felt his left pocket, finding only his wallet. "What the . . . ?"

"What's wrong?" Rodolfo asked.

As Baxter patted himself down, he said, "I must have dropped my phone or something . . . I . . . where the hell is it?"

"Probably back in the office. Don't worry, we'll only be a little while."

"Yeah . . . it's fine." But was it? Baxter felt all around the seat but came up empty. He thought back to their tasting. Had he set it on the table? No way. He never forgot his phone. What in the world? He was tempted to ask if they could turn around, but that seemed ridiculous. Alan and the other guys were still sleeping anyway. Surely Baxter could make it another hour or so.

After a few minutes of beating himself up about it, Baxter said, "I really do appreciate you guys letting us into your lives for a few days. I know it's a busy time." They were on a deserted two-lane road, a mountain standing tall in the distance.

"*Sí,*" Rodolfo said shortly.

They were not off to the best start, and it put Baxter on edge. "It's a great thing you have here," he said. "There's something powerful about the legacy of an estate, passed down through the generations. That's not as much a thing back home. Especially in my family. The only thing my parents passed down to me was . . ." He had to really think about it. "A strong sense of not wanting to pass their legacy on."

"Legacy . . . ," Rodolfo said, tsk-tsking, smoke pouring out of his nostrils. "My father was an asshole who cared more about the legacy of the estate than his family. He was a terrible father."

"Though a masterful lover," Baxter added, his index finger pushing an imaginary button in the air with a grin.

Rodolfo didn't find it funny. Baxter thought he might fare better by opening the door and jumping out, but he reminded himself that Rodolfo was Sofia's half brother.

"Sorry," Baxter said, "that was a bit distasteful. But I feel like you're upset that we're here, and I think we should . . . I don't know . . . clear the air."

Rodolfo turned down the volume of a sportscaster shouting about something apropos *fútbol*, or as Baxter liked to call it, Spanish soccer. "What makes you say that?"

Baxter watched the light rain fall on the windshield, and his head jolted forward as Rodolfo shifted up a gear. "Look. Mia, she's struggling right now. And when she found out she had family—something we're on short supply of back home—I figured I owed it to her to bring her here."

"I think that's not the only reason you're here," Rodolfo said.

Baxter glanced at him. "No?"

Rodolfo kept his eyes on the wet road. "It seems very convenient you showed up after my father died. Very convenient. I don't know what you and my mother are up to, but you have no rights to this business."

The accusation caught Baxter off guard. "You think we're here to take your money?"

"Is it not so?" Like he was running a sword through Baxter's chest, Rodolfo stabbed his cigarette into an ashtray full of butts.

"You're way off base," Baxter said.

He saw Rodolfo's cheeks harden with tension, but he didn't speak until they slid to a stop at a stop sign, close to where a bird pecked at a dead possum on the side of the road. "I don't know that you would admit to it."

"I'm serious. I'm not the kind of guy who hides his agenda. I've come here to help my daughter. I don't want your family's money. I just want Mia to know what it's like to have family. She hasn't even seen my parents in two years, and the last time she talked to Sofia's adoptive mother, Dotty, she promised her a visit that never happened."

"I'm sorry to hear that." Rodolfo reached for his pack of cigarettes in his shirt pocket. "As long as you stay out of our business, then we're fine. I like Mia very much."

Baxter returned his gaze to the road. "I've got plenty of drama going on back home. The farther away from it I am here, the better." Even the thought of how the workweek in Greenville would be starting soon jolted him back to seemingly endless work headaches he knew were coming.

"As long as that is true, then I am fine."

"Fair enough," Baxter replied calmly. Having worked with a lot of shady people both in the music and construction business, Baxter always appreciated a guy who laid it all out in front of him.

Rodolfo put the car into gear and pulled away, and the bird on the side of the road took flight.

~

When they entered the small whitewashed town of Cadeir and drove toward the tall steeple that seemed to be the centerpiece, Baxter realized Ester had been right. No way he and his Audi could have survived these skinny streets. After a series of turns, they broke into a plaza with a few tall pines, and Baxter saw the entrance to the church to the right. A group of men sat in cheap metal chairs, talking; a woman escorted an older lady along the sidewalk.

Rodolfo parked his sardine can and pointed down a small alley. "You'll find the drugstore down there. If you need clothes, there's another store a little ways down. I'll wait."

Baxter was happy to get out of the car. As he meandered in the gentle rain past the old men who gave him a kind greeting, he pondered Rodolfo's earlier accusation. Was Ester intending on rewriting her will and leaving something for Mia? If so, Baxter could see why Rodolfo would be upset.

He passed a fish shop where a man sliced through a huge chunk of tuna with a knife longer than his arm. Four feral cats lingered outside the door, as if they were occasionally tossed scraps. In the pharmacy,

Baxter picked up a toothbrush and a few other things. Farther down the street, he poked his head into the clothing store and realized he might as well be shopping on Mars. But he persevered and held up a sweatshirt that read LAS VEGAS VS. THE WORLD in giant block letters. Ugh, no. After perusing for a few more minutes, he gave up and moved to the pants section, where he grabbed the least bedazzled of the jeans and took them behind the curtain in the corner. Shucking off his boots, which he rarely tied all the way, and Jorge's high-cut pants, he attempted for about five seconds to pull the new jeans up his legs. The cut around the ankles was tight enough to cut off circulation.

"Nope," he said to himself, "these are not going to work."

Retreating like a beaten soldier, he found a package of socks and underwear and got out of there, praying Delta would come through today with his bag.

Returning to the square, he was wondering if everyone knew who the stray American was when he came around the corner and saw Rodolfo had gotten out of the car and was speaking with two men who had him backed up against a wall. The taller one jabbed a finger at Rodolfo and said something that looked an awful lot like a threat.

Despite Baxter's growing distaste for Rodolfo, he was still Sofia's family, so Baxter sped up and called across the square. "Hey!"

The men turned as Baxter drew closer. They were older, maybe in their fifties. The taller one stood a good six inches over the other man and his eyes were set deep in their sockets. The squattier man wore a plaid golf cap and a small earring in his left ear.

"What's going on?" Baxter asked, slowing down a few feet away. "You okay, Rodolfo?"

Rodolfo waved him off. *"Está bien."* Then he said something to the men in Spanish as he straightened his shirt.

The taller man replied in a calm, raspy Spanish, and then both of them turned and started up the street.

"What was that all about?" Baxter asked, watching them disappear down an alley.

"I slept with his daughter," Rodolfo said, extracting his keys from his pocket. "Let's go."

⌒

Back at the estate, Baxter speed-walked to the office. By the time Rodolfo came in, he'd scoured the place.

"Find it?" Rodolfo asked.

Baxter pushed up from a crawl under the table where he'd tasted the oils earlier. "It's not here. Do you mind calling Alma to see if they have it?"

"Sure."

Baxter watched him dial and then put the phone to his ear. A quick conversation in Spanish followed.

"They have it," Rodolfo said when he ended the call. "Up at the tractor shed."

Baxter thanked him, headed out the door, and hiked up the gravel road. By then, it had stopped raining, and the sun was trying to poke through the clouds. When he reached the shed, he saw Alma standing on a stepladder with her head under the hood of a yellow tractor. Mia was sitting on one of the big tires and smirked when she saw Baxter.

"What's so funny?" he asked.

Alma looked up with her own smile and waved a grease-covered hand.

Mia said, "I was telling her about how you used to paint your face with shaving cream and chase Mommy and me around the house. And that song you used to sing. 'Shavin' man, shavin' man, comin' for you fast as I can.' It was so *scary*."

Baxter tightened. Was he going to have to speak to the whole family about putting a cork in it when it came to Sofia? He understood that they wanted to get to know her, but not at Mia's expense.

141

"How could I forget?" he said, trying not to suffocate the mood. He did remember. Once he'd cornered Sofia and Mia, singing that silly song, he'd shoot them with more cream from the can, and they'd laugh so hard all three would end up on the floor.

Alma jumped down and landed her two feet onto the straw ground. She wiped her hands on a towel. "What a silly man you are."

"Yeah, sometimes," he said.

"So Mia has something to tell you . . . don't you, Mia?"

Baxter and Alma both stared at a very guilty-looking eight-year-old. After holding out for a few seconds, Mia reached behind her and then raised Baxter's phone up into the air. "I took your phone."

A surge of joy raced through him. "Ah, where did I leave it?"

She shook her head and then said in a sweet voice that left no room for Baxter to get angry, "You didn't leave it. I took it out of your pocket."

His mouth fell agape. "You pickpocketed me?"

A hesitant smile lifted her lips.

He stepped forward, more frustrated with her than he let on. "And what was the purpose of your little ruse?"

A shrug. "I thought it would be good for you."

He took the phone and then looked over at Alma, who was grinning. "You see what I'm dealing with here?"

"A real terror," Alma joked.

He bounced his eyes between the two of them. "Well, if you two troublemakers are okay for a little while, I'm gonna grab a quick ... . *bath* . . . and then find some Wi-Fi. I need to figure out where to stay tonight, and then I have a bunch of work stuff I need to tackle once the day starts back home. I've got a guy who owes me a lot of money and—"

"I thought we were staying here with Alma and Iaia," Mia interrupted, her smile fading away.

Baxter shook his head. "No, honey. That was just last night, because our place fell through. We're being rude." He worried Alma might disagree, but she didn't say anything.

"I don't think we're being rude. And I wanna stay here."

Baxter looked at his daughter, trying to say with his eyes, "Let's not do this right now." She wasn't having it. "Aunt Alma, are we being rude? Iaia said we can stay as long as we like."

"Of course you're not being rude. Whatever is easiest for you."

Baxter went up to Mia and patted her leg. "Let me just think about it, Mia. Okay? We might be more comfortable somewhere else."

She shook her head and came close to a pout. "Please."

"We'll see." He didn't know what else to say. The last thing he wanted to do was upset her after this giant turnaround she seemed to be having. But kids didn't know what was best for them sometimes.

"He is smelly," Alma said, whiffing the air around Baxter and turning to Mia for a laugh.

Mia granted her one. "Super smelly donkey daddy." Her grin gave him an incredible sense of peace. It was interesting how the fogginess of his life cleared up when she was in a good place.

He jokingly shook his finger at them. "Keep having your fun, you two . . . I see how it is." With that, he pivoted and started out of the shed.

Upstairs in his room, the tiny claw-foot tub gawked at him as if it were a person with antagonistic eyes who could see Baxter's hesitation and could sense his weakness. Baxter saw in the porcelain a lion licking his chops. Something inside of him rejected even the idea of twisting the knob to get the hot water going.

It was silly, really, but the idea of sitting there without accomplishing anything, stirring in his thoughts, his feet sticking out over the lip like a numbskull, made him feel sick inside. If you asked Baxter what his worst nightmare would be, he might just paint this exact picture.

As he'd always noticed when he was still, he had this wound-up tension that ran through his body, like someone was cranking tight his nerves. This was exactly why he hadn't read even one book in the three years since he'd lost Sofia. His body needed to be moving. It wasn't always sadness that seemed to be the root of the tension. Most of the time, it was just anxiety and worry.

Like right now, just not having enough to do was forcing him to think about what the heck was going on with Mia. Had he made a huge mistake by bringing her here? Was recalling these memories with Ester and Alma going to backfire? Or was it, maybe, good for her? As much as that didn't feel right inside, seeing her light up so much since he'd first agreed to take her to Spain had given him hope that there was a way. He just hoped he wasn't masking her issues, forcing them to fester underneath the surface.

Accepting that he did smell like a donkey, he finally twisted the knob. Very cold water crept out of the faucet, and in unsurprising Spanish fashion, it took a good three or four minutes before the change in temperature. He plugged the drain with a rubber stopper and decided it could easily take twenty minutes to fill.

While he waited, he mulled over the idea of finding another Airbnb or a hotel. He felt like he was going to lose either way. Mia and the rest of the family would be upset if he did book something else. But he felt completely out of control if he stayed, like he couldn't manage Mia's emotions in the safest way. Not to mention . . . not to mention! Mia was growing very attached to these people. He hadn't really anticipated that. They were a day in, and she was already treating them like she'd grown up around them. What would happen when they left? Would he be putting more loss on Mia?

Then work fears came pouring in, as if they weren't always at the forefront. Four different people owed Baxter money, two of which he'd probably be taking to court any day. And he needed to talk to the Van Coops about a new timeline on their house. They wouldn't be happy that they couldn't move in by Christmas, as he'd sort of promised. And there was the health of Alan's mother-in-law. Of course he cared about

Alan and Amy, but he was also worried Alan might be distracted. And his other three managers. They were good guys, but he wouldn't put it past them to slack off a bit with the boss out of town, leave a little earlier to grab nine holes.

When the tub was halfway full, he slipped out of his boxers—scratch that, Don Jorge's boxers—and stepped into the water. Sitting back, with his legs severely bent at the knees, he rested his arms on the sides and tried to at least pretend to relax. In moments, he was tapping nervous fingers and wondering how this was supposed to be enjoyable, or even healing.

After the longest minute of his life, Baxter slapped the sides of the tub. "Well, enough of that."

He reached for the rose-scented soap and lathered himself up. Then, in a gymnastic series of moves to get the soap off his body, he lay back and flattened his torso into the water as he spread-eagled, his legs kicking up high in what had to be a yoga move.

Continuing in his pursuit for the Olympic gold, he flipped around onto all fours to wet his hair. As he stretched his head out like a turtle under the faucet, humiliation washed over him with the warm water. His lack of grace forced out a self-effacing smile. This was Baxter Shaw hitting bottom, he thought, a man drowning in his own thoughts while washing himself in a small bathtub in a foreign land.

Chapter 15

THE ZOO ANIMAL

With his messenger bag swinging from his shoulder, Baxter left his bedroom and set out to find this holy grail of a spot that promised decent cell phone reception. It was close to seven back home, and one thing among the many he most surely was going to do was call John Frick and make sure he was going to pay what he owed Baxter.

He wore another pair of Don Jorge's khaki pants, and these rose even higher off the ankles, revealing over his unlaced boots a glimpse of Baxter's pale shins in all their glory. But at least he was in new underwear and socks. It was one thing to wear a man's pants, entirely another to wear his underwear.

Ester was walking out the door, too, slinging her purse over her shoulder. "Hey there," Baxter said. "Boy, what a place you have here. We really enjoyed the tour."

She stopped at the front door. "I'm so glad."

"And the wild horses. Right out of a fairy tale."

"They are, aren't they? Mia liked them?"

"She did. We didn't get a chance to pet them or anything but—"

Ester shook her head and said, proudly, "No, Alma is the only one who can get close to them. Everyone else is a stranger."

Baxter offered a smile. "Well, it was a very special experience. Where are you off to?" He opened the door and gestured for her to go first.

"A quick doctor's appointment. Did you make a decision about staying?"

He followed her out. "I haven't yet."

"I do wish you would," she said, speaking over her shoulder to him as she descended the steps. "You really are welcome."

"I appreciate that, and I'll let you know." He didn't mention that he was definitely hoping to find somewhere else, and her pressing him wasn't helping. As his feet hit the gravel, he said, "Anyway, I'm going to find some cell service. It's Monday, so work is stacking up. But I was curious about something. I always feel like I'm prying, so forgive me, but . . . what have y'all been telling people about us? A small town like this, I expect everyone is wondering who we are. I'm assuming the family knows, but how about everyone else?"

Ester shrugged it off like it was no big deal. "Most everyone in the town knows. You can't keep secrets for long around here."

"Oh, okay. Good." Ester had managed to keep her secret for thirty-eight years, but Baxter didn't say so.

"I'm sure small towns in the US are the same way," she said. "Word travels quickly."

"No question," Baxter said. Even Charleston and Greenville, which were so much bigger than Cadeir. People had known he was leaving the band and moving to Greenville almost before he'd decided.

Ester smiled at him. "After a while, you give up on pretending that you're perfect. Do you know what I mean?"

Baxter chuckled quietly. "That's about the wisest thing I've ever heard." The two of them were in an exclusive club, he thought, having both lost their spouses. You could never imagine what it was like until you'd been initiated.

She jingled her car keys. "Almost sixty years on earth teaches you a few things."

They said goodbye to each other, and Baxter watched her drive away, following by foot. When he reached the creek they'd crossed when first arriving, about a hundred and fifty yards from the house, Baxter's chest was really bothering him. Not like heartburn you get after eating a late-night meal at the Waffle House—something he'd done with the band hundreds of times after shows. This was a flutter that made him feel wheezy, like he might pass out.

He figured he'd better stop for a minute, so he sat on the crumbling stone wall of the bridge and folded over his thighs for a minute, taking big long breaths. This heart thing was starting to worry him, like his stress level could lead to a heart attack if he didn't make some kind of change in his life. How had he let it get to this point? It wasn't like he was out of shape at all. Before he'd become addicted to his Peloton, he was a runner and had been religious about getting in eight miles three or four days a week, even during the band's most rigorous tours.

After about five minutes, he seemed to come out of it some and sat up tall and stretched. Birds chirped from their perches on the branches of the trees surrounding him. It must have been in the high seventies in the sun, but it was cooler here under these tall oaks, or whatever they were.

Hearing the creek running below, he swung his feet around and let them dangle over the water that slid over the moss-covered rocks, easing out just as casually as the well water had from the faucet in the tub. Rather annoyingly, nothing was in a rush here. How nice for them.

There was something else that hit him as he gazed down. This was a creek that seemed to cry tears. He wondered if a piece of land had a soul, and if so, did it have a heartbeat, and could it sense loss? Was it also grieving Don Jorge, its steward? And did it have faith in Alma's coming tenure? He could almost feel the pulse of the land in his heart. *Barrump, barrump, barrump.*

As this rhythmic motion thumped within, a song teased his soul, something about a creek of tears creeping over the rocks.

A creek cries like a woman.

And the tears drip down like rain.

Then the moment was gone, and he was left very aware that those were some of the first lyrics that had come to him since . . . well, hell, maybe since Sofia had died.

He continued down the gravel road, the dust rising up into the dry air behind him. He saw past the meadow the neighbor's house—a crumbling old villa the color of sand, built up on a slope looking down over a small patch of gnarly grapevines growing low like bushes. Between the house and Baxter, in the middle of a meadow of tall grass and wild flowers, lay the pile of rubble made of stone and bricks that Alma had told him to seek out.

He pulled out his phone, and as if he were waving a metal detector over the ground and waiting for a beep, he walked while staring at the bars. When one finally appeared, Baxter felt like a fisher whose rod had bent.

"There we go," he said, leaving the road and entering the meadow.

Baxter lost the signal and let out a curse as he moved farther toward the pile of rubble. When a second and then a third bar appeared, he felt like he was bearing witness to a holy apparition. His phone suddenly came alive with messages. Thank God.

First, he called Delta. After pressing multiple numbers and talking to several robots, Baxter began to lose his patience.

Through gritted teeth, he said, "I have pressed zero a thousand times. I want an operator. Give me an operator. Give me a—"

"Please repeat your choice," the robot said.

"Have I not?" Baxter really let her have it this time, emphasizing each syllable with great annoyance. "I want an op-er-a-tor."

"I am unable to understand. Please repeat your choice."

"An operator. An operator. I want an operator. *Comprende.* Operator, operator, operator." He was vaguely aware during his breakdown that he'd completely lost control, and you know what . . . he didn't care. Humans were allowed to lose it from time to time, and this particular instance was entirely justified. The battle lasted a good five minutes before he finally got to the classical music, which meant he was in line to speak with a human being.

Sensing someone watching him, he turned to find an elderly bald man—the neighbor—sitting at a table in the grass in front of his house. He held a glass of wine in his right hand and stared at Baxter curiously. Feeling like a monkey at the zoo, Baxter nodded hello, then turned away.

He put the phone on speaker and set it down on one of the rocks making up the pile. With a string quartet—possibly Bartók—filling the air in the lowest grade of fidelity, he proceeded to set up a makeshift office, finding a good flat rock to rest his derriere, and then opening up his laptop. This wasn't such a bad base from which to work, he decided, as he connected the computer to the hot spot on his phone. In a matter of minutes, he was in business.

Baxter sent an email to his lawyer, warning him that he might need his services for yet another project gone wrong. At any given time, he had at least two or three things cooking with the lawyer, and that hourly rate stung every time he thought about it.

Eight minutes into Baxter hacking away at emails, a man who sounded like he was from the Midwest came onto the phone and asked how he could help. Baxter filled him in, adding that he was wearing a dead man's clothes. The bewildered associate came back and said that he would transfer Baxter to the correct department.

Tranquilo, *Bax. It's all good.*

The classical music broke up. He grabbed the phone and saw that he'd lost a bar. He popped up and moved a few feet away, only to lose another bar. The music of the strings turned to fuzz.

"Please don't let this call drop," he begged God above. "I will not ask another thing for the rest of my life, or at least for the rest of the trip. Please, even the sanest of men has a breaking point. Protect me and give me bars."

Turning back the other way, he proceeded to climb up the pile of rubble, thinking a few feet of elevation might bring salvation. He noticed the neighbor watching him again as he stepped up to the top of the pile. Just as the classical music came in clean, it was interrupted by a voice.

He'd done it! Three bars and he had a human from baggage assistance on the line. This must be the feeling of coming upon a lost shipwreck at the bottom of the ocean.

Balancing on the top rocks like a well-practiced tightrope walker, Baxter quickly explained his situation. "I'm calling to make sure the bag is en route to me down here." Silence. "Hello . . ."

He looked at the phone. The call had dropped.

"You have got to be kidding me!" he yelled into the phone, as if it had actually harmed him—as if the phone gave a blue bloody shit if he reunited with his bag.

Baxter couldn't imagine the show he was putting on for the neighbor, and the thought convinced him he best take a seat and collect himself. The only rational part left in him felt so embarrassed he couldn't even look that way.

Deep breaths. Like the guy on his new meditation app had said a few times: "I embrace uncertainty. I embrace challenge." Baxter said it over and over again, wishing it to be true.

Trying to let his frustrations go, he readied his charm and dialed John Frick. The call went straight to voice mail. The guy was ghosting him.

"Baxter here," he said. "Hey, I just want to clear this thing up with the change order. I'm in Spain with intermittent service, but email or text me with a good time to find you, and I'll reach back out."

During his second call, a client assured him that Alan was the dumbest person in all of Greenville—perhaps even the entire upstate. Baxter did his best to defend his friend while trying not to lose a customer. Next, he spent five minutes getting yelled at by a friend of a friend whose business Baxter didn't want anyway. He wanted to build houses or manage big renovation jobs; he had no interest in hanging televisions or doors, thank you very much.

He eventually called Alan, who let out a chipper hello. "Happy Monday, amigo. I thought you weren't going to work this week. How's the Spanish life? D'you get you a good bo-ca-dee-yo and una cerveza?"

Alan's accent and slow southern drawl, recalling scents of fried chicken, collard greens, and buttermilk biscuits, did nothing but agitate Baxter. But he held back from saying so, knowing the best way to lead his friend was with a gentle hand.

"I did indeed get a *bocadillo*—a very good one. But the logistics over here leave a lot to be desired. The airline lost my bag. My lodging fell through. No one knows the Wi-Fi password here, and the only cell service I get requires me to stand on a pile of rocks. No kidding, I'm balancing on a chunk of concrete with rebar sticking out of it, trying not to lose the call."

Alan laughed like a hyena. "I can't say I feel sorry for you, brother. Sounds to me like God's trying to tell ya something. Do me a favor and take a picture of you standing on that rock."

Baxter shook his head, glancing over at the neighbor, who was leaned back, his feet crossed at the ankles, looking at his vines. "You should have seen me trying to take a bath in their four-foot claw-foot."

"You can keep that picture to yourself, boss."

Baxter's smile faded. "Anyway, I left a message with Frick. You tell me if you hear anything."

"You know I will."

"What else is going on?" Baxter asked.

"All business, aren't you? Everything's fine here; quit worrying. You've only been gone a day."

"Hey, men have lost fortunes in less time."

"Lesser men, Baxter. Lesser men."

Alan knew some of Baxter's story, but he couldn't possibly understand Baxter's fear of going broke and what that would do to Mia—or to Baxter. There was no way he could ever look in the mirror again, knowing how he'd failed as a father and broken the promise he'd made to himself and to Sofia.

It was in this state of mind that Baxter found himself sitting on the stack of rubble ten minutes later, searching the internet for another place to stay. He did indeed find a great spot twenty minutes away—a two-bedroom flat with one positive review about the comfort of the beds—but he couldn't bring himself to book it. He even entered his credit card information, but he just couldn't imagine asking Mia to get packed up, that they were leaving. It would break her heart. How could he do that to her when things seemed to be going so well?

Chapter 16

HE PUTS THE ACTION IN DISTRACTION

All this talk about Sofia was getting to him, and it came to a head at lunch. Ester had made chickpea stew and delicious croquettes with salt cod, and everyone was in a good mood, especially Mia, who was delighted with Baxter's decision to give up on searching for another place to stay. He was actually enjoying himself, feeling proud that he'd lifted Mia up so, but then Rodolfo started becoming incredibly inquisitive, almost as if he was doing it on purpose, trying to upset Baxter.

"So you really were making more money playing music than what you're doing now?"

"No question."

Rodolfo's whole face was covered in lines of doubt. "From what? Album sales?"

Baxter didn't like how Rodolfo's conversations always seemed to be laden with an agenda, but he was trying not to become defensive. "Album sales, yes. We had a few tunes that hit the country charts. You get paid a little for radio play too. But our tours were pretty lucrative once we graduated to bigger stages. And the songs I was writing for people."

"Like who? Would I know them?"

Mia jumped in to defend her father. "He wrote one for Brad . . . who is it, Daddy?"

"Brad Paisley. Rascal Flatts. Travis Tritt. Zac Brown."

"Really?" Rodolfo looked impressed for once. "I've heard of them."

"Yeah," Baxter said, "these were tunes that weren't the right fit for our band, a little too catchy." Baxter felt a sense of pride, talking about the old days, even though he'd done his best to avoid these types of chats back in Greenville.

Rodolfo looked over at Mia. "And what was this like for you, Mia? Growing up with a famous father? Did you go hear him play much?"

Mia nodded eagerly. "All the time. My mom and I went to a lot of shows." She looked at Baxter. "I loved his band."

Baxter turned to her. "Are you sure you didn't just like to hear the bad words?"

"Well, that too." She gave a big smile.

Baxter tried to return one of his own, but his mind was going to war with him. The shows where his family was in attendance were always his favorite. There was nothing like looking over and seeing Sofia and Mia dancing on the side of the stage, or when he'd walk offstage into their loving arms. It was all he'd ever dreamed of, to have family and to be able to share what he loved doing with them. Sofia's and Mia's support meant more than they could ever know, filling the hole that his parents had left so vacant in his life.

Baxter felt a tightness growing in his body, that string winding, making his toes curl. It wasn't just for Mia that he needed to stop this talk. It was for him too. Muttering an "excuse me," he stood from the table and headed toward the bathroom on the living room side of the kitchen.

Latching the door closed, he turned on the water and leaned hard against the sink, his forearms shaking. He stared into the mirror, seeing first that his forehead was covered in sweat. His eyes were narrow and full of fear.

"Stop, Baxter," he said to the man in the mirror. "You gotta pull it together. For Mia's sake, if nothing else."

If Mia wasn't so damn happy, he'd pack their bags and get out of Cadeir as fast as possible. But that would crush her. She had family for the first time in her life, and it was filling her up in ways Baxter had never been able.

He splashed water on his face and then flushed the toilet, just in case someone was listening. When he returned to the table a good five minutes after scurrying away, he felt much more stable.

"You were gone forever," Mia said. "Everything come out all right?"

Baxter blushed hard. "Daughter, thank you for calling me out. Yes, it all came out fine."

Everyone at the table laughed. Baxter faked his own, wondering how it was so easy for everyone else here to talk about a family member who'd been gunned down three years earlier.

While everyone else took a siesta—including Mia, who'd happily retreated back to Ester's room—he hiked up to the tractor shed to collect supplies so that he could work on the roof. The only solution to his own madness was to keep moving, doing something that would keep both his body and mind busy. It wasn't just about this resurfacing of Sofia's memory. It was also that he was now sharing Mia for the first time in his life, and not having her by his side made him feel even lonelier, as if she were being absorbed into the family and leaving him behind.

He located a ladder, a pry bar, caulk, and the other materials required to repair the damaged section of roof he'd seen. Behind one of the harvesters were stacks of terra-cotta shingles. He located a wheelbarrow and got to work.

Even while he worked, he couldn't stop thinking. There was so much on his mind. Sofia. Mia. This trip. He also found himself thinking about the days before he met Sofia, when music was his only love. How wholly focused he'd been.

He slipped into a memory of when Cactus Road had played at the Memorial Auditorium in Greenville. Baxter's hometown. Though he hadn't been much of anything growing up there, he'd become a recognized face as the band grew in popularity. He remembered standing up there on stage, seeing so many faces from his childhood staring up at him, but there was one thing on his mind. He'd invited his parents and gotten them backstage tickets. And they didn't show. He remembered finishing the first set and hoping they'd made it and had only been late. No such luck.

So maybe he did understand why Mia was doing so well. She was getting the attention she deserved from a family she didn't even know she had. She was getting the one thing Baxter had never had: family.

They reconvened at six for *merienda*, one of the five meals—*that's right, five!*—of the Spanish day. Rodolfo had melted down dark chocolate with olive oil, spread it over sliced and toasted baguettes, and finished it with flakes of sea salt. It seemed everyone in the family had culinary talent.

Sitting at the table in the kitchen, the adults gave Mia all the attention, letting her talk about her day on the farm and of life back home: her love of chess and the classes she liked and the movies she watched.

"Mia," Ester said, "what's the best memory of your mother?"

Baxter nearly crushed the slice of bread in his hand and then cast a warning look her way. Had he not been clear with Ester?

Mia didn't seem to mind. "Aunt Alma asked me the same question earlier. That's kind of hard to choose."

Did they not understand how hard he'd worked to help her forget these memories? Or did they not see that asking these questions was like sifting through Sofia's ashes? Sure, Mia seemed fine now, but she was a very good actor. She'd faked not knowing about her mother's death for weeks.

"I remember . . . ," Mia started, placing the tip of her finger on her chin, "how she used to scratch my back. I loved that." Baxter could instantly feel Sofia's painted nails gliding across his own back. "Remember, Daddy?"

"Yeah," but the word barely came out.

Mia looked at her dad, then pinched her nose and said nasally, "And I remember how she used to pinch her nose and talk like this, and I thought it was the funniest thing in the whole wide world."

He remembered that, too, but it didn't seem so funny now. In fact, it felt like the saddest thing in the world.

After the meal, Ester took Mia to the living room to look through photo albums of the Arroyo family. When Baxter was done with the dishes, he joined them on the couch, his thigh pressing up against his daughter's.

"That's Alma and Rodolfo?" Mia asked, pointing to a picture of a young boy and girl with faces painted in mud. Mia seemed to love everything about the past, something she and her father just didn't have in common.

"They were the best of friends," Ester recalled fondly. "Inseparable. And never afraid of getting dirty. I slept with a mop in my hands."

"Is that true?" Mia asked.

"Of course. If you only knew how many times they came in like this . . ."

Baxter noticed another photo. "Is that . . . that's the creek, isn't it? The one down by the road."

Ester seemed to have drifted away, and it took her a moment to respond with an empty nod.

"You okay?" he asked.

"Oh, yes, just thinking back . . ."

When Ester and Mia moved onto the third photo album, Baxter excused himself.

Upstairs in his bedroom, he opened up the windows to retrieve the clothes clipped to one of the two lines. When he grabbed his pants and shirt, the ones he'd worn on the plane, he saw that a bird had let loose its bowels like a plane drops a bomb directly onto the collar of his shirt.

"There we go, Spain," he said. "You're winning by fifty points, and you're still trying to put points on the board." To add insult to injury, as he removed the clothespin from his boxers, he lost hold of them, and they floated down to the leaves below. "Okay, okay, fine," he said. "Have it your way."

Highly aware of his growing inner tumult, he decided it would be wise to take a few moments to meditate, something he'd been attempting for a few weeks now. Feeling like the ultimate dysfunctional Buddha, he sat cross-legged in the middle of the floor and navigated to the app on his phone where he had a few meditations downloaded. Pressing play, he let a soothing voice attempt to take away his troubles.

A few minutes in, a knock startled him, and he quickly reached for the pause button. Apparently, in Spain, a knock wasn't a request to come in but more of a warning, as Alma pressed open the door before he could stand and hide what he'd been doing.

Her hair was wet from a bath, and she'd dusted her freckled cheeks with blush and dressed in a navy-blue-and-white dress, which was a far cry from her work clothes. Oblong gold hoops hung from her ears, and he noticed for the first time other piercings higher up, a gold bead and a pearl. She held a guitar case in one hand and a piece of paper in the other.

"Is that what I think it is?" Baxter asked, eyeing the paper and hoping it was the password to the Wi-Fi.

She stepped farther into the room. "Perhaps. But . . . what are you doing on the floor?"

His face flushed. "Oh, this?" He pointed to his whole situation, the crossed legs and all. "I've been a little stressed lately and trying to meditate some."

Her dark eyebrows furrowed with curiosity. "How American of you."

"Yeah, I guess so. We live in a tofu world back home. Holistic everything. There are more yoga and Reiki studios than gas stations. Matter of fact, I think there are yoga studios in gas stations now. You can get a Slim Jim and unroll your mat all in the same place. Before too long, they'll be performing brain surgery with healing crystals."

She laughed.

He sensed he was talking very quickly but kept going. "Yeah, so this guy Simon on my phone is walking me through, you know, like . . . how to sit with all the uneasy feelings, inviting them in. He just told me to invite fear in for a cup of coffee. No kidding."

Another laugh, one so caring and genuine. She asked, "What are these fears, and what if they don't like coffee?"

There was something nice about talking to her, the way she didn't seem to judge him at all, like it was totally okay to be honest with her, even if it was embarrassing. And she came off as the only one around without some sort of agenda.

He tapped his skull. "There's a lot of fear in here. Mostly about being a good dad and a good boss." Now that he'd opened the gates, the fears came rushing in. "A good friend. A good human. How to balance all that and still live life." Not wanting to get too emotional, he joked, "And bathtubs. I'd have to make room for my fear of taking a long bath. And wearing high-cut pants. I think both of those fears would definitely prefer tea—an Earl Grey served in the afternoon with scones and little salmon-and-cucumber sandwiches on one of those English tea towers."

She was laughing so hard her eyes had reddened. He chuckled. "You asked."

"I like your funny side," she said. "Especially when you're not using your humor as a sort of shield."

The comment cut him down, and he felt suddenly prickly. Was there anyone out there who wasn't psychoanalyzing him?

"Your daddy humor is funny, though," she added, probably realizing that she'd hit a nerve. She set down the guitar. "You Americans and all of your meditation apps. As if we can't walk out the door and take a deep breath for free. Or take a bath."

He dipped his head in agreement and tried not to take her comments so personally. "We Americanos are just trying to figure out ways to speed up slowing down, know what I mean? I need to know exactly how many minutes you need to meditate to enjoy the benefits, so I don't waste a second more. Pretty sure it's nine minutes, by the way, if you're wondering."

She shook her head. "I'm just giving you a hard time. It's good you're meditating."

"Yeah, I guess. There's a lot going on back home."

"As you've said."

"Yeah, yeah, the broken records of Baxter Shaw. Mia doesn't like listening to them either. They're all scratched anyway," he added with what felt like a very childish smile. It was one thing to open up to her, but if he wasn't careful, he'd need a couch, and she'd need a notepad.

He pointed to the window. "So a bird pooped on my clothes. And please don't say, 'Shit happens.'"

"I would not dare." Her smile returned. "Would you like me to run them back through the wash?"

"No, thanks, I can do it." He looked down at the guitar at her feet. "Is that your father's?"

Alma looked at the black case. "Yes, I brought you his guitar, *and* I found the Wi-Fi password." She held up the piece of paper. Baxter reached out for it a little too quickly.

She was faster than him and pulled her hand away. "Not so fast."

"What?"

"It could be nice to stay unplugged for the week. You sure you want it?"

"I don't know that I *want* it, but I need it, believe me."

"Suit yourself." She handed him the piece of paper.

He stuck it into his pocket and glanced at the guitar case, offering a gracious smile. "This was very nice of you. May I?" He didn't want to even look at the guitar, but he felt obligated as he set it on the bed. She sat in the chair to watch.

Unclasping the latches and lifting the top, he found a stunning nylon-stringed flamenco guitar. Even the sight seemed to stir something deep within him, and they weren't all good feelings.

There was no maker's name on the headstock. He assumed by that and the apparent quality that it was a custom build. Considering how Alma was waiting on him, he sat on the edge of the bed, rested the guitar on his lap, and felt the action. The guitar was set up perfectly. He took a minute to tune it and then strummed a few chords. The nylon pressed into his fingers, and he felt high from it. He missed his Martin acoustic, the way the steel strings felt, the way his guitar used to growl in his hands.

Alma sat back and crossed her ankles. "Mia played me the Cactus Road. I like your sound."

Baxter glanced up at her, almost embarrassed at how much emotion was swirling around inside. All caused by a piece of wood and six strings.

"Just Cactus Road. Not *the* Cactus Road." He nervously barred an F at the first fret and whispered a thanks.

"Play something for me?" she asked.

Playing for Mia was one thing. He felt he owed that to his daughter. Playing for anyone else . . . no, he couldn't do it. Music came from his core, his most exposed self, and it reminded him of all the good times with Sofia, those years when she rode with the band on the bus, and then it reminded him of the inevitable conclusion, the ending he'd brought about.

Baxter returned the guitar to its case with trembling fingers. "Not today."

She must have sensed his unease, because she stood and started to the door. "I'm going with some friends to hear a wonderful flamenco guitarist named Javier Martín Saturday night in a cool venue, a cave in Murcia. It's past Americano bedtime, but I think you would enjoy it."

"A cave, huh? Right on. I'm sure I would." He tried to recall the last time he'd seen live music, but couldn't. "But I don't feel comfortable leaving Mia right now, with the nightmares and all."

"I understand."

He appreciated that she didn't press.

After she'd left, he sat on the bed and stared at the floor, thinking. Since losing Sofia, he felt safe only around Mia. Sure, he could pretend all day long and often feel comfortable—and sometimes even enjoy himself. But comfort was very different from safety. The rest of the world and everyone in it seemed so threatening, even if he couldn't explain exactly why, almost like his nervous system had been put on high alert. Not almost; it was exactly how it felt. Life wasn't about seeking joy and living it to its fullest anymore; it was about watching his and Mia's backs.

If only knowing this truth about himself were enough to fix it.

Feeling uneasy, he opened his computer and attempted to log in to the Wi-Fi network. He punched in the password, *EVOO:)*, and waited eagerly.

The computer responded that either the log-in or password was incorrect. "What?" Baxter said with mounting frustration. He stared at the word written hastily on the yellow sheet of paper, then typed it in again. Another error message.

He opened up his arms and hands and looked through the ceiling. "Are you toying with me? Is this really fun for you?"

He wasn't sure whether he was talking to God or Sofia.

Chapter 17

SAGE ADVICE

While Baxter went head-on with Spain in a battle of wills, Mia had settled into her own rhythm. She'd even made it through the last two nights without nightmares, surely due to sleeping in Ester's bed and finding comfort in her grandmother's presence. Ester was doing all the things Baxter wished he was better at, such as getting down on the floor with Mia to put together a puzzle or joining her in a game of make-believe. He'd even admitted to himself that he had a lot to learn from Ester's engagement with Mia.

Another exciting part of Mia's life was that she'd found a friend she called her BFF—her tree-climbing cousin, Alfonso, who was her age and lived only three miles away. He was an only child, too, a wild one for sure, and they'd hit it off wonderfully. Though he was in school, his mother would drop him off every day after siesta so the two could play for the rest of the afternoon.

Alma included Mia every chance she could with harvest preparations, and Mia adored climbing into the Defender to tour the property and take care of the animals and do other chores. Sharing his daughter for the first time was making Baxter lonely, so he'd joined them the day prior to pull the dying vegetable plants from the garden and ready it for winter.

But his mind had been elsewhere. Among other things, he was still struggling with being so far away from work. Every time he got cell service, be it during his sessions at the pile of rubble or whenever he rode into town, he discovered a new fire that needed to be extinguished.

One client, James Blatch, had even blessed him out for going on such a long vacation right in the middle of building the man's house, which served only to prove Baxter's point: you can't leave the country when you're trying to grow a business. He could only imagine the bad-mouthing Blatch must be doing around town. ("I wouldn't hire that Baxter Shaw to build a doghouse for my wife's Chihuahua!")

If only his frustrations with work were the sole cause of his suffering. Everyone was still talking about Sofia, and Baxter had realized there was just no stopping it. Still, his surrender didn't make it any easier, and if it wasn't for Mia doing so well, he'd have already hightailed it out of there.

And of course no one had found the Wi-Fi password, and he'd surely put on five pounds due to all the eating, and he *still* didn't have his bag. Maybe the worst of it was the sitting around doing nothing but talking, and then the siesta . . . A man could be imprisoned for closing his eyes in the middle of the day back home.

Baxter couldn't stand sitting so still, and he sure as hell couldn't stand accomplishing so little. So to keep his mind at ease when not working on tasks for his company, he continued to repair the roof.

Finally, on Thursday morning—their fifth day in Spain—Alberto the Bread Man brought Baxter's bag, and he hoped this would be a turning point in his journey, perhaps a sign of good things to come. He was so excited about his bag that he even asked Alberto to sing him a tune and was gifted a wonderful version of "On the Road Again." Alberto tried to get Baxter to join in on the chorus, but Baxter shook his head. *Let's not get carried away,* he thought.

At the breakfast table crowded with fresh fruit, a tortilla hanging over its dish, and Alberto's pastries, Baxter said to Mia, "Do I finally get a chance to hang with you?"

"Nope," Alma said with a warm smile as she fed Paco bites from the baguette. "She's coming with me. We have some sampling to do. Harvest starts tomorrow—"

"No, no, I have her today," Ester interrupted, pouring herself sparkling water. "I've promised her we'd ride into town to the playground and then go for ice cream. And I thought we'd go by and visit her cousins at school."

As if she were on stage in a play, Alma dropped her jaw and whipped her head toward Mia. "You wouldn't dare abandon me."

They all looked to Mia, who had a Nutella mustache from cramming one of the pastries into her mouth. Baxter knew they were working together to lift Mia up, and he appreciated that, but did they not realize that they were hogging Mia, taking her away from him? And he kind of needed her right now.

"Sorry, Aunt Alma. I promised Iaia. Besides, I have a weakness for ice cream. Ask my dad."

Ester sat back in victory, a proud grandmother knowing she could always win if she wanted to.

Baxter said, "What am I? Chopped liver?"

Mia showed her pearly whites. "You get me all the time, Daddy."

"Chopped liver," he muttered, making a dicing motion with his two flattened hands. "Chop, chop, chop. I'll just go work on the roof and be by myself." He looked over at the black-and-white fur ball sprawled out on the floor. "Maybe Paco will hang out with me."

"You can have me for siesta, and then I'll go with Alma afterward. Is that okay, everyone?" She looked around like a politician. "I'm spread thin here."

Baxter never could have expected that this trip might actually be what she needed, and he wished he could bottle this whole experience and take it back home so he could give her a dose whenever she was down.

Rodolfo entered seconds later, and Baxter said under his breath, "Party's over." He may have jumped to conclusions, though, because he seemed nice enough today, less grumpy than usual. Maybe he was starting to accept that Baxter wasn't after their money.

Rodolfo touched his sister's shoulder, saying hello, and patted Mia on the back and then kissed Ester on the head. After asking her how she was feeling, he looked over at Baxter and even said, "Buenos días."

As he moved a slice of tortilla to his plate, he looked over at his mother. "Corte Inglés agreed to buy the rest of the production."

Ester looked up. "Really? Well done, *mi hijo*."

Rodolfo lit up, and Baxter saw more of the sales guy in the man than he'd seen before, that confidence after one locks in a new deal. "*Sí*. It's not for what we wanted, but I think we take it."

"What's Corte Inglés?" Baxter asked.

Rodolfo turned to him. "A high-end department store that's all over the country. They've been buying from us for a long time but stopped two years ago. I've been trying to get back in ever since."

"How much?" Alma asked, less enthused.

He gave her a brief look. "Four a bottle."

"Four euros a bottle?" Alma's voice crossed the table like the back of her hand swinging at him.

Baxter looked over at Mia, who was listening with rapt attention.

Rodolfo held up his hands. "They're buying quite a lot."

"I'm keen to accept it," Ester said.

As Alma raised her hands, as if to ask, "Are you kidding me?" Rodolfo said, "I agree. With glass and bottling costs coming up next month. Labeling. Paying the harvesters. We need cash."

"You might as well throw it away," Alma said.

"And this is why farmers need to keep their head in the dirt and out of the business. Who else is going to buy it, *hermana*?" He switched to Spanish and the escalation began.

Alma responded with equal acrimony, all in Spanish and moving so fast that Baxter could barely pick out a word.

Ester smacked her hand on the table. *"Basta!"* Ester's following Spanish sped out of her mouth even faster and more aggressive than that of her children.

Baxter pushed up from his chair and gestured for Mia to do the same. "Hey, honey, why don't we let them talk?"

The Arroyos stopped yelling at each other and all turned to Mia. She looked so small in that moment, as if she'd been let down.

Her grandmother reached for her. "I'm so sorry. Having a family business is difficult." She looked back at Alma and Rodolfo. "Sometimes it's hard to find common ground."

Baxter put his hand on Mia's shoulder. "I think we'll just head upstairs for a little while, get Mia ready to go. Right, honey?"

"Yes, sir," she said, standing with her shoulders slumped.

⌇

Baxter spent the morning wheelbarrowing old tiles to a pile behind the tractor shed. It was good exercise, and he eventually took off his shirt to let the autumn breeze cool his skin.

Working on the roof had become a good distraction from his worries, but, admittedly, there was even more to the experience. Being out there with his shirt off and the sun coming down on him had reminded him of growing up on the jobsites back in Greenville when he was young. It was hard for him to believe now, but he'd loved construction work back then, the beauty of working with his hands, seeing a job come together. He could almost feel the power he'd felt as a young teenager when he'd first gotten his hands on a nail gun and an angle grinder. Those breakthrough experiences that had given him a sense of belonging had even predated the guitar.

When he'd moved all the old tiles, he climbed back onto the roof and began to unroll and staple down a new membrane. About twenty minutes into his new task, he heard the leaves crackle below and glanced down to find Alma watching him, her hand shading her eyes. He stopped what he was doing, setting down the stapler and walking to the edge of the roof. "It's hot today."

"*Sí.* You being careful up there? It's a long way to the hospital."

He wiped his brow. "I'm doing my best."

She held up a bottle of water. "I thought you might be thirsty. Can I come up?"

"*Por supuesto.*" Of course.

Once she got up the ladder, she sat three feet from him, handed him the water, and untwisted the cap on her own.

"Not a bad view, right?"

Baxter gazed out over the grove, seeing the tops of the olive trees, a canopy bustling with bugs and birds. "You've got your slice of paradise, that's for sure."

"I was caught off guard by your tattoos," she said, looking back at him.

He glanced at the tattoos crawling up his arms and the ones on his chest. "Yeah, the proof of my misspent youth."

"Oh, these were from when you were young?"

"I'm still young. What are you talking about?" He shook his head at his weak humor. "No, I've collected them over the years, but it started early." He pointed to a series of jagged triangles on his left shoulder. "My friend and I did these when we were twelve or so."

"Twelve?"

He nodded. "With paper clips. Not the wisest idea."

"And this one?" She pointed to a blue-and-red skull on his biceps.

"That's a Grateful Dead thing. Do you know them?"

She shook her head. "I don't think so."

"They were a big influence of mine. Some of the best songwriting of all time. They're my church, in a way."

She smiled. "Did Sofia have any tattoos? I'm starting to see her as kind of a rocker girl."

And there Sofia came, right back into another conversation. Baxter felt like a boxer who didn't even have enough fight left to lift his gloves. "A rocker girl," he repeated with a chuckle. "She was a long way from that. She wasn't a tattoo kind of person. She was so clean. Ate clean, exercised daily, lived clean. She didn't even drink that much. She was good for me in that way, showing me a better way to live, kept me taking care of myself while I was on the road. At least, most of the time."

Alma went on to ask several more questions about his music and then asked one even deeper. "So what's going on with you?"

He met her eyes for only a fraction of a second. "What do you mean?"

"Being here is hard for you, I think. Are you okay?" The way she always spoke was so calming, as if she were an old wise sage living in this woman's body for a while.

He directed his words to the sage, not Sofia's half sister. "You really want to know, huh?"

"Only if you feel like sharing."

As if he had anything else to hide. They'd all seen his pain in the last five days. "I didn't know what I was getting into coming here. I didn't quite realize how much of Sofia we'd be bringing back into our lives. I mean, I knew y'all would want to know about her, which is fair. But, as you know now, it's just not how we've been healing. I've been trying to forget her. Mia too. And here we are in a place that Sofe could have lived if a few things had been different, and here we are with the only people I know who share her blood. And I'm just getting pulled back into the mire of those days. It was hard, Alma. Still is, but . . ."

He blew out a long blast of air. "What's really screwing me up is that Mia's a different person. Or who she used to be before Sofia died. I hear all this talk about Sofia between y'all, and my first reaction is to snuff it out, you know. But now I'm not so sure."

"She is happy, isn't she?" Alma said. He'd told her about some of Mia's troubles, so she was somewhat caught up. She smiled at him and peered deeply into his eyes, like a yoga teacher might, so present in the moment. "And how about you?"

"Me? Wanna know the truth? I'm a wreck. I figured my time here would be good for me. A little vacation. But it's not working out that way. Not that it's about me. I came here for Mia, so to know she's thriving is"—he welled up with tears—"is everything. I just hope taking her away doesn't make it worse."

Alma was quiet for a long time, clasping her hands together and staring out over her trees. Baxter had the urge to speak, but he didn't know what to say. Maybe he just wanted her advice, he realized, as if she might hold all the answers.

The silence was killing him, though. "It's just that talking about Sofia and thinking about her so much tears back open the wound." He held up both hands almost to his temples, his fingers turned to claws. "There's just so much energy running through me, so much . . . anxiety and . . . I guess, anger and sadness. It feels like someone is holding a Taser up against me."

Snapping out of it, he said, "I didn't mean to unload on you. Forgive me."

Her kind smile said it all: she was happy to listen, and there was no judgment. "Sounds to me like it was destiny that you came here."

"Destiny, huh?"

"Sí."

"It's a funny thing, destiny. I'd like to believe it exists." Baxter was no stranger to mulling over the idea. "I've always tried to make sense of it with Sofia. Were the two of us destined to meet, only to lose each other a few years later? Was Mia our purpose in meeting? Was our relationship nothing more than a . . . an instrument of destiny? I don't know. It's a hard thing to figure out." These impossible questions suddenly rushed up from his core and situated behind his eyes. He bit the emotions back and then let out a sigh.

She watched him with what he thought might be compassion. "I think it requires faith," she said ever so quietly, yet surely.

He rolled his eyes like Mia. "Speaking of hard things to figure out. Faith in what?"

"Faith in something."

Baxter thought of an ellipsis that leaves a sentence hanging. *Faith in . . .* Was that what faith was about, knowing something always followed the ellipsis? He felt like he'd lived his whole life since Sofia's death hanging on the last period of an ellipsis, like a song that ends on the four chord, forcing listeners to find their own resolution.

"I do believe—or at least I want to believe—that something very powerful, I don't know what, brought us here, just when Mia really needed it. That email from 23andMe was a heck of a coincidence."

"It's beautiful. And though it might not seem obvious, I'd guess this trip will be good for both of you."

"I guess dragging me away from work was an added bonus." He instantly wished he hadn't summed it up so clumsily.

"And maybe," she said, "just maybe, it's not so bad to talk about Sofia. It's sad to think the only solution to losing someone is to shut them out of your life."

He thought of the picture of Sofia on his bedside table, one of the few pictures that he hadn't thrown away. "That's not *exactly* what we've done." Maybe a little, but he didn't feel like putting up a defense. Every situation was so different. "How about with your father? What's your secret?"

"I'm doing this for him, making oil. That's my way of keeping him alive. But everyone has different ways of healing, I think."

"Yeah, I guess so." Baxter shook his head to clear his thoughts. "What else is there for you? Outside of farming. What do you like to do?"

She didn't give him a hard time for trying to lighten things up. "I love to travel. Usually I can't get away until late November, but I always go traveling to get away and reset."

"I can't imagine being so close to so many great places in Europe. I wouldn't know where to start."

"That's how we look at you Americans, how lucky you are to be close to New York and California and Colorado. I'd love to go to the US one day."

"Yeah, well, don't sell short South Carolina. You should come see us." The invitation slipped out of his mouth unintentionally.

"Now I have every reason to go," Alma said, shocking him. She must not have seen him withdraw. "Maybe one day I can show you around Europe. I love visiting the Christmas markets up north. Mia would too. Vienna, Prague, Budapest. When it's snowing outside and there's ice-skating and Christmas trees everywhere. Desserts everywhere. Mulled wine, hot cider. Everyone is so happy, running around in their thick jackets and wool hats. It's a fairy tale."

"Wait, Budapest. Is that part of Europe?"

"*Sí*, it's part of the EU, but it's less expensive there. A different currency. You can stay in these, emm, great historic apartments for very little. Last time, my friends and I stayed in a place overlooking the Danube with a piano in the living room. We hired a pianist and violinist to play for us . . . for barely anything."

Thinking about all the places he had yet to see, a strange feeling of youthful thirst came over him. "I feel like I've been missing so much." That missed trip to Paris suddenly stung. He and Sofia were only just getting started with their travels.

Alma dipped her head. "You're still young, well, kind of young. Plenty of time to explore."

"Kind of young indeed." Maybe it had been his and Sofia's dream to see Europe, but surely it was one he and Mia could realize instead.

"I guess I've been putting it off," he admitted. "I seem to put off a lot of things that don't serve an immediate purpose."

"This is the American way, isn't it?"

"For some," he said, feeling protective toward his country. "I wouldn't say we're all being misled. It's just a bit more dog-eat-dog over there. A glass of wine is what? Two euros here. Over there, try five or six times as much. Still, it's no excuse."

They watched a bird soar by. "I like you, Baxter. I thought you were kind of bullheaded, but you're soft inside."

He patted his belly. "Unfortunately, I'm a little soft all over . . ."

She shook her head at him, seeing right through him.

Not wanting to be so superficial, he allowed himself to speak the truth. "You know, I think more than anything it was my upbringing that made me a little uptight. I'm not looking for sympathy, but I had a rough go growing up. And it put me in this kind of survivor mode. Actually, about the only time I wasn't in it was when I was making music."

Alma drummed a quick beat on her legs and sat back. "Yeah, Mia says your parents are busy all the time; that's why you don't see them."

Baxter sat back too. "Yeah, that's what I tell her. Let's put it this way. I've barely spoken to them in the past three years. And they made complete asses of themselves on the day of Sofia's funeral."

His parents had raised—if that was what you'd call it—Baxter in Greenville, but after burning one too many bridges, they had relocated to Aiken two hours away. As rocky as their relationship was, he'd cried when he'd told them the news about Sofia and felt incredibly grateful that they were so eager to come to the funeral in Charleston, where Baxter, Sofia, and Mia had been living.

He should have known they'd only make things worse. Spilling out of the car in the church parking lot, his mother was three sheets to the wind, and his father wasn't much better—though Barry Shaw didn't need alcohol to be a jerk. During the wake, Baxter sat with his father on the back porch, overlooking Sofia's garden boxes. After a long rant about all the problems going on in their life, his father had said to Baxter, "Don't hate me for sayin' so, but I think you could have done better anyway. Those West Coast women are so damn opinionated." If it hadn't been for Mia being a few feet away inside, Baxter would have started swinging his fists and might not have ever stopped.

He winced at the memory. "That's why meeting y'all has been so special to Mia. She doesn't have any of it back home. Sofia's adoptive mother is just as checked out." He wiped the sweat off his brow.

"They're missing out, aren't they?" Alma said.

"Yes, they are."

He didn't like thinking about the lack of family back home, because it made him long for it, for Mia's sake—and maybe even his own. "Was it tough to hear that Sofia was out there, that your mom hid it?"

She let out a loud burst of a laugh. "Welcome to the Arroyo family. Another piece of the wall falls. Yes, it's very frustrating to know I had a sister out there all this time. To know that I could have known her. It's sad to think I never will. But my mother had reasons, mostly because she was in a great deal of pain over her choice. No matter how frustrated I am, I'm glad everything has led to Mia coming here. And you, of course."

He looked out over the trees in silence. Two black birds chased each other around one of the trunks of the olive trees. It was a nice thing for her to say, and he wanted to reply that he was also glad that everything had led both Mia and him here, but he didn't want to let the moment get too intimate. Though he wouldn't have admitted it even under torture, there was some attraction there, a faint stirring within.

"Ester's carried all that pain for a very long time," Alma said. "All by herself. How can I be mad at her? Between my brother and my father's troubles and this thing with Sofia, and her . . ." Alma paused, as if catching herself. "She's suffered enough. That's all I can say."

And her what? Baxter wondered. He didn't push, though.

"What is it with your brother?" he asked. "He doesn't seem very happy right now. Is it because of us?"

"No, no. He's just . . . bent out of shape. Isn't that what you say?"

"That's right." He thought back to a song he used to play. *I ain't broke, but brother I'm badly bent.*

Alma shook her head. "For one, my father always talked about having saved some money, just in case the business got worse. So that we wouldn't have to sell the estate. But after he died, we realized there was no savings. That's what has him so upset. We can't afford to mess up right now. It's all about making sure we have enough cash to get us through each stage of production."

"Is everything going to be all right?"

Alma shook her head. "I don't know. That's why we have to take that Corte Inglés deal."

"So why isn't Rodolfo on the road selling?"

"He's been on the road for a good part of the year. I don't know. He just seems distracted. Growing up he could sell anyone anything, but the stuff that happened between my father and him just made him give up."

Baxter wished there was something that he could do to help, but there sure as heck wasn't. He was busy trying not to let his own company drown. "What was it that happened with your father and him?"

"He's always been our mother's boy, and my father rubbed it in his face. He wanted my brother to be me, to be the farmer. But Rodolfo showed no interest in it, always talking instead about moving to Valencia or Madrid. When I was the one who fell in love with the farm, my father encouraged me while doing the opposite with Rodolfo. He'd called him a *marica*, which is like a flower. He'd tell him to go do the laundry or go mop the floors."

She started talking with her hands, very passionately. "Of course, that made him start resenting me. The only time they ever stopped arguing is if they played cards together. When my brother started to get into the business side, which was my mother's idea, it only got worse. To my brother's credit, he tried hard to make them both proud, but my father didn't . . . emm, trust him or have faith in him. My father had always done it all, the farming and the selling, and I think it was hard for him to let go. We were already struggling—the estate, I mean. I do think my brother genuinely wanted to help, but they argued all the time, especially that last year before my father died. A few months before, he and Rodolfo got in a terrible fight, a fistfight."

Baxter thought back to the many fistfights he and his father had had. He could still feel the strike of his old man's knuckles against his cheeks. "That's tough."

"Yeah. My mother and I came home to find them going at each other near the fountain out front. I tried to break it up, but it wasn't easy. That was a very sad day. And probably the day the four of us broke apart for good."

"What was it about?" Baxter asked.

She let out a long breath, as if she'd been holding it in for an hour. "Business stuff. I don't know. They were always butting heads."

As she spoke, Baxter began to understand Rodolfo in ways even Alma might be missing. Baxter's father had been eerily similar, always wanting Baxter to "put that damn guitar down." Even when Cactus Road had signed their first big deal, his father had shaken his head and called him "lucky," told him it wouldn't last. His parents had seen exactly two shows, both of which they'd left early, blaming it on the noise. It was a heck of a thing to not be supported by your parents.

Baxter drained the rest of the water. "Damn the shadows of our youth. So many of us can never escape them. In a way, I feel for him and understand, but I don't think we can use our past as an excuse to be an asshole, forgive my language."

"You don't need my forgiveness. And that's exactly why . . ." She didn't finish.

"Why what?"

Alma shook her head and pushed up. "I don't want to talk about it anymore. I'd better get back to work."

It seemed like she wanted to tell him something, and he couldn't imagine what that might be. "Sorry I brought it up."

"No, don't worry. And thanks for the water." With that, she climbed back down the ladder.

Baxter heard a melody in his head, something he wasn't used to the past few years. And then lyrics rose up out of him, and he whispered them into the Spanish air. "She speaks of destiny, she don't even know me."

He watched her walk away and mumbled, "And I sure as heck don't know her." When she was gone, he said, "What are you hiding, Alma Arroyo?"

Chapter 18

Lonely Hombres

Once it was morning in the US, Baxter walked down the road, crossed over the creek, and locked in a signal. He sat down with his computer on his lap and made the call to John Frick.

Frick picked up on the second ring. "Baxter."

"Hey, John." He could feel the tension in the man's voice. "Thanks for taking my call. I just wanted to talk to you about that change order. I know you're upset."

"You're damn right I'm upset," he spat.

Baxter breathed through his own anger. "Look, you and I sat down and looked at the expenses. You were fine with it. I wanted to slow things down to make sure we were on the same page financially, but you and Nancy wanted to get into that house. I was trying to help you out."

Frick was silent for a moment. "Maybe so, but I don't recall agreeing to an additional $82,342. I remember it being more like thirty-five."

Baxter began to run through everything, the complete change in cabinetry in the kitchen, the upgraded tile floors, the wine fridge. Frick's wife had suddenly wanted Vetrostone *after* the granite had been delivered.

"Yeah, yeah, I get it. I'm gonna pay you, Baxter. If that's what you're worried about."

"A little."

"No, don't worry about it. Give me a couple of days. I don't do people wrong."

Baxter took the sincerity he heard in the man's voice as assurance, and when they hung up, he felt like maybe, just maybe, he'd survive this trip.

He dialed Alan and jumped right into business. "I talked to Frick. He says he's gonna pay. So keep me posted on that. What else is going on?"

"We got this, Bax. You just sit back and drink your sangria and watch them bulls fight."

"If only . . ." Baxter ran through every single project, and Alan gave him a fairly competent rundown, which gave Baxter a bit of a reprieve. Then Alan asked, "You ever read Hemingway?"

"Back in the old days," Baxter admitted.

"I like him, man," Alan continued. "Dude knows how to write. You know he loved Spain. Loved the bullfight. I think it was . . . was it *For Whom the Bell Tolls*? I think so. Pick you up a copy of that and pour a glass of that vino. You'll be in heaven."

"Yeah, okay," Baxter said, but his attention was caught by the neighbor—or *el vecino*, as he'd learned was the translation—staring at a chessboard on his table overlooking the vineyard.

"Look, Alan, I believe in you. I know I don't show it sometimes, but I know you got this." He wanted so badly to believe what he was saying.

"I appreciate that. You know what this reminds me of, Bax, speaking of good writers? Wasn't it Twain who said that thing about spending a whole life worrying about stuff that never happens?"

"Yeah, I think so."

"Mull that one over. All's good here."

After saying goodbye, Baxter ended the call and sighed, trying to let some of Alma's *tranquilo* mindset settle him.

Good lord, he needed to relax. He was gone for ten days, not a month.

The neighbor was still looking at him and then raised an arm to wave him over. Baxter raised his hands, as if asking, "What?" The man waved him over again. What could he want? Baxter crossed the meadow, and when he was about thirty feet out, he raised his hand and called out, "Buenos días."

The neighbor silently raised a glass.

Baxter passed over the man's gravel drive to the front yard. The grass hadn't been cut in a while and was sprouting flowers and grains.

"¿Qué tal, amigo?" Baxter was asking how it was going, flexing his Spanish.

Don Diego sat up from his relaxed position. *"¿Bien, y tú?"*

Baxter looked up to the clear sky. *"Todo bien."* All good.

The man shrugged with a smile that showed one very crooked tooth in the center. *"¿Come te llamas?"* What's your name? He was maybe a little older than Ester—early sixties, probably, handsome in his baldness and dressed simply in work khakis and a button-down that was tight around his small belly. His skin was dark and aged by the sun, as if he'd been working his vineyard all his life. His beard was about as unkempt as his lawn.

"My name's Baxter. And you're Don Diego, *sí*? Good to meet you." Baxter wondered why he'd been called over. He glanced at the chessboard. The pieces looked like they'd been carved by hand, perhaps whittled by this man. Baxter made a hand motion to accompany his English. "You playing yourself?"

Diego jutted out his bottom lip and nodded, then gestured to the bottle of wine by the chessboard. *"¿Quieres bebir?"*

Baxter wasn't sure what to do. He would rather get back to work, but he didn't want to be rude. He remembered what Alan had said earlier about enjoying a sangria. "Yeah, why not? I'll take a sip. It's your wine? *¿Es tu vino?*"

The man told Baxter to sit, then pressed up and went inside. He returned a moment later with an extra tumbler and a chunk of goat cheese on a cutting board and selection of olives in a ceramic bowl. After setting the food down, he plopped into his seat, pulled the cork out of the bottle, and poured Baxter some wine. He spoke for a while in Spanish, and Baxter could pick out only certain words. *Barrique. Vino tinto. Frutas.* He was pretty sure the old man was talking about the wine, telling him how he'd made it.

Baxter took his first sip, thinking this was a much better way to spend the afternoon than dialing into work. "That's good wine. I could get used to this." He found himself talking with his hands to make up for his lack of Spanish. "My daughter plays a mean game of chess. You call it chess, right?"

Diego nodded again, and Baxter decided the man didn't know a lick of English. He did know the universal language of food and wine, and as he sliced the cheese, he said, *"Queso de cabra. Para picar."* He produced a package of toothpicks and offered one to Baxter, shaking the package until one popped out.

"*Picar*, huh? To pick, I guess. Yeah, I eat goat cheese."

Diego stabbed and ate an olive, then spit the hueso to the ground. The action reminded Baxter of Alan spitting his chewing tobacco. A long stray hair hung like a climbing rope from the man's right ear. He pointed his finger at Baxter and then at himself, suggesting they play.

"Sure," Baxter replied.

As they set up the board together, Diego talked. *He speaks like Bob Dylan sang,* Baxter thought, as if words burned his throat. And he clearly knew Baxter didn't understand much of it, but he didn't seem to mind. Baxter was okay listening to him, like it was music, and the awkwardness fell away.

Baxter made the first move, his pawn to A3. Diego stared at the board like they were in the most heated match of their lives. He eventually sat back and crossed his arms, glancing at Baxter as if sizing him up. He finally made a move, his pawn to F6, then asked if Baxter was a friend of the Arroyos.

Baxter shook his finger. *"No amigos. Familia."* Not friend, family. He wondered why the man wouldn't know, especially considering Diego and Jorge had been best friends.

"Familia?" Diego said, looking surprised. He muttered something to himself in Spanish.

Baxter took another sip of the wine, thinking there was something very special about drinking a man's wine as you looked over his vineyard. "Alma said you and Don Jorge were best friends, grew up together. It must have been hard." Knowing his words fell on deaf ears, he distilled his message down to his best Spanish. *"¿Tú y Don Jorge son amigos, sí? Lo siento."*

A hard nod, as if Jorge's death did indeed cut deep. *"Sí."*

Baxter moved another pawn, realizing Diego might not be aware that Ester had given birth to a child that wasn't Jorge's. Ester had said *most* everyone knew. Even if he'd been better at communicating in Spanish, Baxter decided it wasn't his place to share the details.

"Jorge sure did leave a mess over there, didn't he?" Baxter said, knowing Diego would understand none of it. "I wish you could speak English so you could tell me what was going on. Rodolfo thinks we're here to take his inheritance."

Diego let out a grunt.

"Yeah, we're not going to get very far talking, are we?"

Diego shook his head, more Spanish mutterings. For a moment, Baxter wondered if the man could understand more than he was letting on. That surely would be embarrassing. Nah, Baxter decided, moving another pawn.

"Things just seem more complicated than they need to be," Baxter continued. "And Rodolfo seems to me a bit privileged. Here I am, thinking I'd bring my daughter here for ten days of peace, but there's this weird energy below the surface, as if something I'm not privy to is going on."

Diego said his piece, and though he spoke rather slowly, Baxter didn't pick up any of it. It was a tennis match without a ball, but it seemed to be working, both men enjoying the companionship.

They hammered their way through a discussion about whether Baxter had been to Spain or if Diego had been to the US. Both answers were negative. They went a good ten minutes talking in broken conversation, asking questions of each other, all simple stuff. How old are the vines? Did your father make wine? Where is South Carolina? Which American president did you vote for?

Baxter crossed one leg over the other. "It's nice talking to you, Don D.," he said, laughing. "We should do this more often." He realized how truly nice it was just to be sitting out there in nature, sipping on wine, shooting the shit. No agenda. For a second, he almost forgot about everything else going on around him.

Baxter felt so comfortable that he wasn't even thinking when he said, "And that Alma. She's pretty special, isn't she? Like she's got it all figured out."

Taking his eyes away from the board, Diego looked at Baxter curiously.

"Do you know what I'm saying?" Baxter asked, his eyebrows furrowing. "Are you understanding me? You'd better come clean now before I embarrass myself further. Seriously, that's what happens in the movies, a guy like me opens up his soul to this other guy, Don D., only to find out that he understood him the whole time. Don't do that to me, amigo. I'm too fragile."

If Diego did understand Baxter, he didn't let on and put his focus back on the board.

"Women, right?" Baxter said. "I guess that's what I'm saying." He hit the table. *"Mujeres."* Women.

Diego grunted. *"Sí, mujeres."* To women they drank. Then he asked if Baxter was married.

Baxter shook his head, saying in broken Spanish that his wife was no longer living. Diego dipped his chin out of respect, said he was sorry. Baxter braced himself for the inevitable follow-up question of how, but Diego spared him.

Instead, the man touched his chest and said, *"Estoy divorciado."*

With his great linguistic abilities, Baxter figured that meant he was divorced. "No *hijos*? No children?"

The man shook his head and went on to beat Baxter in five more moves.

Chapter 19

She Sees Right through Me

That night, Baxter read Mia a book in his bed and then spent some time chatting with her, making sure things were going well and that she wasn't putting up a facade like she'd done after finding out about Sofia's murder. The chat turned more into an interrogation, but he couldn't find anything wrong. She seemed so darn happy being here with everyone.

In fact, when he closed the book, she asked, "Could I sleep with Iaia again?" How could Baxter say no? As much as he couldn't make sense of it, he wasn't going to take it away.

After Ester had taken Mia into her room, Baxter found himself alone downstairs with Alma. She produced a bottle of red wine from the cabinet in the living room and held it out in front of her. "Shall we have a *copa* by the fire?"

Though it was far from profound, the question was loaded for Baxter. He looked away so that she couldn't see his internal deliberation. Honestly, he'd like nothing more than to spend time with her, but was it the right thing to do? Not that he'd be cheating on Sofia by simply having a drink by the fire. It wasn't that, was it? That it would be with Sofia's half sister complicated things. Something was certainly stirring between them . . . unless he was reading things all wrong.

Maybe he was. She'd offered to have a drink with him, not go on a date. Deciding the one thing he needed to stop doing was overthinking things, he turned back to her. "Yeah, sure." He couldn't hold eye contact with her long, though, so he diverted his gaze to the bottle. "It looks like what I was drinking earlier with Don Diego."

"That's right," she said. He'd told Alma, Ester, and Mia over dinner that he'd been pulverized by the man in a quick chess match.

Alma set a Bluetooth speaker on the mantel above the fireplace and played flamenco music through her phone. "This is the guy I was telling you about, Javier Martín, who I'm going to hear Saturday. He will change your life."

The guitarist tickled out a tune to the slow beat of clapping hands, and the fire sang as they took the two seats facing it. Baxter listened intently, appreciating that she loved flamenco music, an old soul who should have been born decades earlier.

"You sure you don't want to go?" Alma asked, leaning toward him.

Baxter was more than tempted and thanked her, but said, "It's probably not the best idea, leaving Mia. Life-changing is overrated anyway." He said it with a subtle smirk, though he wasn't laughing on the inside. In actuality, even the idea of attending a concert felt like it would hit too close to home, *especially* with her. The more distance he had from the past, the better.

"Don't say I didn't try." She tugged off the capsule of the bottle and made quick work of uncorking it. After filling both of their glasses, she clinked his, saying, *"Salud."*

"Salud." He put his focus on the wine as he let it coat his tongue and burn down his throat. "Yeah, that's good. What kind is it? Don Diego and I, our conversation is a little tricky."

She spun the glass and sniffed the bouquet. "It's a local variety called Monastrell. He grows a nice bobal too. He's a great winemaker. All he and my father did was drink wine and play cards or chess and talk farming. They very much saw eye to eye, so much so that it sometimes upset my mother."

Baxter ran his tongue around his mouth, still tasting the fruitiness of the wine, thinking he'd definitely be expanding his wine selection back home to include Spain. "Yeah, it got a little weird earlier. I didn't go into details, but I told him we were family from America. I guess I was thinking he might know who we were and why we're here."

Alma shook her head. "I don't know what my mother has told him. They may have avoided telling him, just because of how he might judge her."

"Boy, the can of worms I didn't know I was opening by coming here. He was certainly caught off guard when I told him." Part of him felt like he and Mia were trapped in a simmering pot of water. What would happen when the water got to a boil?

"Yeah, I imagine so. Sorry about that." She set her glass down on the table. "The whole thing happened very quickly."

"Don Diego said he was divorced and never had any kids. What happened?"

"She was never right for him. My father didn't like her from the start. I don't know that my mother did either. She left him for another man about ten years ago, and I think he swore off women afterward."

"Poor guy."

She inclined her shoulders. "I think he's okay living a quiet life, making wine, sitting out in the yard, listening to the birds. It's not so bad."

Baxter thought it sounded a lot like Alma, and it also sounded so very lonely. On second thought, it sounded like him too. Still, the opposite of loneliness came with a vulnerability that Baxter knew painfully well.

"How about you?" he asked. "Why aren't you dating anyone?" The question sounded like he was being forward, driving a spear of guilt deep into his chest. "If you don't mind me asking. I'm just making conversation." His backpedaling came off entirely too obvious, and he felt embarrassed, as if he'd suggested he was interested in her.

She smiled into her wine, then pulled one of her socked feet up to the seat of the chair. "He's married to his vines, and I'm married to my trees."

This was why both of them were so good at what they did. They'd made a choice to stick to their passion and didn't let anything get in the way. Well, perhaps Diego had for a few years, but it was his vines that had won out. As jealous as he felt toward both of them, how they'd ended up doing what they were meant to do, Baxter also felt like meeting Sofia had changed everything. He'd had a plan and a dream, but then she'd walked into his life. At that moment, he should have seen that he didn't need the guitar anymore. He should have locked it away in its case and gotten a real job, one that gets you home at a decent hour every day, like every other good father out there.

"Trees are not unlike a lot of men," Alma said. "They stand around doing nothing."

"Ouch," Baxter said, taking one for all the men in the world while still caught up on the jealousy nipping at him. But why? Why was he jealous? He'd trade in his guitar a thousand times to have Sofia and Mia.

"But trees," Alma continued, "at least they don't argue with me or ask personal questions. No offense."

"Oh, none taken. Men are good for nothing. Seriously, look at me. The moment Sofia left, our lives completely fell apart."

"The jury is still out on you," Alma said.

"The jury is still out? Where did you pick up that phrase, Perry Mason?"

"I don't know who that is. My point is, you might be all right."

"Does *trying* count?"

Her chin lifted a hair as she chuckled faintly.

"Somebody must have torn out your heart, huh?" Baxter asked.

Ignoring his question, she said, "And you, you're married to your . . . what? Houses?"

He shook his head like he'd been wrongly accused. "No, not at all. I don't know that I'm married to anything anymore, other than being a father. But hold on, I'm not letting you get away that easily. So someone broke your heart?" Though he wasn't going to say it, he was fascinated by her story. They were both artists, or at least he had been one as well, and in both cases, they'd proved chasing a passion didn't leave much room for relationships. He'd tried to find the impossible balance. What had she done?

Alma sighed, as if she really didn't want to talk about it. Baxter held strong with his stare, though, not giving her an out.

"Fine, you really want to know?" She took a long sip, preparing. "I broke his heart. His name was Juan Carlos, a restaurateur in Alicante. A very big man, as in loud and opinionated, but I liked it. I liked what he had to say. Gorgeous too. I liked looking at him. Sounds shallow, doesn't it?"

"Not really. I liked looking at Sofia."

"He wanted me to move to Alicante, though, live in the city. And I almost did it. Can you imagine me, a city girl?" She set her glass down and then backhanded the air. "You know what they say here? *El amor es ciego y la locura siempre lo acompaña.* Love is blind and madness always accompanies it. I fell for a man who I knew was wrong for me. It serves me right."

And she'd just proved his theory correct. You make a choice in life. The choice he should have made when he met Sofia was to give up music and dedicate his life to family. Because she was worth giving up everything for, and he should have seen it.

"So . . . enough of this . . . this sad stuff," Alma said. "How are you faring with no Wi-Fi?"

He decided to let her get away with changing the subject. He ran a hand over his hair. "No weefee, no luggage. I'm falling apart."

"And yet look at you; you're still alive."

"For now," he said, acknowledging her point with a smirk.

"I'm a bit buried with the harvest starting tomorrow, but I promise I'll find some time to figure it out. I know it's important to you. Maybe I can get the provider to come out."

"It's probably good for me," he admitted, hearing a singer come in to accompany this Javier Martín, who was an astoundingly good guitarist.

"You're the one who said it." She paused with her eyes on the fire, then turned back to him. "No weefee, no luggage, no problem. Doesn't that sound like a country song?"

His smile surfaced. "You're a natural. Just need to work on your southern accent."

"Y'all," she said, her voice a long way from southern, like trying to watch a foreigner crack a boiled peanut.

He waved his hand through the air. "Slow it way down. We might live fast-paced, but a good southern drawl is as slow as the creek down the road." He said with exaggeration, "Y'all would love my olive oil. Not only is it good for ya, but it tastes good too."

She repeated his words, forcing him to smile again.

"Anyway, I want to talk more about music," Alma said. "What was it like to play for a living?"

Baxter stared into the ruby-red wine in his glass. "It was everything I had ever dreamed of," he said, suddenly feeling a guitar in his hands, looking out over the crowd. All this wine was making him sentimental.

"And you really don't feel like playing anymore?"

The flamenco sounds flowed and fire shot up sparks as he fell back into those days. "Touring and all that is a young man's game."

"Forget about the band. Do you not like just playing for you? We all need a way to express ourselves."

Baxter felt his throat constrict. "When we're younger, sure." He heard Javier Martín working his way into a new melody. "Anyway, I like playing for Mia. Like I said, I live through her now. And before you say anything, I realize this admission shows how unhealthy I might be, but . . . raising a child alone takes all you have."

"It's a little sad that you've given up on living."

"Oh, c'mon, I wouldn't say I've given up on living." She couldn't know what it was like to make such a hard choice, to give up his music. That guitar had saved his fucking life.

She bit her lip and nodded, holding back.

"I'm just trying to get by right now," he admitted, wanting to shield his eyes from the sudden spotlight she was shining on him. "The luxury of living is something I'm working on soon."

The pitch of her voice rose. "Oh, there's a timeline?"

"No, there's not a timeline. It's just . . . one thing at a time."

Retrieving the bottle, she refilled his glass. "Sometimes things need to come in parallel, if you don't mind me saying so."

"And what does that mean?" He slung back another big gulp.

She topped off her wine and set the bottle back. "Mia is a very . . . intuitive—is that the word? *Sí*, she's an intuitive girl. She senses when you're down. Don't tell her I said so, but she remembers hearing you cry through the walls after Sofia died."

Baxter could once again hear the squeak of the door hinges as Mia came into the room to see her last remaining source of security crumbling in tears on the floor. He had thought—or he'd at least hoped—she didn't remember those days of weakness. What an epic fail. He'd done so well to hide his grief from her since then, but much of the damage had already been done. She'd already seen how weak losing Sofia had made him.

Alma continued, "I get the sense both you and Mia are on a similar journey."

"What do you mean?"

She tapped the armrest. "Many of us vibrate on the same, emm, wavelength; that's how we're linked. It's what drives us together. There's a reason you met Sofia. The two of you were vibrating on the same frequency. No doubt you and Mia, connected for so many reasons, are vibrating on the same frequency, too—or at least a close frequency. What if helping you might help her? In your band, what was a harmony if everyone wasn't in tune? I know I'm the last person to give advice. I have brother issues and mother issues . . . but I wonder if you can help her just by tuning in to yourself and in to her, sharpening your connection. Maybe tapping deeper into that guy who used to play music. I can see him in you, wanting out."

Baxter ran his finger along the stem of the wineglass. "Oh boy, you're not afraid to speak your mind, are you? Is this the Spanish way? I can't help but notice how few boundaries there are."

"I suppose so. At least in my family. Besides, you seem to appreciate a real conversation. I like that about you." She grinned, and he felt like he was talking to a good friend. In fact, she sounded a lot like Alan, and he knew that was because she was right.

She drank her wine. "Here you are so worried about Mia remembering her mom and her nightmares and her behavior that maybe you're missing the whole point. Maybe all she needs is you. Maybe she needs to see that there is a way past losing someone, especially a wife or mom."

He thought of how in the event of losing oxygen in a plane, you're supposed to put on your own mask before you help your child. Was that the point Alma was making? He couldn't believe Mia had mentioned hearing him cry through the walls. He was still hung up on it.

"Fair enough," he said. "I agree. Trust me, I'm working on it. You see me another year or two from now, I'll eat the longest lunches and take the longest siestas in the state of South Carolina."

She looked over at him with serious concern. "Why wait?"

"Now, hold on," he said. "Don't act like I'm the only workaholic in this room."

"Fair enough, but harvest does start tomorrow."

"And you love it, don't you?"

A lightness came over her. "Of course I do. It's . . . it gives me meaning."

He chewed on the last word. "It's funny how life is like that, isn't it? All any of us need is a reason to get out of bed."

When their glasses were once again empty, she stood and went to the bar in the corner, pulling out a bottle of green liquid and grabbing two glasses from the top of the table. "This is Afilador, an herbal liqueur, a typical drink here." She poured them each several fingers and handed him one. "To working hard."

"Yes, to working hard."

They clinked glasses and took sips. "That's good," he said, smacking his lips in delight, the burn easing by with a sweet herbal taste. As the alcohol hit him, his inhibitions fell further away, and he looked back at her freckled face. "I will admit your occupation is more interesting than mine. More like art."

"Or like music," she replied. It was a fair comparison. "Do you still talk to the guys in your band?" How sly she was to turn the conversation back to him.

"Not as much as I should. We text back and forth a little. I was pretty tough to be around after she was shot. They were there for me, and they know now that I appreciated that, but it was hard to be around 'em. Though I had my reasons, there was still no sugarcoating the fact that I'd abandoned them. I'd make the choice again, for Mia's sake, but I can't help but feel like I let them down. We were a bullet train, just exploding with success. Had even gotten written up in the *New York Times*. And then I left and things fizzled out. It wasn't just because I had left. If any of us had left, it would have been the end."

As he said that last bit, he relived the haunting feeling of letting the guys down, telling them he couldn't keep going. They'd made it, burst through all the hurdles to finally arrive, and it was Baxter, the one who'd pushed the hardest, who'd ultimately called it quits and run away.

"I don't understand why you quit playing entirely. I would have thought a musician would play more after losing someone they love."

Javier Martín and his band switched songs, and Baxter felt each note pry into his core, asking him the same questions.

"You'd think that, wouldn't you?" He couldn't go back there without revisiting the day Sofia was shot, their last band practice. He'd not played a note with the fellas since, and it was sad as hell. "For me, letting go of music felt like the only answer. When I used to play, I sang from the depths of my soul, giving it all I had, and when I picked up my guitar later, just before I'd officially left the band, I got the sense that my soul had been spooned out like a . . . like an avocado. I had nothing left. Good heavens, Afilador works quickly."

"It's a truth serum."

"Apparently." He took a big sniff of the Afilador, soaking it in. "Sofia had become my muse. One of the lasting images I have is her standing on the side of the stage with her thumbs up. Without her, what was the point?"

Alma showed her sad smile. "She was your cheerleader."

"Exactly. Besides, I knew I had to leave the band for Mia's sake. It wouldn't have been a good life for a little girl. Better to just walk away and put everything I had left into her."

"It's very admirable. You know, Baxter the Tool Man, you come off rather harsh, but I can see why Sofia fell for you. In addition to being handsome and having cute dimples, you're a good man. Rough around the edges, but a very good man. A good father."

A good father. Her words rang in his ears. He wasn't so sure she was right. "Rough around the edges, huh? You do know your American slang."

"I told you. American television." She set her elbow on the armrest, then rested her chin on her fist, her eyes penetrating his. "And I'm sure your status as a rock star didn't hurt either. You up on stage with your guitar and your swagger, all the girls waving their arms. I'm sure you broke many hearts when you married her."

He blushed. "Sofia would have loved meeting you."

"And I her," she whispered, "but I suppose that wasn't part of the plan."

"If there ever was one."

"Have you ever met anyone else?" Alma asked. Her head was propped up by her arm, her chin against her palm, her eyes on him. "Do you and Mia talk about that?"

Baxter crossed his foot over the other knee. "I've dated a little bit, never brought anyone home. I don't want to do that to Mia."

"Do you think she'd really care?"

"I'm not sure." The idea seemed to grab at his throat. It was a lot more than Mia. Maybe he was just another cliché of a widower, but he sure as hell couldn't let himself fall for someone again. He didn't have the strength to lose anyone else.

She sat up and pulled her hair behind her ear. "You're very in your head, aren't you? Always thinking."

"You know what they say in my line of work? Measure twice and cut once. Does that make sense?"

"*Sí*. How very safe that is."

"That's the point, I guess."

She thankfully let him escape the spotlight. "How's your Spanish coming along? Are you rolling your *R*s yet?"

"Rolling my *R*s?" he said through a laugh. "I'm five days in. I don't even know what *R*s to roll. You should have heard me trying to talk to Don Diego."

"Try it," she said. The idea apparently amused her, as her whole face lit up.

He'd had enough to drink that he didn't think twice about an attempt, but what came was a sound more like a plane taking off in his mouth.

Her cheery and beautiful face let out a burst of laughter, and he thought her laugh was so big for such a petite woman. But it was pure, too, and very much music to his ears.

"It's more with the tongue," she said. "Not your throat. Like this." She purred out a long string of *R*s.

He tried to imitate her, another botched attempt, and they laughed together this time.

"Put your tongue just behind your teeth and let it flutter." Another purr of *R*s, her tongue flittering in her mouth.

He tried to roll his *R*s again to no avail.

"Keep practicing," she said. "You'll get it."

He couldn't do it, Baxter finally decided. No, not roll the *R*s—that was not what he was thinking about. He couldn't be down here for another moment. It wasn't just that he sensed Sofia's ghost watching them, but he couldn't stop thinking about Mia. What in the world would she think of the two of them drinking and laughing together so late into the night? No, no, no, not a good idea at all.

He set his glass down hard, almost breaking it, and then pushed up from the chair. "I think it's time I retire."

She clapped her hands together. "Oh, that's right. It's Americano bedtime."

"Hey, we'll see who's up for the sunrise," he said, looking down at her.

She shook it off. "I'm a sunset kind of girl."

"Yeah, you are," he said, not knowing exactly what he meant. Sure would make a good song, though.

As he broke up the fire with the poker, he heard in his head a tune: *A sunset kind of girl* . . .

Setting the poker back down, he wobbled between her and the fire, and as he felt the warmth of the flames on his skin, he felt her take his hand. They looked at each other for what felt like a long time, and he waited for her to say something, anything to cover up the sound of his loudly beating heart.

And then she gave his hand a squeeze and flapped one of her eyelids open and closed. "Buenas noches, Baxter."

Chapter 20

FINGERS ON THE STRINGS

Upstairs, with all that alcohol running through him, Baxter couldn't stop staring at Don Jorge's guitar case. He was sprawled out on the bed, his shoes still on, his hands behind his head on the pillow. The house made its night noises, as if it truly came alive once the humans closed their eyes.

What was it about Alma that made him want so desperately to bring passion back into his life? She had a way of pushing him without force, like a magician might levitate an object without contact. The sour taste that lingered all the way down in his soul was indeed jealousy, because he'd tasted that level of artistry himself and he missed it desperately. This part of him felt like he needed to prove to Alma—and to himself—that he wasn't all dried up, that he'd once mattered too.

There was more, though. If jealousy was sour, it was the sweet taste of making music that pulled at him. He craved to play even a note or two that, if he let himself go, could rise up from deep within and travel through his fingers to the guitar in a way that would remind him that there was indeed magic out there. Back when he'd been on fire in his field, playing music was like stepping into another dimension, as if the moment he'd played the first note of the day, he was opening up a door and stepping into space, being pulled up by his essence into the vastness of all that was out there.

He'd not known this feeling since he'd put away his Martin guitar, but he could still remember it. He could feel what it was like when he was tapped in, when even one note sounded as beautiful as a symphony, when the strum of a chord was enough to make his knees fall out from under him or enough to make him weep with wonder.

Tonight he wanted that feeling more than anything, and that guitar locked away in its case beckoned to him. It might have been the alcohol, certainly the lingering sounds of Javier Martín's guitar in his ear, and unquestionably Alma's queries about the man he used to be. No matter the combination, it was enough for Baxter to push up and cross the room.

Yes, he'd played for Mia, but that had been different. He'd done that for her, at her request. Tonight was about him. He wanted to see if he still had it.

He unlatched the case and stared at the guitar for a little while. Nerves teased him, as if he were staring at the knob of a door that led into the unknown, and he wasn't sure if he was capable of twisting it, let alone going through.

And yet his need to see if there was anything left in him gave him the strength to place his hands around the neck of the guitar and lift it up and out of the case. Memory clips passed by his inner eye: he and his band taking the stage and Baxter lifting his Martin off the stand and pulling the strap around his neck.

He could hear all the fans who knew the words to their songs cheering them on, ready to take a journey with them. Because that was what it was . . . all of them were there because they were sometimes lost in the swamp of their day-to-day, but there was something about the communion that took place between the artists on the stage and the crowd that lifted them collectively out of their own stormy lives.

He sat down on the bed with the guitar in his hands. The crowd noise and the memories disappeared, and it became him and his instrument. And he was full of belief, knowing that all the little worries in life didn't matter. And best of all, Mia . . . she was doing okay. His guitar was in his hands, and she was doing okay. They were here in Spain, and she was thriving. She was going to be okay.

He placed his left ring finger on a B-flat and picked the note with his thumb. Ahhh . . . that simple sound that encased all the beauty of the world within it. And it was bluesy as all hell, and he bent the string a little to let it really get at him, tugging at the man who was still somewhere in his brittle skeleton.

Playing a series of notes this time, a simple improvised melody, he felt an overwhelming sense of . . . was it joy? His mouth fell open at the possibility. He did still have it, this key to the great unknown. It was swinging from his neck on a thin thread, but it was still there. There was no ego here. There was no proving anything to anyone. This was who he was, and dammit it felt good, like mainlining a drug that he'd given up years ago.

Though he could fingerpick a little, he was most comfortable with a flat pick, and with Don Jorge's guitar on his lap, he felt his right hand hoping for one, as if the guitar were asking him to grant a wish.

Reaching into the guitar case with surprising urgency, he lifted open the center flap and felt around. He found an extra pack of strings, fingernail clippers, a tuner, and a small Dictaphone recorder, but no picks.

Curiosity got the best of him, and after pulling out the digital device, he turned it on, and the screen came alive. He pushed play, and in a few seconds he could hear Don Jorge tuning up. It was a very eerie feeling but also exhilarating, and he almost dashed out the door to find Alma. She would surely appreciate hearing her father play again.

Deciding not to bother her, Baxter lay down on his back with the guitar on his chest and the Dictaphone in his hand. He closed his eyes and listened to the dead man start into practicing a strumming pattern. Alma had been right. He wasn't very good, but he seemed to be determined, which was the next best thing, and Baxter thought it was beautiful, hearing a man of Don Jorge's age learning the guitar.

Baxter must have listened for a good three minutes, imagining what he had been like. He thought about Don Jorge's relationship to his trees. It was no wonder the man hadn't been the best father or husband. How could one really give his all to both?

Like a wet blanket thrown on a fire, these musings suddenly stamped out Baxter's wonderful feelings from a moment ago. The guitar resting on his lap felt like a slithering snake, and he pushed it away, almost knocking it off the bed before catching it at the last minute.

With his heart racing, he raised a hand to his face and pinched his temples. This was exactly the penance he would pay for returning to those old days in his mind. *All or nothing.* The three words that defined his relationship with the guitar.

A knock came on the door. Had Mia had a nightmare?

It took another knock for him to realize that the sound had come from the recording. Baxter stared at the Dictaphone and listened as Don Jorge stopped playing and said something in English like, "Come in."

A door opened and closed, and then Don Jorge spoke. The only word Baxter recognized was *dinero.* Money.

The person who had entered spoke. It was Rodolfo.

Baxter sat up, staring at the Dictaphone as the discussion quickly elevated until Don Jorge was screaming damn near at the top of his lungs. Baxter couldn't pick out even a word. He rewound a few seconds and tried again.

This time, a word stuck out in his mind: *robando.* He knew it because he'd had to use it months earlier to deal with some copper that had gone missing from a jobsite, and the English word was so close to it. *Robando* meant robbing or stealing. Was someone stealing from them? Or was Rodolfo stealing from his father?

The recording abruptly stopped. Perhaps Don Jorge had realized he'd been recording.

Now Baxter had a totally different reason to go play it for Alma, but he resisted the urge. If anything, this would be a sad reminder of her father and brother's relationship, and it would be no way for her to start her harvest.

He played the recording several more times, fighting off thoughts of his own father while piecing together more of a translation. Eventually, he realized he'd better put up the guitar before he woke and found it on the floor broken in half. He returned it to its case, put the recorder on the bedside table, undressed, and climbed into the sheets, hoping he could get a few hours of rest and maybe even sleep off his coming hangover.

But it took him a long time to fall asleep, because he couldn't stop wondering what the two men had been arguing about. He kept thinking about what Alma had told him on the roof, how Jorge had always talked about having some savings set aside, savings that they'd never found. Had Rodolfo stolen it from him?

If so, this was even more reason to get Mia out of there sooner than later.

Chapter 21

The Polyphenols of Life

He woke with a headache and the taste of guilt in his mouth, surely as bitter as a raw olive plucked from a tree.

He hadn't figured out the afterlife, and he had no idea what he believed, but he'd certainly had moments in the last three years when he was sure Sofia had been in the room. He could remember the chills that came over him when he'd felt her brush by one night as he limped toward their bed in Charleston, a stir in the air in a breezeless room. "Are you there, Sofe?" he'd asked.

Was she here in Spain with them? Could she see or hear his thoughts? Had she seen him laughing so with Alma? Or was she long gone, either paired up with an angel in heaven or folded into dust? Maybe she was nothing more than pure energy, recirculating back into the ethers. Either way, how foolish and small to think she would be concerned about her husband back in the real world. If anything, she'd be watching Mia, not him.

Baxter rolled over, trying to find a modicum of comfort on the hard rock that was his mattress. Rays from an orange sun shot through the cracks in the blinds, telling him it was time to get up and accomplish something. Even if he had nothing to do, he couldn't quiet the drill sergeant in his head, calling him lazy for letting the sun precede him.

He fell back to the night before, listening in his intoxicated state as Jorge and Rodolfo argued with each other. Why was Don Jorge so angry? What had Rodolfo done?

His head on the pillow, he played the recording again, hoping he might be able to understand more in this sober state, but the words were still a foreign blur.

Except for two words: *dinero* and *robando*.

It would be so easy, Baxter thought, to go downstairs and play the recording for Ester. He could smell the burning fire and knew she was drinking her sweet coffee. But he thought of what Rodolfo had said about staying out of their business, and Baxter reminded himself why he was here: to help his daughter. Better if he kept the recording to himself, at least for now.

He did, however, want to know the gist of the argument. With a clearer picture of the drama here, he'd get a better sense of how to contain it until their departure. And there was something else: Sofia would have wanted him to figure it out. Always believing in doing the right thing, she never would have allowed even her own half brother to get away with stealing from the family. So for Sofia's sake, and also Alma's and Ester's, Baxter decided it was his duty to investigate.

Looking on the side of the recorder, he pulled back a rubber flap to figure out the required cord needed to transfer the file to his computer. From there, he could send it over to Alan back in South Carolina, who could get one of the framing guys to translate it for him.

⌒

In the kitchen, Ester was creating another one of her marvelous tortillas, poaching sliced potatoes in a cast-iron pan filled several inches high with a dark-green olive oil. From there, she'd strain out the oil, let the potatoes cool for a little while, mix them with eggs, and then cook them in a cast-iron pan like a frittata. The idea of tearing into a tortilla greatly appealed to the hungover part of him.

Mia sat at the kitchen counter and was extra bubbly, having had a good night of sleep without any nightmares. While she fed Paco torn pieces from Alberto's *chapata* bread, she taught Baxter and Ester about mermaid's purses. "That's what they call the egg cases, Iaia. They're like these weird sacs—not exactly chicken eggs. The sharks lay them at the bottom of the ocean. After a few years or something like that, the cute little baby sharks swim out."

"Cute?" Baxter said. He thought her inability to understand time was much cuter. She often said things well beyond her years, but she didn't yet totally grasp how hours and days and years fit together.

Mia said to Iaia, "It's only certain kinds of sharks. Some are born in the mom's belly."

Baxter was often blown away by what Mia could remember from years earlier. "We used to find them on Folly Beach, didn't we, honey?"

"That's right."

Baxter surprised himself with a memory that felt nice as it left his lips. "Your mom knew all that stuff, didn't she? She could name every bird—"

"Every shell," Mia added proudly.

He saw Sofia lifting a horseshoe crab out of the sand and showing it to Mia. They were both water signs, Baxter and Sofia. Where he was a Pisces and found tremendous peace in sitting there soaking up the sound of the waves, she was a Scorpio who always wanted to be digging into the sand or plunging into the water. He remembered the look on her face when she came up from duck-diving her Al Merrick board into a wave as she worked her way out to the lineup. It was as if God was talking to her down there under the water. Then she'd go on to ride waves better than anybody else out there.

He almost enjoyed the memory until he thought about what he'd done with her boards, how he'd given them to one of her surfer buddies.

Dammit, he should have held on to them and let Mia learn on those boards.

Iaia, who seemed especially chipper today, turned from her position watching over the frying potatoes. "One day, you'll have to take me to Charleston."

"Yeah," Mia said excitedly, "you'd love it. We can show you the house where I grew up, where my mom used to garden. You'd love the food: pimento cheese, deviled eggs, grits casserole, fried okra, catfish."

Ester watched her with happy eyes. "I have no idea what these things are, but I trust you."

Mia set her elbows on the counter. "Maybe you could come for a long time. Or even come live with us, if you want to. We have a *huge* house."

"All right, Mia," Baxter said. "That's enough."

"What?" she said.

Baxter gave her a look. It was one thing to offer a polite invitation, but what if Ester actually took them up on it? They'd never be able to let Sofia go if their house became some sort of American outpost for the Arroyos.

When Alma came down, she greeted Baxter just the same as she always did, a sweet smile and a "buenos días," making him wonder if the previous late-night talk had even happened at all. Of course she had other things on her mind, as it was the first day of harvest.

She looked very cool and practiced, and when Baxter asked her if she was nervous, she shook her head and smiled. "I live for this."

He'd probably answered the *exact* same way a hundred times when people had asked him if getting on stage made him nervous, and he once again found himself feeling a hint of jealousy. He thought back to the night before, the way Don Jorge's guitar felt in his hands. And he remembered hearing Javier Martín playing so wonderfully. Part of him really did want to go to the concert.

All or nothing, he reminded himself.

Starting her routine, Alma reached for the olive oil near the stove and painted it onto Mia's smiling face and then rubbed it onto her hands. She did the same to herself, leaving a sheen on her freckled cheeks.

Baxter realized he'd been looking at her when Alma turned his way and held up the bottle. "Give me your hands." She rubbed them with a generous dose of the oil, meeting his eyes and giving his hands a little squeeze at the end. Then she leaned over and painted his face with her fingers, Mia laughing all the while.

"You look much younger, Daddy."

"Do I? I feel like someone's about to sprinkle rosemary on me and throw me on the grill." He turned to Alma, still feeling the place where she'd squeezed his hand. "How long do you have between picking and getting the olives to the mill?" She'd talked more than once about the importance of crushing the freshly picked olives as soon as possible.

Alma poured herself a small glass of orange juice and shot it back. "Four hours maximum. Once we start, it's a race to get things done." She set a hand on Mia's head. "Do you and your dad want to harvest one of the first trees?"

Mia turned to her aunt. "For sure."

"Come find me up the road in about thirty minutes, okay? I have to run."

—

When Mia went upstairs to get dressed, Baxter found Ester in her office, a small room down a hallway past the kitchen. She sat at a secretary desk with a tall hutch, its slots and open shelves spilling out with loose papers, pens, and the ilk. Paco lay at her feet and lifted his head at the intrusion.

"Can I ask you about something?" Baxter said, glancing around the room, noticing on one wall several photos of family and a painting of

Mother Mary. Below them a Spanish novel lay open-faced on a baroque sofa with elaborately carved wood and gold-tasseled pillows.

Ester turned and lowered her reading glasses to the tip of her nose. *"Claro que sí."* Of course.

He put his hand on the doorframe. "Your neighbor, Don Diego. I don't know if I mentioned that he and I played a game of chess yesterday. I realized as he and I were talking—or trying to, considering the language barrier—he doesn't know who we are. I told him we were the American side of the family. He seemed kind of surprised, so I left it at that. Have you spoken to him? Since he was so close to your husband, I want to avoid putting more of my foot in my mouth. I thought I'd better let you know."

She'd been nodding the whole time, and when he finished, she removed her glasses, letting them rest around her neck by a beaded string. "I haven't spoken to him about it, but I'll catch him up today." She rubbed her eyes. "Honestly, I've been putting it off, because I know he won't be happy with me for keeping it from Jorge."

Baxter dipped his head. "I'm sure he'll understand when you explain that it happened after you'd gone to school. Everyone else seems to have taken it okay."

She gave a half smile that faded as quickly as it came; then she turned back to her desk. "I'll talk to Diego today."

Baxter thanked her. "Everything okay? I hope I didn't mess up by telling him."

"It's fine, don't worry about it." She didn't bother turning back to him.

"Good. So we'll see you in about fifteen to go find Alma?"

Another nod, even more subtle this time.

～

With Paco and his wagging tail following along, they went to find Alma. It was a little after nine. A patch of gray clouds crept in from the west, one of them momentarily blocking the sun. Past the garden and around a bend in the grove, Baxter heard the machines running and followed their sound. They soon found Alma on the gravel road, pointing to a few trees and talking to a group of harvesters wearing neon-green vests and holding long black sticks. Behind them were the two yellow umbrella harvesters.

Baxter and company watched from a distance as Alma orchestrated her harvest like a maestra conducting her symphony. Men climbed up into the mechanical harvesters and drove toward the first trees. The harvester closest to them moved slowly to grip the trunk with its giant pinchers; then the umbrella tarp opened up and formed a full net around the base of the tree. Alma and three other harvesters surrounded the tree at a safe distance on the other side. The machine shook the tree, and Baxter could feel tremors in the ground thirty feet away. At the same time, Alma and the other men and women hit the higher branches. The olives rained down into the black tarp, and Baxter's and Mia's mouths fell agape at this incredibly foreign vision.

For thirty minutes they watched with astonishment as the harvesters moved from tree to tree, collecting their bounty. Baxter couldn't stop watching Alma, who seemed to be having the time of her life. No, she was definitely not nervous. In fact, she was exactly where she was supposed to be.

Breaking away from the action, Alma approached Baxter and Mia with two poles and a net folded up in her hands. The three of them spread the net around the base of one of the trees. Alma explained that she didn't like to use the mechanical harvesters for the older trees, as they were more fragile. She took one of the poles to demonstrate her method.

"You don't want to break any of the branches, but you don't have to be gentle. Strike them so that the pole moves along the branch and doesn't crack against it." She wound back and slapped the tree, and olives poured down onto the black net. She did it again and again with the expertise of one who'd been doing it all her life.

Alma handed the pole to Mia. "Do you think you have it?"

"I think so." Mia struck the tree, but only a couple of olives fell. Alma stood behind her and placed her hands next to Mia's. They whacked the tree together with a much more successful result, and Mia squealed with delight. Baxter cheered her on.

As he tried his hand at it, Alma said to Mia, "Remind your father he needs to use more of his brains and less of his muscle. Don't let him break my trees."

"Good luck teaching him," Mia said. She hit a branch and knocked down more olives.

With his pole ready to strike, he said, "I'm being gentle, ladies."

"No, you're not," Mia said. "You're playing baseball over there."

Baxter feigned offense as he tried again.

"There you go, Daddy. Practice what you preach; brains over brawn. That's what you say to me."

He side-eyed her with a grin.

Alma patted Baxter's back. "I'll return in a few. Mia, keep an eye on him."

As she raced off, Baxter and Mia continued their work. Whack, whack, whack; the olives showered down onto the tarp.

～

"This is the life," Baxter said after a while. "What do you say, *mi hija*? Decent vacation?"

She stopped to look at him, her breath heavy. "The best of the best of the best. I don't ever want to leave."

Her response was a little bit more than he'd been searching for. Maybe he had done something right for once, taking her here. He was surprised to hear himself say, "If only your mom could see us now. I don't know if I told you, but she wanted to go to Spain."

Mia lowered the stick, resting one end on the ground. "Wait, what?"

"Yeah. We'd always wanted to do Paris for our honeymoon, but when she got back the tests and learned that she was Iberian, she was suddenly talking about the Costa del Sol. All the time, the Costa del Sol."

"Where's that?"

"Way south, near the bottom tip that almost touches Africa. Marbella is where she wanted to go. I forget what they're called, but there are these beautiful mountains just on the other side of the city. So stunning. She had this kind of . . . uh . . . hoity-toity side to her. She liked the idea of a marina full of yachts and a big promenade dotted with seafood restaurants and expensive shops. She wanted to shop in the morning and then eat langostinos while looking out over the Mediterranean toward Africa. Then take a siesta in a fancy hotel. The Spanish in her was strong. I promised her that we'd go and . . . we just never got around to it."

That was around the time Sofia had gotten pregnant, Baxter thought.

"Maybe we could go next time?"

Seeing his daughter gobble up his words, a lightness seemed to come over him, as if he might float away. "Yeah, I think that's a great idea."

Mia gave a very genuine smile, and Baxter swelled with pride at what he and Sofia had created. "I'm so proud of you, sweetie. Your mom would be too. Here you are in a foreign country with people you barely know, and you're bringing everyone together. You should see the way Iaia lights up when she's around you. This is what it's about, honey, giving back, doing things for other people. You've come here to fulfill your mother's dream, and you aren't afraid at all. And now you're giving Iaia new life, not to mention Alma and the rest of your family too. I don't know if I have anything left to teach you. If you want, you can go ahead to college. Though, as I've said, you know I'm following you wherever you go."

Mia leaned on her pole. "Is that really true? What about work?"

"Are you kidding me? You think I'm going to let you leave Greenville without me? By the time you really go to college, when you're eighteen, I'll be retired. Even when you get older and fall in love—God forbid—and get married and have kids, I'll live next door." He was getting emotional now. That was what he and Sofia had always joked about, that they'd follow her wherever she went.

"I swear to you, I will be the best grandfather in the world. I'll be like Iaia, playing on the floor with your kids, stacking Lincoln Logs or LEGO bricks or whatever it is they'll be doing in twenty years. Probably building holograms or something else futuristic. Work won't even be in my purview. My job will be grandfathering."

Mia lifted up her pole and started looking for more olives in the tree. There were still areas dense with clusters. "You'll be a great one, just like you're a great dad." Her compliment was a kiss on the cheek. "And I want to be with you always, too, but we'd better get back to work."

She swung back and yipped with excitement as she made a success-ful connection. "Did you see that? Let's see what you got."

"You're on." Baxter gripped the pole hard and wound back and struck the tree, causing another downpour of olives. But something else happened, a pop in the shoulder that hurt like hell and spread down his back like fire.

"Are you okay?" she asked, hearing him wince.

Baxter reached for the pain just below his neck. "You might have to finish on your own." As Mia returned to her work, he sat against the trunk of another tree, massaging his shoulder and watching his daugh-ter until Alma returned.

"Your father already ran out of steam?" Alma asked, shaking her head at Baxter with a beautiful grin.

Mia turned to her, jabbing her pole in the dirt. "He hurt his shoulder. I had to do the whole tree myself."

Baxter pressed up to a stand. "Mia challenged me, and I think I swung too hard."

"Pobrecito," she said, puffing out her bottom lip in jest. She patted his cheek. "This is why women rule the world."

⌐

Less than four hours after they began harvesting, a caravan made up of Alma's Defender and two flatbed trucks loaded with bins of ripe olives drove toward Cadeir. Baxter was glad to see that his phone got service not long after they reached the main road. After listening to his voice mails, he took the opportunity to pull out his laptop and plug into his hot spot. The first thing he did was send the audio file from Don Jorge's Dictaphone to Alan and ask him to get one of the guys to translate it. Rodolfo's warning about minding his own business played in Baxter's head, but he couldn't help himself. His curiosity about what the two men had been arguing about was a pesky mosquito that wouldn't go away.

They pulled into the parking lot of an old stone building on the outskirts of town. Other than a gas station with an outdoor café across the street, there were no other buildings in sight. A barrel-chested man stood under an open garage door. He and Alma exchanged a wave.

"That's Joaquín," she said. "His great-grandfather used to crush my great-grandfather's olives. And probably used to yell at him just like I yell at Joaquín."

Baxter and Mia watched as Alma orchestrated the show, first inspecting all the equipment, and indeed scolding Joaquín when she saw something she didn't like. After hosing down a big tank herself, Alma watched as Joaquín climbed into a forklift, lifted the bins one by one, and drove them through the garage door toward a line of waiting machinery. Alma called Baxter and Mia over and explained the process as if they were looking through the glass of a car wash.

"I told you," she said. "He's lazy. The hoppers weren't even clean. This is why I want my own mill one day. But now we're ready."

Once Joaquín dumped the olives into a hopper, a conveyor belt ran them under a leaf blower that started the cleaning process. Afterward, they were dropped into a water bath before continuing to a vibrating screen that removed any last dirt. From there the olives went into the hammer mill crusher.

"A problem comes up at this point," Alma said a few minutes later, watching her olives turn to paste. "The olive and water molecules are too small and have become hard to separate, which is why we need the malaxer." She led them to the next machine, where they could see paste filling the tank. "This will help the oil molecules bind back together, so we can separate the oil and water."

She checked the temperature with a temperature gun and said over the loud noise, "We have some warm water running through the walls around the paste, but we have to be careful it doesn't heat the oil too much, or it will hurt the flavor." Once the tank was mostly full, she hit a switch, and several large blades stirred the paste.

From there, the paste was run through two more centrifuges. The whole process took about forty-five minutes, and Baxter enjoyed watching Alma walking the tightrope of harvest, a phone in her hand to manage the workers back on the estate while making sure the process here at the mill ran smoothly.

And then the big moment came. Baxter and Mia joined Alma and Joaquín to watch the long silver cylinder spout, waiting for the finished oil. It came out in a cloudy bright green, and everyone in the building clapped and yelled. Alma produced a small wineglass and stuck it under the oil, filling it halfway. She took a closed-eyed sip and then grinned with satisfaction. Mia followed suit, looking equally happy.

When Baxter took his sip and the oil coated his mouth, he was bowled over. The spiciness and bitterness burned, but only slightly, and the herbal and grassy flavors made his mouth water. But more than that, he was tasting something far greater than a cooking ingredient. This oil had captured the Arroyos and their land so precisely, like the perfect photograph taken in the perfect light. He wondered if it would taste this way back in Greenville, when they opened a bottle upon their return. Would he so instantly be ushered to the estate and all its divinity?

"What do you think?" Alma asked.

Baxter thought he'd only ruin the experience with his limited vocabulary. How could anyone describe such flavor? Hell, it wasn't even about flavor. It was an experience, a story told in a moment. So with the reverence he felt it was due, he simply patted his chest and smiled.

"I know," she said with obvious satisfaction. "You'll never have anything better in your life than great oil on the first day of harvest." She took an empty glass bottle and filled it up. "This will be for tonight."

Baxter felt something stirring inside of him, as if that sip of oil had broken him free in some way.

Chapter 22

A GROWING DISTURBANCE

At dinner, with candles flickering between them, Alma, Mia, Ester, and Baxter sat chatting after a long meal. Rodolfo had just left. Paco searched for scraps around their feet. Mia sat on Baxter's lap and regaled them with a story about how one of her classmates had gotten locked into the bathroom at school.

Crumbs and flakes of salt covered the table from where they'd broken Alberto's bread and dipped it into the new oil, or *nuovo*, as Alma had called it. Their bread plates carried a bright-green sheen from where puddles of the *nuovo* had been lapped up. Along with the bread, they'd had a salad dressed with lemon and oil, and chestnut soup topped with fresh chestnuts that had fallen from the trees near the garden.

"Ester," Baxter said, "yet again one of the finest meals of my life."

"We sure could use you back home," Mia said. "We have more than enough room."

Ester chuckled. "Wouldn't that be fun?"

Mia showed a smile that could melt a glacier. "For as long as you want."

Ready to leave the conversation behind, Baxter said, "Mia, it's been a long day. I think it's time to brush your teeth and hit the hay. Can I tuck you in?"

"No, no," Ester said kindly, opening her arms from across the table. "You had her all day. If you'll allow me, I'd like to read her a book, and then I'm going to go to sleep as well. How does that sound, Mia?"

"Sorry, Daddy," Mia said, twisting to him. "Catch you tomorrow?"

"Suit yourself, little princess," he said, letting Mia go to her grandmother. He had to admit it wasn't the worst thing in the world to have a little help for once.

"You okay?" Baxter asked Ester, thinking it was quite early for her to retire.

She nodded. "Long day, that's all."

Ester and Mia went hand in hand up the stairs, leaving Alma and Baxter to clean up. Baxter felt instantly awkward in the kitchen. Hiding these forbidden feelings was easy enough to do with Ester and Mia around, but in the sudden quiet, he felt exposed. She was Sofia's half sister, for God's sake.

With these thoughts weighing him down, he helped Alma carry the dishes to the sink, and then he turned on the water to start the long process of waiting for it to warm.

"Don't worry about me," he said to her with a sly smile, "I'll just be here until sunrise waiting on hot water."

"So funny, aren't you?" Alma collected the silverware from the dishes and set them in the sink, brushing so close to him he could smell the orange scent of her hair.

"Mia sometimes thinks so. Seriously, you can go ahead and hit the sack. I know you're tired."

"I'm fine," she said. "I enjoy doing the dishes."

"That makes one of us." He turned to see her scraping the salad bowl into the trash, the last of the shaved carrots and olives. "You know, if you had a disposal, you wouldn't have to do that."

She cut him a look. "And if you'd stop fighting Spain, you might see she'll open up to you. You don't need hot water or disposals or hot sauce or dryers to be happy."

"Maybe not, but you do need pancakes. And Cheez-Its."

"I know, I know . . . and big cars and automatic transmission. The list goes on." She set the bowl in the sink, her body close to his again. "Don't worry, you'll be back home soon enough."

As if to prove a point, he said, "Being here is good for me. And though the idea frightens me, you make me want to make music again—or at least to be creative again." He shook his head. "I thought that part of me was gone, but seeing what you do . . . tasting that oil today. Good God. I want to make something."

She didn't say anything, so he kept going. "But it's scary. Music isn't something that I can just dabble in. It was my everything, and if I start playing again, I'm worried I won't be able to stop."

She laughed.

"What's so funny? I'm serious, like maybe I should pick up metal-lurgy or . . . painting."

"Maybe finger painting," she said, and he could sense her smiling without even looking at her. "You don't have to go jump back on a tour bus tomorrow, do you? One step at a time. Why don't you come with me tomorrow night? To see Javier Martín. I'm telling you . . . he might have the answers you seek. Just get back into that world a little. Put down your triple whatever Starbucks drink and take a breath; it's not all or nothing."

That sure was the way it felt.

"Look at you," she said. "You're coming alive. Just the idea of get-ting music back in your life is lighting you up. Look at your eyes. You need it."

He blushed, uncomfortably so. She pointed a finger at his chest. "When will you ever get this chance again?" she asked. For the first time since he'd met her, Alma was pushing. "My mother will take very good care of Mia."

He could barely look at her, but he did.

"Do this for you," she said.

More than anything, continuing to say no would prove to her that he was completely dried up, and he didn't want her to think that. So he held up his hands and said, "Oh, what the hell . . ."

⁓

It was a little after ten the next day, and Baxter and Mia were returning from a hike through the forest. The sky was striped with cirrus clouds; birdsong filled the air. They were holding hands, and Baxter couldn't have been more at peace. This was life at its best. They'd stopped several times to watch birds or to study the tops of the mountains. They'd even seen a deer.

"Are there olive trees in the United States?" she asked as they left the trees and joined the gravel road that led back to the villa, which had just come into view. Binoculars hung from Mia's neck. A pink headband held back her wild hair and added to the green and violet and navy blue of her attire.

"Sure. I don't think on the East Coast, but definitely in California. Why?" Baxter watched a plane cross the sky, painting a puffy contrail to the east.

"I'm just trying to figure out what I'm going to do when I get older. Would it be okay if I was a farmer like Aunt Alma?"

"Of course it would be okay. You can do whatever you'd like. I was hoping you'd lean toward bullfighter or chess grand master, but an olive farmer is cool too. Alma's kind of amazing, isn't she?" Baxter could see her face in his mind's eye, and he shook his head at the absurdity of life, Sofia's half sister affecting him so.

"It's in my blood, Dad. What if we came back for most of the summer, like the whole summer, and I could study under her? Then we could come back again for harvest. I won't miss any school, so you won't have to worry. In the meantime, I was thinking it would be neat if we could start a garden. It was her first job when she was my age."

219

"I think a garden is a super idea."

Mia nodded, and he saw a sudden shift in her demeanor, her head lowering, her pace slowing.

Baxter stopped. "What?" She sometimes did this, looking for attention, but he knew there was substance behind her mood now. "What is it?"

She stared at her white shoes, and he saw her laces had come undone. "I don't want to say."

He knelt to give them a quick tie. "Oh, now you have to say. You think I'm letting you take another step. C'mon, cough it up."

When he stood again, she raised her gaze, her brown eyes a window to almost everything he cared about in this world. "Well . . . I wish we could stay longer."

"Oh boy." Couldn't they catch a break?

"I'm not trying to be a jerk. I know we can't. I know you have to get back to work. And I'm very happy you brought me here. It's just I hate that we live so far away from our family."

Worry came alive in his chest, the idea that she could slide back so easily to the way she'd been. "I know you do. And I do, too, believe it or not." Surprised he'd said it, he looked at her. "They're good people, aren't they?"

She nodded subtly.

Baxter could already see his little girl gazing sadly out the window as they waved goodbye on Tuesday, shedding tears on the way to the airport in Madrid.

"C'mere," he said, pulling her into a hug. He squeezed her tight, feeling her heartbeat against his. "Something tells me Spain is going to be a very big part of our future, no matter what. I don't know why we wouldn't come every year. Hey, what if I found a Spanish teacher who would come to the house?"

"For both of us?" she asked.

"Yes, for both of us. I can't let you have all the fun. I mean, it might take me twenty years, but I'm willing to start learning." As he said it, the idea warmed his heart, something they could do together, a way to hold on to what they'd found here.

"Wanna hear me roll my *R*s?" Without a response, he tried again to let his tongue flicker against the back of his teeth, but he felt like a cow chewing on cud.

Just as Mia let out what seemed like a genuine laugh, a very angry voice stung the air. They both turned to see Alma and Rodolfo facing each other outside of the offices. Alma was jabbing a finger at him, screaming at her brother, who had his hands out to his sides.

A protective instinct came over Baxter as Rodolfo started firing back. Even if he *could* understand Spanish, Baxter was too far away to make out what they were arguing about.

"Why are they yelling, Daddy?"

"I have no idea." But he knew he didn't want Mia involved. This was exactly what he'd been trying to avoid. "Let me see what's going on. Would you stay here for me?"

"But, Daddy."

"Please, honey. Just hang here for a minute. I'll be right back."

With Mia watching him, Baxter jogged down the road until he was close enough to say something. "What's going on?"

"My brother es *un idiota*," Alma said, turning toward him.

"*¿Yo soy idiota?*" Rodolfo said back and then added more venomous Spanish.

Baxter stopped close to Alma, who stood by an ivy-covered brick wall that stretched out away from the house. "You okay?"

She nodded, but she was beyond distressed. Spinning back to her brother, she launched into another verbal attack. Veins rose on Rodolfo's forehead as he yelled back at her.

"Hey!" Baxter said, hearing the growl in his own voice. "You don't talk to her that way."

Rodolfo whipped his head toward Baxter like he was pointing a gun. "I told you to *stay* out of it!"

Baxter stepped closer. "Where I come from, you don't speak to women like that."

Alma side-eyed him. "I don't need to be rescued, Baxter. This is our business."

He raised his hands apologetically. "Okay." He glanced to see Mia watching them. Feeling like he'd certainly overstepped his bounds, he started walking back that way, albeit slowly.

Listening over his shoulder, he heard Rodolfo yell something at Alma in Spanish. She responded with equal viciousness. As much as Baxter wanted to intervene, she'd made her point clear. He listened to their voices trail off as they took their argument inside of the offices. When he looked back, he saw Ester staring down from an upstairs window.

—

"What happened, Daddy?" Mia asked when he reached her.

"I don't know, honey. Brothers and sisters sometimes fight. Let's not worry about it. Why don't we just keep walking for a while?"

Baxter led Mia past the house and down the road to the area with cell reception. He figured he could make a couple of calls while they were killing time.

He hadn't even been thinking about Don Diego, but the man was sitting there at his table, as usual. An idea came to Baxter. "Hey, honey, wanna go play some chess with the neighbor? I bet he'd love it. He seems kind of lonely."

"Yeah, I guess. Well, actually, sure."

"He's good, though. Don't get discouraged if he beats you. He's had a lot of practice, and he's way better than me."

"I'm way better than you, too, Daddy. It's a large club."

He rapidly spun his head her way. "Wow, ouch, and wow. Don't you forget, little lassie, I taught you everything you know."

She took his hand. "I'm just kidding. I think you're a great chess player. Just a little distracted. The only reason I beat you is because you're always looking at your phone."

He was listening to her, but most of him was focused on the feeling of her little fingers interlaced into his. She needed him and counted on him. And loved him. He could feel all that and more surging through him and rising up his arm and settling into his heart. It was a daunting responsibility, and he hoped to God he was up to the challenge.

Diego sat with crossed arms at the table, looking out over his vineyard. "Don Diego, I present to you Grand Master Mia Shaw. Do you want to play a game of chess?" Baxter pointed to Mia and then to him.

"*Sí!*" The man thrust up from his chair and bowed, reaching for her hand. He didn't stop at shaking it. He pulled her in and patted her hand, telling her in Spanish it was a pleasure to meet her.

She instantly warmed to him, responding, "*Encantada.*" Good to meet you.

Delighting at her linguistic efforts, Diego made quick conversation in Spanish, asking her age and if she liked Spain; then he gestured for her to take a seat across from him. "*Uno momento,*" he said, holding up a finger and then racing inside.

Don Diego came back out a moment later with a tray carrying a carafe of water, a basket of bread, a bowl of grated tomatoes mixed with oil, and a shaker of salt.

"Oh, wow," Baxter said. "How'd you do that so fast?"

Of course, Diego didn't understand what Baxter had said. The man excused himself again and came back out this time with the chessboard. He set it on the table between himself and Mia, and she helped him arrange the pieces.

As if he were her boxing coach, Baxter sat in the third chair and inched toward her side. With the language barrier, there wasn't much to do but get started, so she made the first move. Don Diego chuckled proudly as he shifted his pawn and waited for her response. He glanced over at Baxter, saying something about the serious look in her eye. They'd both learned to talk with their hands, as it helped break through the communication barrier.

"I told you," Baxter said, knowing Diego wouldn't understand but saying it anyway, "she's not one to take lightly."

As the two faced off, Baxter excused himself to make a call. It turned out most of the property on the side of Diego's house carried a strong signal. Though it was only past six in the morning in South Carolina, Baxter knew Alan was up.

"Hey, Baxter. Good morning."

"Mornin'," Baxter responded. "I'm not waking you up, am I? I figured you'd be eating lunch by now."

"Nah. We're up. Actually, we're leaving the hospital. Amy's mother just passed."

Baxter stopped in the grass. "Oh, brother. I'm so sorry."

"Yeah, thanks. But don't worry. I got things under control here."

"Oh, c'mon, Alan. You take care of your family. I'll book a flight home right after we get off the phone."

"Nah, Bax. We've known this was coming. Don't cut your trip short."

Baxter was already thinking about what he'd say to Mia and the rest of the family. "I appreciate that, but you need to be there for Amy. It's no big deal for us to come home a little early."

"Baxter, I'm telling you right now, everything is fine." He launched into what they had going on the next few days: the spec houses, a few inspections, a big project in Spartanburg starting up.

"Alan, thanks for covering for me, but I'm telling you . . . if you want me to come home, I'll be there. All the stuff we're doing doesn't matter as much as family." He really meant that. Being here among Sofia's people, among Mia's people, maybe even *his* people, was giving him a sense of belonging that he didn't know existed. That was what family was supposed to do, wasn't it? He'd never really known it until now.

"And that's why I think you need to stay where you are," Alan said.

Baxter nodded. "I'll talk to the other guys and make sure they step it up."

"They already are, Bax. Don't worry, we're working hard for you."

Baxter greatly appreciated the comment and their dedication. Alan was very possibly capable of running the show with Baxter out of town, and he regretted ever doubting him.

"Oh, and I got your email about the recording," Alan continued. "What's that all about?"

Baxter glanced back at Diego and Mia, who were focused on the game. He walked toward the property line to escape earshot. "Honestly, I don't know, but it's not all peaches and cream over here. I can tell you that. Long story, but one of the guys is causing all kinds of problems, and I just want a better hold of what's going on. They're speaking so quickly I can barely pick up a word."

"Okay," Alan said. "Let me take the kids to school, and I'll get on it."

"Yeah, no rush. Take care of your family. The rest can wait."

"I appreciate it."

Baxter ended the call and returned to the chess table. "How we doin' over here?"

Neither of them responded or even acknowledged his presence. Baxter saw that Diego was going after Mia's king aggressively. His bishop was dangerously close. Mia had left her knight exposed, but Baxter didn't want to correct her. Instead he sat and watched in silence.

Diego handed him the basket of bread and told him to eat up. Thanking him, Baxter spread the grated tomatoes over the bread and then topped it with flaked salt. He took a bite, thinking this was one of the things he'd surely take back to the US. Why had he never thought to grate tomatoes?

Breaking Baxter's concentration, Diego started into a question he had to repeat in multiple variations before Baxter caught the drift. Mia beat him to it, though, and said, "He's asking how old Mommy was when she died."

Had Baxter been more proficient in Spanish, he might have said that Diego was overstepping his bounds, that the question certainly wasn't one for Mia's ears, but looking over at Mia, Baxter seemed to be the only one bothered.

"She was thirty-eight," Mia said nonchalantly, then cast a look at Baxter. "What's that in Spanish?"

"*Treinta y ocho,*" Baxter said.

Diego grunted sadly in response.

Baxter gave a shrug, pretty much saying, "C'est la vie." As if it were that simple. And yet it was. Death was an inevitable part of life, and sometimes it came sooner than you hoped.

As Baxter washed his first few bites down with water, he noticed how Diego and Mia were both leaned over the chessboard, stroking their cheeks with their index fingers. He thought it would make for a heck of a cool picture, so he stood and nonchalantly extracted his phone back out of his pocket.

Before he could grab the shot, Mia looked over to him, ready to smile for the camera.

"No, no, no, keep doing what you were doing."

She returned her eyes to the chessboard, but the moment was gone. Diego had already sat up, too, and was capturing one of her rooks with his bishop. *"Jaque mate,"* he said.

Mia looked over at Baxter like she'd failed him. He, in turn, glared at Diego, who should have given her a break.

The man held out his hand, and Mia graciously accepted. "Good job, señor."

Chapter 23

Music Heals the Soul

Always the safari guide standing up in the Jeep, pointing out elephants in the room, the first thing Mia asked Alma when they got back to the house was, "Are you okay, Aunt Alma? What happened?"

Ester was there with Alma in the living room, the two of them clearly into a deep discussion. Baxter had noticed that Rodolfo's car was gone.

Baxter said, "Honey, that's not our business."

Alma glanced at her mother and then knelt down and put her hands on Mia's shoulders. "Yeah, *cariño*. I'm sorry you had to see that. Your uncle and I are arguing about work. *Ven aquí.*" Come here. Alma lifted Mia up into her arms. "Can you believe your father is going to a concert tonight?" she asked.

"Why can't I come?" Mia asked, her arm around Alma's shoulders.

"Tonight is very late, more for adults, but next time I promise I'll take you. I think you would love flamenco." Alma lightly pinched Mia's nose. "Deal?"

Mia nodded and then said strongly, "I am glad my dad's going. It'll be good for him. He needs some fun."

Baxter looked over at Ester, who watched with crossed arms. She gave a weak smile to Baxter and turned away.

What in the world was going on?

He didn't find out until he and Alma climbed into the Defender around nine that night to pick up her friends and then make the long drive into the neighboring *comunidad* of Murcia.

"There's something I should tell you," Alma said. "An offer came in to buy the estate."

Baxter bent his head to her. "Oh . . . is it for sale?"

She nodded sadly, and he felt left out of a very important issue that must be at the forefront of the family's mind. "I had no idea."

She met his eyes and then returned them to the road. "It's from a group from Jaén who will destroy this place. But if she can get them up in price, my mother will probably accept."

The news that the estate was for sale had come out of nowhere, and now Ester was about to sign it away. Was this what he'd sensed had been off since his arrival?

He didn't even know where to start with his questions. "How long have you been trying to sell it? I kind of figured you were tied to this place?"

The headlights sprayed onto the dark and winding road as he waited for her to answer. "Yeah, I am," she eventually said, "but my mother decided earlier in the year, probably even as we buried my father."

He felt a prickling sadness. He'd come to like it here and had even found an attraction to the land and the villa. Selfishly, he also felt sad for Mia, who was looking at this place like a new discovery that would become a part of their lives, like a lake house you visit in the summers.

Then it occurred to him how much it must hurt Alma. She was losing her land just like he'd lost his music. "I'm sorry," Baxter whispered. "It must be really hard."

She shrugged. "What do you do?"

"There's got to be something, if you don't want to sell it. This is your family's land. Why is your mom so eager to get rid of it?"

"It's complicated. Mostly because she doesn't think the two of us can run the estate without her, and without killing each other. And she's probably right. The same thing happened with my father and his siblings. To avoid this exact thing, my grandparents made the decision to give the estate to the oldest—my father. To an extent, it worked. They kept the estate alive but destroyed the family. My uncles barely ever talked to him again; only one sister came to the funeral. He even wrote them occasional checks, which they happily cashed, but the damage was done. Ester has this high hope that one day my brother and I will actually get along. She thinks selling the estate is the answer."

"It doesn't seem like your brother wants to be involved. Why don't you buy him out or find another investor?"

"We tried for a while, believe me. The problem is we're not making enough money." She laughed half-heartedly. "Who would want to invest in an old estate that's falling apart? The only lucrative part of this business is the land."

"Why not sell half the land?"

She shook her head. "No, it's protected. We aren't allowed to divide it."

Baxter wished he knew someone who could help, but he understood their dilemma. If the business was lucrative, maybe he could talk someone back home into investing into the romance of the olive oil business, but he was having a hard time seeing any upside of such an investment. She hadn't mentioned a price, but he could only imagine it was well into the millions. What a shame. It would have been so nice to know he and Mia could return every year, such an easy way to fill his daughter's cup.

"That's not right. There has to be a way to help you keep what's yours. I know how much this land means to you."

"It's not mine, though." She took a big swig of her water from a bottle in the cup holder. "It's my mother's."

He turned her way. "Yeah, I get that you're not an owner yet, but I'm not sure land deeds are the only way to measure ownership, especially in the case of a piece of land that runs in your genes. If I was your mother, and if Rodolfo doesn't want to be involved, I'd let him go. Give you the estate."

"My mother would never do that. You see how much she supports him."

"Then it's him who should give it up, give it to you."

"Right," she said sarcastically. "He feels he's entitled to his part of the inheritance—and I guess he is."

Baxter pulled at his seat belt to loosen it. "I get that he thinks he deserves money, and your mom doesn't want to kick him to the curb, but what if he agreed to be a silent partner, and you pay him dividends?"

She shook her head. "We explored that option. I begged for it, but he hates the idea, and then he blows up and my mother ends up crying and . . . you know, it's a cycle that never ends—unless my mother sets us free by finally removing the burden. Believe me, I appreciate you caring, but you'll drive yourself mad. My brother hated my father and he hates this place, and nothing will change that. And that's why we have to sell. Simple as that."

"What is it with your brother? I get that your dad was hard on him, but he's gone. Why not move on?" Even as he said it, Baxter knew that he himself hadn't moved on from his own troubled relationship with his father.

"I don't know. He wants to be set free. I've never seen him work so hard in his life since my mother gave him the green light to find a buyer."

"What is he wanting to do?"

They came around a big bend. "He says he wants to open up a men's boutique in Madrid. Hand-tailored suits, fine shoes and scarves, that kind of thing."

Baxter still couldn't believe the topic hadn't been discussed until now. "What will everyone do? What will *you* do?"

"My mother will probably go to Madrid with my brother. She says she misses the city, but I think she also wants to be there for him too. And I . . . I'm not sure. Well, of course I'll keep farming olives, but I don't know where."

He couldn't shake the idea of how wrong it was that she'd lose her land. "The buyers will probably want to keep you on, no?"

She looked like she'd taken a bite out of a rotten apple as she said, "To make lamp oil and ruin my family's name? No. I have no interest." She gave a shrug, like it didn't matter. "I don't know what I'll do."

"Oh, c'mon," he said, seeing through her for once. "I know you're all about living in the moment and focusing on this harvest, but what are you going to do once all this goes away? Do you really think you can find something as special?" He'd come to admire her so much as an artist, and to see her relenting so quickly was upsetting. "I'm here to tell you giving up your passion can crush your soul. You finding a new farm would be like me trying to go out and find a new band. I'm not sure it's that easy."

She shifted in her seat. "You're really going to make me think about it?"

"I mean, c'mon. Don't tell me you haven't."

"Maybe a little," she said. "I've had some job offers, but I suppose I'll have the money to buy land, so I'll look around, see what's out there."

"Here in the Valencia *comunidad*?"

"I have no rules. I've thought about Italy, but I also feel very tied to my homeland. To España. There's some very good land for olive trees in Andalucía, and as you know, it's the home of flamenco. And it's hotter there, so the trees ripen faster. I'll finish earlier in the year. As long as I find a place with the same duende as here."

"Duende?" Baxter asked.

"Yeah, you know, like magic or . . . emm, like the source of life, a direct connection to God. Javier Martín, this guitarist, he has duende. You'll see."

⌐

They first swung by to pick up childhood friends of Alma's, a couple with two children back home with a babysitter. The Spanish guitarist Tomatito played from the speakers, setting the mood for what was to come.

Baxter couldn't stop thinking about Rodolfo, wondering about the contents of the recording and thinking about the way he'd exploded at his sister and how it had sounded so much like the way Rodolfo had screamed at his father on the recording. Baxter was starting to see that it might be best for the family to dissolve the business. How heartbreaking, but what was there to do? Perhaps it would be wise for Baxter to stay out of it and let Ester finish what she'd started. No question she lived very intentionally and lived her life like a chess match, pondering deeply every move.

The first part of the drive was Alma letting off some steam about her brother and about the offer that had come in, explaining that the potential buyers were infamous in the industry for counterfeiting oils. Ester had immediately countered, and they'd quickly countered back. Now Ester was in control. She had two days to accept, and if she did, they would close in the middle of January.

Alma's friends listened intently and caringly, and Baxter sensed they were solid humans. You could tell a lot from a person's friends. Eventually, Alma apologized for her rant and let it go, reaching for the stereo and turning up Tomatito, letting the music ease her.

Baxter could see how important music was to her, as if it healed her. He knew all about that: He'd found salvation with a guitar in his hands. It was a shame it wasn't that way anymore.

Alma's friend Vero, a petite woman with jet-black hair cut perfectly at her chest, asked, "You played country music?"

"No," Baxter said, trying to let go of all the thoughts rattling around. "This was alt-country or . . . some call it Americana."

"What's the difference?" her husband, Vincente, asked. He wasn't much taller than her and had a three-day-old beard with a few gray whiskers. He wore jeans so incredibly tight that Baxter worried his head might start turning blue.

Baxter turned back to look at Vincente. "In the music world, it's the difference between Willie Nelson and John Hartford and guys who sing stuff like 'Achy Breaky Heart' and 'Honky Tonk Badonkadonk.' Not that I'm criticizing. As long as they're playin' what fills them up, great."

"Wait," Alma interrupted. "There's really song called 'Honky Tonk Badonkadonk'?" The way she pronounced it made everyone smile.

"Oh, that's just a start," Baxter said. "May my Nashville friends forgive me for saying so, but there's a lot of bad country out there. But people can't get enough. If you want to live on an estate in Leipers Fork outside of Nashville, drive a Hummer, buy a yacht to put at your lake house, all you have to do is write 'She Thinks My Tractor's Sexy.'" When everyone laughed, he tossed out a couple of more. "Or 'Truck Yeah' or 'Alcohol You Later.'"

Baxter broke into an improvised song. "I like it when you wear my boots . . . and nothin' else, when you drive my truck . . . and crank it up, when the tailgate's down and the radio's up, playin' that cheesy countryyyyyy. Yeah, cheesy countryyyyy . . ."

"Oh my goodness," Vero said, "you have a good voice. And I like that song. Who sings it?"

Baxter was still laughing, feeling good to be doing so. He couldn't believe he'd sung in front of someone other than Mia. "I'm ashamed to say I just made it up, adding to the long list of bad country songs. So much of it all took a turn for the worse sometime in the nineties." He raised a finger. "I know I'm sounding jaded, but I'm being honest. Alternative country is where most of the renegades went. The stuff we played, it had heart. We could make you laugh and cry with a couple of lines. And I tried not to write hooks that were too catchy. We made you work to hear the good in them. You had to seek it out. Know what I mean?"

He recalled the day he'd found his bandmates practicing at Drew the bass player's house after Sofia's death. He'd arrived without his guitar, and he suspected they knew what was coming. He'd barely been able to look them in the eyes as he confessed that he was leaving the band.

"Ah, we're not letting you leave that easy," Drew had said. "Don't worry. Just take the time you need."

Baxter had shaken his head. "No. This is it. We're gonna move to Greenville and start over." He'd told them that he was buying his old boss's business and hanging up music. "It's time I focus on Mia."

They'd all nodded and accepted his decision and hugged him as he'd left. But the tears had fallen hard as he'd driven back home to pack up his things. To give away Sofia's things. Cactus Road had been so good to him. Those guys were his first family. And he'd left them without a singer, an abandonment he still was unable to shake.

Vincente said, "You are an artist, *tío*. You'll have to play for us sometime."

"I lent him my father's guitar," Alma said, "but he's shy about playing it."

Baxter cut a look at her. "I'm out of practice."

"Thank goodness for Spotify," Alma said, reaching for her phone. "Let's listen to some of the Cactus Road. I like this one album, *Songs for When You're Hurting*."

"Not *the*," he said. "Just Cactus Road."

She chuckled.

He wagged a finger at her, more focused on the fact that she had clearly been listening to his music enough to know which album she liked most. "And how about we keep Tomatito on and save Cactus Road for another day?" He'd not intentionally listened to his old band since he'd walked out on them.

Protests came from the back seat, both Vero and Vincente insisting Alma play Baxter's music. For once, Baxter stopped resisting, and somewhere in the far depths of his soul, he grew eager to listen to the music he and his brothers used to make. It was a good thing, because Alma had already pushed play.

The first song from *Songs for When You're Hurting* was a tune called "Bad Decisions" that Baxter had written at a beach house on Daufuskie Island, where the band had holed up to write. He kicked it off with a bluesy guitar lick, and then the drummer and bass player and pianist joined in to establish a rhythm that would shake your bones. Baxter had always loved playing with those guys because they could play on the back of the beat like no one else in the business, and it always brought out a certain attitude when he sang, something laid back and confident, like they were taking over the world but were in no rush in doing so.

And then the Baxter on the album started singing, "A long line of bad decisions . . . and unrealized ambitions, got me raising my suspicions about it all . . ."

Flooding over him came a surge of longing as deep and painful as how he felt about Sofia, but there was also a spark of light, too, the thrill of playing music with those boys, their young and eager souls giving it their all. They'd had some damn good times, and he wouldn't trade them for anything.

What a hell of a thought that was. Sofia had never once suggested he leave the band. His guilt about it was only his doing, and maybe he'd been wrong these past three years. Because they'd been onto something, and as he heard the music he and his brothers had made, he was sure that they'd been following their destiny.

Chapter 24

FLAMENCO

Ten minutes off the highway, a small, sleepy town tucked into the valley of several jagged rock faces emerged. A church steeple topped with a giant cross glowed in the moonlight. Alma weaved through the center, past the church, and drove them up a gravel road cutting into a canyon in the desert. They soon came upon a series of adobe-style cave houses built into the hills. In some cases, only the chimneys of the houses were visible, protruding up from the earth like telescopes. She parked in a dusty lot filled with cars, and they joined a group of people walking up through a line of cacti and olive trees to the rock cliff ahead.

They followed a series of overhead lights down steps lined with a wooden railing into the earth. Loud talk and laughter and the clink of glasses and the dank smell of the underground rose up from below. Three stories down, they entered a large cave, where sharply dressed Spaniards gathered at candlelit tables loaded with tapas and carafes of sangria and wine. A host took their name and then led them to a four-top about ten feet away from a small stage where four empty chairs and a guitar on its stand waited for the performers.

Baxter had never seen anything like it, and he was too taken aback to even speak until they'd sat and Vincente had ordered them sangria. He looked over at Alma with a smile, and she smiled back. "Not bad, right?"

"To think I almost didn't come."

She reached for his arm. "I would have made you, even if it meant dragging you."

What he couldn't get over was that though he'd left Mia with sitters for work reasons, he'd not once since Sofia died left her behind to go do something for fun. That idea didn't seem healthy now.

For an hour, the four of them drank sangria and ate *padrón* peppers, *patatas bravas*, octopus, and cuts of different sausage. They fell into a conversation about spirituality and religion, speaking freely in a way one can do only in a cave late at night. Baxter was on fire and felt young again, soaking up the others' thoughts with great interest before sharing what he'd come to believe himself.

As a quiet and collective gasp filled the cave, a dapper man spilling over with charisma weaved through the tables, and Baxter knew it was Javier Martín. Everyone clapped as they noticed him. He climbed the steps of the stage and reached for his guitar. Baxter twisted his chair around to face him, remembering so well when he'd been the one onstage.

The guitarist wore black pants and polished black shoes decorated with silver tassels, with a long gray blazer over a black shirt unbuttoned to the bottom of his rib cage, showing a thin gold necklace. Baxter remembered his own wardrobe of worn-out Frye boots, blue jeans, and a button-up shirt with the sleeves rolled to his elbows.

Martín acknowledged the crowd's applause, and when the cave went quiet, he said a few words in Spanish as he tuned his guitar and arranged the microphone. Baxter unquestionably sensed the duende that Alma had spoken about.

The guitarist crossed his right leg over his left and got situated with his guitar. He glanced back at the crowd with a grateful smirk before closing his eyes. Every sound seemed to be sucked out of the cave. And then he opened his eyes, and they were different from a moment earlier. This was a man possessed, and even in this silence, nothing for him existed but the music. Baxter felt a desperate need to be sitting up there next to him.

Martín began to tickle the strings, and a miraculous sound rose into the air. Baxter was transfixed from the first note. Seconds in, Martín showed impressive chops, flinging his right hand up and down, his left hand moving almost as fast, drawing out melodies and counter melodies and even rhythm at the same time. It was utterly jaw-dropping.

Just when Baxter didn't think it could get any better, a man in a white shirt, black pants, and equal charisma to Martín came from the back, clapping a very strong Spanish beat with impeccable timing. He took the stage and sat down. He stopped clapping long enough to adjust the microphone, but you could see he was in the groove, his whole body moving. When he started singing, Baxter just about fell out of his chair—as if the earth had stopped spinning.

His singing was like Native American chanting, so beautiful and soul stirring. Baxter never could have played so well or so deeply, but his thoughts didn't last long because these two men took him away, the music so incredibly rich and percussive and foreign and wonderful. They played like they were brothers and had played all their lives together. This was as close to a holy experience as Baxter had ever had.

His love for music came back to him like a boomerang striking him in the chest, and he was nearly out of breath when they wrapped up the first tune. That was what it was like, playing music for people. It wasn't an ego thing. When you were plugged in like Martín, you were breaking bread with the stars, sharing something cosmic and ethereal. There was nothing like that communion between an artist and the audience, when the great muse took over the bodies of the band and pulled the souls of the audience up there with them, the stage becoming a church celebrating the unity of life.

As tears ran down Baxter's cheeks, the audience let out a thunderous applause that shook the very walls of the cave. *This* was exactly why he'd started playing music in the first place, because for Baxter, there was no place that took him deeper.

"Are you kidding me?" he said, leaning over to Alma, who looked pleased that he was so happy.

A smile split her lips. "I know." He could see she was equally affected.

Baxter turned back to the stage just in time to hear the guitarist kick off another tune, something even more aggressive—foreign melodies raging over foreign beats. Baxter instantly fell back into the music, and he thought he had fallen in love with flamenco, and this would be a passion of his forever. Not the playing of it, as he didn't think he could ever achieve such mastery, but the listening of it, because he wanted to feel the way he felt right now, bursting with the attitude and audacity and spunk of a Spaniard, his whole core feeling awakened, as if nothing else in the world mattered but this moment; and that there was so much beyond our control and so much out there to believe in.

Nothing human could create these sounds—those bold and golden tones—without a higher power flowing through them, and Baxter knew he was in the direct presence of God. This was the kind of music that required a seat belt for the soul, and Baxter found himself uncaring about going home and about his job and even the money he'd put into those spec homes. All he cared about was the essence of life, the marrow of it, and he cared about living every moment as if it were his last, just like he'd felt when he'd taken the stage every night with Cactus Road. He'd figured it out, the *it* being just about every damn thing, and if only Mia could see him now . . .

And then . . . more clapping and all the heads in the cave turned. A woman in a red-and-yellow dress, her dark hair tucked into a low bun with a side part, strutted toward the cave with more attitude than any performer Baxter had ever seen. A red flower was tucked behind her ear. Chill bumps fired on his arms, as if only the sight of her was enough to evoke more magic in that cave. She tapped castanets with her fingers, and her timing was also superb, and the look on her face was so serious, as if she were living this music like her life depended on it.

She stepped onto the stage and Baxter's eyes lowered to her black shoes, and when she stomped, the whole stage rocked, and the cave echoed with the beat of her foot—her face shaking with each collision. The guitarist strummed hard, and the singer clapped and broke into a new tune, and this woman in front of Baxter danced the darkness out of that cave, her hands moving her dress like a matador swung his cape. He'd been teased by the earlier tune, thinking something heavenly was happening. Only the start of it. They were in it now, and the music had blasted Baxter out of his chair like a cannon had shot him into the clouds.

Her feet hit the stage with such power that he could feel the energy travel over the stone floor and then rush up his legs, making him a captive to her rhythms. He wanted to stand up and shout, to dance or to scream. He'd woken from a dream he'd been dreaming since Sofia had died. He'd been protecting Mia in all the wrong ways, and all he had to do was just live and to live hard and ride the world like he was riding a bucking bull like the old days and then . . .

He turned to Alma, whose eyes were closed, and she was equally mesmerized, and he couldn't take it any longer and he took her hand, and as her eyes opened, he leaned over and pressed his lips to hers and . . .

. . . and the world made sense, and her lips felt like the key to a door that had been locked forever. He felt tears spill out as he pulled away from her and stared into her green eyes that glowed in the twilight of the cave. The musicians played harder, and the dancer stomped, and the bass of her stomping shook Baxter's whole body, and he let out a smile.

He kissed her again, and Alma put her hands on his arms and pulled him closer to her. *She* kissed him this time, and Baxter lost all sense of reality as he dove into her, full-on with everything he had. He felt his chest pumping hard and his heart soaring, and he was exactly where he wanted to be, and nothing in the world mattered.

Then the woman let out a final stomp, and the music stopped, and silence wrapped her fingers around the cave, extinguishing it like it was a candle blown out by a gust of wind.

Baxter drew in a deep breath and found Alma's green eyes again and took one last sip from this moment, because he felt fear returning almost as quickly as the silence, and he didn't want to let this go. It was like he'd been falling and okay with the fall, but then all of a sudden comes the tremble of turbulence, and he wanted to reach for something to hold on to.

Not yet. Because it all, everything—all of it—made perfect sense, and he'd remembered what it was like to live, what it was like to be young and free and open armed to whatever may come.

⌇

Back in the car, Baxter saw Alan had called. Wasn't that how it always worked, reality crashing back in? Everyone was high from the experience, people still spilling out of the cave with true smiles, knowing they'd all touched the stars tonight. This was exactly why Baxter had devoted most of his life to music, because for him it was the one bit of proof that there was something bigger out there.

Tonight had reminded him so in a big way, and he wanted to white-knuckle that feeling and make sure he was able to take it back with him to Cadeir and then back to Greenville, where he could change the way they were living. How, he wasn't sure. Less fear, that was the only way to sum it up now. Less worrying about the seat belt and more enjoying the thrill.

He sure as heck didn't want to get pulled back into the real world so quickly by listening to Alan's message. Instead, he ignored it. This was what a Spaniard would do, let reality wait until tomorrow, until mañana. And more to the point, tonight was about the music, and he'd remembered how powerful it could be, how alive it used to make him feel.

Alma seemed to have let go of everything that had happened earlier in the day with her brother and the offer coming in. Every once in a while, as they chatted with her friends in the back seat, she'd cast a look at him rich with all kinds of feeling, and he ached to get back home so that they could be together. And it wasn't lost on him that he didn't feel guilty or fearful either. He didn't feel guilty that he'd taken a big step toward moving on from Sofia or that it happened to be with her half sister. And he wasn't worried about what it would feel like to lose her, having to go through losing someone else he loved. He wasn't even worried what Mia would think, because she would most surely want him to feel like he felt right now.

It was one of those nights you wanted to last forever.

～

They returned to the estate a little after four in the morning and shared a glass of wine downstairs at the kitchen table. Not once did they talk about the kiss, only about music and life . . . and then about the end of the estate.

"The estate has given to this family what it was supposed to," Alma said, curled up on her chair, "and now it's time to move on."

Baxter shook his head slowly. "I wish I had an answer, Alma. I wish there was something I could do."

"It's okay," she said. "This is the way it's supposed to be." She seemed unfazed. How was it that she could so easily let something go? She was just light as a feather, both inside and out, and especially after her fix of music, she appeared to have no problem letting the wind take her the way it was blowing. Though it might have driven him crazy yesterday, there was a part of him that admired it today.

Still, he wanted to help her. Baxter wished like crazy he had the money, but he was tied up. Even if he were more liquid, he couldn't afford to take such a risk. He needed the cash for his company and for Mia and her college and a wedding and a down payment on her first house.

"What would it look like if you stayed here?" he asked. "If your brother and you both wanted to keep the estate. Let's just say, for the point of the conversation, that you were able to mend your relationship. What would you do differently? What's your vision?"

A devious grin alighted her lips. "*If* my brother and I could get along, then I suppose I'd have wings, too, and I'd take off from here and fly like a bird over Spain and all of Europe. We'd have world peace and everyone would be rich and olive oil would be as loved as it once was in the old days. I'd . . ."

He grinned back at her.

She sat up and tried again. "There are many ways to improve. The first thing I'd do is try to start saving so we could handle a bad year. As you saw, we need our own mill. It's the only way I can make the best oil in Spain. It would also increase profits. And I always wanted to open up the estate to ecotourism—a way for us to help educate about real olive oil, an idea my brother hates. I wanted to build guesthouses with a restaurant and a tasting room where we could teach people about good oil and its unbelievable health benefits. We could put it up there near the garden. Italy does an amazing job with their *agriturismi* but, for some reason, it hasn't caught on as strongly in Spain. Perhaps we are more, emm, *cerrado*, like, closed off."

"Have you tried convincing your brother?" Baxter asked. "Is that even a possibility? The thing that's so frustrating is this entire decision could be made between the three of you. All you need is common ground."

Alma's face said it all. "There is no convincing him. All he cares about is selling. I don't want to try to change his mind anyway. I'd love an ending where I remind him of our happy days growing up and we see his heart turn and he opens up his arms to me. 'Let's do this together, *hermana.*'" Alma smiled at the absurdity. "He is too hardheaded and righteous and . . . and this is why my mother is probably right. After she's gone, it will only get worse."

Baxter lifted his hand and let it drop. "Your mother is a long way from being gone."

Alma looked away, her head slowly shaking.

He sighed. "I really am sorry. I don't have any brothers or sisters, so I can't relate in that way, but if I had to work with my dad and mom, we'd kill each other."

"Anyway," Alma said. "We can't save the world tonight, and I have a lot of work to do tomorrow."

"Yeah. Thanks for taking me. It was darn near life-changing, truly, and that's coming from a guy who said life-changing was overrated."

She lightly patted the table and started to stand. "It's nice to see you this happy."

"It's nice to feel this happy." Baxter watched her rise, wondering if she'd come round the table to kiss him. He couldn't stand the idea that they'd never touch again.

Looking down at him from a safe distance, she said, "Have a good night," and then she turned away.

I get it, he thought, as she disappeared out of the kitchen. No matter what had happened in the cave, where in the world could it go between them? Especially in this house with Mia and Ester sleeping upstairs.

Pushing up, he set the glasses in the sink. He'd not felt so alive in so long, and he didn't want to lose it. Deciding he wasn't done and still feeling music shimmering all around him, he crept up the stairs to retrieve Don Jorge's guitar.

Energized by the chill of the early morning, he crossed through the electric fence and strolled into the groves as if he were following someone he couldn't quite make out, a vision that kept waving him on. The sun had not yet climbed over the mountains to the east, but it had created a mild amber hue that colored the fog that drifted through the trees like ghosts.

Stopping in front of a gorgeous old tree so twisted it looked to be corkscrewing itself into the earth, he lowered himself to the ground and rested his back against the trunk. Ripe olives dangled over him. He heard the coo of a dove and twisted his head to see the lone bird resting on a branch above him, calling out her morning song.

Baxter should have been tired, but he was awake, so very awake. He could still hear the music and see the passion in the dancer's face, and he could still taste the sweetness of Alma on his lips. He sat there in utter amazement, breathing in this place, thinking the whole country was holy ground.

If there was any one thing he could do for his daughter, it would be to continue being the man he was right now, the one less bound by fear. And that started with working and worrying less, but it didn't stop there, because they needed their thirst for life back. He needed to show Mia who he'd been before Sofia died, the man Mia was too young to remember, the man who could walk out on stage and open up his arms to complete and utter vulnerability.

The sun finally broke over the mountain, an orange disk rising in the blue, scattering the fog. A dog called out and the dove cooed, and then the rooster started up his alarm. Another morning on the estate, another morning in Spain.

He unlatched the case and pulled out the guitar, resting it on his lap. A sense of relief and calm came over him, as if he'd found something he'd lost. For a moment, he wondered what Sofia would think. Would she be okay with him playing again? Surely so, as long as he didn't let his music get in the way of his relationship with Mia. No, he'd never let it be a wedge again.

As Baxter fingered chords and drew out a melody with his hands, he felt Don Jorge's presence. This land had bubbled in his blood. Baxter felt him through the guitar and through the ground and through the trunk of the tree upon which his back was pressed.

Then a whisper came down from the trees, and Baxter knew he wasn't alone. It wasn't like the vision that had led him here, either; it was something much more tangible, a presence as real as he was, as real as the other souls on this farm. He heard a whisper, and though he couldn't hear the words, he knew the message: *It's not too late to live.*

It's not too late to live.

Baxter broke into a rhythmic chord progression in G, a tune he'd never played before. He watched his hands move and heard the music rising up into the groves, but he wasn't in control. Something else was playing him, something much stronger than him. His mouth opened and words came out, first softly, a morning melody like the dove's coo, but several lines in, his voice opened up to what was trying to come out.

He didn't know how long he played, but it was a long time and several songs, and he felt hoarse in his throat, but a transcendent energy coursed through him.

He'd not played music like that in many years, and he was reminded why he'd played in the first place. It wasn't only that music had given him a way to express himself and a place to go when it hurt, but music had given him a way to touch the intangible, to know there was a point to all of this, that even when it got hard, there was some sort of reason for it all.

Chapter 25

A Spanish Telenovela

When Mia climbed on top of him, he felt as ancient as the old villa in which they were in. Though he was used to operating on a lack of sleep, today was ridiculous.

"Daddy might be sleeping in today," he said, pulling her in. "Let's doze off for another hour. It's Spain. *No pasa nada.*"

"Nada chance, Pops. It's already eight. Time to rise and shine."

He rubbed his eyes. "What if you gave me an hour? You can watch whatever show you like, do whatever you want. Daddy didn't sleep much."

"It's Sunday. We have church in an hour. Then the whole family is going to lunch at a hotel, and there's supposedly a huge playground. Alfonso says it's the best in the entire world." She patted his chest. "You just need some coffee and a slice of tortilla."

"Oh, is that what I need?"

"Among other things."

Her chipper face really was enough to get him up. The idea that she'd been waiting for him to wake from his grief came alive in his head. All that stuff that had happened last night, the feelings he'd had. Were they the ones she'd been having since almost the moment they'd first arrived? Were they both onto something?

"Why don't you get dressed and clean up? Give me five minutes, okay?"

They looked at each other and smiled, and he wondered if she could see how he felt inside.

"By the way, no nightmares last night?"

"No, sir. I slept great!"

As she darted off to her room, he shook his head, hoping this was the start of their new lives. He let his head fall back into the pillow. Could he get just another hour before he had to go forth and live this life that he'd tasted the night before? He surely wasn't getting any younger.

When was the last time he'd stayed up to see the sunrise? Probably ten years ago, that night with Sofia, a staycation in Charleston. They stayed at the Planters Inn, dined at the Peninsula Grille, followed by dancing—so much dancing—and eventually ending up at Waterfront Park, dangling their feet over the seawall. Like they were twenty years old again. He let himself fall into it, feeling the way Sofia's body felt against his, with their arms locked, as they looked out over the harbor, the sun inching up over the horizon, the water on fire.

"I wonder if we'll still do this stuff when we're older," she'd said to him.

Baxter looked at her like she'd asked if he'd ever retire. "What? Watch the sunrise?"

"Dance all night, watch the sun rise. Live out loud."

Baxter had stared into the universe of her eyes. "That's the one thing I know about us. As long as we're together, we're gonna keep riding the world like a bucking bull, and that's exactly why I love you."

"And that's exactly why I love you," she'd replied. "You're the only mess I want to make."

His mouth had fallen open. "What in the world is that supposed to mean?"

"You're just everything I ever wanted, that's all." And then they'd kissed, and he'd tasted a future life that he never could have dreamed of from that mattress on the floor in his tiny room in his parents' trailer.

You're the only mess I wanna make, he thought. He still didn't know what it meant, but now he wanted to understand more than ever. He felt his eyes wet the pillow. That might also have been the first night they'd ever spoken of having children.

Hearing their daughter call for him from the bathroom ("Time to get up!"), he whispered, "I miss you, Sofe. It's one hell of a mess we made, for sure, but I'm doing my best to clean it up."

Mia came into the room. "I can't hear you."

"Nothin', honey. I was just talking to myself." *To your mother.*

By the time he made it down the stairs, Alma had already gone to work. As she had told him last night, she was harvesting some of the Arbequina olives today and was excused from church. As he slurped his coffee and recounted to Ester and Mia his evening of music, he found himself grasping to remember the feelings he'd had, because it kind of felt like a dream now.

Ester helped dress Mia, as it was all Baxter could do to get ready himself, and soon the three of them piled into Ester's car to ride into town. Baxter wished he could talk to Ester about the offer she was about to accept, but he had to hold back. Ester squeezed into an impossibly tight parallel parking space, and they worked their way through the narrow streets toward the towering steeple in the middle.

It took a while, though, for two reasons. Ester was moving very slowly, blaming it on her back, but also they couldn't get very far without someone she knew stopping them. It was a good thing they were early, because these were not brief chats. Ester would introduce Baxter and Mia, and her friends would greet them excitedly, seemingly not judging Ester for her sins as a teenager.

Baxter slowed and let everyone get ahead of him so that he could check his messages, most specifically Alan's from the night before. At the last minute, he hesitated, wondering if this was really a good idea. But more knowledge could only be a good thing; he pressed play.

Alan's southern accent came rushing over. "Jeez, dude, what kind of Spanish telenovela you got going on over there? I got Luis to translate it for me. I don't know whether you want me to get him to write it down or you just want the CliffsNotes. Anyway, I know you're sleeping, so just call me when you get up."

That's it? Baxter wondered. Alan wasn't even going to share any of the details? Baxter was tempted to wake his friend up but then thought of what he'd felt like the night before and said to himself, "It can wait a little while longer."

After a lengthy but nice service, Baxter and Mia found themselves shaking more hands and kissing more cheeks, and if it was even possible, meeting more family. It must have taken them an hour to get back to the car. They finally drove to a nice hotel on the outskirts of town. It was a white building, more colonial looking than anything else, with a giant expanse of a lawn that had been meticulously raked of leaves. Churchgoers piled out of their cars dressed in their best. The adults seemed to race for the tables almost as quickly as the children ran toward the very impressive playground. Chasing Alfonso, Mia shot off as quickly as any of them, and Baxter was so happy to see how comfortable she felt.

Baxter tried his best to be cordial and even upbeat despite his body telling him to hit the sack. When he saw Rodolfo dressed in a handsome gray suit with a red handkerchief protruding out of the pocket, his mind went straight to Alan's call the night before. What in the world was on that tape?

They sat at one of the many long tables inside a large banquet room, and a server poured bubbly cava, which was Spanish sparkling wine. It didn't take long for the conversation to steer toward the sale of the estate, and Ester caught everyone up, briefly making eye contact with Baxter in what felt like an apology for having excluded him. She was checking a few last things with her real estate agent and lawyer before accepting the offer, but she expected to do so today. Soon the table was full of more food, and despite the knot in his stomach over the sale of the estate, the Spanish part of him was thrilled to be facing such a feast.

With a full belly an hour later, Baxter excused himself to call Alan. The anticipation had become too much. Walking outside, he saw Mia standing next to Alfonso, his arm around her, and Baxter paused to take in the sight for a moment. Mia looked fearless over there, unfazed by the hell they'd been through, as if all she'd been waiting for was a big dose of family to surround her and lift her up.

What did Baxter need? Surely more than a night in the cave. He hated the idea that he might be dragging his daughter down. He couldn't allow that for another moment.

He went the other way down a long walkway that opened up to a pool, which was closed for the season. The lounge chairs were stacked on one side next to a collection of umbrellas.

"Hey, amigo," Alan said.

Baxter paced alongside the pool. "Hey, brother, how's your family? How's Amy holding up?"

"Oh, you know. We've had better days, that's for sure."

Baxter nodded, as if Alan could see him. "So . . ."

"Yeah, so the recording. I'll tell ya. There's a lot going on there. I'm assuming that's what you want to talk about?"

"If you have the time. I know you got a lot going on."

"It's a nice distraction," he said. "Seriously, you're right in the middle of a telenovela. I'd be careful. Who is the older one? What's his name? The guy with the raspy voice."

"That's Don Jorge. The father who died last year."

"Okay, yeah, Don Jorge. Luis says he's talking to his son, right? Rodolfo?"

"Yep, you've got it figured out." A bird that looked like a Carolina wren landed on the stack of lounge chairs and looked at Baxter curiously.

"Don Jorge is not happy with his son."

"No, he is not. Any reason?" Baxter thought of that word: *robando*.

"He's asking where the money is. Apparently, Rodolfo is stealing from him . . . or from the company. Two hundred thousand euros."

Baxter was slightly shocked that he'd been right. "That's what I thought I heard. Two hundred thousand?" Poor Ester and Alma. His shock gave way to anger. What in God's name had Rodolfo been thinking, taking advantage of such good people?

"Bax, are you pulling my leg with this recording?"

"I wish I was." He suddenly held a stick of dynamite threatening to tear the family apart—a family that was instrumental in lifting Mia out of her grief.

Something occurred to him, though. Was Ester already aware of what Rodolfo had done? Surely she had access to the bank accounts. She was the boss. Was this why she was selling? Did she know that her son had stolen money? Was she bailing him out? Did Alma know? Nah, no way she knew, or she wouldn't have given up her fight. But Ester . . . if for some reason she didn't know, then she should.

"Anything else?" Baxter asked.

Alan cleared his throat. "Don Jorge says he was goin' skiing the next morning and that he wanted that money back in his account 'fore he gets back. When was this made?"

Baxter exchanged a look with the bird still watching him from the chair. "If he was going skiing, it could have been right before he died. Don Jorge went down in a plane on the way to the Austrian Alps in early December." A chill ran up Baxter's spine as he wondered if Don Jorge had died the day after this exchange with his son.

"You can't make this stuff up, can you? What you gonna do about it?"

That was the question, wasn't it? Either hold his tongue for two more days and get the hell out of there, or jump headfirst into the affairs of Sofia's family. As much as he wanted to hide the drama from Mia, and as much as he didn't want to break Ester's and Alma's hearts and even risk breaking apart their family, he was pretty sure he wasn't getting on that plane Tuesday without, at the very minimum, sharing this recording with Ester and Alma.

"If I was smart," he said, "I'd get in the car and drive back to Madrid. But these are good people here. I need to figure out a way to help. Whatever that might be."

"Just be careful, amigo."

What in the world had Baxter got them into?

Chapter 26

No One Loves Like a Mother

When they returned to the estate, they dropped Mia off in the lower groves to help Aunt Alma, which gave Baxter the opportunity to talk to Ester. Deciding he'd better wait to play the tape until they got inside, he said the most obvious thing. "So you're selling?"

They bumped along the road in her Jeep. "Looks like it."

"I was wondering what was happening around here."

She cut a look his way; her gold earring danced. "I didn't want to complicate things by telling you."

You are as complicated as me, he thought. "It's none of my business anyway. So Madrid, huh? That'll be a change."

Ester let out a quick and sharp laugh. "A good one, I hope. I think the city might be nice for a while. It will be fun to see Rodolfo grow his business."

"You have to be sad, though."

"Of course. I've spent more than half of my life here. But as you can see by the way my children bicker, the end has most certainly come."

"I get it, believe me. No judgment here. My family couldn't have run a Laundromat together."

They rode in silence for a while. He wondered if the contents of the tape might change her plans.

Don Diego's house came into view on the right. "He's a good guy, isn't he? Don Diego. Other than the fact that he didn't let Mia win. Did you get a chance to talk to him? How'd he take the news of you having a daughter?"

He thought he heard her laughing to herself. "Yes, I talked to him. He was protective of Jorge at first, but he understands. You get our age, you become hardened to a lot of things."

"Yeah," Baxter said, "I know what you mean, and I'm only forty. I feel like I've been kicked around so much that all's left is a battered slab of flesh."

Ester actually laughed, as she pulled her eyes away from her neighbor's house. When they parked, Baxter said, "There's something else I'd like to talk to you about." He felt the Dictaphone heavy in his pocket.

Ester seemed to find what he'd said amusing, offering a chortle that moved her shoulders up and down. "Is this about Alma?"

"Alma?"

She dropped her keys into her purse and cracked open the car door. "*Sí*, you and my daughter. The one still alive."

"I, uh . . . what?"

She exhaled sharply, one hand still on the door handle. "Have you not accepted your feelings for her?"

The question stung like a bee. In a flash, he felt guilty and even ashamed. "My feelings for her?"

She looked at Baxter the exact same way Sofia had looked at him when he played dumb. There'd been a few times—maybe more than a few—when Sofia had become jealous when some of Baxter's female fans had approached him on the street or on the stage after a show. Sofia would say, "She was hitting on you . . . right in front of me."

Baxter would shake his head. "No, she just likes the music."

"Oh, c'mon. Your music's good, but I can tell she wants more than that."

He'd shrug. "Nah."

"Don't play dumb," she'd say. "As long as you remember who butters your bread, I don't mind them looking."

"Oh, I know exactly who butters my bread. And I'm very particular with my butter."

They'd share another smile, and he'd know that she kind of liked dating the guy who took center stage and sang his heart out. He also knew that those girls could flirt all they wanted to, but none of them would even so much as distract him for a second from the woman he would spend the rest of his life loving.

For a moment he wondered if Sofia was there looking through the eyes of her mother as she'd asked if he had feelings for Alma.

"Dios mío," Ester said, as if she wasn't going to entertain any more of his shenanigans. "I'll just wait until you're ready."

Baxter shook his head, deciding he wasn't going to let out a lie but that he wasn't quite ready for an admission either. "I can't go there." He heard his words come out a bit sharper than what he'd meant, as if he'd spit them out with finality. "And that's not what I wanted to talk about."

She finally opened the car door all the way and stepped out. "Then what?"

"Let's go inside."

―

As they sat down at the breakfast table, a wooden bowl of oranges and a couple of heavy secrets between them, he was second-guessing his decision to play the recording for her. Yes, it might help her change her mind, but was he about to pull back the curtain on something that could ruin this family? Was it worth it? Or . . . if Ester was aware of Rodolfo's crime, then what? Was Alma the only one in the dark?

Ester waited patiently until he finally opened his mouth. He was unsure of what might come out. "I've . . . I've found something and feel it's very important to show you. But it might be painful."

Ester's forehead wrinkled with concern. He was reminded of telling her about Sofia's death, and he hated that he was about to bring more devastation. But he felt he had to protect both Ester and Alma. He extracted the Dictaphone from his pocket.

"I found this in your husband's guitar case, and I listened to it to hear him play, but heard something else too."

She stared at the machine, and Baxter didn't see anything hardened about her then.

With a deep draw of air, he said, "I think your son has been stealing from the company."

Her head kicked back in surprise, and he wondered if it was a true reaction or a well-executed act. He pressed play and set the recorder on the table between them. After tuning his guitar, Don Jorge started up with that strumming technique for a few seconds. Ester listened with what seemed like both bewilderment and great concern, surely wondering what was coming.

And then the knock on the door. Rodolfo.

As the two men screamed at each other, Baxter watched Ester fold in, her whole body. He was at once reminded of hearing Sofia's voice after she'd gone. It was the message she'd left on her voice mail: *You've got Sofia. If I'm lucky, I'm out on the water. Either way, I'll get back to you as soon as I can.* Baxter had listened to it so many times, he could still remember the faint sound of a car horn halfway through her message.

All the way up until the day Mia had found him crying in his room and he'd decided to wipe away the memories, he had listened over and over to her message, as if it were the only thing he really had left of her. Sometimes, he'd even left messages of his own, asking her—no, begging her—to come back to him. But he'd gone to Verizon after his decision and had them delete her account. It was the only way he knew to make sure he didn't listen to it again.

He hated kicking up this same pain for Ester.

When the recording stopped, Baxter looked at her. A frown had turned down her lips as her eyes stared off into space. *Did she already know?* he wondered again. If so, she belonged on Broadway.

"I'm sorry," he said.

She didn't move or utter a word.

Baxter let her process things for a while, then said, "Perhaps I should leave?"

Ester stopped him by raising a flattened hand. "You understand what they're saying?"

He shook his head, realizing he hadn't been ready to answer the question. Not wanting to tell the truth, that he'd circulated the recording back home, he said, "Enough of it. He was stealing."

Ester nearly bored a hole through the table with her stare. "This was the day before my husband died; he's talking about taking the plane."

"How was he doing it, the stealing?"

She shook her head. "He has access to most of our accounts. All he has to do is approve a transfer with his phone, if that's how he did it." She lowered her head again in thought. It was so quiet Baxter could hear the house shifting. This was more like it, Baxter thought, the truth of family. Even the seemingly good ones like these Arroyos couldn't escape the lit fuse growing shorter.

"I don't want Alma to know. I don't want you to tell her."

Baxter felt his head snap toward her. Her reply was so quick he wondered if she'd already been deliberating the decision. "What? Did you know, Ester?" He couldn't help but ask. As much as he'd come to like her—maybe even love her—he wasn't sure that he totally trusted her.

"No." She rubbed the space under her eyes. He wanted to go to her and offer a hug, but that felt strange. He'd invaded their business in a serious way.

"You can't keep this from Alma," Baxter said, thinking of the damage he'd caused in lying to Mia about how her mother had died. "You have to make it right. She deserves this property." Baxter almost said that Rodolfo should be arrested but held back. "Your son might need help."

"Help?" she said, looking up. "What kind of help is there?"

Baxter thought about her question. He felt like he was overstepping his bounds. "I don't know."

Ester's face tightened. "Don't you see, Baxter? This doesn't change anything. This house is a dollhouse from the outside, but it's full of snakes on the inside, just as Rodolfo says. It's Jorge who made him this way. My husband is the one who ruined this family."

Baxter took a moment before responding. "No matter what you do with the papers, you have to tell Alma."

Ester's eyes narrowed at him. "And you're one to talk. You lied to Mia about Sofia's murder. Sometimes lies are the only way. I do *not* want you telling Alma. Do you understand me?"

As much as he didn't want to say so, he had to. "I don't know that I can keep it from her." Then he braced for her response.

Ester's face turned icy—nearly blue, and bitterness rose from her mouth. "Do you understand what would happen? This would destroy any chance of them having a relationship. Irreparable damages." She hit the table so hard the Dictaphone and the bowl of oranges shook. "I will die knowing my son and daughter will hate each other forever, that *everything* I've done as a mother was a failure."

Good God, she wasn't holding back now, and he hated that he'd done this to her. Feeling like he needed to be the strong one, he said, "For one, you're too young to talk about dying. And I don't know if there is anyone on earth that can empathize more with the fear of failing as a parent, which makes me more than qualified to assure you that you are far from a failure."

Baxter clasped his hands and leaned toward her, lowering his voice. "And as far as their relationship and it falling apart, I get that too. You guys have something beautiful, and there's still plenty of time to make things right. This doesn't have to be the end."

She shook her head in frustration. "This doesn't change anything. Yes, perhaps my son needs help, and I will figure that out, but I am still selling this property. I am accepting the offer tonight, and we will be done with it by January."

Baxter pressed his hands down on the place mat, his stomach pressed up against the edge of the table. "Tell me this . . . why haven't you accepted the offer yet? You've been sitting on it for days."

She slammed her fist down even harder this time, and one of the oranges jumped out of the bowl. "Because it hurts, Baxter. This isn't an easy decision, dammit."

Baxter put the orange back. "I completely understand." And he did. Forget her feelings toward her husband. This land clearly meant something to her, and it undoubtedly meant everything to Alma. On the other hand, the issues surrounding the estate were slowly severing the last ties of their familial bond. Ester was damned either way.

"I very well may tell her, but in my own time."

"Yes, ma'am." He wanted to tell her how much lying to Mia about Sofia still plagued him, but he didn't want to stand at the pulpit and preach, as if he had all the answers. Unsure of what to do, he sat back and said, "I think it's way too much to process in an instant. Think it over. I know you'll do what's best." He hoped so, at least. "I'm here to help any way I can. I've only known y'all for a few days, but I care. You are my family because you are Mia and Sofia's family. I want what's best for all of you." Calling them family out loud seemed to soothe him in a way he could never have imagined.

Ester set her elbows on the table and buried her face in her hands with a sharp intake of air. Baxter stood and set a hand on her shoulder for a moment. He hated being the one who had brought her to this point. Part of him wished he'd not ever opened Don Jorge's guitar case. Was this yet another warning of what happens when he let music into his life?

Leaving the evidence on the table, Baxter lightly squeezed her shoulder. "Let me know what I can do."

He started through the kitchen, but he didn't get far before she said, "Baxter."

"Yeah."

"Sit down."

Baxter pivoted and returned to the table. This time, he sat with his hands in his lap.

She sat back, and her eyes bounced from one place to the next for a moment, finally settling on him. "I'm dying."

His head kicked back. "What?"

She bit her lip, almost chewing on it as thoughts seemed to spin in her head. Was she sick? He thought about her bad back and her avoidance of alcohol.

Finally, she said, "I have coronary heart disease. I had a heart attack last year and had surgery. Double bypass."

Sadness washed over him for so many reasons. Because he cared about her. Because she was a good person. A great mother who cared so much for her family. "But you're . . . you're young. How in the . . . ?"

"My doctor says it's stress that may have caused it. That and genetics."

"How are you dying then if you had the surgery?" he asked.

"It seems the damage has been done."

Baxter saw in her eyes the possibility of death, and the notion of her soul leaving this place settled in the pit of his stomach. Death, death, death. This whole world was just everyone waiting to die.

"What do you mean 'the damage has been done'?"

"It means I won't live forever, that's for sure."

He shook his head, not only at the news but at the fragility of life, of how easy it was to get knocked off your feet for the last time. You just never knew when it was coming. Back before Sofia, he'd always watched or read in the news from a distance as someone lost a loved one. He never could have imagined it would be Sofia. Those exact same thoughts came back to him with Ester. How could it be her who was destined to meet an early end?

And what did this mean for Mia? She'd finally found a grandmother who was actually a real grandmother, and now she was going to lose her? It was too much.

He didn't want his face to betray such thoughts, so he pushed them away. "How long do you . . . what are they . . . ?"

She filled in the blanks. "Hard to tell. I'm on medicine and following orders, eating well, exercising, and trying to manage the stress. But it might not be enough."

Baxter realized he'd just done the worst thing for her stress, exposing her son for the man he truly was. He wished like all hell that he could unplay the tape.

"A heart transplant seems to be the only answer," she said.

He sat up with a cinder of hope coming alive in his heart. "There you go. I had a client who's doing great after one. That was a few years ago." He realized as he looked at her now that he didn't blame her for the choices that she'd made, and he wished he hadn't jumped to such quick conclusions about her. She didn't deserve what she'd been put through.

"We can certainly be optimistic."

"Good." He felt his head going up and down. "I'm very sorry, Ester. I can't imagine what you've been going through. Is this why you found us? Is this why you did the test and why you're selling?" Another thought occurred to him. "Do Alma and Rodolfo know how bad it is?" Even as he asked, he knew the answer. If she'd had a heart attack and surgery, then yes, they knew.

She smiled to herself and then raised a hand to her chin pensively. "Yes, they know, and yes, this is why I looked for Sofia. Before it was too late. Of course, I had no idea it would be too late to find her . . . but . . . I found you and Mia. As far as the estate, well, as you know, there are so many reasons, including that I didn't want to burden Alma and Rodolfo with the war that would have ensued if we didn't deal with it now."

As selfish as it might have been, he thought of Mia and how devastating this news would be to her. He supposed the answer was that a few days together would be better than none at all. It was the same for him too. He was very glad to know this woman, and each day brought them closer together. Ester was the mother-in-law of one's dreams.

"Life," he said, as if the one word summed up everything spinning around them.

"It doesn't stop coming at you, does it?"

"No, ma'am."

She pulled her hair behind her ear, then said out of nowhere, "I want to give Mia part of the inheritance. Part of the proceeds of the estate."

"You don't have to do that. We're fine."

"This is not for you," Ester said. "This would be for Mia . . . and for me."

Ah, he got it. How could he argue? And Baxter couldn't help but think that Rodolfo had been right . . . part of his inheritance was at stake. Nothing was black and white, was it? He shouldn't have judged the man so quickly.

"She is as much a part of this family as my children. Had I not given up Sofia, she'd have been here now, and . . ." Ester swallowed back her anguish. "She'd be here now, and she wouldn't have been shot, and I would have known her."

Baxter reached across the table for her hand again. He wished there was something he could say, but he thought better of even trying. In a way, they were both living life staring into the empty glass of regret, and there were few lonelier feelings in the world than knowing you could have done things differently.

She squeezed his hand as if they were sitting next to each other on a plane during terrifying turbulence. "The truth is that my heart is broken because of what I did to Sofia. It has burdened me for too long, and I'm not sure I want to live with it much longer. She was my daughter, and I did the one thing a mother should never do: abandon her."

Baxter's eyes suddenly leaked tears. "Oh, Jesus, Ester. Don't say that. It's not true. I'm sure you gave her up for adoption in hopes she'd have a better life than the one you could give her. And maybe she did. She found me, and we were meant to find one another. And she had Mia, who was the light of her life. It was destiny that you give her up in Madrid so that she could find her way to me. Everything was worth it to have Mia." He felt tears slide down his face. "Don't you beat yourself up over a decision you made when you were a teenager."

Baxter stopped and breathed in through his nose.

Ester's face was covered in tears, too, and she mopped them away with her hands. "Thank you for saying so. You have no idea what it means. I am glad she found you. So very happy. I just . . . I wish I could have known her. I wish I could be with her. And perhaps I will one day soon."

"The one thing I know," he said, "is that she is here. With both of us."

When she'd gotten it together enough to speak, Ester said, "There's a part of my heart that *is* still strong, and that is the part I will be taking with me when I go. It will be filled with the love I have for my family. Every one of them, including you, Baxter Shaw."

"You saying that means more than you could know. Thank you." He wiped his cheeks. "You're a good person, Ester. A very good person, and I have no doubt that Sofia is thankful for what you did."

Ester started and stopped. Finally, she got out, "At least she didn't have to deal with this . . . all this that's going on here. I don't know what to do." Then a whisper: "I don't know what to do."

Baxter wished he had the answer, but he didn't.

Chapter 27

Tears of the Lonely

Alongside his sadness for Ester, a seed of regret grew through the rest of the afternoon, so much so that he found himself strolling down the driveway in complete and utter disarray.

What had he done bringing Mia here? How dare he think he might be equipped enough to provide the true remedy for her aching heart? Though he wanted to believe that he'd done the right thing somehow, all he could see was the error in his ways. Mia lost her mother, for God's sake! She was grieving. And all he'd done was make it worse. Children weren't fucking resilient! That was what parents told themselves to feel better after they realized the extent of their failures.

Children needed to be protected. You didn't test your theories on them like lab rats. You gave them a safe place to grow and taught them how to one day face life's difficulties. You sure as heck didn't take a young girl who lost her mother to a foreign country to meet relatives without vetting every bit of the process.

What was he thinking? That they'd walk into an estate of super-humans with no struggles of their own? How had he forgotten that everyone has agendas, and everyone has their secrets? This was no light matter; it was life and death, and he was stringing Mia along.

Reaching the creek, he swung his legs over and sat on the crumbling stone wall. The creek was only a few feet below his toes, and it slid by like the tears that had been shed in the kitchen. Even the estate had its problems. He was glad he and Mia were able to see this place, but he wished it wouldn't be the last time. Not only for Mia's and Alma's and Ester's sake, but his as well, for even as hardheaded as he was, he could feel this place working its magic on him like a sorceress casting healing spells. He was changing, soaking up some of the Spanish air, the Spanish way. At least, that was how it had seemed for a little while. Now it felt more like a deception than anything else.

And what did any of it even matter if Ester was going to die?

Baxter wished there was something he could do about all of it. Well, maybe he could help with the estate, though the hope was looking more and more like a pipe dream every day. But he sure as hell couldn't save Mia's grandmother. *A heart transplant,* he thought. How successful were they? What were her chances?

He felt so very far away from the man who'd broken through in that cave as the flamenco music had taken him away. God, he wished he could tap into that man, but it had been a farce, like some fake life, a blanket of lies. He wished he could go grab Mia and run, get out of there before all of this came falling down on him.

Bottom line: losing Ester could absolutely crush Mia.

He understood why he and Mia had been left in the dark about Ester's health. It wasn't her responsibility to disclose her sickness. How could she have known experiencing more loss would be the single-worst thing that could happen to Mia?

Baxter felt himself spiraling down, falling all the way back to whom he'd become after Sofia was shot. He could hear the gunshots again, leaping out of the phone. He shook the memory away.

The only thing that made sense was the creek rushing by below him. He could hear and feel those tears like they were his own.

The one thing Sofia had said was to take care of Mia, to give her the best life he could. One simple request. And he'd fallen so miserably short, taking things into his own hands. What kind of father ripped his daughter out of school and therapy to go chase a hunch? A father who had no idea what he was doing.

He hadn't even gotten to the most embarrassing part, that he'd also let himself have feelings for Alma. Forget about the distance and the fact of her being Sofia's half sister. He didn't deserve love again. That was it. What? So he could hurt more people? Good God, what if Mia had seen them kissing or even flirting?

A stinging pain filled his chest. "What have I done?" He pressed his hand against his rib cage and then let out a long exhale, tasting the bitterness of his mistakes.

The fixer, the title Sofia had always called him. Whenever she was having a bad day, he'd try to fix it, ask her what was going on, and then diagnose and attempt to remedy the problem.

"I don't want you to fix it," she'd say. "I just want you to listen."

Here he was fixing again, his clumsy big hands fumbling around without any precision. Brawn before brains. Mia's struggles weren't about fixing, were they? You didn't fix your daughter's grief. How had he not seen it? He could almost see Sofia wagging a finger at him, telling him how disappointed she was in him.

Mia didn't want to be fixed; she didn't need to be fixed. She needed a father who would listen. How had he missed all the signs? How had he forgotten what Sofia had always said?

And now it was too late. His fixing things had gotten them in one heck of a mess that even he, the great fixer, couldn't fix. He'd done quite the opposite, actually.

Maybe he should go get Mia right now. Their flight was in two days, Tuesday morning. What if he called the airline and changed their flight? He could say something came up at work and that they had to take off early. He could probably find a red-eye out of Madrid—or even Barcelona. Hell, they could just go get a hotel somewhere else. Mia would be sad, of course, and certainly mad at him, but they could escape before all of this blew up in their faces.

And how could Baxter face Alma and spend time with her for the next two days without revealing the truth? Hell, how could he look Ester in the eyes, knowing the game she was playing?

The best thing to do now was get out of the way . . .

He pulled at his hair and looked down into the water, seeing his reflection. And he was disgusted by it, by the man who could have prevented all this had he not been so selfish.

Another image appeared, one of Sofia on the beach, the little bump that was evidence of their daughter starting to show.

The cheerleader she was, Sofia didn't want him to leave Cactus Road. "No, Bax," she'd said, touching her belly, "I can handle her. You go on tour and keep writing songs. Do what you're meant to do." When she'd said it, he'd tasted victory. He remembered casting a look over the Atlantic, thinking that he was off the hook, that he hadn't been forced to make the decision. If he had been, what would he have said? He wasn't exactly sure, which wasn't a good enough answer.

It didn't matter that he'd done his best when he finished his tours. "But when you're home, you're home," Sofia had continued. "We will support your music always, but when you get off that bus, you give us your all." And he had, or at least he thought he had.

But his all wasn't enough. It never had been.

The crunch of gravel stole him from his misery, and he realized his face was covered in tears. He quickly wiped away the evidence with his shirt and turned. It was Alma's Defender. Mia sat in the front seat. He looked away and drew in a few deep breaths, shaking off the feelings inside.

As the Defender slid to a stop, Mia poked her head out the window. "What you doin', Daddy?"

He stood and went to the window. "Just hanging out."

"You okay?" she asked.

"Yeah, of course. Okay? I'm fabulous." If only she knew. He looked past her to Alma. "Hey."

"Buenas," she said, and he thought she could surely sense the pain he attempted to hide. And seeing her, he knew what he'd felt for her was now dead—it had to be.

He looked away, unable to shake the idea that he was keeping such a secret from her. Even if he knew it wasn't right, Ester had asked him to keep quiet. Whom should he betray? Alma had her own secrets too.

He forced himself to look at her. "Are you done for the day?"

"Yep," she said, "we just left the mill."

Mia held up a bottle full of a beautiful neon-green oil. "Look what I have. Wanna try?"

Baxter put his hand on his daughter's cheek and turned up his lips. "You know I do. Will you give me just a few minutes? I have one last phone call."

Chapter 28

NUOVO

The call to Delta was as punishing as one could imagine. He would have gladly paid the nearly $200-a-person change fee for the 11:00 a.m. flight the next day, but they wanted another twelve hundred for the fare difference.

If they still had a few days to go, he might have considered it, but to get them out only a day earlier wouldn't have been worth it. Instead, he decided he'd stick with their flight on Tuesday but leave Cadeir in the morning. He wasn't exactly sure how he'd pull it off with Mia but would start early by telling her and everyone else that something had come up with work. Then, at their hotel in Madrid, he could figure out how to explain that they were still stuck on the same flight.

Of course, yanking her away early could have the opposite effect and hurt her even more, but it was a chance he had to take. Yes, he knew that lying wasn't always the best way . . . but in this case he was pretty sure it was. Whatever it took to protect his daughter.

Satisfied he'd at least found an exit strategy, having booked a night at a hotel near the airport with an indoor pool that might make Mia happy, Baxter walked into the house thinking all they had to do was make it through the night.

As if it would be so easy. He'd forgotten that Ester had a dinner engagement with friends that would keep her out late, which meant

Mia wouldn't get to spend their last night hanging out with or sleeping with her grandmother. Not that Mia would know that it was their last night.

He was gentle on her as he helped her get ready for bed. He could sense she was sad they were leaving soon, so instead of losing his patience after asking her six times to brush her teeth, he brought her the tooth-brush and offered to help. He finally got her into bed around nine, and he read to her for a while, and then she asked for him to sing to her.

As Baxter lifted Don Jorge's guitar out of its case, he thought of Alma downstairs, probably still watching television. He'd been unsure how to handle the situation with her, so he'd decided the best thing to do was avoid it. "Mia's a little sad about leaving," he'd whispered to her as Mia was walking up the stairs. "I'm probably going to stay up there with her. Make sure she sleeps well. See you bright and early."

"*Vale*, have a good night. Buenas noches." For a moment, he'd thought Alma looked disappointed by his decision, but he blamed it on the crazy voice in his head that had once told him it would be a good idea to kiss her.

He sat on the edge of the bed and twisted his body toward Mia so that the guitar faced her. As he tuned up, she asked, "Daddy, when do you think we can come back? Do we have to wait until the summer? What about spring break? Isn't it in March?"

The guitar suddenly felt wrong in his hands, and he didn't feel like playing. "I think we can talk about spring break."

"Yay," she said. Her breath smelled of bubblegum toothpaste. "Aunt Alma says everything gets pregnant in the spring. The dogs, the horses, chickens. I love babies. I want puppies to climb all over me."

He strummed the guitar, and the chord reverberated within him. Was there really a difference between lies? Was there gray area, or was it black and white? The truth or a lie?

He knew the answer.

No, he couldn't lie and tell her they had to go home for work. Nor could he keep hidden the sale of the estate. The guitar in his hands felt like its own form of truth serum, so much more powerful than the Afilador.

If he really wanted to be different when they returned, then he needed to be a new man, one who wasn't trying to protect Mia from everything.

Determined to get something right, he said, "I have to tell you, kiddo. Looks like they're selling the estate. We might have to visit everyone at their new house."

Her innocent eyes peered up at him. "What?"

"Yeah, I know . . . it's sad, but I think they're ready to move on."

As her bottom lip jutted out, he felt so bad for her. Sure, it was just a piece of property, but he'd seen her come alive here. She might see the estate as not only where her entire Spanish family gathered, but also a place that still gave life to her mother.

"Wait, so we're never coming back here?" She looked to be on the verge of tears.

"Probably not." As he shook his head, he caught himself scrambling to make it all better. He'd promised her a puppy once things settled down at work, but maybe that would make her smile now . . .

And yet what could be better proof that he'd lost control of the situation than him trying to plug his leaky ship with a puppy, as if it and its floppy ears would fix all their worries? At that point, why not plant olive trees in their backyard in Greenville, figure out how to make tortillas the way Ester does? Hell, why not get cardboard cutouts of Ester and Alma, set them up in the living room?

A puppy, he thought, shaking his head. And he hadn't even told her the worst of it yet, about Ester. What would he use then, an elephant?

Enough fixing.

He brushed his hand through Mia's hair. "I'm sad about it too. I was looking forward to coming back. But no matter where everyone moves, we're going to find them and visit as much as we can. How about that?"

She slowly inclined her shoulders and then let them fall. "That sounds okay."

He pinched her cheek. "You're a tough girl, you know. Tougher than me."

"I guess," she said in a melancholy tone.

"It's true," he said, pulling his hand away from her face. "I don't know if you feel like listening, but . . . can I play you a tune?"

An ever-so-slight nod as she muttered, "Yes, please."

Doing the only thing he was ever good at, he let his right hand pick up a rhythm on the guitar. He played a tune from the old days, but his head was elsewhere.

What in the world would Mia think if she knew that he'd kissed Alma? Or that he had feelings for her? Feelings for Sofia's half sister! He couldn't imagine admitting it to anyone. Even the idea that Ester had picked up on it made his blood curdle.

He played two more songs, and when Mia yawned, he played her the "Unicorn Song," singing the chorus while on the brink of collapse.

When Mia dreams she dreams of butterflies
And she drifts away to this lullaby
When she wakes she's glad to be alive
And her mommy and daddy are right here by her side . . .

By the time he'd finished, she was sleeping. He remembered playing the song for Mia for the first time, Sofia singing with him. *Mommy and Daddy are right here by her side.*

Were they? Were they really? Or was it just a broken daddy who had let down his wife and little girl? Where was Sofia in all this? Was she in this room? No, he wasn't feeling her tonight. He and Mia were alone.

Baxter watched her sleep for a long time with his guitar in his lap. Alma was still downstairs, and he didn't want to see her. He didn't want to talk about Ester being sick or the estate going away. And he didn't want to have to pretend that all was well, that he hadn't found a recording revealing her brother's crime, or that he'd booked a hotel in Madrid for the next night, that he and Mia weren't leaving.

Baxter watched Mia's chest rise and fall. He looked at her beautiful face, the most beautiful face in the world. What kind of God would allow this being to suffer so? He strummed the guitar and sang, "All you do is take and take and take, you take it all away."

What am I doing? he wondered, pulling his hands away from the strings. "What happened to me?" he asked himself out loud.

He strummed a minor seven chord. "What happened to me? Does anybody know?"

He was silent for a moment, as if someone might answer.

"What happened to me," he sang, "as if I don't know?"

Baxter pinched the bridge of his nose and folded over Don Jorge's guitar.

"My little girl," he whispered in quiet song. "I'm sorry I let you down."

He reached out and touched the big toe of her right foot that poked up through the blanket. Where did they go from here? What could he do differently?

As if the guitar held the key, he strummed a few chords, searching for something, wishing words to rise up out of him.

And they did . . . Ester's words from a while ago.

"When you get my age, you give up on pretending," he sang quietly. Suddenly he felt immersed, like his eyes were waking, his whole body waking, the black-and-white filter draped over him like a blanket of chains slipping off. He felt something stir inside, and the word *truth* rose up within him, as if he'd not known the truth until now. Seeing the way Ester had begged him not to tell Alma had held up a mirror and showed him how dangerous it could be to avoid the truth. And telling Mia the truth moments earlier seemed to have shaken something loose.

No more secrets, he thought. *Not anymore.*

He began to see visions of how he'd been living so wrongly, and then Alma returned to his mind, and almost instantaneously a song came out of him, one he knew was a gift from on high.

"I'm stuck on the page of a painted world, I'm falling in love with a painted girl." The words kept rising and the chords seemed to lead the way, his hands moving without his direction. Someone was playing him, like back in the old days. He was immersed, a puppet to the great songwriter in the sky.

When the song came to its own conclusion, the lyrics still hung in the air. It was so clear to him now. He hadn't been truly living since losing Sofia, and instead he'd been trapped in a painted world. And Alma . . . she was nothing more than a painted girl, a fiction he'd created to fill the immense crater that Sofia had left. But at least he'd caught himself in time . . . and that idea gave him hope.

"Sofia?" he said quietly, slightly aware he was losing his mind. "Sofia, are you there?"

Chapter 29

THE TRUTH LIKE A SNAKE

Baxter woke afraid, and he grabbed for something and came up with a handful of white sheets in both fists. The sun slanted through the window and cut a line across the bed. It must have been at least seven in the morning. He gently turned to his side to look at Mia. She'd slept through the night again. Her nightmares were going away.

If only she didn't have to find out all the truths today. But she did. He knew that now.

The truth.

He had to stop worrying and fixing and protecting and tell the truth. How could he ask Ester to come clean if he wasn't telling Mia about Ester being sick? Or if he was pretending he'd changed their flight? He could still see Ester shrinking in on herself yesterday, and the sight worked to break him away from his own shadows. This was what happened when you lived a life of trying to control the uncontrollable. Hell, he was even experiencing early symptoms of heart issues. Was he on Ester's exact path?

The truth wasn't always easy, but it had a way of making things right. What if this was the last time Mia saw her grandmother? Wouldn't she want to hug her a little tighter, spend a little more time saying good-bye? You're damn right she would. Baxter would do anything to redo those last days with Sofia, to slow them down and savor them.

There were so many things devastatingly wrong with how he'd been attempting to process his grief. How in the world had he not seen it? His false feelings for Alma might be the worst of it, but there'd been countless examples before then. And what was he thinking trying to sneak Mia out of there this morning?

He had failed a million ways, but at least he could do the right thing now. He wasn't sure how to tell Mia that her grandmother was sick. It would be almost unbearable, nearly as bad as telling her about Sofia's murder. But he knew that he would do it today, hopefully with Ester by his side.

When Mia woke a few minutes later, he moved her hair from her eyes and kissed her forehead. "Good morning, little princess."

"Good morning, Daddy." She said it very sadly.

"What's going on?"

"What do you think? We have to leave tomorrow."

He pressed his eyes closed, collecting himself, making sure his reaction was true. When he opened them again, he said, "I'm not ready to go back home either. But we have to."

"I know."

"That's why we need to make today the best ever, right?" To her nod, he said, "Let's do that. Let's make it the best day of the whole trip."

He was struggling with how hard it would be to break the news as they walked down the stairs to the smell of coffee and fire. If she was down now, how much worse could it get? Still, he couldn't keep protecting her.

It looked like Alma and Ester were into a serious discussion when Baxter and Mia entered the kitchen. Alma smiled at him, and he found it hard to make eye contact with her as he mumbled a good morning.

Mia slumped into the stool next to Ester and said with great melancholy, "Good morning, Iaia."

Ester put her hand on Mia's back. "What's going on, *pobrecita*?"

"She's sad about leaving," Baxter said, answering for his daughter, who had chosen not to speak. "I told her that you were selling too." He reached for two glasses and began to fill them with water.

Both of the women sighed audibly, showing Mia, whose head was down, the vast abundance of their care.

Alma came around the counter. "This is why we've decided to do something very special today." Was Alma reading minds? He and Mia had just had that conversation.

"What?" Mia said, lifting her head heavily, like a weight was tied to it.

"Well," Alma said, "you can't come to Spain and not see the Mediterranean. My favorite place in the world is a little over an hour away. It's called Xàbia. They have amazing playgrounds and a beautiful coastline. Delicious ice cream. And you can take your shoes off and walk in the sand. What could be better?"

Mia was skeptical. "But I thought you had to work."

"Family is more important than olives," Alma said. "Besides, I have to prove to your father that he's the only workaholic in this house."

"Ouch," Baxter said, the jab hurting more than she probably intended.

"Let me get my guys started," Alma said, "and we could leave by noon. What do you say, Baxter?"

As if he had a choice. "If Mia's in, I'm in."

"Okay," Mia said, looking slightly brighter.

Baxter decided that he had to be strong for Mia. Enough wallowing in his own stuff. He leaned across the counter, trying to get her attention. "Hold on. Is that a smile I detect?"

She side-eyed him.

"Don't you dare smile."

She was trying not to.

"Nope, don't do it. Don't make me whip out a dad joke."

She was fighting it back now, the corners of her mouth turning up. Ester and Alma were already grinning. Baxter thought about what

Alma had said, how he used humor as a shield. No, that's not what he was doing now. He was using humor to lift his daughter up. There was a difference.

"I'm warning you," Baxter said. "The Mediterranean isn't even pretty anyway; it's basically sludge. And the ice cream tastes like mushy peas. The playgrounds are all falling apart, like dangerous." Mia was breaking, and he pushed her harder. "Ready for dad joke 764?"

"No, please don't, Daddy. You're going to embarrass yourself."

He had her now. "Why would you give a T. rex Tylenol?"

Mia rolled her eyes, bracing for it.

"Because he went for a run and he's dino-*sore*."

Mia suddenly bloomed like a flower, her smile stretching wide.

"Ah, there it is. My beautiful girl."

Her smile might fade later, but that was life, one long series of ups and downs.

⌣

The four of them came into Xàbia from the north, Baxter up front with Alma making small talk, and Ester in the back with Mia tucked up against her. They passed countless olive and orange groves. Scattered among them were extraordinary vineyards set in soil as red as flames, with vines that looked similar to Diego's, short and stubby like bushes. The palm trees grew in abundance, too, and it truly felt like paradise, this Xàbia. The low-rise stuccoed buildings all had terra-cotta roofs and showed a heavy Moorish influence, with fancy ornamentation, horse-shoe arches, and mosque-like angles and curves.

The Mediterranean soon came into view, its bright-blue splendor glimmering like a sea of diamonds. Xàbia was tucked into a large cove, protected by cliffs on either side. Alma explained that the beach was to their right, marking the southern part, and then three kilometers north was the port, where another collection of restaurants and hotels stood.

"I could live here forever," Baxter whispered, taking in the sights.

"Now you see why all the Madrileños come here," Alma said.

"Madrileños?" Baxter asked.

"People from Madrid, the *pijos*."

"*¿Pijos?*"

"The . . . how do you say . . . the people with money who have beach houses and big rings and fast cars—"

"Ah, I get it," Baxter said. "Big rings and fast cars."

"*Pijos,*" Mia parroted, looking out through the windshield.

"Don't let her translate that," Ester warned.

Alma drove them along the water toward the port and stopped halfway up, where it was quieter, a few walkers and joggers, no restaurants, only low-rise condos with dreamy balconies and vacation villas decorated with purple and pink geraniums. The coastline was made up of a sandstone shelf that dropped off into the sparkling, transparent sea. Up a little farther, boats bobbed in the port under the watchful eye of the magnificent houses perched on the cliff.

The salty wind blew in from the ocean, slapping waves against the shore. Baxter pulled a sweater over Mia's head and took her hand. They walked toward the water, navigating the shelf.

Alma pointed to one of the many etched-out areas in the dark rock where the rising water had created pools. "Romans used to cut out blocks of the sandstone to use as building materials, and they used the resulting pools as baths when they filled up during high tide. This was all a giant spa."

Listening to her reminded him of how her passion had been so instrumental in guiding him back to the guitar and to maybe even his life, and he regretted how he'd used her as an anecdote to his grief. She didn't deserve that.

"The Roman empire sent their generals to Valencia after they retired," Alma said. "I imagine many of them came here." She pointed out over the clear blue water. "And out there about two hours by boat is Ibiza. But I like Xàbia better. It's more, emm . . . *cómo se dice* . . . quaint."

Though he was half listening, he was also wondering what he'd been to her. Had he led her on? Was she hoping that there would be more between them? Probably not. She might not have even thought of him in that way since their kiss, so why was he still so hung up on it? Surely guilt, he decided.

When they reached the water, Baxter picked up a rock and skipped it toward Ibiza, thinking he could feel his soul healing with each wave.

The sun shone on him hard, and he felt a great moment of lightness as he put his focus on the feel of his daughter's hand secure in his. They were on this ride called life together, and surely he could make it work. The answer started with the truth and accepting that he couldn't always fix every situation, but there needed to be more. To be a great father, he needed to put all the pieces together. Alma had made the point that Baxter needed to live again, that Mia needed the old Baxter most of all. His living again might be the final piece to his life puzzle.

What did it mean, to live again? What was his truth?

As if the answer had been waiting for him to ask the question, he felt music teasing his soul, and lyrics rose from his core and up to his lips. It was a wonderful feeling, the sense of a song coming on, and he opened up his heart to it.

There came a time when it was over
And I looked back to where I'd been
The way I drove myself crazy
over things I didn't understand
Well, settle back
Easy Sunshine,
Lose yourself in the rising tide
There's no way to know what's coming
We're just along for the ride.

As the song drifted away out over the sea, Baxter felt someone take his other hand. He slid his eyes right and was startled to see that no one was there. And yet there was someone there, and he knew it. Sofia's hand felt as real as Mia's. It was the three of them again. And right then Baxter knew that it had been Sofia who had somehow orchestrated this whole thing, somehow found a way to send that email from 23andMe. *Nice one, Sofe.* And he thought he might know what she was getting at.

For one, might it be that she was giving him his music back? He felt so musical inside now, melodies dancing in him like the old days. Perhaps it was okay that he'd chased his dream with his band, even after meeting her. That was what she had wanted. No one can control life. The day she'd been killed wasn't proof that he'd made all the wrong decisions. It wasn't Baxter being punished for his selfish choice. That man and that day was just a part of life that can happen to anyone.

Goose bumps rose on his skin as he bathed in the love rising up from Sofia's and Mia's hands. With this trip that she'd surely orchestrated, Sofia wasn't only showing Baxter that her death wasn't his fault, and not only was she giving him permission to play music again, but she was also telling him to live again.

Alma touched Mia's arm. "Tag, you're it." Then Alma was off, running along the sandstone shelf, leaping over pools of seawater where tiny fish and shrimp swam in circles, waiting for the tide to set them free.

With a smile so strong it could have divided the sea, Mia raced after Alma in an eruption of giggles, yelling out to her aunt, "Oh no you don't!"

Baxter turned to Ester, whose black-and-silver hair blew in the wind. "I need your help with something, and it's very hard for me to ask. Something that might be too much to ask . . . I'd like for us to tell her today."

"Tell who what?" Ester asked, which was a fair question. The secrets were so many that specifics were required.

"I'd like us to tell Mia about you being sick . . . if you"—he raised a hand—"if you're okay with it." He needed her to be okay with it.

Ester looked to the horizon and nodded, as if she'd known it was coming.

Baxter hoped what he'd said and was about to say wasn't him still trying to fix things. The truth seemed to supersede all else. "And maybe it's the time to set free everything bothering you. What if you told Alma about the recording, about Rodolfo stealing? Forgive me for saying so, but you and I are so alike, so full of love, but what if we've been trying too hard to protect our children? If you're selling, you're selling. Accept the offer, but—"

"I accepted the offer this morning," she interrupted.

Baxter felt like he'd been punched in the solar plexus, and it hurt despite the fact he knew it was coming. "Okay, but what about the truth? I can barely look at Alma, knowing what I know. Please consider telling her. She deserves to know. You'll feel better, getting it off your chest." He readied himself to be scolded.

Ester drew in a long breath of salty air. "I will tell them everything today."

Peace washed over him. "Really?"

"Our talk yesterday forced me to do a lot of thinking. My lies have gotten me in enough trouble."

"I know the feeling." He put his arm around her waist and pulled her in. "No one said it would be easy, did they?"

She whispered, "No."

He could only imagine what she'd been through lately, and a wave of sympathy came over him. "Sofia would have loved you, you know? I mean, of course, she would have loved you because you were her mother, but because of who you are too. She would have loved how great you are with Mia and how much you fight for your children."

"I don't know how it's even possible," Ester said, "but I miss her every day, and I barely knew her."

"I think it's not only possible but probable. A mother's bond to her child starts in the womb, not once the baby is breathing. And I know you have the same bond with Rodolfo, no matter what he's done."

She nodded painfully, as if it was the hardest truth to admit in the world. "I lost my Sofia. And I lost my husband." She began to break up. "But I can't lose my only son. I just can't."

Baxter squeezed her tighter, wishing there were something he could say. Instead of pushing his own agenda or trying to impress his limited wisdom upon her, he gently kissed her on the head. "I understand." And he did a little bit.

"There's something about the water," Ester said, "like it has all the answers. Even if I can't reach them, I see them out there, stirring in the waves."

Letting his arm fall from her waist, he returned his gaze to the sea. "It's always been that way for me too."

They smiled at each other. He thought he understood her so much more than he had when they'd arrived. Not only because she was a Pisces, as they'd figured out a couple of days earlier, but because he realized she was confused too. *Sometimes we think those older than us have it figured out, but that's not always the case.*

"How do you say 'the sea' in español?" he asked. "*¿Mer?*"

She shook her head. "*El mar.* But if you're a poet, you can get away with using the feminine form. *La mar.*"

Baxter tried it on. "*La mar.* I like that. The sea is most surely a woman, isn't she? Just like every good boat out there."

"That's it."

Baxter said, "I'm so glad we came. Not just for Mia. Of course, for Mia. But for me too. Meeting you and Alma and the rest of the family has helped me understand Sofia and come to grips with losing her. I feel like . . . I don't know, Ester . . . like this was all meant to be. Whatever led us here, our lives are richer because of it."

She chuckled. "And mine as well. I was over the moon to meet Mia, but I never thought meeting you would have such a great impact on me." She reached for his arm and patted it. "My Sofia was a lucky woman."

Baxter blushed, but he stopped himself from making a joke about not exactly being a bouquet of roses. This was one of those times when it was okay to feel. He didn't need to deflect the emotions swirling around.

As he thanked Ester for the compliment, a memory came to him, and he bit back a swell of anguish. He could see Sofia in the coffee shop where they'd met, and he remembered how they looked at each other. He was holding his guitar, and she'd approached with the best pickup line in the world, one prophetic as hell, come to think about it.

He remembered on that back patio how from the second their eyes locked, they were in trouble. It was in the way she was smiling at him without breaking eye contact, as if they were best friends already. He knew he was giving her that same look of familiarity. And there was an undeniable undercurrent of sexual tension, even in those first seconds.

"Stop it," he told himself, only realizing after he'd set the words free that he'd said them out loud.

"What?" Ester asked.

Attempting to hide the incredible sense of longing scraping at him, he steadied his tone. "Sorry, just talkin' to myself. A songwriter's habit." It had been admittedly nice at times to have relived some of these memories of Sofia, but Baxter was looking forward to leaving it all behind and getting on with life.

Chapter 30

THE TOWER OF POWER

They climbed back into the car and drove up to the port, where there was a broad, palm tree–dotted walkway that threaded between a rocky beach and a long line of restaurants, where people sucked down café con leches, Cokes with lemon slices, and even cervezas or vino, and they ate toast topped with scrambled eggs, shaved *jamón*, or grated tomatoes.

Alma led them down the steps to the pebbly beach, where she dropped to her knees and began to dig. Baxter jabbed his hands into his pockets and watched with Ester as Mia raced over to join Alma. A young boy swung a plastic sword farther down, fighting invisible pirates. Past him a woman sat between the legs of her lover as they watched a swarm of sailboats dancing about in the heavy wind.

"C'mere, Daddy!" Mia called, waving him over so that she could show him something. "Look what I found."

Baxter made his way and squatted to see that she had a handful of wonderful discoveries, including shells he'd never seen before and old bits of patterned terra-cotta tile, worn and rounded by the salt water. "These are amazing, honey," he said, picking up a piece of green sea glass.

"Want to dig with us?" she asked.

"Yes, of course." How many times had he watched her dig, watched her play, stood on the sidelines as the adult?

They searched for treasures and then sat together on the pebbles, studying their finds and watching the sailboats run east with the cool November wind. He saw that his sweet daughter's cup was so full, and he savored the moment with everything he had.

They eventually returned to the car and drove down to the Playa de Arenal, which was the sandy beach tucked into a rocky cove on the south side. Another string of restaurants with ample outdoor seating lined the walkway, facing the sand and sea.

Mia's eyes went straight to the rope tower rising over the sand. Several kids played there, swinging and climbing.

"Can I go play?" she asked, tugging her daddy's hand.

He studied the tower, thinking that it was very high—too high. One boy was all the way at the top, and Baxter thought it would be an arm-breaking fall if there ever was one.

"I'll go with her," Ester said. She pointed to an outdoor table at the restaurant closest to the tower. "Why don't you two find us a table?"

Baxter tightened, hoping he wouldn't have to explain to Alma what he'd realized about her. If it came to it, he would be honest.

Looking over at Mia, he said, "Honey, promise me you won't go more than halfway up."

"I promise." She whipped around and jumped over the wall down into the white sand and then dashed toward the tower. Ester followed at her own pace.

Alma ordered them grilled sardines and *dos copas de vino blanco* (two glasses of white wine) from a British server. As Ibiza-like electronic chill music played from somewhere inside, Alma explained that Xàbia had always attracted expats, and he'd get along fine speaking only English here.

"So it's like Spain with training wheels," Baxter said, feeling rather light and tranquil, despite the lingering remnants of their kiss in the cave hovering above their heads. The more important matter was that Ester was on his page, and there'd be no more secrets soon.

Alma acknowledged his humor only slightly and then began to tap her fingers against the table, as if she was waiting on him to say something. But what? Did he really need to spell it out? Not that she was asking for anything more of him. He thought back to the lyrics from the night before. *I'm stuck on the page of a painted world. I'm falling in love with a painted girl.*

Baxter shifted in his seat, rearranged the silverware, and eventually focused his gaze on Mia climbing up the first rungs of the tower. Ester had taken a seat on a nearby bench.

Nary a word was shared between Baxter and Alma until the server returned. After sipping the cold and crisp verdejo, Baxter broke the silence. "What's Valencia like?" He was referring to the capital city a little over an hour north (and obviously going for lighter conversation).

Alma laughed to herself, as if she knew exactly what he was doing. Thankfully, she played along. "It's quieter than Barcelona or Madrid, but it's still faster than I'm used to. Very beautiful. They have a park called the Turia, the old riverbed that runs for several kilometers through the city. You can bike and run through there. On the end near the water is the opera house and the City of Arts and Science and the aquarium. The architecture is very . . . maybe you would say, futuristic, like *Star Trek*. And the restaurants are amazing."

"I'd like that." He had one eye on Mia, who'd apparently made friends already.

"So," Alma said, clearly tiring of the trivial, "are you mad at me for not telling you about my mother?"

So much for small talk. "No," he said, "I get it. We were just strangers coming into your world. I probably would have done the same thing. The more important thing is that I'm so sorry you're having to go through it. I know it's gotta be hard. She's way too young."

Alma turned so that she could see Ester on the bench. "Yes, she is."

"I want to tell Mia today," Baxter said, moving along. "I told Ester that."

Alma faced the table again and began to twist the stem of her glass, considering what he'd said. She eventually looked at him. "I think it's a good idea."

Baxter gave a nod. As they stared into one another's eyes, he wished he could tell her about Rodolfo, as he felt this growing sense of betrayal. It was enough to make him look away. "I know I did the right thing by bringing her here, but now I feel like I'm going to tear it all out from under her. It's like I've given her this great gift, and she's blooming, but I've given her a whole new set of problems by taking you and Ester away. And maybe even Spain away." He shook his head.

"Stop," she said.

He cursed under his breath and sipped his wine. Then he looked at her again. "I'm just in this stage where I'm wondering what the hell is going on. Have I been the best father I could? While I'm wondering all these things, why didn't I find y'all years ago? We would have been coming here all along. Y'all have given Mia a sense of belonging that's been missing dearly. That's what scares me most. Is she going to be all right going home?"

The idea of going back made him feel like he was taking Mia to a foreign land. A part of him sensed that she belonged here with the Arroyos, and he saw a flash of someone who raises a wounded animal, plucking it from the wild. Eventually that animal gets better, and if she has wings, she needs to fly, and if she has a mother, she needs to go see her, and if she has a herd, she needs to run with it. He wondered if Mia indeed needed to run with her own herd. Where would that leave him, though?

Alma watched him curiously, as if she was waiting until his mind had slowed down. When he found the courage to make eye contact again, she said, "Mia's going to be great wherever she is." For some reason, Baxter believed Alma's words. The painted girl spoke anything but painted words.

The server returned with a bowl of olives and six large grilled sardines. Alma stabbed one and dropped it onto his plate, then took one for herself. Baxter wished he knew what she was thinking, because she seemed as pensive as him, so quiet and reserved.

Instead of prying, though, he held up his fork and asked, "How do we do this?" Perhaps it would be better if they pretended like they'd never kissed.

Alma masterfully pulled off the meat from one side, then lifted up the bone to free the rest of it. Baxter copied her and took a bite, the saltiness of the sea pairing exquisitely with the verdejo.

"Are you kidding me?" he said, the astonishing flavor pulling him back to the now.

She responded with a chuckle. "I know."

God, he was going to miss this life.

After a second sardine, Alma washed it down with a sip of wine. "You're a very good man, Baxter the Tool Man. I think you've raised a wonderful girl. Quit beating yourself up."

He wiped his mouth with a napkin. "You know what. Starting today, I think that might be the mission."

"I'm happy to hear that."

He shared a look with her that seemed to go on and on. He saw flashes of their time together in the past days, and he thought about how much she had impacted him. It might have been Sofia that had gotten him to Spain, but it was Alma who'd taken the baton, a relay of sisters. Alma was the one who'd helped him begin to understand the Spanish way. She was the one who'd shared her father's guitar and introduced him to flamenco music. And it was Alma, too, who had shown him that you can't fix everything. As much as she loved her estate, as deep of a connection as she felt, she'd somehow accepted that it was time to move on. Her surrender was admirable.

"Some things you just have to let go, don't you?" He wasn't speaking to Alma.

She didn't realize he wasn't speaking to her and replied, "What's that?"

He looked across the table at her. "I was just thinking how amazing it is that you're able to let go of the estate without it killing you. I've seen how passionate you are, and yet you can let it all go. I didn't even know that was a thing. You're an inspiration, Alma."

She took his compliment graciously with a humble "Thank you."

"There's something about letting go," he continued. "That's what I've learned about being here. We can't control everything around us. We can't write our future. Sometimes we just have to let go." He raised a finger, thinking of his music. "But, at the same time, there are things that you have to hold on to as well. I suppose you have to be good at knowing which way to go."

"I think you're right," she said, swirling her glass with a sly grin.

Happy. He felt so happy all of a sudden, like he was onto something. Finally the mysteries of the universe were unraveling. Sofia would quite possibly forgive him for his mistakes along the way, including the kiss with Alma. Perhaps it was Baxter who needed to forgive himself, too—for all of it. The beautiful thing was that he had time to turn their life around, and he'd caught himself before it was too late. And now he knew how to do it. God, maybe he should back *way* up and rethink things. Rethink his life.

Rethink his and Mia's life.

Their gated life.

He looked over at Mia dangling halfway up the tower. With a burst of inspiration, as if he were pecking out of his shell, he stood and said, "I'll be right back." He broke into a run across the sand. He felt free, just like he had in the cave. When he got close, he smiled at Ester and reached for the first red rope.

"Hey, Daddy!" Mia called down.

"See you at the top?" he asked, starting to scramble up, feeling the pain in his shoulder flaring up but not caring enough to slow down.

"You're coming up?" she asked skeptically.

"I'm going to the top. Come join me."

"Seriously?" If Mia's smile was the indicator, he'd finally figured it out.

How about this for letting go? he asked himself, fueled by the strange design of life he was suddenly enjoying.

Giggles spilled from Mia's mouth as they climbed, father and daughter, one rung at a time toward the top of the tower—toward a new beginning.

Once they'd arrived, both of them holding on to the top rope, he leaned over and kissed her head. "This is the life, isn't it?"

With bright pearly eyes, she seemed too shocked by his actions to even respond.

They spun their heads around, taking in the sea and the tall cliffs and the electric blue above. For the first time since a dying Sofia had called him from the parking lot, Baxter felt as carefree as a child.

"Things are going to change, honey," he said. "We're gonna go back to a new life in South Carolina. No more working so hard. No more putting off life, okay? I swear to you. I'm so sorry for being gone. But I'm back and I see now. I see so clearly."

"What do you mean?" she asked.

"Don't let me give you any more excuses. It's time to start living. We're going back to Greenville with a new perspective, and we're going to seize back our lives. No more working on the weekends. No more meals standing up. No more building cookie-cutter houses. No more living life on the go. We're going to take Spain back to South Carolina."

She was looking at him like he'd gone crazy.

He was wondering if he'd just written the worst country song on earth. *No more working on the weekends, no more meals standing up . . .*

He laughed to himself. "What I'm saying is . . . this trip has changed me, and you're going to see a new dad when we get back."

With a quizzical look, she said, "Sounds good to me."

He looked back toward the table near the restaurant and saw that Alma had followed him over and sat next to Ester. They watched with broad smiles. And as he bounced his eyes between the two, he decided that the future of the estate wasn't something that he needed to try to fix. If the time had come, then so be it.

Chapter 31

Undercurrents

"I need to talk to the two of you," Ester whispered in the foyer as she set her purse down on a long and skinny oak table. They'd just gotten back from Xàbia, and Mia had raced to the restroom.

Baxter glanced at Alma and back at Ester. "Okay."

Keeping her voice low, Ester said, "I wonder if we might get her comfortable in my bed to watch a movie; then we can talk down here."

Baxter felt a surge of nerves cascade up his back. Though he was glad that Ester had found the courage and that all the truths would soon come to light, he knew it wasn't going to be an easy last night in Spain.

When Ester suggested to Mia that she cuddle up in her bed with Paco and watch a movie, Mia was thrilled. Perhaps the one thing more persuasive than sugar or puppies was screen time.

As they ascended the stairs, Alma and Baxter sat down at the small table in the kitchen. "What's this all about?" she asked.

Baxter met her eyes, refusing to hide or cower away. "I think it's about figuring out the future."

Alma nodded and reached for one of the oranges in the bowl. She dug her fingers into the rind and began to peel it. "It's going to be okay, Baxter. Just be there for Mia. We all will."

He thanked her. "Strangely, I feel okay with Mia finding out."

While they waited for Ester to return, the undercurrents swirling between them were enough to make Baxter want to push the pause button and go hide in a closet. They talked about the harvest, and she told him that she had only a few days left and that it was one of her best. She was ecstatic with how her team had worked together in their last effort and said that the oils tasted better than they ever had.

Though he knew she was being sincere, the entire conversation felt incredibly superficial. Had Mia been there, she would have sprung up from her seat in their safari Jeep and said, "All I see is elephants! You two! Have the dang conversation. Daddy, tell her what you're thinking. Are you really going to leave things this way? Just apologize, if that's what you feel like you need to do." And to Alma, she might say, "Just admit that you're not attracted to him, that you let him kiss you because he sprang it on you while you were both caught up in the magic of that cave."

"Perhaps it's because I know this is our last harvest," Alma said, barreling on despite the undercurrents, "but in the oils I can taste . . . emm . . . the power of one last effort. My father was not perfect, but the best of him did something very special for the olive world, and I know he would be proud. Not of me, that's not what I mean. But of what our family has done for so many years, to get here. Of course, he'd be destroyed that we're selling to those *gilipollas*, but he'd know the time has come. He'd get it. Nothing lasts forever."

Hold on, maybe she wasn't thinking about what had happened between them. It very well could all be in his own head. It wasn't a kiss on her mind; it was making good oil. Hoping she was oblivious to his Old Faithful–worthy geyser of mind chatter, he collected himself and said, "I suppose you're right. He'd be proud of you, though, Alma. He'd be so proud."

She continued to peel the orange, staring at it like it was a crystal ball. "Thank you, but I don't need you to say that."

Of course she had other things on her mind. It was a kiss, not a proposal. She'd probably not even thought about it since, and here he was worried that he was going to break her heart. Oh boy, he still had a lot to learn. No, she wasn't waiting on him to explain his take on their relationship. Like any good artist, she was focused on her work. And that was when it hit him that none of this was about him. What a fool he could be. The poor woman was about to find out something awful, and he was trying to twist these last hours in Spain into being about him.

She was a very good person who'd recently lost her father, and she was losing their estate, and in a few moments she was about to find out that her brother had been stealing from them. No, this wasn't about Baxter at all.

Shaking all the heavy thoughts from his purview, he leaned forward and spoke from his heart. "I'm saying it because I believe it, not because I'm trying to . . . I don't know . . . make you feel better." As she lifted her gaze from the orange, he refused to look away, and in her green eyes he saw so much sincerity and kindness and warmth, and he hated that she was about to be caught unawares.

Ester came in moments later and joined them at the table.

"I have something to tell you, Alma," Ester said. Baxter started to stand, to get out of the way, but Ester motioned for him to stay. She uncurled her hand to reveal Jorge's Dictaphone.

"What's that?" Alma broke apart the orange, filling the room with its scent.

"Baxter found this in your father's guitar case a few days ago. Before you get mad at him for not telling you, I wouldn't let him. Despite how much he urged me to. I've been trying to figure out what to do, how to tell you."

"Tell me what? What's on the recording?" She held halves of the orange in each hand. Drops of juice had dripped down onto the table.

Ester looked at the Dictaphone. "Your brother has been stealing from the company."

That got Alma's attention. Her head snapped to her mother. "What?"

This was incredibly hard for Ester. Baxter could see it all over her face. "They are fighting, your father and brother on the tape. And your father accuses Rodolfo of stealing. And he admits to it."

Alma sat motionless, staring into her mother's eyes. Baxter wanted to reach for her hand, just to show that he was there for her, but what in the world would that do? He was just some knucklehead from South Carolina who'd screwed all this up in the first place.

After a few beats of silence, Alma said, "Play it."

Ester pressed the play button and set down the Dictaphone next to the collection of peels from the orange. The sound of Don Jorge tuning his guitar rose up into the air. Baxter couldn't help but watch Alma as she listened, her eyes locked on the black device. She moved her gaze to her mother when, in the recording, her brother knocked on the door.

When the recording ended, Alma pulled her hands to her lap. She stared at the table for a long time. Baxter tried to feel with her what she was going through and knew it all too well, the overwhelming sense of betrayal, a family falling apart.

Alma's silence forced Ester to speak. "Baxter brought it to me yesterday. Of course I was going to play it for you but was waiting for the right time."

"The right time?" Alma said, her anger flaring. She cut Baxter a look. "You've known about this? Both of you have?" What followed was a string of Spanish that Baxter knew was not anything kind, and he accepted all of it as duly deserved.

"I told you," Ester said. "I wouldn't let him say anything. If there's anyone to blame, it's me."

Alma shook her head and said something to Ester in Spanish.

"In English," Ester said. "Baxter is family."

The word *family* was cold and hot at the same time. Ester was very kind to include him in such a way, and he did feel like they'd opened their arms to him, but he wasn't so sure that he deserved it. If it wasn't for all his meddling, they wouldn't be having this conversation.

"I went to the bank yesterday," Ester said. "I never thought to look at the transfers from last year. I just thought your father had failed to save as much as he'd told me over the years. But there are two large transfers two days apart. Close to three hundred thousand euros total."

Baxter sat back. Wow, that was a lot of money.

Alma switched back to Spanish for a moment, spitting out something to her mother. Ester responded with equal anger, first in Spanish, then back to English. "I don't know how. He's the salesman. He had access. All he had to do was use his phone number to make the transfers."

"Have you spoken to him yet?" Alma asked.

Ester shook her head. "No. I wasn't sure what to do. I wanted to talk to you first."

Alma's eyes narrowed as lines creased her jawline. "He is not my brother. Not anymore."

Her sharp and speedy disavowal of Rodolfo hit Baxter hard in the chest.

"We need to talk to him first," Ester said. "We can't make assumptions."

"Assumptions?" Alma pointed to the recorder. "There are no assumptions to be made. He's been stealing. He's admitted it. And you're ready to bail him out once again." Venom surged through her words.

Ester dropped her head, as if she knew that was coming. "We need to talk to him, to help him."

"All you do is help him! Ever since he was a baby. He doesn't want to work, so you make excuses. He won't do his homework, so you do it for him. He doesn't want to be a part of this farm, so you sell it." Alma balled up her fists and swung at the air with a curse in Spanish.

"He's damaged and he hurts inside," Ester said. "Your father never gave him the love he deserved, so it's been up to me to make up for it. Do not dare blame me for that."

Baxter tended to agree with Alma. Though he could empathize with both Ester's attempts to make up for Don Jorge's poor parenting and Rodolfo's struggles to find a place in the world, Baxter would never condone theft. The shadow of a lousy father was cast wide, but it was not inescapable.

Ester pressed her eyes closed. "We have to talk to him."

"What is there to talk about?" Alma asked. Baxter thought she might upend the table at any moment.

"He's your brother, Alma. He deserves a chance to make things right."

"There's no making things right with him. Don't you see?" She jabbed the table with her finger. "You shouldn't be selling the estate. You should let me take it."

Baxter almost whispered that he agreed, but he reminded himself of his decision at the top of the rope tower, that this wasn't his fight.

Ester shifted in her seat, as if she was searching for a way to rid the pain. "He is your brother, and he is my son. He is not something you throw away. We will talk to him tomorrow, and I will figure out what to do. He will pay back every dime with his part of the inheritance. That I assure you."

As Alma shook her head over and over in anger, Baxter calmly placed a hand on the table. "I'm gonna let y'all talk, okay? I'm completely here for you if you need me, but I brought this on, and I just . . . it's not my pla—"

"No," Ester said, cutting him off. "There's something else, and you need to hear it."

As if it was an order, Baxter settled back into his chair. What now?

"Oh, *Dios mío*," Alma said. "Of course there is. What else has he done?"

"This has to do with me," Ester said, her voice suddenly becoming strained. She reached for her throat. "I need a water."

Baxter rushed to the cabinet and found a glass. He filled it from the purified water tap and took it to her. She drank a long sip, like she'd nearly died of thirst.

"What can I do?" he asked, wondering if there was medicine she needed.

She touched her heart and closed her eyes, clearly waiting for some pain to pass. Quiet seconds ticked by. "I'm fine," she finally said. "And you've already done so much, Baxter. You've helped me understand that I can't keep hiding the truth."

She sat back and crossed her arms. "Which brings me to something I need to say. I need to tell you both a story." Her eyes seemed to lead her back through time. "When your father left for Germany, for school, we had broken up, as you know. And shortly after, I became pregnant with Sofia. I told you that it was a onetime thing. It was more than that. A relationship that was very complicated, but it was a man I loved. A man I loved as much as your father—or more. You know, they say you only have one love in a lifetime. I don't think it's true. Not always."

Ester slid her eyes to Alma. "I've loved two men in my life."

"What are you talking about, Mama?"

Baxter was equally perplexed as he waited for more.

"I never cheated on your father," Ester continued. "I may have lied to him, but I never cheated. We'd decided to break up. Perhaps my feelings for this other man had been growing, but I never would have acted on them." She added in hindsight, "I don't think I would have."

Then she said, "Only after Jorge had broken up with me and I was still here in Cadeir. Only then did I let myself truly fall for Sofia's father. And it was beautiful. It was autumn here, the leaves like they are now. Knowing we had to hide our love for each other because of this small town, we snuck around." A smile lifted the corners of her lips. "He would steal kisses from me at night. Or take me walking in the mountains. Or we might leave for the day or the weekend. No one ever knew. There was something beautiful and exhilarating about that."

"Who is he, Mama? Do I know him?" Alma pulled her hair behind her ears, her furrowed brow showing bewilderment.

Ester kept speaking as if she didn't hear Alma's question. "And it wasn't just lust. That's what I knew. I felt for him in a similar way that I felt for your father. The way you do when you find your soul mate. The problem . . . was that they were best friends."

Though Baxter suspected what was coming, it still hit him like a bucket of ice water over his head.

Alma sat up. "What?"

"This man that I loved, he was Diego. Sofia's father. Mia's grandfather."

It was as if the room had been blasted by dry ice, every bit of it frozen. Alma with her mouth agape, her eyes full of shock and staring at her mother. Ester, with the weight of the world leaving her, the expression on her face one of surrender. And Baxter, his hands on the edge of the table, his gaze lost in the grains of the wood.

He'd known it, but the idea had been too preposterous, a silly contrivance of the imagination. He thought back to the way Mia and Sofia had leaned over the chess table so similarly, and he remembered the curious question Diego had asked about Sofia's age when she'd been killed.

"Does he know?" Baxter finally asked, thinking of the conversations the two men had shared. He'd been talking with Sofia's father. Good God.

Alma was still staring at her mother in disbelief. Ester turned her exhausted eyes to Baxter. "Between spending time with you and Mia and then my call to him, I think he figured it out. He's been calling and texting me. Unsure what to do, I've been ignoring him, putting it off. I thought that maybe he'd let it go."

"How could you lie about this?" Alma asked as she thrust her hands above her shoulders. "For so many years. Who are you? It's all lies."

Baxter fell back to the day he'd told Mia about her mother's murder, and the deception materialized as a sharp burn in his chest. He wanted to take Alma's hand and say, "It's not all lies. Parents just make mistakes sometimes." But he stayed out of the way and then found himself thinking about Sofia and how she could have met both of her parents all along.

Ester looked at her daughter with great strength. "I didn't tell anyone about Diego and Sofia because it would have destroyed your father. It would have broken his heart to know that I'd slept with Diego. He would have lost his best friend, and he never would have taken me back. You and your brother never would have been born."

Alma was clearly fighting back tears.

"What happened?" Baxter asked. "Between you and Diego?" Though the previous conversation had less to do with him, this topic had everything to do with him and Mia, and he wanted to know more.

"As soon as I realized I was pregnant, I told my parents. They would have figured it out. And they pulled me out of school and sent me to the convent in Madrid. And they forbade me to see Diego until after I'd had the baby. They were so ashamed and didn't want everyone in Cadeir to find out. I told Diego I'd made a mistake seeing him and that it was over. I pleaded with him to never tell Jorge and to let me go. He cried that day and begged me to stay with him. He even tried to find me, but my parents wouldn't tell him where I'd gone. After I had the baby, I moved to England to go to Cambridge. I couldn't face Diego, so I made up excuses to avoid coming back to Cadeir. I still loved him and missed him so much."

Ester drew in a slow breath. "And I wanted to tell him about the baby, but it was too late. Sofia was long gone, I knew. I didn't want him to hate me. My four years at Cambridge were plagued by this pain.

Jorge had come to see me throughout, missing me, trying to get me back. I wouldn't allow it. I still loved Diego.

"My last semester, a month before graduation, I heard that Diego had gotten engaged. I knew he'd been dating someone—a girl we'd gone to school with—as I'd been keeping up through my friends here. It broke me. I had plans to stay in England and go to law school." A sigh. "I didn't have it in me anymore. I didn't want to go home, and I didn't want to stay. I didn't know what to do. And that's when Jorge came back to me. He slowly gave me life again."

Ester lifted an open hand. "The rest, you know. He proposed, and I left England for good. As difficult as it was, I agreed to move back to Cadeir. Jorge had no choice. By then his parents had left him the estate. So I had to come back here and live right next door to Diego and watch him with another woman. It was at our wedding here on the estate that I saw Diego for the first time in years. I could barely look at him."

Alma looked all over the place, putting together the pieces. "He's been living next to us all this time. And, what, you still love him?"

"I always loved him."

Baxter propped his elbows up on the table and massaged his face. He appreciated Ester sharing the story, and he felt her pain, and he couldn't imagine how hard her life had been back then. But he was focused on his daughter.

He said to Ester, "I want Mia to know."

"I do too," Ester said quickly. "That's why I'm telling you. And I want to tell Diego. This ends today." She sighed and looked at Alma. "All that I can say . . . all that I can promise . . . is that I will never lie to you again."

Alma stared at her mother, and Baxter wondered what she might be thinking. Was she skeptical, angry, afraid? He recognized in Alma's face the same look of confusion that Sofia had showed when she spoke about how her mother had ambushed her with the news of her adoption, all forced to the surface because Sofia had expressed interest in doing a

DNA test. In fact, Alma looked more like Sofia right then than she ever had before. They might be different in so many ways, but the way they needed to trust the ones they loved was indistinguishable.

Alma stood. The chair legs scraped against the tile.

Ester reached for her daughter. *"Cariño."*

Alma shook her off and stalked across the kitchen, saying something in Spanish over her shoulder. Baxter was pretty sure she'd said that she needed some time. The front door squeaked open and then shut closed, and the house went silent. A moment later, the Defender out front came alive, and Baxter listened to it crush gravel as Alma sped away.

Among the many thoughts tugging at him, the prevailing one was that he should go after her. She didn't deserve any of this, and he wanted to take her in his arms and tell her that he knew what she was going through and that it would be okay and that he was sorry for his hand in it. He even felt for the keys to the Audi in his pocket.

But then the absurdity of it crashed down on him. She wasn't Sofia. She wasn't his wife, his partner. He wasn't supposed to be there for her, to go after her—not now, not after he'd crossed every boundary in the world and kissed her.

So instead he let go of the keys and took hold of Ester's hand. "She'll be okay. It just takes time."

Ester patted his hand and said somberly, "If only we had more."

Chapter 32

Coming Clean to Mia

They sat on the front steps, Mia between Baxter and Ester. Their thighs touched. They faced the lawn and fountain and beyond into the groves. The waning sun hid behind a patch of dark clouds. Paco sat between Mia's legs, and she stroked his fur. Baxter could sense Mia's nerves, as if she was aware of the gravity of the coming conversation.

After a brief chat about the film Mia had been watching, Ester dropped the hammer. "With you leaving tomorrow, I need to tell you some things. *We* need to tell you some things."

Baxter felt his nervous system calm, as if he was indeed letting go of the consequences, knowing with all of him that they were doing the right thing by catching Mia up to speed.

"Your father," Ester said, "he doesn't know it, nor would he believe it, but he's had a big impact on me this week. We get along well together. And what I know, Mia, about your father, is that he loves you, and he loved your mother with all of him, every last bit of him. And you know your father would do anything for you, right? I'm the same way. I'd do anything for my children."

Ester paused as if she'd lost her train of thought. "There are some things you need to know before you leave, and they will make you sad. But I want you to show me how strong you are. Somehow, you've come back from losing your mother, and you are a bright star for us all to gather around and find strength in. I want you to be at your brightest right now. Can you do that?"

Mia looked to Baxter and then to Ester. "Yes, ma'am." Hesitance seared the tone of her words as she pulled at her hair.

"Give me your hand," Ester said, lifting up an open left hand. Mia took it and Ester squeezed. "Can you stay strong for me?"

Mia nodded.

Baxter put his hand over her jeans on her shin, assuring her that he was there for her too. The air escaped his lungs as he waited for Ester to continue. He sat up and put his arm around Mia and then extended it so that he could touch Ester's shoulder. He hoped it might be enough for her to know that she wasn't alone. That neither of them was alone.

A long silence followed, then, "I have a sick heart, Mia, and they have to perform very serious surgery on me to give me a new one."

Mia turned concerned eyes up to her grandmother. "Why is it sick?"

"There are a lot of reasons. I suppose, in the end, stress, bad choices, a long life of trying to keep everyone together, no matter what it took. I had surgery late last year, and it wasn't enough. My only chance now is a heart transplant. That means they will take out my sick heart and replace it with someone else's healthy heart. It's risky surgery, but people can often go on to live very long lives afterward."

"They're going to take out someone else's heart? Then they'll die, won't they?"

Baxter was feeling heaviness in his own heart. He thought he'd better take this question. "The heart will come from someone who passed away, Mia. Someone who had a healthy heart. It's a very special thing, the greatest gift you can give someone."

"That's right," Ester agreed. "I'm on a list, and when my times comes, they will call me. And the heart that's meant to be for me will be waiting. It is very special."

Mia suddenly thrust her arms out and around her grandmother's neck, her voice laced with sadness. "I don't want you to die, Iaia."

Ester's eyebrows crinkled like tinfoil, and she cried into Mia's neck. Mia and Baxter broke down too. He wrapped his arms around both of them, smelling Ester's flowery perfume and sensing the power and love of the three of them. Baxter felt the wetness of Paco's nose on his hand as the dog attempted to squeeze in as well.

Dammit. Why did it have to be this way? Why did death have such an impossible grip around life? There was still one more truth stuck in its cage, but the setting free of this secret was the one he'd feared the most.

"There's one more thing I want to tell you," Ester said when they broke apart from each other. She laughed sinisterly, and Baxter knew exactly why. All this protecting had led to lies that had formed like a tumor that now needed to be cut out. "You know Don Diego, who you played chess with? Our neighbor?"

Mia said through her sniffles, "Yes, ma'am."

"He's your grandfather." Baxter saw a visible tension drift away from her body, as if she'd been touched by an angel.

Mia's head shifted back. "My grandfather? You mean my mommy's dad?"

"Yes. Don Diego is Sofia's father."

"I don't understand," Mia said.

Ester took Mia's hand again. "Yes, I know. You see, I was dating Alma's father since I was very young. But when he left to go to school in Germany, I fell in love with another man. His best friend. And I made a mistake one day and kissed him. Not too long after, I found out I was pregnant with your mom."

"You got pregnant from a kiss?" Mia asked.

"Well . . . a little more than that."

"That's what I thought."

Baxter shared another complicated chuckle with Ester.

Ester let go of Mia's hand and rubbed her own face. After a big sigh, one rife with the letting go of the last of her secrets, she said, "I never told anyone except my parents until today, when I told your aunt and father. I was too young to have a baby, and so I gave her up for adoption. And I spent the rest of my life regretting it." Suffering poured out with her words. "And the rest of my life loving a man that lived next door who thought I'd given up on him."

Was she really still in love with Diego? Baxter wondered.

"Do you understand what I'm saying, Mia?" Ester asked.

Mia glanced at her father, then back at Ester. "He's a very good chess player."

Baxter felt a bit of relief as Ester patted Mia's back. "Just like you." A pause. "I want you to know it's okay to be angry with me, Mia. It's okay for everyone to be angry with me. All I could do is to make it right now, and I have Baxter to thank for that. He helped me see so many things."

Baxter and Ester shared a smile, and he knew then that she was the closest anyone would ever come to being his mother. He cared for her more than the ten days they'd known each other should warrant.

"Why didn't he say anything?" Mia asked.

"He doesn't know," Ester admitted, then added, "but I'm about to walk over there and tell him. I wanted to tell you first."

"He's going to be mad, isn't he?"

Ester groaned, as if the answer to that question was now on the forefront of her mind. "Yes, he is. He will have every right to be. But you know what? I think he will be happy too. Diego is a very good man, and he's been lonely a long time, and when he finds out that you, our little American miracle, came from all of it . . . I think that's what he'll focus on."

"If you're Iaia," Mia said, "is he Yoyo?"

Baxter and Ester laughed out loud yet again, one of those laughs when nothing made sense, and all you could do was laugh at the absurdity of the human condition.

Ester said, "Do you have any more questions, or can I go talk to him? I think he might want to come see you afterward."

"Really?"

"Of course, really."

Ester started to push herself up, and he leaped to his feet.

No mother deserved to suffer for thirty-eight years over such a brave choice, to give up everything in hopes that their child might find a better life elsewhere. In this particular case, she did! Baxter thought of all the good that had come from Ester's decision, including this little girl right here.

He started to say all this, that it was okay what she'd done, but instead he took her hand and gently pulled her up to a stand.

Chapter 33

Jacque Mate

They watched Ester walk with a light step down the gravel road. She crossed the bridge of the creek and then disappeared behind a patch of trees as she cut into the meadow toward Diego's house.

"Is she going to be okay?" Mia asked.

Baxter turned back to her and put his arm around her. "Maybe for the first time in years. Just think. The next time you see Diego, you'll both know that he's your grandfather. How amazing is it that you keep collecting new family like other kids collect Pokémon cards? It's exciting, yeah?"

She peered up at him. "Yes, sir, it's pretty neat."

Jokes weren't going to cut it this time. "Do you wanna go inside and talk about it?" He knew that it wasn't his job to fix her feelings, only to be there for her as she experienced them.

"If you want to . . . ," she said.

"I kind of do." He placed his hands on both of her shoulders. "It's a lot. And aren't we lucky that we have each other to lean on?"

In the house, she walked slowly, as if she didn't know where to go, small steps to nowhere. Baxter watched with hope and even faith, knowing that she was strong enough to get through anything.

They came into the living room, and both sat on the couch under the portrait of Don Jorge. Paco sat at their feet. She curled up next to

Baxter, and he pulled her in tight. It was nearly silent, only the sound of air moving back and forth, as if the house were breathing relief.

"I don't know where to start," he said. "What are you thinking? What do you feel like? You know, I could say I'm sorry that I brought you here. I could say I'm sorry I didn't consider what we could be walking into. But I don't know that we had a choice. In a way, I feel like we're meant to be here. As much as all this hurts us, we have family that needs us right now."

Mia pulled at a thread on his jeans. "Do you think we can take everyone back to Greenville?"

"Oh, how I wish, dear one. Alma has olives to farm. Your grandmother has her doctors here." Baxter didn't mention Rodolfo.

Mia sank deeper into the couch. Surprisingly, Baxter also found himself wishing that Ester and Alma moving to South Carolina were a possibility. Peeking into an impossible future, he saw Mia and him in a couple of months pulling up to the Greenville-Spartanburg Airport and waving at their Spanish family, who were coming out of baggage claim, ready to start a new life.

There was room in the house—plenty of it for this nonnuclear family. Ester could take the basement with the kitchenette. Alma could stay in one of the guest rooms upstairs or . . . no, he stopped himself from thinking of the other possibility. Why couldn't he let go of these sinister thoughts? No matter how much shame he felt for feeling them, they held strong against his pushing them away.

But then he brought Mia into his vision, and he saw Mia and Alma starting a garden in the back near the fence. They could have that entire area. And Ester would adore their back patio and the golf cart. She could no doubt make friends at the club, and quite possibly find a very good heart doctor and have a better chance at a transplant.

He almost smiled.

Baxter could hear his neighbors now: "Yeah, that Baxter Shaw brought home a whole Spanish family. It's enough to write a book about."

"What do you think they're talking about?" Mia asked, looking toward Diego's house and tugging Baxter back to the present. "Is he, like, yelling at her?"

"That's a good question." He bit his bottom lip and tried to put himself into Don Diego's skin. "It's safe to say he won't be happy, but she had her reasons. Perhaps he'll understand. He's got a certain wisdom about him, I think, like he might just get it."

Baxter leaned toward her. "What I do know is the dominant feeling he will have is joy. Because he's finding out right now that he has a granddaughter, a beautiful and sweet granddaughter who isn't too far away from whupping his behind in chess. For a lonely man who was divorced and never had kids, I imagine there's not much better news to find out in the world. If I was him, I'd come running over here."

Mia's mind seemed to move a mile a minute. "What if he doesn't? What if he doesn't want to see me?"

Baxter thought about her question and answered honestly. "It's a valid concern. His loss, if that's the choice he makes. And maybe we won't blame him, will we? He's probably going through a lot of shock right now. If he decides it's too much to see you, then we won't fault him. I'm sure you'll know it has nothing to do with you. Right?"

"I guess so."

Baxter squeezed his hand around her shoulder a little tighter. "It's true. In case you haven't noticed after a front-row seat to watching me, being an adult is tough. Since we have kids, we're supposed to be grown up and show them the way, but"—he lowered his voice—"here's a little insider tip: we have no idea what we're doing."

Mia smiled and raised her hands. "I hate to break it to you, but every kid knows that. But . . . at least you pretend to, Daddy. And sometimes you get it right."

Baxter felt his shoulders bounce as he laughed at his ever-more-wise offspring. She had a point. "No more pretending, kiddo. The truth is that I don't have all the answers. I don't think anyone does. You know,

I guess it's like that batting average of a baseball player. A few strikeouts is okay as long as you get some hits and even some home runs in there."

Mia twisted to him. "You hit a lot of home runs."

Baxter smiled so hard his face hurt. "If I'm hitting any home runs, it's because I have the greatest daughter in the world. You're throwing me fastballs right over the plate. I'm proud of you, honey."

"I'm proud of you, too, Daddy." Again they hugged, and it was all he wanted to do.

After a good two minutes, Mia said, "You can let go now. Or we might end up stuck together."

He released his hold. "That wouldn't be so bad, would it?"

She shook her head.

Baxter wondered where Alma had gone. Was she okay? And like Mia, he wondered what was happening down the road. Diego didn't seem like the kind of man who had much anger in his heart. Loneliness, yes. Anger, no way. But strength? Did he have the strength to get past Ester's enormous lie in order to recognize what was truly important?

Figuring they'd better do something to pass the time, Baxter said, "You know what we should do? Maybe start thinking about dinner. Something tells me Ester won't feel like cooking, and Alma will probably come in late. What do you say? Do you think we could cook for everyone? No matter what happens, tonight is definitely still a celebration. A few tough spots aside, I think it's been the best trip I've ever had, and I just love you, darling. I love you so much it hurts, and I'm so glad that we were able to find your mom's family and that I'm finally waking up to see that we're loaded with good. Our life is just getting started, right?" He squeezed her again.

She nodded. "Daddy . . ."

"Yeah?"

Mia turned and climbed onto his lap and put her little hand on his cheek. "I love you."

Nothing had ever hit Baxter harder. "Oh, baby doll," he said, "I love you too."

⌇

They were making dinner, Mia and Baxter's best efforts at putting something together with foreign ingredients, when they heard the front door open and close. It made them both jump, as the anticipation had been building for more than an hour.

"Who do you think it is?" Mia whispered. She was at the sink, peeling a carrot.

Baxter was trying to make ranch dressing with something that tasted similar to sour cream. Setting down a spoon, he turned to Mia. "Should we go find out?" He took her hand, and they went into the living room.

Two people stood there, Ester and Diego, their hands dangling at their sides. Ester looked more relieved than anything else. Diego's face told an entirely different story; he was in such shock that, had he any hair, it would have been blown back. He carried a folded chessboard in his arm.

Five or ten seconds of pure silence must have gone by as the four of them looked at each other. Then the first thing that moved other than Paco's tail was Diego's mouth. Baxter hadn't seen such a smile in his whole life—not even from Alberto the Bread Man. Diego slapped his bald head and looked down at Mia as if seeing her for the first time.

Mia, never shy when it came to this kind of thing, said, "Are you my grandfather? *¿Tu eres mi abuelo?*"

Diego opened up his arms and stepped forward, saying *"Sí, creo que sí."* I believe so.

Baxter and Ester watched as Diego lowered himself to the ground, both his crackling knees landing on the hardwood floor, and he gestured for Mia to come to him. She didn't hesitate, as if she'd known him forever and had been separated from him for only a while. In a second, she was wrapping her arms around her grandfather's neck as Diego whispered what were surely kind words to his granddaughter.

"It was only supposed to happen now," Baxter said to Ester as he sidestepped to her.

"I hope you're right."

"I know I am."

Mia and Diego were having their own conversation, or trying to. Mia's Spanish had come a long way in nine days, but it wasn't enough. So she did the thing that made the most sense to everyone. She pointed to the chessboard in Diego's hands and asked, "Wanna play? *¿Quieres jugar?*"

No doubt the world was a wild and crazy place, and as Baxter and Ester sat at the dining room table, watching Don Diego and Mia play, he thought what a blessing that he'd come across Sofia in the first place. What a blessing he'd gotten the time he'd had with her—that they'd had with her.

Because it was enough.

It wasn't enough, but it was. Because that was the way it had happened, and her time on earth had come to its end. Where she was now was where she was supposed to be, and he was supposed to be exactly *here*.

What a blessing that they'd been able to create this wonderful and beautiful being who was now coming out of her own grief and lifting up everyone around her while she was at it. No doubt this forty-pound human had changed Ester and now Diego in ways that might not have been possible without her. The same was true of Baxter. One little girl with all the power in the world, changing people with her own courage.

Let go of the things that don't matter and hold on to the things that do. That thought that had come to him at the beach made more and more sense every time he thought of it.

Baxter had to let go of what had happened to Sofia, and he had to let go of the idea that the two of them were supposed to grow old together. But what about her memory? Of course, they didn't want to forget her, but he wasn't so sure that they needed to keep plunging into the memories like a favorite book you revisit. No matter how much growth Mia had experienced here, he still had to be careful not to let her slip back to her old ways. And that was what memories did, didn't they? Pushed your head back under the water in an attempt to drown you.

No. That wasn't true. It was the old Baxter talking. How could he possibly think that the memory of Sofia could be anything but pure and wonderful? After all, her memory was all they had left of her, and the last thing she would ever want was . . .

Lights suddenly lit up in his mind, so bright he could have fallen out of his chair. He could so clearly hear what Ester had said earlier about having two loves in a life.

The last thing Sofia *ever* would have wanted was for her memory to hold him back. And that was when it hit him. He'd missed part of her message, of why she'd orchestrated this life-changing endeavor to Spain. She wasn't only putting a guitar in his hand once again, and she wasn't only urging him to live again . . . she was giving him permission to love again. And the way to do that was *not* by forgetting Sofia and burying her memory deep in the attics of his mind. It was by cherishing their love, holding it secure in his heart, while also opening himself up to the possibility of meeting someone new. Perhaps the real question was: Did he have the strength to risk losing again?

Alma appeared in his mind. Maybe he'd already met that someone new. But wasn't she the painted one in his lyrics? Even if she wasn't, the two of them were an impossibility, so why was he even thinking of her? He was losing her before it even began.

Then it hit him. True, they might not have much of a future together, considering the distance between their homes, but at least he could admit and revel in the attraction they felt toward each other. Even if they never saw each other again, she was the one who'd lifted him up and helped him open his heart again. There would always be that between them. She'd always own a little piece of his heart.

He shook his head at the dazzling mystery and wonder of life. He even laughed out loud as he caught a glimpse of the future, Alan asking, "D'you have you a good vacation, amigo?" Oh, how absurd and how impossible to answer.

Letting go, Baxter said to himself. It was a practice he'd have to continually work on. No doubt going home would give him his challenges, and he wasn't such a rookie of life that he thought everything would be different, like the flip of a switch lighting up a dark room. No, he'd have to work at it.

Today, though, he had the tools to decipher what needed to be let go. He also knew what he needed to hold on to with all his might. Family was at the top of the list. Baxter thought of his old bandmates from Cactus Road and Alan and the other people who'd been there for him, and he knew that friends were up there too. Friends and family. What could be more important?

Startling Baxter, Mia struck the table. "No! Why did I do that?"

Ester and Baxter looked at the board just as Diego said, *"Jaque mate."*

Mia's cheeks trembled with frustration, and Baxter could see she was fighting off tears. He wanted to say, "Hey, Don Diego, haven't you ever known a little girl before? Wouldn't hurt to let her win."

Diego wasn't a cold man, though, and when he saw that Mia was shaken, he reached across the table, gesturing with his fingers for Mia to take his hand. She was hesitant at first but took a deep breath and reached for him. Baxter saw her tiny young hand meet his weathered fingers in a wonderful embrace.

Diego showed off his crooked tooth with a broad smile. "You very good, Mia. Very good."

"Gracias."

He smiled again and let go of her hand.

Mia stared at the board for a while. Clearly deciding she had no way out, she toppled her own king. "Again?" She looked at Ester. "How do you say *again*?"

When Ester told her, Mia made a circling motion with her finger at Diego. *"Otra vez."*

Diego raised his hands. *"Claro."* He let loose another smile.

As the two lost themselves in a match, Baxter had to ask Ester, "So . . . how did he take it?"

Ester answered with her eyes on Diego. "He knew," she said. "He had heard that I had family from America coming, and that made him curious. When he met Mia, he put it together."

Baxter recalled his and Diego's time together, and then the day he brought Mia with him. "I'm surprised he didn't say anything."

"He was going to." She said quietly, "He was angry with me. But I suppose he understands too. Jorge never would have forgiven us. We wouldn't be here now."

"None of us would," Baxter said. "Do you love him? Have you always loved him? Has he loved you?"

She sighed. "Of course I've always loved him . . . and I should have told him. We never talked about it again, though. I got back together with Jorge, and that year was buried in time."

"And now?"

"We'll see."

Baxter knew exactly what she meant.

Chapter 34

THE GROVE

After Don Diego had gone home and Ester and Mia had gone to sleep, Baxter took Don Jorge's guitar out into the groves and sat against the trunk of an olive tree. The stars glistened loudly. An owl hooted from somewhere deep in the forest. A bottle of Don Diego's bobal and a half-filled glass rested beside him. There was that feel in the still air that any day now, the true November cold would arrive.

His fingers were chilly but working well enough to hold the chords. And he'd warmed up his voice and had been singing for a while, recalling tunes that he thought he'd forgotten, the words coming back like they'd only been hiding shallowly under the surface, patiently waiting for his return.

He'd been singing with his eyes closed, and as he sang the last words of a Tom Petty number, he opened them to find Alma standing a few feet away, a purple wool blanket wrapped around her shoulders. The sliver of the moon hung over her left shoulder like a Christmas ornament.

"Hi," he said.

"Hi."

"I was wondering if I'd see you before we left."

She nodded. "I just needed to clear my head."

He could almost see the confusion of today swirling in her eyes. "Are you okay?"

"Will you just keep playing?" she asked, stepping into the moonlight and lowering herself to the ground several feet in front of him.

And that was what he did. Her blanket wrapped around her, Alma listened to him for a while, and her watching him brought out the best in him, and he gave those next few songs all he had.

When he finished and set the guitar down by his side, she whispered, "That was wonderful, thank you."

He sat back against the trunk. "Thanks for listening. I haven't played for someone like that in, well . . . you know, years."

"How'd it feel?"

"So good. And that you were the one I was playing for, even better." She bit her lip and looked away.

"What can I do for you?" he asked, wishing he could take her in his arms but unsure of what she wanted. "I know today was a lot. I'm so sorry for not telling you about your brother, and I'm so sorry you didn't know about Diego."

She laughed to herself. "None of it had to do with you."

"A little bit. I probably should have left that recorder in its case."

"I'm glad you didn't."

The thing she'd told him by the fire that night, about him and Mia vibrating at the same frequency, popped into his head. He was pretty damn sure he and Alma did too. He could feel the energy between them, and he was pretty sure he could feel her pulling him toward her. She was nothing like Sofia, nothing like any woman he'd ever met. A heart of gold and the passion of an artist; the ear of a therapist and the fire of an alt-country singer—not to mention damn fine taste in music. She was an enchantress to him, a wonder that drifted through the forest, untouched by the outside world.

She moves like leaves, he heard in his head, *and she sits silently like a tree.*

He smiled to himself, absolutely craving her.

"What?" she asked.

He laughed loudly this time. "Oh, I don't know. Life's just funny, isn't it? Never in a million years could I have imagined sitting among these trees, thinking what I'm thinking."

"And what is it you're thinking?"

Truth, he heard a voice say.

He suddenly felt nervous like he had when he'd asked girls on dates when he was young. That wasn't going to stop him, though. "I'm thinking that I'm not ready to go home, and I'm not ready to say goodbye to you. I'm thinking that you're one of the most amazing people I've ever met." Maybe they didn't have much of a future, but that didn't change how he felt, and he wasn't going home without telling her.

Alma blushed, and it was the first time he'd ever seen her do so. And he felt his cheeks swell with joy. He felt no guilt at the admission. So what she was Sofia's half sister. Life was as twisted as the olive trees surrounding them. That was what made it beautiful.

He said to Alma in a slightly jittery tone, "I care about you, Alma. I know it could never work between us, and maybe you don't feel the same way anyway, but . . . I wanted to tell you before I leave. You helped me see color again. It's like my heart was sitting on the ground, dusty and lifeless. And you picked it up and kick-started it."

She was watching him with those kind and warm eyes, and when he paused, she gave a faint smile. He wasn't sure if it was one of charity, her mind scrambling to figure out how to let him down gently, or if perhaps she was glad he'd said it.

He picked up his glass and took a sip of wine, thinking he must sound crazy, saying all this to a woman he'd known for only a little while. "You grabbed me by the shirt collar and dragged me up into the sky . . . pointed me back down at the life I've been living. Let me see it from another perspective. From a more important perspective. And I'm so grateful."

She pulled the blanket tighter around her. "I think you're giving me a little more credit than I deserve. You just needed to get away from it all for a little while."

"Maybe so, but more to my point: I leave here tomorrow, and I don't want to without you knowing how I feel. There was a moment when I worried I'd just . . . I don't know, I was worried I had somehow tried to replace Sofia with the next closest thing . . . her sister. Half sister, whatever. It's not like that, though. I like you a lot because of who you are. Because of who I am around you. Because of who we are together."

She watched him pensively, and he couldn't bear her silence, so he kept talking. "We might be an impossibility, but I need you to know that you'll always have a piece of my heart. Oh, c'mon, say something . . ."

She finally broke into a full-fledged smile. "I was wondering if you'd let me speak."

"Please . . ."

"You're not wrong," she said.

"Not wrong about what?"

"About us. There's a little thing happening."

"A little thing happening?" he asked, feeling his jaw drop an inch.

He saw in her face that she was having fun with him. "*Sí.* There's a chance I might shed a tear when you leave."

"A tear for me?"

She shook her head. "Is it so hard to believe? I like this Spanish Baxter, the one who rambles under an olive tree, the one who has a better sense of humor, the one who . . ." Her voice trailed off and she looked away, out through her trees.

"The one who what?"

"I don't know."

"What?"

She finally turned back to him, then looked at the guitar. "The one who isn't afraid of a guitar. I hope you don't lose touch with the Spanish you."

He looked down at the guitar. He certainly wasn't afraid now. Bringing it back to his lap, he said, "So you think I'll just slip right back into the man who came here ten days ago?"

"Do you think ten days changed you?"

"It put a big dent in me, that's for sure. Or I should say polished me back toward shiny. I told Mia that I'm going back a changed man, and I mean it. No more pushing off living."

She looked at him like she almost believed him, and he thought that he wanted nothing more than to prove to her that he was indeed a new man.

He strummed a C with his thumb, locking eyes with her, drawing energy from her beauty. There were a melody and words in his head. He sang, "I'm not ready to say goodbye, when this night could last forever. I'm not ready to say goodbye . . . to you." It was a C to G to B-flat to F, and the next time around, he picked out the melody as he strummed. Then he sang another chorus, and her smile stretched wider, filling him up.

If he didn't put that guitar down and go to her soon, he'd lose his mind, but he kept playing, improvising lyrics as freely as he had back in the old days. She hugged herself and closed her eyes, and on her strikingly beautiful face he saw a contentment that settled every cell in his body. He could have played for her until the sun rose and then again and again . . . but he tried not to let the thought lead him astray, because he'd be on a plane in a few hours, wondering if it had been only a dream.

When he finished, she said with great amusement, "I thought your songs weren't supposed to be so catchy."

"Yeah, well . . . this is the problem with falling for someone," Baxter said. "You start to get all mushy." *No holding back now,* he thought. Not when their time was limited.

Alma stared at him for a long time, and he could see in her inviting eyes that she felt the same craving that he did. The silence between them was a magnet, drawing him to her. He was about to go to her when she said, "You really think you're falling for me?"

He let out a breath, as if he'd been holding it for several minutes. "There's no thinking about it. Yeah, I'm falling for you. And you've turned me into the Burt Bacharach of Americana. Didn't you hear what I just sang for you? What else do I need to do to prove it?"

Alma started flat-out giggling, and he was thrilled to see that he could make her laugh like that. He used to be able to do that to Sofia too. And he'd had this same conversation with Sofia, always teased her about it.

As Alma wiped happy tears from her eyes, Baxter heard himself speaking to Sofia years before, "Don't you make me soft." They were sitting on a bench at the Battery in Charleston, watching the boats cruise by. "I don't want to sing about hearts becoming whole," he told her. "Bob Dylan would crucify me. You gotta let me keep the blues."

Sofia had reached over and touched his heart. "I think you've got enough blues in here for several lifetimes of songwriting. Never forget where you came from."

Back in the present, he listened to the last of Alma's giggling and realized it was okay that he was thinking of Sofia, and accepting the idea seemed to drop him even deeper into the moment, allowing him to let go of any last remnants of resistance.

"I've never heard you laugh like that before," he said.

"There's not many who can make me," she said. "The Burt Bacharach of Americana. Baxter the Tool Man. You have a whole bag of personalities."

"Yeah, I do, don't I?" He had a grin, but he was being sincere as he said, "But I think they all like you."

"Oh, do they?"

"Yeah, and they're all sad we're leaving." It was now or never. He set the guitar back down, folded forward, and moved toward her. When his face was close to hers, he said, "But at least we have right now. Maybe that's enough."

"Is it?" she whispered, opening up the blanket to him.

He shook his head. "I guess sometimes it has to be."

Their lips met, and his soul danced as hard as that woman in the red dress in the cave. He and Alma might not have a future, but they had right now. She fell back against the ground and pulled him down with her, and they kissed and pressed against each other with a desperate passion.

When they briefly broke apart, he took in the beauty of her, not wanting to ever forget this moment. He kissed her forehead and cheeks, and then with his finger he drew a line down from her lips to her chin and along her neck to where her shirt was buttoned. He pressed his hand against her chest. He could feel the rapid beat of her heart, and it was a song.

A song that he'd take with him on that plane.

Baxter woke early to the cold of the morning. He held Alma in his arms, the purple wool blanket wrapped tightly around both of them. Another blanket that he'd retrieved from her truck lay under them. The birds sang a melody that sounded like hope as he came alive like a bear after hibernation. The sun, the glorious orange sun, had risen over the mountains, and its rays reflected off the drops of morning dew that had collected on the ground around them.

This was a sunrise he'd never seen before, a graffiti of brilliant colors imprinted on the sky. This was a sunrise that came from within and from up high, and he thought there could be no better sign to show that he was finally living again.

He kissed the top of Alma's head as she stirred.

"Oh, look at that," she said, pointing in the opposite direction of the sun. Baxter followed her gaze and saw that there were several of the horses standing maybe fifteen feet from them. One shook his head and let out a neigh.

The sun reflected off their coats as they stood there without a shred of timidity, looking toward Alma—their leader, the *granjera* of the estate.

"Go say hi," Alma said.

Baxter shook his head. "And scare them off?"

"They're not scared of you today."

He pushed up and walked carefully and quietly in their direction. He could sense Alma behind him, watching.

"Hey, guys," Baxter said. "Buenos días."

To his surprise, the horses didn't shrink away. He reached out to the one closest, a tall black horse with a brown spot under its eye. He set his hand on the horse's forehead.

"You're really letting me do this," he whispered.

"Looks like someone's no longer a stranger," Alma said, coming up from behind him. The horses circled them, and she put a hand on another one's neck. *"Esta es Baxter,"* she said. Then she turned to him. "A sunrise like this makes it hard not to have faith, right? Even for a skeptic like you."

"There's not much skeptic in me this morning," Baxter replied, again rubbing the nose of the horse and then looking up toward the resplendent sky again. Faith seemed to come so easy right then.

A moment later, the smell of burning wood wafted by, and Baxter turned to see there were lights on downstairs. "Your mom's up."

Alma smiled sadly. "I should go see her."

Baxter took her hand. "Just a few more minutes here, then we'll go inside." He pulled her toward him and put his cheek to hers. *"Tranquila."*

"¿Tranquila? Really? You're suddenly Spanish?"

Her breath on his ear teased a chill up his spine. "Tryin' to be. Spanish on training wheels." As the sad idea of saying goodbye to her cut into him, he knew that his heart was on training wheels too.

Chapter 35

Family Ties

Ester sat by the fire, her feet crossed at the ankles. She held a mug of coffee in her hand, a tornado of steam spinning above it. As she turned, Paco sprang up from her feet to greet them.

Alma petted the dog and then kissed her mother on the top of the head. Baxter heard apologies in Spanish as the two of them conversed. Ester switched back to English and said to Baxter, "Rodolfo will be here in a few minutes. I want us all to talk to him about the tape."

"You want me there?" Baxter asked with surprise as he came to stand next to Alma with their backs to the fire. He'd much rather they have the conversation once he and Mia had left.

"Yes, I do," she said, setting her mug down on the table. "Diego just came over and took Mia."

"Wait, she's up?"

Ester nodded. "He'll bring her back in a little while. As I have already told both of you, Mia will be a part of the inheritance, and that means that you need to be a part of the decisions."

"I'm not sure Rodolfo is going to like that," Baxter said, noticing the warmth of the fire on his hands and on the back of his neck.

"I'm not sure I care what he likes right now."

Alma held up her hands with a sadistic grin. "Whether you like it or not, you're family now, Baxter. Even the horses think so."

Both women stared at him until he relented. "I'm happy to be here and help however I can."

A few minutes later, Baxter returned from the kitchen with coffee for Alma and him and joined the women back in the living room, taking a seat in a chair to Alma's right. Ester sat across from them on the sofa, under the painting of Jorge, whose eyes were suspiciously real, like the *Mona Lisa*'s. The standing lamp cast an orange glow over Ester and showed a very weary and worn-down woman, the rims of her eyes the blue of old blood, her cheeks nearly gray. Seeing her this way, Baxter was glad that he was there. He wasn't sure that he had much to offer, but perhaps there was strength in numbers.

On the wooden coffee table between them was a stack of Spanish flag coasters and two thick books of paintings, one of Goya and another of Dalí. Baxter pulled two coasters off the stack. "Can I get you anything, Ester?"

She shook her head and glanced toward the hallway that led to the front door. He could see that all she really wanted was to get this over with. He wouldn't go as far as to say he could empathize with Ester and her worries, but he got it. As easy as it was to say that Rodolfo belonged in jail, Baxter well understood that your own child had a place in your heart, no matter what they might do. Ester loved Rodolfo, and nothing would ever change that. In a way, Baxter was envious. His parents had never given him such unconditional love.

"Do you know what you want to say to him?" Alma asked.

Ester's shoulders slumped. "I think he deserves a chance to explain." Baxter noticed for the first time the scar from her surgery rising up her sternum. She must have been hiding it with scarves and more conservatively cut dresses until now.

"To explain?" Alma asked. "What could he possibly say to make this better?"

"*Yo no sé.*" I don't know.

327

Rodolfo quickly sniffed out some sort of ambush and said something along the lines of, "What's going on?" He smelled of strong cologne and was dressed in very tight jeans, an ironed blue shirt, a scarlet scarf, and a gray sports coat.

Ester asked him to sit. His seemingly permanent scowl forming even deeper creases, he said he would pour himself a cup of coffee first. Baxter took the time to throw another log on the fire.

When Rodolfo returned, he sat next to his mother on the sofa. Baxter noticed the familial triangle that had been formed with the painting of Jorge making the apex, the patriarch's eyes peering over them, as if waiting to see what transpired.

Ester clasped her hands together in what Baxter saw was a very tight grip, the veins in the top of her wrists swelling. Turning to Rodolfo, she said, "I've been going over the bank accounts, and it seems we're missing some money."

It was an interesting approach she was taking, as if she wanted to see Rodolfo squirm before playing the tape. Baxter watched him for signs of surrender or retreat.

The man took the path of overreaction, his face contorting in such a way that made him look like the worst actor to ever grace the screen of a telenovela. His chin retreated to his throat so much so that Baxter thought he might damage his trachea. Flattening out the creases of his jeans, he said, "How would there be money missing? How much?"

Ester pulled air in through her nose. "Nearly three hundred thousand euros. Two transactions."

Rodolfo looked to Alma for the quickest moment, then back to Ester. "I didn't know we had that much. What accounts?" Sweat collected on his forehead, making it glisten like a newly paved blacktop. The only noise in the room was the serpentine hiss of the fire, as if it were coiled in the corner, ready to strike.

As a log dropped, Ester lowered her hand from where it pinched her mouth and chin. "Did you take the money?"

Rodolfo pointed to Baxter. "Why is he here? This is none of his business."

Baxter pushed the question off to Ester, who answered, "It very much is, and I want him here. Did you take the money?"

Rodolfo's face looked like it had suddenly been whipped with the sharp tip of shame. He started to speak, but Ester held up a finger. "No, no. Don't lie to me."

"I have no idea—"

"*Silencio!*" she snapped, making Baxter jump. From the pocket of her robe she drew out the recorder and placed it on top of the Goya book. The sight of the damn thing made Baxter wonder again if what he'd done was merely destroy these people. It was hard in that moment to see any of the good in his interference.

Rodolfo looked at it cluelessly, asking what it was in Spanish. "*¿Qué es esto?*" Baxter could see that his breathing was shallow and forced. He might not know exactly what might be on that Dictaphone, but he damn well knew he was in trouble.

Ester pressed play, and the scene from the day before Don Jorge's fated flight came to life. Everyone stared at the Dictaphone, as if it were a small person on the table speaking. Perhaps the truth was that no one wanted to look at Rodolfo, to see him falling apart.

When the heated part came, and on the recording Rodolfo had admitted that he'd stolen the money, right when it sounded like Jorge hit the table with his fist and launched into a vicious verbal attack, Rodolfo angrily reached for the recorder and pressed the stop button.

"How dare you steal from us!" Ester shouted at him as he recoiled back to his sitting position.

"I had no choice," Rodolfo growled back.

Ester threw up her hands.

Rodolfo attempted to calm her by pressing his hands down through the air. "Please, Mama. Take some deep breaths. This is not good for your heart."

"My son stealing from me? No, it is not." She could have burned him with her glare.

Inheritance or not, Baxter still felt like he had no place being here, but per Ester's request, he stayed still and watched the three of them battle it out.

"I was protecting you." Rodolfo looked at Alma. "I was protecting us."

Ester turned up the volume to her voice to match her anger. "And *how* were you protecting us?"

Rodolfo took a moment to collect himself. He seemed reluctant to speak, the slight shake of his head showing more frustration than guilt. "My father was gambling, Mama. He was losing everything."

"What are you talking about?"

"I didn't want you to know," Rodolfo said. "Your heart." He shook his head. "I didn't want you to know."

Baxter looked over at Alma, who sat there in shock, watching and waiting to hear more. Had they gotten this all wrong? Had he misread the signs?

Rodolfo took a handful of his well-manicured hair above his forehead. "He lost nearly all of our savings. I found out while going through the financials. He was taking out big withdrawals in cash from the bank in Gandia. I confronted him about it. He tried to deny it, but I threatened that I would ask you. He admitted that he'd been gambling and losing. And he begged me not to tell you. I didn't want to tell you either. That was the one thing we agreed on. You had just had the surgery." The conviction in his posture and tone were not an act.

"Remember the day we hit each other?" Rodolfo asked both Ester and Alma. "That was the day he admitted to it. I told him he had to stop, and he said it was his money. So I took it from him. I transferred it to my account."

The fire moaned as Baxter looked up to Don Jorge on the canvas. The man looked so perfect up there, a passionate farmer dressed in his finest clothes. A man who had reinvented olive oil in this region.

Perhaps he wasn't so perfect. Or . . . Rodolfo had prepared the ultimate lie, one that would be hard to prove.

"Do you have the money?" Ester asked suspiciously.

He shook his head. "No. They came for it, the guys he was playing Truco with. I told them that it was his debt, not ours, and I refused to pay." He held up his hand. "And they cut off my finger."

His claim was a grenade that exploded between them. Had those men truly cut off his finger? Baxter saw no signs of lying in Rodolfo's eyes.

Ester's cheeks turned to stone. "Do not lie to me."

Rodolfo reached for the cross dangling around his neck. He kissed it and looked at his mother. "I swear to you. I wanted to tell you, Mama, but I thought it might kill you. And I didn't want you to hate your husband. So I decided to handle it myself. You and Alma would never have to know. After they cut off my finger, I gave them everything. We still owe them another two hundred thousand euros. I was going to pay them with my part of the inheritance, from selling the estate."

Baxter sat back and ran a hand through his hair. Was this why Rodolfo had been so worried about Baxter intervening? "So the men I saw you with in the town . . . ?" Baxter asked gently, tasting the regret of judging Rodolfo earlier.

"That's them," Rodolfo said. "They're very bad guys."

The missing finger proved that.

Rodolfo adjusted his watch and looked back at his mother. "We needed to sell anyway. The business is tanking. It's been tanking for years. I just saw the opportunity to fix this on my own. I'm sorry I didn't tell you. I didn't know what to do."

Ester seemed to shake off the surprise that had dizzied her as she said, "I thought you stole from us."

"I would never steal from you, Mama." He reached for her hand. "I just don't want you to be stressed. I want you to get better." Sadness pulled at his face. "I wanted to take you to Madrid so that you'd be close to your doctors and so that I could look out for you."

Ester burst into a cry and began to kiss the place where his finger had been. "I can't believe you did this for me."

As completely screwed up as this moment and these revelations were, Baxter saw only the broken pieces of a family coming back together, and it was beautiful.

Rodolfo slid toward her and patted her back. "It's okay. Everything is okay. He had a problem, and I am fixing it. They will leave us alone once we pay the rest. And it will be over."

"This is not your problem," she said. "It's *our* problem."

Baxter reached for Alma's hand. "You okay?"

Her head was moving back and forth, the shock of this moment surely dizzying her. She nodded to Baxter and then said to her brother, "If you're lying about this, I will kill you."

Rodolfo let go of his mother and stood and went to his sister. He knelt on the ground before her. "I wanted to tell you, but I thought I could make it go away. I know how much you loved him. And I didn't want it to break your heart."

"You were going to let me hate you?"

"I would do anything for you," Rodolfo said. "You're my sister." He choked up as he said the words, and Baxter became even more sure that Rodolfo was telling the truth.

Alma's eyes moistened, and she slid off her chair and came to her knees and hugged her brother. The sight made Ester cry even harder, and she stood and went to them.

Baxter watched them hold each other with all they had, and he suddenly saw his younger self folded into a corner in his room, feeling so utterly alone as his parents screamed at one another. No one had ever come to him and pulled him up off the floor. No one had ever held him like this, until Sofia.

Rodolfo had done all this to protect his mother and sister. Maybe not the brightest decision in the world but damned admirable. No wonder he'd been an asshole. The guy was holding all this pain about what his father had done. He was suffering alone—alone like Baxter had been for so long.

This is what family should be! he wanted to scream, and the idea of leaving saddened him even more. He'd been worried that Mia would be looking out the back window of the Audi with a broken heart, but no . . . it was him. He saw that boy in the corner now on his knees in the back seat of a car, waving goodbye to the only family he'd ever known. And in this exact moment, Baxter understood what the word *family* truly meant.

Chapter 36

TIME TO GO HOME

It was time to go.

An hour had passed since they'd played the tape for Rodolfo and unraveled the last secrets of the family. Diego had brought Mia back over. Everyone Baxter and Mia had met in the last ten days was now there, the extended family, including Alberto the Bread Man.

Marshmallow clouds hovered above them. The air smelled of fall and burning wood and of the promise of winter. Leaves drifted down around them.

With the Audi packed and already running, Baxter and Mia offered last hugs and kisses to the kind people swarming around them. Baxter saw in the faces of Ester and Alma and Rodolfo the same lightness that he himself felt. There was indeed some weariness, too, but it was the lightness of hope that reverberated around them most strongly.

Baxter kissed Ester's cheeks. "We'll be back as soon as we can, okay? Take care of yourself in the meantime."

"I will. And you take care of Mia."

"Yes, ma'am . . ."

She must have seen the sadness that had suddenly come over him. "Don't worry," she said. "I'll be here when you get back."

"You'd better." He was already missing her.

Ester took his hand. "And thanks to you, you'll have your bedrooms waiting on you."

Baxter's face turned to confusion. "We will?"

"I'm not ready to sell, not quite yet." She looked over at Diego, who was speaking with Mia. "I have a lot to think about . . . and I don't need the pressure. Diego said he'd lend us some money. I told him no, but he's insistent. I just need to get out of the contract, which I'm sure I can figure out. Then maybe we can get through my surgery and see things more clearly on the other side."

"I'm really thrilled to hear it, Ester."

"All's well that ends well, right?" She let go of his hand and turned to Mia, who was walking over with Diego. He was another man who had a lot to work out, but his smile indicated that he welcomed what may come.

Mia rose up into Ester's arms. "I'm gonna miss you, Iaia."

"Me too. Please, Baxter, get this young lady back to me as soon as you can."

"You know I will." Baxter turned to Diego and shook his hand. "I hope to get back here soon, Don Diego. I'm very appreciative of the wine you gave me, but it won't last long. I'm gonna need a refill."

"*Sí,*" Diego grunted with his smoky voice.

"And next time you see Mia, she's gonna bring the heat to that chessboard. You be ready." Baxter was pretty sure Diego had no idea what he'd just said, but it didn't matter. The two of them had learned to communicate without words. To that end, Baxter pulled him into a hug and told him to take care of Ester.

Moving on, Baxter found Alma waiting for him by the Audi. He put a hand on the hood and said casually, "So . . . it was good to meet you."

She gave an all-knowing smile and then a shake of her head.

"Yeah," he said, wishing he could kiss her one last time, but he could feel the eyes of all the Arroyos watching them. "I hope y'all figure out a way to keep the estate."

"One year at a time, right?"

"That's right." He stepped forward and hugged her, taking in the moment so that he would never forget it. "Thanks, Alma. You're one of a kind."

"Aren't we all?" she said as she let go of him. "Isn't that the point?"

He took in her smile, intending to revisit it later. "I suppose it is."

And then he saw over her shoulder Rodolfo standing by himself on the outskirts of the crowd. "I'm gonna say goodbye to your brother now. Don't be a stranger, all right?"

She patted his shoulder and said in a massacre of the southern dialect, "Y'all come back now, ya hear?"

He gave her one last look. "You never told me you saw *The Beverly Hillbillies.*"

"I didn't tell you a lot of things." With that, she gave him a wink and turned away.

What a woman, he thought, shaking his head as he approached Rodolfo. He stopped three feet from him. "I can't say enough how sorry I am. I very much admire how much you care for your family, for your mother and sister."

Rodolfo didn't say much, but he shook Baxter's hand. *"Gracias. Hasta luego, hermano."*

Despite everything that Baxter had done and everything Rodolfo had gone through, he'd just called Baxter a brother. And that meant a lot.

After they embraced, Baxter called out for Mia. "You ready, sweetie?"

She nodded glumly and gave one last wave to everyone. Her cousin Alfonso looked the saddest, standing there with a frown. She took off a bracelet that she'd made and gave it to him, and that seemed to brighten him.

And then Baxter and Mia climbed into the Audi. "Okay, chica, are you ready? Let's get this big American SUV on the road."

She was waving like mad at the family circling them. As Baxter began to pull away, Mia stuck her head out the window and yelled, *"Hasta luego!"* Baxter heard all kinds of joy in her voice, and he knew that she'd grown up more in these ten days than she had in her whole life.

And she wasn't the only one. With their newfound family disappearing in the rearview mirror, Baxter felt more than ever that he was absolutely capable of being the father that Mia deserved, and he would start right this minute.

As Mia sat back down and clicked her seat belt, he said, "Hey, wanna hear a dad joke?"

She cut a look at him. "Some things never change, do they?"

He inclined his eyebrows and simply shook his head.

"On with it then, Daddy. I'll brace myself."

Chapter 37

ONE MORE THING TO DO

The morning after they returned to Greenville, Baxter squeezed his truck into a parallel spot on South Main Street. Stepping out onto the street, he swung his messenger bag over his shoulder, helped Mia down, and led her a block down to a coffee shop called the Ugly Mug. Through the glass window, he saw several tables occupied by people staring at their laptops and sipping specialty drinks.

"This, honey pie, is where I met your mother."

"How come you never brought me?"

"It was all too painful. I should have."

He opened the door for her—the door to the past—and the scent of freshly ground coffee rushed over him. The pastries caught both their eyes as they approached the counter.

"Good afternoon, can I help you?" a barista with a yellow ribbon in her hair asked with the kind of energy one has only with access to free shots of espresso all day.

Baxter looked down at Mia. "For the princess?"

She scanned the glass case and stopped on a decadent strawberry cheesecake. "Could I please have that one?"

"I don't think it will be as good as Iaia's cheesecake, but of course you can." Baxter added a cup of coffee and a bottle of water.

Once he'd settled his bill, he led Mia to the back of the restaurant and into the courtyard. A tall fence wrapped around the space, making it feel very private. More than twenty potted plants bathed in the sun in one corner, their leaves still wet from the earlier rain. A small concrete fountain bubbled next to them.

November in Greenville was a treat, and he was shocked to see only one other table occupied. He'd been here plenty of times over the years, and he was thankful Starbucks hadn't knocked these guys out of business, and even more so that the same rickety cast-iron table and two rusty chairs where he and Sofia had first shared a moment remained.

Baxter pointed. "I was sitting right there when your mom came up to me, took the other seat."

Mia looked that way as if he'd just told her Tinker Bell was hovering above the table.

"It was right there when we both fell in love." Baxter could see his younger self turning to see who had interrupted him, feeling the butterflies in his stomach. He'd never forget those inquisitive and thirsty brown eyes, as if she were right on the cusp of figuring out the whole world.

Baxter set the tray down. "Why don't you sit where your mom sat?"

Mia delightedly eased into the seat, as if trying it on for size, breathing in the same air.

"Pretty wild, isn't it?" he asked, setting down his bag and taking the seat opposite, remembering the feel of his guitar in his hands.

"I was sitting in this chair with my guitar, writing the last lines of a song. My notebook and pen were right here." He pointed to a spot on the table, seeing in his mind the dog-eared and coffee-stained notebook where he'd written many songs. "I had a big huge cup of black coffee."

"And Mommy?" Mia asked with a mouthful.

"I noticed out of the corner of my eye someone was coming toward me. She was the most beautiful girl in the world—looked just like you—and without hesitation, she sat down. Right in your seat. Like she knew me."

Mia listened to him the same way she did when he read her bedtime stories. "What happened next?"

Baxter smiled and felt it in every cell. "I wasn't exactly sure what to say. She was so pretty that she made me nervous. She, on the other hand . . . was very confident. Dressed in a business suit, a sly and comfortable grin. Not only did she make the first move by sitting down, but she was the first to say something." He paused for dramatic effect.

"What did she say?"

"With her little smirk—the same one you like to throw at me—she said, 'I think you're a little out of tune.' I think I fell in love right then."

Mia let out a proud chuckle. Baxter laughed with her. It was the best pickup line in history and prophetic as hell for what he'd become after her death: an out-of-tune widower trying to figure out life and himself while somehow trying to be a role model for a daughter who needed him more than ever.

He sat back and crossed his ankles. "I was nervous, but I was also a little cocky." To Mia's gentle grin, he said, "I was pretty used to people coming up to me, you know, telling me they liked our music."

Mia set down her fork, which she'd licked clean. "Would they ask for your autograph?"

"Sure. But not your mom. No, ma'am—she'd never heard of us. Before that moment, I was totally okay having a girlfriend here and there but never settling down. My guitar was my wife. Oh boy was I wrong. If I'd had a ring in my pocket, I would have dropped to one knee."

What an idiot he'd been to keep these memories from Mia. *And* himself. How great it was to speak so openly about Sofia without it tearing him apart.

"And then what happened?" she asked.

Baxter pinched his chin. "Well, I tuned my guitar. She was right."

"And then?"

"She asked me to play something for her, 'cause she was having a rough day."

"What did you play?" Mia almost put her hand in the cake as she leaned toward Baxter.

"The song I was working on. 'Regret Is a Broken Mirror.' You know that one. When I finished, I held out my hand and said, 'I'm Baxter.' We talked for a while, and the next thing we knew, the sun was easing between those two buildings, falling out of sight."

It was time to show her what he had in the bag. Unlatching the snaps, he drew out the exact notebook he'd been writing in that day. As he set it on the table and began flipping through his scribble, he said, "Eventually, she said she had to go, and I asked for her number."

When he got to the page, he pointed to where Sofia had written her name and telephone number and then kissed the space under the digits with her lipstick. Mia reached for the notebook with eager anticipation. He felt a lightness spread over him as he watched his daughter put her fingers on the lipstick and then trace her mother's writing.

Baxter allowed himself a moment to really feel into Sofia's energy. "It's like she's here, isn't it?"

Mia nodded, the pad of her index finger now touching Sofia's bottom lip. Baxter remembered how Sofia's lips had felt on his, how she'd kissed him for the first time two days later in Charleston.

"Why was she here if she grew up in California?" Mia asked, still looking down at the notebook as if her mother were looking back at her.

"That's what I asked. What was someone like her doing in Greenville? She was so *not* Greenville. The only person in the whole town without an accent. I think that's what got me first, a far cry from a southern belle. She had your olive skin and coffee-colored brown eyes and she . . . she was just everything I'd always wanted. I was supposedly her kind of exotic too. She loved my accent, my biker boots." He lowered his sunglasses to the tip of his nose. "My southern charm."

Mia let out a masterful eye roll.

He readied his fork for a bite. "She told me she was from the West Coast, across the entire country from South Carolina. She'd just done an interview for a marketing gig in Atlanta and was driving to a second interview in Charlotte. Isn't it amazing how the world works?"

He jabbed his thumb at his chest. "I happened to be in Greenville for the first time in a couple of years, *happened* to be visiting because it was your great-grandmother's birthday. And I *happened* to have chosen this coffee shop to go write a song. At the same time, your mother, who had never been to Greenville in her life—who didn't even drink coffee—was here because she'd gotten hungry while driving through. She just *happened* to want to see what downtown looked like and decided after her lunch to grab a mint tea. Then, for some wild reason, when the barista—just like the one who helped us earlier—asked if she wanted her tea in a to-go cup, she'd shaken her head, said she'd drink it here. Then both our worlds changed forever."

He beamed at the good that had come from that day. "How amazing *all* that had to happen in order for you to be sitting here right now." He jabbed a finger at the table. "Because of all that, you and I have each other, and we now have the Arroyos and Diego. Actually, it was that day that she told me that she was adopted and that she'd like to find her family. Well, we found her family for her. We've finally found *our* family, kiddo. And I'd do it again and again and again, go through it all, to be here with you. Now that's the truth, my little love." Baxter wiped a happy tear from his eyes. "Now you know."

It was okay. He was talking about the old days, and *he* was okay. There was nothing he could have done to change how their lives had played out. Things happen. It was how you dealt with them that defined your life. He knew that now. There was no time for regrets, because regret was indeed a broken mirror. It wasn't like he'd run out of time. Mia was eight, still so young, and they had so many more memories to explore.

"So you wanna know why I brought you here," he asked, "why I really brought you here?"

"Why, Daddy?"

"Because I thought your mom should be part of the decision."

"What decision?"

Baxter sat back and couldn't help but let a smile come over him. He'd been thinking a lot about this idea.

"What if we went back to Spain?"

"I know, I know. For Christmas."

"No, that's not what I mean. Do you know what a gap year is?"

She shook her head.

"It's something a lot of people do when they're younger, like right before or during or after college. It's a big life reset, where you go spend a year living an adventure. I was thinking you and I could take a gap year in Spain."

"Wait, what?"

Oh God, the look on her face filled him up. "I promised you . . . things were going to be different. I don't want to live a gated life anymore. You've been right all along. I work too hard. It's really me that needs the reset. I was thinking that I could sell the company to Alan. He just inherited some money from his mother-in-law, and I know he'd be interested. We could sell the house—it's too big anyway—and put everything in storage. And then we go spend a year in Spain and figure out what in the world it is we really want, what *really* matters."

Mia's little eyes had expanded into Ping-Pong balls, and she was speechless.

"And Ester has a big surgery coming up. Don't we want to spend time with her? Don't we want to spend some more time with our family? We could find a place somewhere in Cadeir, a little villa not too far away from the estate. And you can go to school with your cousins, learn Spanish."

"*Sí, sí!*" Mia said.

"Yeah, me too. I just think it could be the greatest thing you and I have ever done. It's something we'd cherish for the rest of our lives. It'll take a lot of work, getting a visa and selling everything, moving everything into storage. But I think we could get to Spain in a couple of months. We could watch the olive trees come alive in the spring and go all the way to harvest. You could help Alma after school and on the weekends."

"What would you do, Daddy? You might get bored."

"That's a good question. I was thinking about asking if I could borrow Don Jorge's guitar and start learning flamenco. You know the guitarist I saw in the cave, Javier Martín? He lives on the coast in Andalucía. I was thinking I could take lessons from him, drive over there once a week."

"Who are you?" Mia asked.

"This is just me," Baxter said. "Little ol' me. So what do you say?"

"Do you have to ask?"

"And there's one more thing," Baxter said. "I thought we'd go by the church tomorrow and visit your mother's columbarium. I had an idea I wanted to run by you."

"What?" she asked.

"You'll see."

Back in the truck, Baxter and Mia were driving toward the church when his phone rang through the truck speakers. It was Alan.

"Do you mind?" Baxter asked her. "He's probably wondering where the heck I am."

When she nodded, he pressed the green button. *"¿Qué tal, tío?"*

"Didn't you get back yesterday? I figured you'd be barking orders by now. All that rioja and tapas must have slowed you down."

"If you only knew," Baxter said. "Hey, I have a proposition for you."

"What's that?"

Baxter looked his daughter straight in the eyes, and another big fat smile came over him. Then he proceeded to take another big step toward reclaiming their life.

Epilogue

La Familia

One Year Later

Fall was once again upon them, and Baxter could already sense the rhythm of the seasons in his bones. He was feeling more Spanish by the month. It had been an exhausting year in a lot of ways. Selling a company and a house. Moving to another country.

Reframing the exhaustion, though, Baxter saw it as one of the most freeing of his life. As he'd finalized the sale with Alan and worked on each step of the visa process, he couldn't believe he was doing something so wild. It was, however, by no means uncalculated. He had plenty of money to buy them a couple of years of adventure before he needed to get back to work. He'd probably return to the construction business, but on better terms, building houses he believed in, and he'd thought once or twice about going back to Charleston, if Mia was up for it. Either way, there was no need to worry about it now, as they'd already decided to stay on until at least the end of Mia's school year the next June.

Fortunately, they returned to Spain in mid-January and had time to spend with Ester before her heart transplant. On March 12, six days after the surgery in Madrid, she suffered a major and heartbreaking complication with the primary graft and the donor heart. Baxter, Alma,

Mia, Rodolfo, and Don Diego spent two weeks in Madrid, hoping and praying that the doctors might save her.

Three weeks later, they wheeled her out of the cardiac unit of the Gregorio Marañón Hospital and, in the parking lot, she stood and walked to Alma's car on her own. It was a victory that all the family and friends who'd come to see her weren't sure would ever happen. Though her recovery was slow, Ester was doing better by the day. Baxter knew that she'd surely found strength in the way Alma and Rodolfo had worked to repair their relationship; she'd also found it in a budding relationship with Diego. He'd been absorbed into the family, becoming a loving grandfather to Mia, and Baxter often sat at the dinner table in a state of amazement of the way things had worked out in the end.

Especially when Ester had announced she and Diego were getting married. He was going to sell his place and move into the estate. He'd formed a partnership with the Arroyos (of which Mia was included) and was helping fund everything that Alma had wanted: a new mill and a tasting room and a restaurant. Having let go of the idea of moving to Madrid, Rodolfo was happy, too, and his relationship with Alma had come full circle. He'd promised her that he would never compromise her vision of the estate, and she'd said that she couldn't run the estate without him.

Baxter had been having the time of his life studying flamenco with Javier Martín, which included a deep dive into listening to all the great names. Baxter had become so obsessed that he began to question 23andMe and wondered whether he might have some Spanish blood from somewhere way back when. Though he had a long way to go, he'd finally reached the point where he could play a few songs comfortably. His skill didn't matter. All that mattered was that he was feeding his soul and having a damn fine time doing it.

As a funny sidenote, he'd discovered during his first lesson with Martín that the guitarist was happily married with four children. That confirmed what Baxter had already figured out. As long as there was balance, one could always be both an artist and a family man.

Baxter had also been writing music again. He found himself constantly hearing melodies in his head and was always eager to get a guitar in his hands. Having struck up renewed relationships with his former bandmates from Cactus Road, he often shared with them new tunes that were bubbling out of him, and he thought he might attempt to sell a few songs down the road.

He'd also been helping with some of the construction around the estate. Baxter had learned so much from the local builders, and the mill project was nothing short of a work of art. If all things went well, they'd have it up and running by the summer, and Alma could press the olives in it the next fall, about a year from now. What Baxter never thought could happen was he was reminded of the love he'd had for building when he was younger. That was why eventually starting up a new contracting business didn't sound so bad.

Today was the last day of harvest, and bottles of the new oil were scattered on tables crowded with tapas such as cured meats, *ensaladilla rusa*, Manchego cheese, olives, and salted Marcona almonds. Four mostly empty bottles of cava rested in ice buckets. Ester's brother was cooking two giant pans of *fideuá de mariscos*, the paella-like dish made of broken spaghetti. Mouthwatering langostinos and mussels and clams were artfully arranged on the top with slices of lemon, and their scent mingled wonderfully with the autumn air.

Mia sat at one table, facing her grandfather, playing a round of chess. There was a pink polka-dot bow in her hair, and she was growing up so quickly: nine going on twenty. Under Don Diego's instruction, she'd become a much better player and was even known to win on occasion. Her Spanish had gotten much better, too, and the two could chat over a chessboard for hours. Ester sat next to Mia, quietly cheering her on with a smile richer than any other Spaniard alive. On the ground to the right of the table, Paco pawed at Mia's new puppy, a water dog named Lila.

Alberto the Bread Man sat in a chair next to Baxter, who held a guitar in his hands. They'd been playing a lot of music lately, the two of them. Though Baxter's Spanish wasn't coming along as quickly as Mia's, he was able to communicate enough with Alberto to discuss their dreams of forming a band one day soon.

"Daddy," Mia called out as they discussed which tune to play next, "will you play some flamenco?"

"Oh, I don't know if I'm ready, honey."

"Creo que eres." I think you are.

She didn't have to ask again. Baxter turned to Alberto, who clearly understood, because he'd already raised his hands and begun to clap. Baxter took a moment to collect himself, feeling into the bread man's beat. He then opened up a song using the pulgar technique with his thumb, drawing out a basic melody. After a tap on the wood of the guitar with his ring finger, he broke into the compas strumming that he felt most comfortable with, and he was actually impressed with himself as the sounds left Don Jorge's guitar.

Alma joined Alberto in the clapping, both perfectly timed into the Spanish rhythm, as if the Spanish were born with this beat in their hearts. Then the whole family was on their feet, dancing and clapping along with Baxter's playing. He had played for crowds around the world, big ones, too, but none could ever match the friends and family surrounding him now.

Dancing along with her grandmother, Mia launched hearts at him from her eyes, and Baxter very much felt like he was onto something. He might not have it all figured out, but he had his hand on the tail of something grand.

~

After everyone had left, they took two cars to the cemetery, as they had one more person they wanted to share this last day of harvest with. They walked past graves peppered with falling leaves the color of pecans, bananas, and pomegranate. Mia rode on Rodolfo's shoulders, Baxter and Alma held hands, and Ester rested her hand in the crook of Diego's arm. Baxter thought they made a great couple. If only she could have lived a second life and given their love a lifelong chance. But, just as he'd had his time with Sofia, Ester was blessed to still have time with Diego.

The steeple from the church in the center of Cadeir poked up over the trees in the distance. There was a purple hue to the air, and it was cold out, but cold in a way that felt exhilarating, the kind that arches your spine and gives you energy. Bouquets of fresh flowers decorated many of the headstones, and despite it turning dark out, several people were also out there, surely saying prayers and last goodbyes.

They came to a stop at Sofia's grave, which was two rows away from Don Jorge's. Baxter and Mia had moved her ashes from the church in Greenville to where they thought she might feel most at home, to where she was bound by blood.

Don Diego set down a bouquet of November wildflowers that he and Mia had picked from the meadow near his house. Then he kissed his hand and touched the gravestone, whispering something only he and his daughter would ever know.

As Diego backed away and slipped his arm around Ester, Mia said to Baxter, "You know what I've realized?"

He pulled her in. "What?"

"I think Mommy is very happy in heaven. She was just waiting for us to catch up."

Baxter looked at his daughter through instantly wet eyes. "It's amazing it's taken us this long to figure that out, huh? What a wise observation, my little lady. That's all she was doing, waiting for us to catch up."

Mia turned to her mother's headstone. "Mommy, Daddy and I miss you so much, but we want you to know we're very happy. Don't worry about us." She cupped her hand and whispered, "He's in good hands."

Smiling, he looked at the grave, realizing he was finally okay with Sofia being gone. It would always be there, the hurt of it, but he'd learned to turn the hurt into a reminder to live life. In that spirit, he said to Mia, "Olive you, honey."

Every one of them laughed at Baxter's dad joke, and he felt proud, even when Mia said, "*Olive* you? Really?" She turned to Alma. "Do you hear this?"

"Let's face it. He'll always be a work in progress," Alma said.

"Isn't that the truth?" Mia shook her head and let her eyes roll up.

Baxter put one arm around Mia and pulled Alma in with the other. Alma motioned for Rodolfo and Ester and Diego to join them. As they did, Baxter felt as whole as he ever had, and that was something he never could have imagined.

"Olive all of you," he said, and there was no shielding his emotions with humor. To be sure they really knew it, he said, "I love all of you, my family."

With a proud smile on her face, Ester let go of them and stepped forward. "There's one more thing to do." She drew a small bottle of the *nuovo* from her purse and poured the oil over the grass next to her daughter's headstone, closing the loop and bringing Sofia home for good.

Baxter tightened his arm around his daughter, and when she looked up and offered him a smile, he knew for sure that Sofia hadn't gone too far at all.

Acknowledgments

I've written a lot of words in my day, but I come up far short when I attempt to express my gratitude to the people who contribute to my books and my life. For so long, I thought that writing was a solitary endeavor; I couldn't have been more wrong.

Andrea Hurst, where to even begin. I can't imagine there are many agents out there like you. Thank you for always steering me well in my life, in my career, and in my stories. If you only knew how many times I've turned to my wife after our calls and said, "Don't ever let me take her for granted." I'm so grateful for the relationship we have and the trust that we share. Perhaps more than anything, I feel blessed to create with you, and that's what we do. So many of the best ideas in my books come from one of your brilliant bursts of inspiration that leads us into brainstorming.

Chris Werner, my editor at Lake Union, who gave me the shot of my dreams. I'd been watching Lake Union for a long time, hoping I might one day be a part of the team, and now it's happening, and it's everything that I'd hoped. I'm so appreciative for the tremendous effort you put into my books, from the team you have built around me to the Brilliant (with a capital *B*) editing suggestions that you share in the most eloquent of prose. I find that with each draft I submit, the predominant thought in my head is: "I hope I make Chris proud." Thank you to the entire Lake Union team; you are a joy to work with.

Tiffany Yates Martin, one of the best developmental editors in the business. I'm not exaggerating when I say working with you feels meant to be. I love working with you, and there are few better feelings than scanning your initial notes and knowing that we are on the same page and that you have given me a crystal-clear path in how to elevate my manuscript—or perhaps better said, how to knock the darn thing up into the sky. You are an unsung hero and belong at the center of the stage. Thank you for being such a great teacher and for pushing me to my best and for always going well above and beyond. Knowing you are my safety net, I'm almost getting too comfortable jumping into the unknown.

Leaving the story behind and zooming out to a wider perspective, I want to thank Ruth Chiles, who came into my life at the exact moment I needed her. You are my shaman and sage, and you've given me faith in myself and in everything else out there. My appreciation and admiration are infinite.

To my beta readers, who selflessly raise their hands every time I'm in need. After almost messing up this time, I want to make a promise to you right here: I'm going to do everything I can to always find a way to include you in my works in progress, because you—each one of you—always make my books better in countless ways. This one is no exception. I do not take you for granted.

To my buddy John Frick, an amazing contractor in Charleston who builds anything but cookie-cutters. Thank you for letting me pick your brain, and even more, thank you for your friendship. I hope the story stretches a smile across your face.

Joanne Lacina, owner of Oliveoillovers.com. How could I know that our serendipitous connection years ago would turn me into a complete olive oil fanatic? I'm so grateful for the oily wisdom you have bestowed upon me. And thank you for introducing me to some of the masters in Spain; I'll never forget my visits with them. How lucky we Americans are that you bring us the amazing olive oils of the Old World with such passion and care. If anyone reading these words is interested in expanding your knowledge, Joanne and her company are the place to start.

To both Jorge at Masía el Altet and Rafa at Oro del Desierto, thank you for taking the time to share your estates with me. I am now a devotee for life, and I can't wait to follow your steps as you continue to blaze trails in bottling terroir oil that rises up from the soul of your land.

Zonia Horn, as you might have detected, you really helped me step into Baxter's skin. I'm so grateful for our time together in Spain. You are an amazing friend and mother and human. Thank you for everything, including the rolls of cookie dough that never quite made it to the oven, as I always just ate them raw.

To my friends and family, especially those of you who don't have to read my books but do. If you only knew what that means to me. Thank you for loving me even when I'm so deep into a novel that I can't seem to pull my head up long enough to return the love the way you deserve. Maybe the words in my stories can start to make up for it. I am so blessed to have you in my life.

I feel like I forgot a couple of people. Hmm . . .

Oh! My wife and son. Mikella and Riggs Walker. What a grand journey we're on. Everything I do is for you, and everything that I do well is because of you. Thank you for your endless patience and stratospheric love. And thank you for reminding me of the importance of having fun. You give my smile muscles a workout.

And to the booksellers and book clubs and all the readers out there, it is you who give me the courage and opportunity I need to tell stories for a living. As they say here in Valencia, *muchísima gracias*. I am lifted up by your correspondence and with each time you buy or sell a book or share it with your friends and family and followers. The best way to pay you back is to keep giving my all to every novel, so that's exactly what I'm gonna do. And I'm just getting started, amigos.

About the Author

Photo © 2018 Brandi Morris

Boo Walker is the bestselling author of *The Singing Trees*, *An Unfinished Story*, and the Red Mountain Chronicles. He initially tapped his creative muse as a songwriter and banjoist in Nashville before working his way west to Washington State, where he bought a gentleman's farm on the Yakima River. It was there, among the grapevines and wine barrels, that he fell in love with telling high-impact stories that now resonate with book clubs around the world. Rich with colorful characters and boundless soul, his novels will leave you with an open heart and a lifted spirit. Always a wanderer, Boo currently lives in Cape Elizabeth, Maine, with his wife and son. He also writes thrillers under the pen name Benjamin Blackmore. You can find him at www.boowalker.com and www.benjaminblackmore.com.